New York

Also by Terence Clarke

Novels:

My Father In the Night

The King of Rumah Nadai

A Kiss for Señor Guevara

The Notorious Dream of Jesús Lázaro

Story Collections:

The Day Nothing Happened

Little Bridget and The Flames of Hell

NEW YORK

Stories by

TERENCE CLARKE

ASTOR & LENOX

New York

ISBN (print edition): 978-0-9860582-7-1

Published by Astor & Lenox, San Francisco, California, USA.

To contact the author or publisher, please visit http://astorandlenox.com. Requests for author appearances, educational and library pricing, and licensing regarding Astor & Lenox titles are welcome.

Cover illustration by r. black. (www.rblack.org), commissioned by Astor & Lenox.

Photo of Terence Clarke by Nancy Dionne (www.nancydionne.com)

For Beatrice Bowles
amor de mi vida

The true New Yorker secretly believes
that people living anywhere else have
to be, in some sense, kidding.

—John Updike

CONTENTS

EVERYONE IN L.A.

Pat, a many times unpublished novelist, descended the steps to the Canal Street station.

How can they just keep me there like that? he asked himself. He had been in the office since seven the previous morning, a Manhattan branding firm famous for putting California start-ups on the map and preparing the websites and marketing for major IPOs. A few of the skinny, Levi's-clad employees at those now publicly traded companies were in their mid-twenties and had come into, Pat knew, millions of dollars. They rode scooters up hallways rather than walked, having put a very small percentage of their stock option fortunes to work at the Amazon.com scooter store. Pat preferred walking, and was doing so just now, headed home at 1:22 a.m.

Because he worked for the branding firm and not the start-ups, Pat wasn't one of these nouveaux riches. Wealth evaded him. Nonetheless, like his clients, he wore a pair of slim-cuffed jeans, a cowboy shirt hanging out over his belt—red with white stripes over a white T-shirt—and a very cool black wool porkpie that a former girlfriend (a marketing manager at MTV) had bought for him at Arnold Hatters on Eighth Avenue, the day it had closed a year ago. He loved the hat. Even more, he enjoyed the cobalt blue corduroy sport jacket he was wearing, from the Kmart on West Thirty-fourth. Sixty-five bucks. Quite in keeping with Pat's tastes.

Although he was a marketing writer for the branding firm, glistening across the surface of Pat's talent was the understanding that such writing was—way down deep—not much. He knew that branding was important. Facebook, for example, was an iconic name, its presence immediately recognizable around the world because of that clever letter *F* logo. Apple, too, with that clever apple. But for Pat, Charles Dickens was more important, and Charles Dickens had never needed a branding firm. In *Great Expectations*, when Abel Magwitch takes Pip up by his heels on the Kent marsh, or when the same Abel struggles up the gloom-sequestered stairs to Pip's rooms many years later to identify himself as....

Pat looked around. He imagined for a moment that someone nearby on the platform could make out his thoughts, and that he might be in danger of revealing to that person who Abel Magwitch really was.

He felt a stale wind blowing in his face. The approaching uptown 1 train—a narrow tsunami—hurtled like abrupt thunder into the station.

When the doors to the train car slid apart, Pat was confronted by a tall young woman dressed in 1950s pink pedal pushers over a pair of platform high heels that otherwise looked like sandals from a Roman gladiator movie, a T-shirt with the face of Lady Gaga silkscreened upon it in red and purple, a Balinese vest of many colors, very curly hair—dyed to resemble that of Lucille Ball—tied up in a knot above her head, yellow-framed sunglasses, and an unlit cigarette hanging from her gloss purple lips. She was speaking to someone on a cell phone.

"Like, duh! What else would you expect?"

She was more or less blocking the door, indifferent to the profanities that floated about her from passengers trying to get around her, to get off the train. For the moment, Pat could not enter the car, and when the opportunity to do so finally arrived, the woman did nothing to accommodate him. He edged past her and around the large Macy's shopping bag hanging from her arm, which took up what space the woman herself did not take up.

"No! Don't you see? The whole thing is that Mitch had those looks, and that Lila was too much in love with him to protect herself."

Silence.

"Yeah, I know that. But Lila didn't."

Pat stood clear of the closing doors and sat down a few feet from the woman on the phone. The train took off toward Houston Street.

There was more information after that. Lila was identified as a loser from Chicago, and Mitch, who was her boyfriend, was described as "one of those actor clowns from L.A., like everyone in L.A."

Pat placed his laptop case against his stomach and folded his arms before it. The train roared, but he was so close to the woman in the doorway that he was kept awake by her conversation.

"Listen, I know Mitch." She grimaced, her lipstick quivering with momentary rage. "I even went out with him."

Pat banged to the right and the left as the train raced up the tunnel.

"You did too? When?"

The doors opened at Houston Street, and the woman refused to relinquish her place, causing more profanity.

"Yeah, but, like, you didn't, you know, hook up with him the way I did. I mean, did you, Richard?" She hurried into laughter. "Yeah, I did! But it never amounted to anything."

The doors closed.

"No, he couldn't get it up."

The train rattled into motion once more.

"Yeah, that's right. Like everyone in L.A."

Pat fell into a reflection about Mitch. Someone about thirty years old probably, perhaps a young Johnny Depp in the sense of being self-involved and resplendent in his handsomeness. Cocky, too. Sought after. Well reviewed.

Not like Pat. Pat's novel had so far been turned down by seventeen publishers. The three literary agents who had represented it all respected his "finely honed, measured talent," as one put it. But he knew that they all wished he would write less well. His little book about a nun in Oakland, California benefitted, the publishers said, from "Mr. Cronin's obvious talent, his sumptuous knowledge of life within a Catholic convent, his unusual ability to present kindness and religious solicitude in a compelling way..." and so forth. "But it'll never sell," one publisher wrote. "The trouble is, there's no market for this kind of, uh, quality undertaking, Pat," one of the agents said on the phone, asking if he could write something a little gutsier, with more murder and rapine. “What about one of those priests that can’t keep his zipper shut?” she suggested. “Pat. That would sell!”

Pat glanced from the corner of his eye at the young woman on the phone. He wondered if he himself would wish to get it up with someone who spoke so abrasively, had so little concern for who was in her vicinity, and now laughed very loudly as she opined, for her correspondent Richard, that Mitch’s girlfriend Lila had always “like, you know, sucked.” There was perhaps a reason for Mitch’s unresponsive affections.

“And besides which, someone that looks as good as Mitch won’t hang around for long with someone who looks like Lila.”

Well then, Pat wondered, what would jealous Lila do to capture Mitch?

He imagined Mitch done up in chaps and cowboy boots, way out west.

“You don’t understand, Lila.” Mitch looked off into the sunset. “Sure I love you, but…”

They were riding on two horses—Lila’s a calico paint, Mitch’s a fine palomino—across a vast meadow of subtle, waving grasses in the background of which was some portion of the Rocky Mountains. Lila, a whore from the little Montana town of Darby, had spent an evening with Mitch in one of the rooms upstairs at the Sawmill Tavern. Mitch was an out-of-work cowpoke whose very smile caused women’s hearts to grow disheveled and, suddenly, to undress themselves.

“You need a woman, Mitch.” Lila frowned, her fingers adjusting the lace collar on her store-bought Kansas City dress. She was a woman jealous of whatever exotic cowpoke desires pulsed through Mitch’s blood. Her lips, a little like Scarlett Johansson’s, softened like lipsticked butter. “You need what a woman can do for you.”

“I’ve made up my mind, Lila. We’re taking that herd to California, and a woman doesn’t belong in a place like that.”

“Mitch—”

“There are Cheyenne and Apaches all along the way. River crossings. Avalanches.” Mitch removed his cowboy hat, slicked his hair back with his left hand, and replaced the hat. “There won’t be any turning back. Not by me, not by anybody.” He looked aslant at Lila, who rode the horse like a man, not being the kind of woman who paid attention to ladylike equestrian probity.

"You ever seen what an Apache does to a white woman?"

Lila swallowed, chagrined by the thought of such a horrid fate.

"I'm not taking a woman with me through Indian country."

Rattling the Macy's bag with fresh frustration, the woman leaned forward, as though sharing a sadness with the cell phone. "And you know, Richard, that when he got here to New York, the first person he met was me...and *then* Lila."

Pat grumbled. He had Mitch and Lila going in the wrong direction. So now Mitch, he decided, was a two-bit hood in Lower Manhattan, a mole for the police in their dealings with the Irish Westies.

"That's when you went out with him?" The train's rumble made it difficult to hear. "You met him on the subway?"

Pat smiled. Yes. Mitch was trying to whack Goofy McMeany, a numbers runner and former priest who had controlled the operations on the far West Side, around the Javits Center. "Couldn't keep his zipper shut," it was said of Goofy, and he had infuriated Mitch when he had insisted on going out with Lila.

"But Lila was cuter then than she is now." The woman placed the cell phone itself in her Macy's bag, its earphone cord dangling into the bag's maw. She removed the sunglasses, and Pat realized that she really was quite beautiful, a kind of Middle Eastern curve to her eyes, a little bit of Istanbul in them, a little Xanadu maybe.

But Pat figured Lila to be very cute indeed. She wore a tight, long skirt that undulated down her legs, a white cashmere sweater that reminded Pat of the Himalayan cat that he had had as a child. Salty. Lila in her sweater exhibited all the sensuous, curve-governed finesse that Salty had had, including the ability to curl up on Pat's lap.

"All that glorious hair of his? Mitch didn't know what to do with it."

Glorious, Pat thought. Mitch's hair was probably so full with fine curls and rugged Italianate body that, along with his dark, Argentine-style, polo-playing beauty and threatening smile, his hair caused Lila to faint.

"Well, do you know what, like, the last thing he said to me was?"

Pat pondered the possibilities.

"He said, 'Tiffany…'"

Tiffany! Pat thought. Faded neon lights raced by, one next to another, attached to the tunnel wall outside the subway car like narrow, scribbled stars in the firmament. *Well*...Pat grumbled to himself, thinking. So this time Mitch and Tiffany would be in a Yellow cab. Mitch, leaning close on the back seat, held her hand as she wept. The stars outside, over the Hudson River, had none of the fast-moving bravado of the neon lights in the tunnel. "I could have been a contender for you, Mitch," Tiffany whispered.

Or maybe Tiffany, at a deserted oasis in the Sahara, would be watching the lush Arab sheik Mitch Sharif riding on a gorgeous Black Arabian stallion, far to the horizon, beyond which, a small dot of darkness, he disappeared. "*Salam alaikum*, Tiffany."

Or maybe Tiffany Bennett at Pemberley with her uncle and aunt, discovering that the handsome, cold-hearted Mitch Darcy was the owner of this astonishment of a country manse and, moreover—if her uncle and aunt were to be believed—a fine gentleman of upstanding morals and comportment, rather than the arrogant, prideful lout saved from himself only by the fact that he had ten thousand in sterling a year. This information left Tiffany at odds with herself about what she thought about Mitch. She chastised herself, adjusting the pretty green parasol that rested on her left shoulder, a girl so young, so well raised, and yet so prejudicial.

"He said, 'Tiffany, I don't get you!'"

Pat felt like a private eye, listening in on a tapped line. Tiffany's friend Richard was doing all the talking now. The car was crowded, many people standing as it approached Forty-second Street. But a semi-circular empty space buffered Tiffany from the other passengers, a kind of barrier that they had made in order to not have to listen to her conversation. It served little purpose, the barrier. If you were in the car, you had to listen to Tiffany.

"And, you know…you know how aggressive women are, once they get here to New York. They just go for it, and that's what Lila did." Tiffany leaned her forehead against the glass in the door. "Just went for it." Her shoulders slumped, and the Macy's bag began to slip. "Like I wasn't even there."

The car rocked to the left and right. Pat realized that Tiffany had begun weeping, and he imagined her now walking up Saint Mark's Place toward Tompkins Square, dressed differently than she was on the subway car. A bit less casually. An FBI agent. A fashionable business suit, maybe, classic black pumps, the Macy's bag. She and Mitch had been having a glass of wine at McSorley's, and Tiffany had been hoping that that would be the moment when Mitch asked her to marry him.

Mitch, also dressed in a business suit, a youthful, morally vacant, devastatingly good-looking day trader, had learned just that afternoon that the Chinese whom he had convinced to buy junk-bond stocks (the proceeds from which would effectively cover the losses he had sustained in Europe)....

Pat thought about it a moment. *Yes.*

Before he met with Tiffany, Mitch, deeply compromised and suddenly realizing that he was a fool in mortal danger, was standing on the corner of Wall Street and Broad, taxi traffic rumbling by as he awaited the signal, when an impeccably dressed young Chinese fellow stopped next to him and whispered to him that he was a dead man.

So asking Tiffany to marry him was not the most important thing on his mind, which Tiffany did not realize. And then, as she followed Mitch up Saint Mark's Place, trying to hold back tears, she saw Lila, waiting on a bench outside one of the basement shops on the street, gorgeous in a kelly green silk dress and simply ravishing red pumps, her legs crossed, a sensuous tableau sculpted to perfection, smoking a cigarette. Clearly waiting there for an assignation with Mitch, Lila arrested everyone's attention. No one, not even Mitch, electrified the people passing on the street the way Lila did.

Tiffany stopped, her shoulders erect, her hopes dashed. And as Mitch approached Lila, offering her his hand, a black limo pulled up to the curb and someone inside gunned Mitch down. The screeching tires of the escaping limo did little to distract Tiffany from the agony of seeing Mitch's blood smeared across the side of the parked car down which he slid.

Tiffany groaned. "Oh, Mitch."

The train entered the Forty-second Street station and the doors opened.

Tiffany was silent now, but she was even less able to move out of everyone's way as she openly, quietly sobbed. "Oh, Richard...." Tears soiled her eye makeup, and she appeared ready to flee the car, to run up the platform and throw herself before the lead car, Anna Karenina, Pat mused, mulched by the 1 train.

"No, he never said anything about love, Richard. Least of all to me."

Her knees seemed to buckle, and she leaned to the side, taking hold with her right hand of the one free plastic grip suspended from above. The paper handle of the Macy's bag rested in the crook of her arm. Turning her head toward Pat, she caught him watching her. Tears streamed from beneath her sunglasses. Tender, in sudden, deep, embarrassed sadness, remorsefully, she smiled at him.

The doors closed and the train took off. Now Tiffany remained silent. Pat did not know if Richard was still on the line. She appeared to be listening, but she said nothing. She brought a crumpled tissue from a pants pocket and dabbed the makeup from below her eyes. The train arrived at Seventy-second Street, Pat's stop.

He had continued watching Tiffany with surreptitious interest. Once she ceased speaking, other passengers on the car ceased paying attention to her. The loudness, the abrasiveness, the silliness was now gone. Instead, Pat sensed in Tiffany the rapid decline into a bloodied reality, that of the loss of wished-for love. Mitch had never said anything to her about love, and now Pat realized that, judging from her demeanor, Tiffany cared a great deal about love. Lila...Lila was the victor. Tiffany, rude, angry, judgmental, and profane, was the defeated, and now was suffering deeply for it.

The doors opened. Pat stood and adjusted the porkpie on his head. He secured the laptop case strap over his right shoulder and, turning to the door, realized that Tiffany was preceding him onto the Seventy-second Street station platform. She walked quickly toward the narrow stairway that causes such a bottleneck for passengers attempting to get up to Broadway, no matter how many or few of them there are. Pat ascended the stairs right behind her. Her high-heeled sandals clapped against the cement. Her cell phone remained in the Macy's bag. She turned toward the doorway leading out to the street.

"Pardon me."

She looked back over her shoulder at him. Her face was splotched and blotted, a wreck. But she smiled once more.

"I'm sorry to interfere." Pat reached for the door and pushed it open for her. "But I…I saw how upset you were on the train. I mean no harm, but—"

"What do you want?" Tiffany stopped in the doorway as they were passing into the bleak, dark noise of Broadway. Other passengers, swearing, swirled clumsily around the couple.

"Can I walk you home?"

"Look, I don't need your help."

"I know, but…" Pat looked up the street.

"Even though…"

Tiffany sighed and stepped with Pat toward the street corner. She stopped there, gazing for a moment at Verdi Square. Pat often sat on one of the benches that border this small, verdant triangle. He would be seeking advice from the great composer, whose operas about clashes between ancient nations and the ruin of painfully gained love had often, since he had first discovered them at university, moved Pat deeply. What Pat missed in his own life was such love, and suddenly, awaiting the rest of Tiffany's brush-off, he realized that his writing missed it as well. The wish for the white, blinding, blood-messed clash of love and the securing of it. Joy. The loss of it. Anger. "Write about that!" he whispered to himself. The mortified heart. Betrayed forgiveness. Joy.

Tiffany glanced back at him. She removed the sunglasses and placed them in the bag. She looked down at the sidewalk. She waited, and continued waiting. "Even though it's awfully kind of you to ask." She shifted the bag from one shoulder to the next, and glanced once more at Pat. "Yes, you may."

THE HIGH LINE

Pollard held his attaché case before his chest, warding off the first blow, a wild haymaker from the homeless man dancing about before him.

"What did I do?" Pollard cowered behind the case.

The man took another swing. Like the first one, it collided with the case, and Pollard fell back against a wooden park bench.

"Stop!"

His umbrella flew into the rain. The attaché case fell half on the walkway, half in the plot of flowering succulents that bordered it.

"*¡Puto!*" The attacker pointed an index finger at Pollard. Middle-aged and stringy thin, the color of his skin like dried-out coffee, he was frayed and bent. He wore a soaked cloth jacket dirtied at the cuffs, faded and beat up. A wool watch cap, red on one side and black on the other, was similarly scruffy and inundated. His eyes had no focus, their black pupils surrounded by red-flecked white. His voice had taken on the crudity of whiskey- and cigarette-induced decline.

"I own this High Line, man! What're you *doin'* here?"

"I…"

"I live here, *cabrón!* I own this!"

The man lunged at Pollard again, this time reaching for the lapels of his overcoat. Pollard pushed the attacker away and fell against the bench once more.

The assailant wiped his lips, turned, and ran down the High Line toward Fourteenth Street. His footsteps clopped heavily through the puddles, noisy breathing coming in gasps. He yelled and made an obscene gesture at Pollard.

"¡Gringito maricón!"

His jacket flew out behind him. The retreating voice yet surged once more—*"¡Mama ñema!"*—from the top of the stairway leading down to the street.

Otherwise, it being early on a stormy Sunday morning, the High Line was almost empty.

Pollard's breathing was strained. He took up the attaché case from where it had landed in the succulents, whose small white, yellow, and red flowers gushed from them, carefully tended, shivering in the rain, charming.

A couple in raingear, several yards away, had seen the scuffle and appeared afraid to approach him. Pollard waved to them. "I'm okay," he said. Rainwater pooled on the surfaces of his rimless glasses where they lay on the concrete.

The couple retreated. During the fight, Pollard had thrust his hand against the bench back, slamming it into the thick, curved wood. A rip gleamed from the sleeve of his overcoat. Otherwise, his double-breasted gray suit and navy blue tie—with the exception of the black overcoat, the only mention of color in his appearance—had survived the scrape without much of a scrape at all. Yet he stood silently, wondering *What's that guy got against me?* And *What's a* mama ñema?

The High Line was A. Pollard O'Rourke's favored route to work. He was a principal in the corporate law firm O'Rourke Testi Moody Grumbold, and the offices took up an entire upper floor of the High Line building on West Fourteenth Street. He and the other 106 attorneys represented Fortune 500 interests against those that would keep them from their goals. The Justice Department, for example. The Democratic Party. Global warming nuts. Pollard was not a cold man, although you would think that he was, were you to read the briefs and memos that he wrote, or to sit in on a meeting with him. He had been so devoted to the flinty eminence of his firm for so many years that his youthful exuberances were now overtaken by the need to appear unjudgeable. He was tough on everyone, even his clients, who absorbed his dismissive demeanor because, in court, he won. Pollard was brilliant, stony, ruthless, and unafraid. Generally, other firms did not enjoy taking him on because, more often than not, they lost.

He lived in a large brownstone on East Seventy-third near the park, and was now a widower, his wife, Cassandra, having passed away in 2011. It was she who had predicted great success for him, just after he had graduated from Columbia Law School in 1975. They were engaged on that very day, and Cassandra declared to her girlfriends at the party that her Pollard, already so tuned in to the rigor and sacrifice that would be needed to become a famous lawyer, would indeed become more famous than any of his classmates. Cassandra had been devoted even as a young woman to the public good—to which Pollard had paid little attention his entire life—and felt that her husband would need someone like her to steady what she sometimes called, exhibiting a large smile, "Pollard's fervidly litigious inflammations." Pollard had always enjoyed the phrase.

Never in his life did A. Pollard O'Rourke care about the welfare of the crazy, the poor, the disenfranchised, refugees from foreign wars, or immigrants legal or illegal. Cassandra did all that, through the Church and Catholic charities. But now she was gone, and he knew that in his heart he had valued his wife's involvement, even though he had seldom spoken to her about it. Above all, he never once criticized her for it. He knew why. His heart would have suffered alone, were it not for his wife. Cassandra saw in Pollard qualities that he barely saw himself, a vision of him that he deeply appreciated. The fact was, she had loved him, and now that she was gone, he saw how his own heart, to his surprise, mattered to him also. He had followed its counsel whenever it came to his wife, although he now worried guiltily that having opted simply for silence when it came to her charity work hardly constituted a commitment to what she was doing. Pollard missed Cassandra, her caresses of him, the ways she could release his hunched-over emotions. He still thanked her time and again for supporting him in a profession that required the mordant implacability that most people felt made up his entire personality.

His driver chauffeured him every day to the Thirtieth Street stairway to the High Line, and he walked the rest of the way to his offices. The

High Line allowed him to stroll. Before he was assaulted, he felt no need to worry about his mortality up there. Such lovely views, enhancing the quiet peace of the river to the west. Since his childhood, the High Line—or as it had been called back then, the West Side Freight Line—had been one of the Manhattan wonders that amazed Pollard.

The morning after he was attacked, he told his driver to take him all the way to his office. As they drove below the High Line, it was impossible not to stare up at it through the limo's darkened roof window, trying to make sense of the attack. Pollard found himself also, with considerable pleasure, going over the three different versions of the High Line he had known.

When he was a small boy in the late 1950s, his father, James O'Rourke—the founder of the law firm of which Pollard was now senior partner—occasionally brought him on the subway to look at the elevated train tracks on the West Side. Hand in hand, he and his father stood on the sidewalk below and waited for the slow freight trains to meander by, up above. The trains appeared gargantuan to little Pollard, huge metallic animals grinding with thrilling menace through the sky. The boy worried that they might fall down from up there, and the destruction that he imagined frightened him time and again as he saw himself and his father ground under by falling railroad cars filled with fruits and vegetables, lumber, fish, panicked chickens, and bawling cattle, the exploding train engines scattering in flames across the streets below.

The boy loved the fear, holding tightly to his father's hand as the grinding roar passed above them.

He especially enjoyed the many large goats up there, tan and white. He and his father would see them grazing along the tracks. James explained to the boy that a lot of weeds grew from between the tracks, and that goats were the cheapest and most efficient way of keeping those weeds at a minimum. Pollard wished to go up and see the animals, which was not permitted. But his father asked around and found that there was a vacant lot toward the old docks at the foot of Twenty-fifth Street, where a cyclone fence kept the goats in. He then made it a regular stop, for Pollard to look at the animals.

A shack at one end of the lot protected the goats against the winter cold. But in the warmer months, they came out into the open, which was strewn with a layer of wood chips, and lay there in the sun, chewing. Pollard imagined that the goats were fans of his own favorite Wrigley's Spearmint gum. His father had first suggested the idea, getting a laugh from the boy. The goats chewed with regal disdain, occasionally looking toward Pollard and his father and the other few viewers as though they—the goats—were celebrities, Pope Pius or John Wayne. You had to be important to be a goat.

Twenty-five years later, the newlyweds Pollard and Cassandra came across town a few times to the Meatpacking District on a Sunday—driven there in a Town Car that would wait for them—to the same spots that he had enjoyed with his father. The railroad had been abandoned, and the trestles now were rusted behemoths on which could be found only silence and, now and then, ghostly men walking. The iron supports were covered with graffiti, and indeed the neighborhood was now dangerous. Garbage in piled plastic bags glutted the curbs and corners. Especially in winter, the neighborhood had an air of ruin and empty anger that made Pollard think they should tear these tracks down and do something to spiff the place up.

But he didn't really want that, and Cassandra especially didn't want it, because the goats were still there. Strolling along the railroad tracks up above, an occasional bell ringing from one of the necks, they were herded, in Spanish, by an old man with a stick or a young man with a stick. Cassandra worried for these fellows, who seemed to know the other people walking on the tracks. The goatherds would stop to talk with one or two of them, the goats pausing and grazing as the conversations carried on. Bits of English and Spanish dribbled down from the filthy heights.

A policeman once explained to Pollard and Cassandra that those others were bums, homeless guys, junkies. "You know, nowhere to go, losers." He told the couple that they were never to even think about trying to go up on the tracks. "I'm not talkin' about the guys with the goats. But with those others," he glanced upward at the bottom of the rail bed, "you might not make it back."

The driver took them a few times to the goat lot, and although the goats were there now and then, the goatherds were not. Finally, the district became so notorious for attacks and drug abuse that Pollard stopped taking his wife there altogether. The Meatpacking District was abandoned, and the rust-bitten railroad stood as a sign of its own imminent destruction.

But the West Side Line did not come down. After several years, the structure was saved by civic enthusiasm and millions of refurbishment dollars donated by the sort of culture-attentive people Cassandra knew and liked, to whose efforts Pollard suspected she offered assistance. Restored as a vernal walkway and called the High Line, it now produced only raves of wonder from its visitors and was the cause of a complete re-do of the neighborhood below. When he leased the offices on Fourteenth Street, Pollard exclaimed at the amazing hubris of the leasing guy when he quoted the square-foot fee. His scolding, shaking head had no effect on the leasing guy, and Pollard, realizing that he should jump quick, signed the papers. Now he was glad he did. The rent he was paying was a song compared to what other tenants, who had not at first jumped, were now paying.

Cassandra passed away just after the first stretch of the High Line opened, before Pollard decided to move to the new offices. He knew his wife would have been the first to suggest he get dropped off several blocks away from the offices, to take a morning walk among the trees, flowers, and grasses—every morning—up above.

After the attack, it took him a few weeks to resume those walks. He did not encounter his assailant again, and eventually lost the fear that the scuffle had caused in him. He did wonder why the guy had fingered him. The randomness of the violence still made no sense. Pollard had been walking alone in the rain, his thoughts on the paperwork he had to do. He resented having to spend a Sunday—bad weather or not—on such pedestrian, plodding efforts as going over corporate billings, grinding his teeth as he thought about people like Barack Obama, and grumbling about the ever-rising costs of his business. Previously he had preferred Sundays that were devoted to wandering the city with Cassandra. He had loved walking around in the Manhattan parks and finding some special little café or park bench on which to have lunch with her. They had frequently discussed things like the latest at The Frick (Pollard's personal favorite), the Staten Island Ferry, the Metropolitan Opera (Cassandra's favorite), or whether fun had to always be reserved *just* for Sundays.

Cassandra had the good fortune to have been raised up the river, in Croton-on-Hudson. Her father's gardening talents especially had made their small Tudor house on a hillside a few miles from the village into a kind of thoughtful English manor. For her, it was something a little out of Beatrix Potter or Jane Austen. Cassandra's own specialty lay in understanding how gardens work, and less in writing stellar masterpieces. She had a sense of color and flow that allowed her to turn the garden that she planted behind the brownstone she and Pollard owned into a little Hudson River painting. But this particular painting changed every day on its own, without the bother of having to consult Albert Bierstadt or Frederic Edwin Church. Cassandra sometimes hoped that those two men, whose art of the Hudson River Valley she revered, would rise from the dead and join her on the back stairs of the brownstone, stretched canvases at the ready, straw hats in place, and brushes primed.

Pollard once asked her why she so loved gardens.

"It's the stories in them." He had predicted the answer. Like Pollard, Cassandra was a reader. But unlike his preferred Roman history, ancient war, and weaponry, her preferences in books had always been for myths, the turn to love, fruition, animals, birth. Especially the universal beginning that was held to, she believed, by every belief. "Mother Spider's story sings through her web, Pollard." Cassandra blew softly into the web they were examining that particular morning, in Central Park. The web glittered with small water drops, minute diamonds in the morning sun. "No matter in what language she spins it. The minute it comes from her, the story is there." Cassandra's grin made a bit of fun of him. "If you get what I mean."

He didn't, but he knew that Cassandra would try to help him toward getting it.

Pollard's caring for the new High Line had been established the very first time he and Cassandra had walked it, a few days after it had been officially opened four years ago. It now was a slim, narrow park that had transformed the broken-down meatpacking and warehouse neighborhoods through which it ran. On a given day, tourists flocked to it, and for once in his life, Pollard didn't mind a crowd. The completely unique path curved through and around multi-storied buildings, floated through them, as it were, above the street noise, in friendly clarity. For Pollard, it was the best thing that had happened in New York City—except for Cassandra—since he had been living here, which was from the day of his birth.

On another Sunday a few months later, a blue one glimmering with morning sun, Pollard was headed to the office once more, for more drudgery, when he spotted his assailant.

This time, the High Line was filled with tourists and numberless New Yorkers. The man was sitting on a bench near the top of the Fourteenth Street stairway, reading. He appeared not to have changed his clothes since the day of his dispute with Pollard, although his clothing was now at least dry. A backpack lay at his feet, and he was the only person seated on the bench. The passing crowds clearly feared him, because he was also muttering—raving, actually—although the voice conveyed nothing from the magazine in his hands. It was, rather, a whispering rattle of incomprehensible observations, one following another as though he were explaining himself to himself.

A small cowbell rested next to him on the bench.

While raving, he studied the magazine, turning its pages carefully and leaning forward to read. His head turned back and forth over the print, his eyes quivering with excitement. Now and again, he spotted a young couple with kids and would take up the cowbell, to ring it. It was a kind gesture but a frightening one. He addressed the parents, waving to the kids and ringing the bell.

Everyone avoided him, but indeed he did not represent the danger that he had when he had assaulted Pollard. Withal, he appeared screwy but peaceful. Recognizing him, Pollard crept past, worried that the guy would see him and fly off once more. But the assailant uncrossed his legs and recrossed them the opposite way, turning from his right to his left and then back again, babbling and reading. Now and then, he broke into laughter.

Pollard stepped toward a bench across the walkway and sat down. Sunlight fell across the front of his buttoned-up suit coat and tie. He shielded his eyes so that he could watch his attacker carefully. Now and then, the man looked up to wave some more at passersby, who would look implacably ahead. He seemed unoffended and would then continue his reading.

After several minutes' assuring himself that the fellow was—well, maybe—harmless, Pollard set his teeth, took hold of his nerves, and stood up. He felt much more secure than he had in their previous encounter because so many people were flowing by, providing possible help if Pollard were to need it. He passed through the crowd to the other bench, and sat down a few feet from his assailant. He dropped his attaché case to his feet.

"Hello."

The man looked up from the magazine.

"Do you remember me?"

A look of fevered interest fell across the man's face. "No, man."

"Can I ask your name?"

"Neftali."

"Okay, I—"

"But my nickname is Eshu."

"Why's that?"

"I don't know, man. It's just a name. Everybody calls me that." He sat back and thrust a hand into the left pocket of his jacket. "It's New York. You know, everybody got a nickname in this town." He glanced toward Pollard. "What's yours?"

"Me? Pollard O'Rourke."

"No nickname?"

"No. Just Pollard."

"What's it mean?"

"I don't know. It was my grandfather's name."

"What'd you say it was?"

"Pollard."

"Like the parrot."

"Uh...well..."

Eshu grumbled. "Okay, I'm callin' you Pollie, even though you ain't no parrot."

Pollard sat back and gathered the front of his jacket around him. "So, how are you doing?"

Eshu shook his head. He laid the old, ripped copy of the *Economist* on the bench. "I'm okay, man. What about you?"

"I'm fine."

Eshu leaned over the magazine and continued reading, as though to get rid of Pollard.

"What are you reading about?"

"I don't know." Eshu pointed at the magazine. "None of this shit means anything to me."

"Why are you reading it?"

"I don't know."

Pollard looked off into the distance, toward the river. "You don't remember me, do you?"

"Come on, man! I don't."

"You attacked me a few months ago."

"No, I didn't."

"I'm afraid you did." Pollard pointed across the High Line to the bench where he had injured his hand. "It was right over there. Don't you remember?"

"No."

"I just...I just wanted to ask you why you did that."

Eshu closed the magazine and put it down to his side. "I don't know what you're talkin' about."

"You don't."

"Just leave me alone, Pollie!"

"But I want to know who you are."

Eshu waved his hands about before him, uttering a profanity. "I'm the raven, man. I'm the leaf off the tree. What do you think? I'm the guy who tells the joke. I make you feel good."

"Eshu."

"I'm the love-maker, the earth shaker—"

"Please."

"I'm the zombie. I'm the Zulu."

"Wait a minute."

"And I bet you some kind of lawyer, ain't that right? A cop or somethin'."

Pollard, who usually monopolized the conversations he had with other men, was unused to repartee like this. "I guess I am, yes." This Eshu came from some place, somewhere, that he Pollard would never ever have visited. The leaf off the tree.

"A cop?"

"No...no. A lawyer," Pollard said.

Eshu fell into silence and stared at Pollard. The whites of his eyes were still sprinkled red. The gaze riveted itself to Pollard's eyes and seemed to want to burrow into them. Pollard remained silent. He did not turn his gaze aside, until Eshu finally threw up his hands and took up the magazine again. *"¡Carajo!"*

"Wait a minute. Do you live around here?"

"Me? Why?"

"I don't know. It's just that I've been coming down here for years."

"Not as long as me."

"Since I was a kid."

Eshu pouched his lips tightly together. "Yeah, but you never lived down here."

"That's true." Pollard sat back and crossed his arms. "That's—"

"And I been living in this shithole since I got here."

"Where from?"

Suddenly, Eshu's few teeth shined from his smiling mouth. *"¡La República Dominicana, carnál!"* He tapped the palm of a hand against the magazine.

The cover showed the world being swept up in the claws of a crazed, enormous, multi-colored American eagle.

Later that afternoon, Pollard sat on a metal chair in Bryant Park, eating a tuna sandwich. Two young men, clearly boyfriends, sat on a bench nearby, two large plastic bags from Bed Bath and Beyond at their feet. They were going over the cookware they had just bought, chatting excitedly about the meals that would come from it and the laughter from the parties they would have.

Pollard recalled a conversation of similar happiness that he had had with Cassandra, a few years before. It was the last time she had been able to tell him that she loved him, sitting on a bench beneath a tree in this same park. Cassandra was very thin, and walking any kind of distance was so difficult for her that they had changed their favorite Sunday venue from Central Park to this smaller one. Here, Cassandra could take Pollard's arm, and they could stroll as they had been doing for so many years, just not nearly as far.

She was worried, as frequently was the case, about Pollard. "What will you do when I'm gone?"

She would be gone soon, they both knew. Pollard had asked Cassandra, many times recently, if she realized how much he still cared for her. His affection for her was—by others—so unexpected a feature of their relationship that barely anyone knew of Pollard's almost devastating worry about Cassandra's illness, and what was about to happen to her.

He took her hand. "I'll worry about you some more."

Cassandra lowered her head as she examined the backs of her fingers. The gesture was a familiar one to Pollard, the quickened settling of her glance on some as yet unrevealed thought. He knew that she had something to say that was compelling to her feelings. When they were a younger couple, he often intervened in such moments, hurrying to ask her what was wrong. But even when there was nothing wrong, Cassandra would wait until the thought was completed in her mind, honed properly, and clear. She was not afraid of Pollard, that she would incur his anger or anything of the sort. She merely wanted to say what she really meant to say, rather than allow an utterance—in such an intimate moment—to be false or half-intended. In the last many years, Pollard learned to wait for Cassandra to utter the suggestion or to wind out the tale.

"I wish you wouldn't worry, Pollard."

"Oh, it's just that—"

"Because I'll get to see whether..." Cassandra labored with the phrase, short of breath. The completed sentence came out nonetheless with a kind of whispered freshness. "I'll find out whether any of the stories are true."

Cassandra was wearing a red beret that held to the right side of her head like a 1920s flapper cloche. It was, she said, the best she could do now that her hair was mostly gone. Her hair had been dark brown and full with the invitation to be taken up in Pollard's appreciative fingers. Cassandra had always cared for her appearance, and now grumbled at the deterioration that the illness had caused in her during the previous year and a half. Pollard had also learned during that time how to express his own affection for her in ways that he had been unable to previously. She suggested that his new verbal affability was such a surprise that it was simply too unlike Pollard. Maybe he was trying a little too hard to make her comfortable. This was an accurate observation, but Pollard persisted. Trying too hard or not, he would tell Cassandra how he felt rather than let her intuit it, as she had done so well throughout their marriage.

"I predict..." She held his right hand. Sunlight mottled the walkway before them, the morning bright with fresh color. "I predict that you'll go on for years, Pollard."

"But doing what?"

Cassandra lowered her head once more. She let go of Pollard's hand and folded hers together on her crossed right knee. Gazing at the public library building across the way, the view cluttered with hundreds of strolling visitors, children, tall trees, benches filled with chatting couples and friends, she took in a long breath, and let it out as though it were freeing her.

"You'll tell about the beginning of the world."

"Money, you mean." He grinned.

Cassandra sighed. "Yes, I know you could talk about that, but—"

"It's the basis for everything, you know."

"Oh, but Pollard."

"Can't do anything without it."

"Pollard...."

He stopped.

Cassandra took his hand again. "Pollard, I so care for you. You've been so kind to me." She sighed, an exhalation of regardful exhaustion. "But I need just one more thing from you." Cassandra patted Pollard's fingers. "I need you to listen to this."

Pollard kept silent, waiting.

"You know how much I care about the stories. All those myths that mean so much to me. The way the universe began. The great egg. The coupling. Earth and sky."

Pollard had heard Cassandra's telling of such stories since their first meeting. She had been reading them since her childhood. Because of her, he himself read—in secret, to be sure, not wanting his attorney friends to suspect such softness—about every sort of tribal beginning, every explanation of the birth of animals, the seeding of celestial plants, the jokesters, the birds, the jackals and gods. Oracular mysteries and the upsetting of heavens.

"All I want, Pollard... Please. Don't forget how much I love those stories."

"Of course I won't. I—"

"The story has everything, you know."

"Yes, I—" He stroked her fingers with his own, precise in his care for her illness-informed delicacy.

"You've taken such care of me," she said. "It's true."

"No, I've been—"

"Yes, okay." The index finger of Cassandra's right hand caressed the underside of her gold wedding band. "But so *loving* a difficult man. So... radiant, Pollard."

"Radiant!" he whispered.

"I'm afraid so. You're argumentative, Pollard. When you come home, I can tell how much you've boiled and steamed that day."

Pollard smiled.

"I've sometimes felt imperfect." She studied the wedding band a moment. "Marred. Not up to what you've wanted."

"Please."

"But you've given me what I always wished for."

"Cassandra, I—"

"Love, Pollard." She put the fingers of her right hand to his lips. "Yes. Love. Dented, but reparable. Almost always."

The next time Pollard spotted Eshu, it was a weekday. He watched as Eshu stood, stuffed the cowbell into his backpack and walked, with what appeared to be an aching back, along the High Line, toward uptown. He was heavily involved in conversation with himself. Pollard let him pass, and then followed him.

At the foot of the Twenty-sixth Street stairs, Eshu appeared unaware of the traffic rattling past. He crossed Twenty-sixth, making the finger at the two Yellow cabs that honked at him, and then paused for a moment to talk with a street hot dog vendor in very rapid and gargly Spanish. The umbrella over the stand carried the stand's name, in large red colors: *Perros Calientes Osvaldo.* The vendor, in his twenties and dressed in perfectly turned-out New York football Giants sweat clothes, a pair of black and blue Nike Jordan Melo basketball shoes, very dark black-rimmed sunglasses, a necklace of seashells, and a black beret, continued talking with Eshu as he prepared a hot dog. Pollard could not understand what they said, since for most of his life he had considered the Spanish language beneath him. Now he wished he hadn't thought so ill of it, wishing he could understand what a hot dog vendor might say to someone like Eshu. The man passed the hot dog into Eshu's hands, and waved him away, laughing, not taking any money from him.

Eshu walked very quickly, his right shoulder lower than his left, one hand holding the backpack close. He finished the hot dog, tossing the wrapper to the sidewalk. Several yards further along, he paused in the middle of the block to speak with himself, his left hand held high and making a fist, then an accusatory pointed weapon, finally a caressing palm running itself over his chin.

Eventually, he arrived at, and entered, a one-story brick building that had a sign up above. Pollard could not remember this part of Twenty-sixth Street from his childhood, except that all the buildings then had the same single-story plainness that this one still had. Now, with so many new restaurants and shops, this appeared to be one of the few such buildings left on the street. The bricks were painted brown on the outside, although the paint was chipped everywhere. The sign over the entrance appeared new. Bright red lettering formed an arch over a rendition of a candy-apple red 1968 Chevrolet Impala convertible with the top down, and two brightly smiling dark-haired girls in sunglasses waving at passersby. The lettering announced Basoalto Auto Repair and Wrecking.

The flat-roofed building had a double entrance—on one side, cars pointing in; on the other, cars pointing out.

"Can I help you?" A large man in Levi's and a blue work shirt, carrying a clipboard that held several sheets of paper, approached Pollard. The shirt pocket was embroidered with his name, written in script: Raúl Basoalto. "Somethin' wrong with your car?"

"No, I..."

Raúl's dark brown skin was mottled with black freckles on both cheeks. He had a mustache.

"I'm here because I'm concerned about...about Eshu."

Raúl looked over his shoulder into the garage, then took a rag from a back pocket of his Levi's and wiped his hands. "What about him?"

Pollard, too, looked into the garage, but saw nothing of Eshu. "Well, he...he—"

"What are you, from the city or something'?"

"The city."

"Yeah, you know, Public Assistance? Public Health?"

"No, I—"

"Then why do you want to talk to me?"

"Well, I followed him here."

"Followed him!"

"Yes, I—"

"Look, man, I'm his brother." Raúl waved his hand to the rear, into the shop. "I own this place." Five mechanics were working on several cars. "Is he in some kind of trouble again?"

The shop was not well lit, with only one window, covered over, in the iron door that led, Pollard guessed, to a back office, or maybe outside. Everything in the shop seemed in its place. Raúl's set jaw bespoke the importance he placed on his business. He had once been a muscled man, Pollard guessed, now softened by middle age and a life of work in the garage. He wore heavy-rimmed eyeglasses and a plastic sleeve with three ballpoint pens in his shirt pocket.

"No, no trouble," Pollard said. "I—"

"So what about him?"

"He's been up on the High Line, yelling at people."

Raúl's hand dropped to his side, the papers on the clipboard folding over upside down.

"I think he's endangering himself."

Raúl exhaled, a combination of distressed anger and acquiescence to unwanted news. "Yeah."

"People are afraid of him." Pollard put a hand on the rear fender of a late-model Cadillac parked in the entrance. "Even me. I was afraid of him."

"Was?"

"Yes. He attacked me."

Raúl looked to the back of the shop, and then gestured up the sidewalk. "Okay. Come on. Let's take a walk."

The two men entered a decrepit Polish diner a few blocks away and sat at the counter. They ordered coffee. The diner was clean enough, although everything in it was so lined and pouched with age that what appeared soiled—the linoleum floor, the dishes and cups, the guy at the stove—was actually just old.

"What's your name?"

Pollard began the reply, but then thought better of it. The waitress brought the coffee.

"Pollie," Pollard said.

"What do you know about Eshu?"

"Hardly anything." Pollard lifted the cup to his lips. He had also ordered two slices of buttered toast. The butter lay before him, in a pool on the toast. He had described the attack for Raúl, whose worry, and even anguish, were immediate. Raúl, a spoon in his right hand, leaned forward over the counter as Pollard described in more detail what had happened.

"I only know that he's crazy. I mean, excuse me for that. But he could do real harm to himself."

Raúl nodded. When he sighed, his jowls, covered with a few days' growth of graying beard, sagged. "Why does a guy like you care, though?"

"Like me?"

"Yeah, you know, the suit, the tie..." Raúl pointed to Pollard's attaché case. "That thing." He studied the case a moment. "What you got in there?"

"Papers. Nothing."

"So why does Eshu matter to you?"

Pollard understood the reason for the question. "A year ago, he wouldn't have, but—"

"Then why now?" Raúl took a sip from his coffee.

Pollard did not have an immediate answer. It had not actually occurred to him that he was worried about Eshu. He had not realized the movement of his heart, because he had so little experience of that movement in any instance but those with Cassandra.

"You know, he gets a lot of kindness, Pollie, from people who've known him all his life. But—"

"Not from people like me."

"No." Raúl's lips turned down, a passing across them of ironic humor. "I don't think Eshu's ever met anyone like you."

Pollard nodded agreement. "Or me, him." He took up a piece of toast, turned it on end so that the butter could drip from it to the plate, which it did in a slow yellow drool. Eventually he lifted the toast to his lips.

"He's always been bats," Raúl muttered. "My older brother. And I knew that, even when I was little. He couldn't do anything. He just wandered around. Got in the way." Raúl took up a spoonful of sugar from a small covered bowl, and poured it into his coffee. "But our parents loved him. Everybody did."

"What about your parents?"

Raúl smiled, studying the coffee. "My father, he got here from Quisqueya." He turned toward Pollard. "You know where that is, right?"

"No, I—"

"Dominican Republic!"

Pollard nodded.

"And then he brought our mother here, a long time ago. They were young."

"And you were born here."

"Both of us, yeah." Raúl stirred the coffee a bit more, its profound darkness giving off a rising of steam. "My father liked cars. A good mechanic." His head flowed back and forth in a sighing nod. "But, get a job?

Nah, if you were like us...you know, goin' around in Spanish everywhere and..." Raúl pointed to the skin of his right forearm. "This color..." He placed the fingers of his right hand against the side of the cup, caressing it. "I had to go with my father every time the police picked Eshu up, when we were kids. You know, like, when I was eight or nine, because my father, he couldn't get the English. Neither of them, him or my mom, neither of them could get it."

"But you—"

"Yeah, because I was born here. So the cops would read the paperwork to me, and I'd translate it for my father, and then we'd be able to get Eshu out."

"How often did that happen?"

"A couple times a year." Raúl sipped from the coffee. "I bet I've met every social worker in Manhattan for the last four decades." He broke into a saddened grin. "And by the time I grew up, you *could* get a job. My father had taught me about cars, you know, enough to get on in a garage that a couple of those Irish guys owned."

"Where?"

"Right here. My place." Raúl laughed. "You know, they were payin' protection to the Westies. So their business was pretty good. The Flynn Brothers."

"Where are they now?"

"They're both gone. Joe Flynn sold me the business before he died. He was a good guy."

The crusts of Pollard's toast lay mired in butter.

"So my father couldn't get work. And Eshu, he didn't know from nothin'. Everybody was worried." Raúl finished the coffee and replaced the cup on the counter. The spoon inside it rattled around like a small bell. "And then my father got the goats."

Raul asked for another cup of coffee.

"Even in the seventies, see, there still were animals in pens and yards, here and there all over Manhattan. Chickens, turkeys, sheep. All kinds. So my father couldn't get a job, and he noticed guys up on the elevated tracks, with shovels and clippers and stuff, cutting back the weeds. And these were substantial crews...seven, ten guys, back and forth, up and down from one end of the line to the other."

He poured a little milk into his coffee.

"And my father, he and his father had always had goats back home, and he knew that you didn't have to pay them no wages, and that they were far better than a bunch of guys with shovels. So he went to the rail yards and talked to somebody." The milk swirled about in the coffee like tumbling clouds. "Who knows how he found the guy to talk to? But he did. And they said they'd give it a try if my dad could supply the goats. And he knew a guy down in the West Village, some kind of a farmer or somethin', I don't know, who had some goats. And they worked a deal. He'd rent the goats, with an option...an option—"

"To buy."

"Yeah. And you know, eventually, he did buy them, and then some more. So..." Raúl beckoned toward the guy at the stove and ordered a couple of fried eggs, sunny side up. "So then, he had a job, and so did Eshu." He reached to his right for a bottle of catsup. "You know, Pollie, my father was good with the goats. But Eshu...Eshu, he was great."

"How so?"

"He talked to them. None of the rest of us could understand him half the time, but they could."

"But how did you.... How did you know?"

"Because—I swear to you, Pollie—because *they* talked to *him*."

Pollard saw Eshu again the next day. This time he wasn't reading. Rather, he lay on one of the wood chaise lounges on the High Line, sunning himself.

"I know you're from Quisqueya."

Eshu had entwined the fingers of both hands behind his head. He wore a pair of cheap sunglasses. He was not wearing his wool cap, and Pollard noted that his hairline had receded quite a bit, and that his hair color was cobbled here and there with gray.

"You know about Quisqueya?"

"No." Pollard stretched his legs out on another chaise, next to Eshu's, that was also facing the sun. "It's next to Haiti, I know that."

"Yeah, but nobody goes to Haiti." Eshu lowered his head. "That place… you saw that earthquake." He laid his head back against the bench headrest and allowed himself to become bathed in light. "That was God's laughter, man, that earthquake."

"You know, years ago, I used to see an older man and a kid, a teenager, herding those goats up here."

Eshu did not reply. His face remained immobile, his hands behind his head. His lips began working against one another, as though some sort of fever were building in his mind. Pollard leaned toward Eshu, his hands held open, the fingers splayed.

"Was that you, Eshu, back then, up here?"

"Don't ask."

"No, come on, was it? Were you the kid?"

A gleam of spittle rested on Eshu's lower lip, which he wiped clean with his left hand.

"Was that your father?"

Eshu raised the hand once more to the back of his head. Sunlight glistened from the lenses of his dark glasses. The image of the round sun itself, halfway up the sky on this late morning, popped from the surface of each lens like a burning coin.

"Eshu…."

The suns began to quiver. Eshu brought a fist to his mouth, and held it there. A gasp came from him. Pollard realized that it was an expression of grief.

"Yeah, man. So what?"

"Well, I…" Pollard gathered his hands, watching as Eshu ground the fist against his tightly closed lips. "I loved those goats when I was a kid. My wife loved them."

Eshu's glasses quivered with new ferocity. The sun was rising. "Me, too," he whispered.

"So it was you and your father."

"Of course it was, *cabrón*. What did you expect?"

"What was your father's name?"

"Eshu, man. Eshu Senior."

"A hot dog, please," Pollard said. "Catsup, mustard, and relish."

"Somethin' to drink?"

"Yes, a Coke, please."

The young man set about preparing the meal.

"Can I ask your name?"

"Listen, pal, it's up there." The vendor pointed at the umbrella.

Pollard looked up. "Osvaldo. And you've been doing this for long?"

Osvaldo took a bun from a heated metal drawer, and then swirled around with a pair of tongs in the boiling water kettle, searching out a frankfurter that was fully cooked. "Gotta make a living," he said without looking up. He paid little attention to Pollard himself, treating him, actually, as though the attorney were some kind of Upper East Side rich idiot slumming down here on the West Side, and therefore to be ignored.

"Eshu told me about you."

Osvaldo looked up from the can of Coca-Cola now in his right hand. His sunglasses glared. "You're Pollie?"

Pollard took the Coke. "That's me."

An immediate change altered Osvaldo's demeanor. "He told me about you, too." He stuck his hand out in greeting. His smile revealed bright teeth perfectly aligned. "It's nice to meet you."

"It is?"

"Yeah. You been nice to Eshu, and…you know, that can be tough sometimes."

"I do know that."

"But he told me you know about the goats."

"I do." Pollard lowered his attaché case to the ground.

"Yeah, you saw them even when old Eshu was alive."

"I did."

"I wish I'd known him." Osvaldo looked over his shoulder at the High Line, which was, as usual now, the source of laughter and celebration thirty feet up, children shouting. "When they put this new High Line up, they made it illegal for the goats to go there. So, Eshu was out of a job." He took up the bun and began making a hot dog for Pollard.

"Pardon me, I don't like a lot of bread in the bun. Could you…could you—"

"Dig it out?"

"Yes, please."

Osvaldo nodded. He picked at the center of each half of the bun, removing much of the white-paste bread. "You got to realize that Eshu never actually had a job after the trains stopped running in 1980. And his father died a couple years after that. I mean, nobody paid him any more. And in those days the railroad tracks were really bad. I mean, it was junkie heaven up there. But Eshu kept going, and took the goats with him, because he knew—at least he told us kids that he knew—all along that the tracks would be open again some day, and that they'd need the goats." Osvaldo showed the dug out bun to Pollard, seeking his approval. "You see what I'm sayin'?"

Pollard nodded. He took up the catsup bottle and passed it to Osvaldo.

"So he's been pretty angry about this." Osvaldo pointed with the catsup bottle over his right shoulder, up at the tracks. "He doesn't fully get it that his being angry doesn't mean a thing to the city guys who run the High Line." Osvaldo laid a trail of catsup into the long crater of the lower bun, a kind of abstract expressionist garnish. He plopped a frankfurter into the bun as well. "He doesn't like suits."

"The clothes they wear, you mean."

"Yeah. But I really mean the guys that wear them. You know, bureaucrats and stuff. Business guys." Osvaldo pointed with the semi-completed hot dog at the front of Pollard's suit coat. "Guys like you." He looked away briefly, grinding his teeth. "No disrespect, man. But you know…suits!"

"So, no goats."

"That's right." Osvaldo held up a bottle of relish and raised his eyebrows at Pollard. Pollard gave his assent. "And it drives him nuts."

"Yes, he seems pretty hurt."

"Hurt? What do you mean?"

"Damaged."

"No, man." Osvaldo spooned a large glob of relish across the hot dog. "He's the air itself." He hurried the paper wrap around it. "Especially when I give him one of my dogs. Shifty. Cloudy."

He handed the hot dog over, and Pollard passed a ten-dollar bill into Osvaldo's hand.

"He always tells me that. He once said the hot dog makes him static, you know what I mean?"

Pollard held his breath. The hot dog warmed his hand. What was this language?

"He told me lots of things when I was a kid. Smoke. From human fires, see?" Osvaldo's bright teeth flashed, perfect. "Food. Dreams. Stories, man."

Pollard surveyed the red meat, the fern-colored relish, and the blood-seeming catsup.

"You eat that dog and you'll get what I'm sayin'." Osvaldo examined the bill in his fingers, and then handed it back. "Hey, you need this more than I do."

The next few days, Pollard waited for Eshu on the Fourteenth Street bench, but he did not show up. Pollard sat reading—the *Wall Street Journal.* The *Post.* The *Economist*—and no Eshu. He decided to get a hot dog.

"I don't know," Osvaldo said. "Sometimes he just gets moody, you know? Gets into himself." The hot dog vendor tapped the side of his head with an index finger. "Thinkin'. 'New words,' he says. 'Somethin' new up my sleeve.'"

Raúl had a similar response. "There are times when you just can't reach him, that's all."

"What, you don't know where he is?"

Raúl chuckled. "No, Pollie, I mean, you talk to him, but he's just not there. He's gone."

"I see. But, can I see him?"

Raúl grumbled with unexpected impatience. "He doesn't want to be bothered."

"But—"

"Pollie. You just got to listen to me about this. Eshu's thinking about things. He's, like, in solitary, you know? Contemplatin' stuff."

Pollard went to his office, and then returned to the bench every morning and every afternoon for the next several days. His desk took on an uncustomary messiness, its usual pristine orderliness suffering some sort of distraction. Paperwork remained outside the manila folders in which it had hitherto been so carefully organized. Parts of documents fell to the floor. He missed the wastebasket when getting rid of stuff, something that had almost never happened before. Pollard spent long periods of time looking out the window. Standing in the glass-intensified light, watching the passing crowds on the High Line down below, he sighed with the continuing absence of Eshu's raggedy speech and drooped shoulders.

He went out one day at lunchtime, to get a hot dog from Osvaldo, when, suddenly, like a strike of hurried lightning, he heard the dissonant jangle of bells coming up the Twenty-sixth Street stairs, the scattered clopping of dozens of hooves, the confused baa-ing and cacophony of animals hurrying up from the street. A dozen goats burst onto the High Line.

Eshu came up behind them, a long stick in his hands, his voice shouting out orders at the goats in no perceptible language. He was herding them, directing them, consoling them.

There was immediate delight among the children on the High Line. Held back by their parents, taken up into their parents' arms, they nonetheless were charmed by the animals, amazed by them. Eshu herded the goats into a circle and started inviting people to come look at them. Especially the children, who seemed so much better prepared to be entertained by the goats than were their parents. iPhones came out. Cameras, pictures, laughter....

Just as quickly, a phalanx of policemen came up the stairs. They charged the goats, the children now being grabbed up by their parents, pulled away, pulled from harm.

The police ran for the goats. They carried billy clubs and wore flak jackets and helmets with plastic face guards.

"Hang on, guys," Pollard shouted. None of the officers acknowledged him. They surged ahead, intent on the goats. "This isn't necessary."

One of the policemen approached him, pointing at him with his billy club. "You! Sir! Get out of the way."

Pollard grabbed him by the elbow. "Son, you don't need to do this." The cop punched him in the ribs with the end of his stick, and Pollard went down.

The goats stampeded. Eshu had lost control of them, and the animals scattered, seeking alarmed escape. The neck bells rattled and rang gracelessly. Parents ran away with their children. Some hid behind benches. Others sought the stairways leading to the street below. The goats appeared to turn on the tourists, to attempt to defend themselves against them, although Pollard, rolling over in pain and watching, could tell that they were themselves just scared of the rampaging police. The goats were trying to get out of the way. They were as afraid of the cops as the tourists were.

As the goats scattered, so did Eshu's mind. He attacked the police with his stick, flailing at them with it. A few of them retaliated, and Eshu took two severe blows. A club to the head brought a spatter of blood down his face, and as he knelt to try to recover himself, he was kicked from behind. He sprawled on the walkway but recovered so quickly that he once more rose up and continued shouting, still attempting to fight the police off. But they backed him from the walkway, into and through a large plot of flowers, toward the side wall of the High Line. Continuing to defend himself, Eshu was staggered by a rough blow to his left shoulder.

Pollard stood, holding his ribs, bent over in pain. "Officers! Stop!"

Eshu raised a fist. He railed at the cops, shouting that they were nothing but *maricones* and *mama ñema*s. Finally, lurching backwards, driven and shouting the whole way, he fell over the low railing to the street below.

The following day, a spontaneous altar arrangement appeared before the entrance to Basoalto Auto Repair and Wrecking. The central object was a cross made from spliced-together pieces of painted wood, nailed upright to a wooden plank. To either side of the cross was a black-and-white photograph of Eshu in a metal frame. Or at least Pollard supposed that they were of Eshu. One showed him at the age of about fourteen, dressed in a suit coat, a white shirt and tie, glaring at the camera. He looked like he had just won a prize at school, the look on his face of dazzled hilarity. The other photo showed him standing on the railroad tracks of the old West Side Freight Line, about twenty years old, two goats posing with him, all three, as it were, smiling for the camera. Both photos were brown-yellow with age. A collection of candles had also been assembled, many of them now lit, big and small, slender and fat. Wax puddled up and down their shafts or at their feet, bunched and piled. A dozen new votive candles sat in a cardboard box to the side, to be lit, Pollard assumed, by passersby. A few art objects also lay about the altar, small statues of the Virgin Mary, little skulls made of hardened sugar and painted with food dye, an old rosary, and many, many indistinct amulets, stones and shells.

Osvaldo had wheeled his stand to the sidewalk outside the garage, and was open for business.

A line had formed at the stand. A lot of children accompanied by their mothers stood behind homeless men and women and other general passersby, while a half block away, a group of chatting New York City firemen approached. Pollard knew there was a station on West Thirty-first Street.

He stood to the side of the stand. He felt all right, although his bruised ribs had been wrapped at the hospital the night before. Quickly, the line grew and grew.

Osvaldo shook Pollard's hand. He had heard about the lawyer's attempt to protect Eshu. Pollard sipped from the cold Coke that the vendor had given him.

"Listen, Osvaldo, could you give everyone a dog today? Everybody who comes here?"

"Of course, I always do that."

"But I mean, on the house, like you did for me the other day."

Osvaldo placed a hand on the counter top, his gaze centered on Pollard as though the attorney were out of his mind. "Listen, there are going to be hundreds of people here today."

"Hundreds!"

"Yeah, everybody knew Eshu."

"I…I know that."

"You're talkin' thousands of dollars."

Pollard lowered his attaché case to the sidewalk, hunkered down and opened it. From among the half-dozen manila folders holding sheets of paper covered with tight, word-processed paragraphs—many, many paragraphs, one after another—he took his billfold and, turning his back to the ever more lengthening line, removed ten hundred-dollar bills. "I'll pay. This'll get you through the morning, won't it?"

Osvaldo gawked at the bills. "Sure, but—"

"Keep a tab." Pollard looked back over his shoulder at the line, now being joined by some uniformed bus drivers, a few street workers in neon-yellow-striped jackets and hard hats. There was even a policeman, a Latino of some sort, who had removed his hat and was saying with obvious feeling to one of the bus drivers that this was a disaster, that it shouldn't have happened, that.... The policeman shook his head, grimacing and appearing to Pollard to be anguished, perhaps in mourning.

"I'm good for it," Pollard said. He pushed the money into Osvaldo's hands, and glanced into the garage. "I've got to go to the bank, and I'll be back this afternoon. But first, I want to talk with Raúl."

Raúl lowered his head, his hands in the pockets of his work pants. He leaned against the fender of a blue Volvo.

Pollard buttoned the suit jacket. "You know, I've never paid attention to crazy people on the street."

"That's for sure, a guy like you." Raúl gestured toward the sidewalk outside, and the now joyful crowd that was gathered around Osvaldo's stand. A few musicians had arrived. "You don't have to, like we do down here."

"But you paid extra attention to Eshu."

Raúl nodded as he studied a couple of spots of engine oil on the shop floor. His teeth worked, causing his mouth to shift back and forth. "You'll never get how much we loved him, Pollie."

Pollard suddenly went back over his years at O'Rourke Testi Moody Grumbold, and how few of the conversations that he had there were like the ones he had had with Eshu, Raúl, and Osvaldo. None, in fact. "Look, I miss Eshu," he said. "How many times do you get to talk with the raven?"

Raúl grinned. "He told you that, too, eh?"

"Yes. Or the Zulu? Or the zombie?"

A long silence ensued, during which Raúl mourned.

"What can I do, Raúl? Please."

Raúl removed his glasses and wiped the front surfaces of them against his shirt. He replaced the glasses. "You're a lawyer, no?"

"Yes."

"All right, come with me."

They walked to the back of the garage, to the single iron door with a small window in it, the one taped with cardboard. As they approached the door, Raúl looked over his shoulder toward the shop entrance, toward the firemen waiting with the rest of the throng for free hot dogs. Seeing that everyone outside was for the moment occupied with the party atmosphere, he reached for the doorknob and gestured to Pollard to follow him.

A sparse vacant lot, surrounded by the backsides of other low brick buildings, contained a large shack in one corner. More a small barn, it featured a couple of oblong tin water buckets in front and several shallow metal bowls with animal feed of some sort. Six very old goats lay in the lot in the morning sun. Grizzled, all of them.

"These are all that's left." Raúl looked toward the door, which had closed behind him. "You know, they were too old to get to the tracks yesterday, even though, man, I can tell you they wanted to go. We used to be able to keep the goats in a vacant lot, which our father did for years, and then Eshu after him. Over on—"

"Twenty-fifth."

Raúl looked up, surprised. "You been there?"

"I used to go and visit them."

Raúl scratched his head, shrugging. "But now, we're not supposed to keep them. The city would get after us if they knew. So…" He approached one of the goats and leaned over to pet the animal. The goat stopped chewing for a moment, enjoying the affection. "The neighbors, they keep it quiet, too. They like the goats. They…they…" Raúl sighed, lowering his head.

The goat sought another caress.

"Would you help us with the city?" Raúl stood back and placed his hands in his pockets. The goat observed him, the animal's look that of a companion offering solicitude.

Pollard leaned over and pet the goat as well. "So that you won't have to give them up?"

"Yeah. We want to keep them here." Raúl studied the animals, and

Pollard easily saw how much they meant to him. "All of them." He fingered the ballpoint pens in his shirt pocket.

Pollard barely hesitated. He knew that Cassandra would have enjoyed being here, and suddenly felt that, in fact, she was. "Sure, I'll do it."

"We don't have any money to pay you."

"Nah. The money doesn't matter, Raúl."

The vacant lot, the shed, and the plainspoken wood chips that covered the ground began to change. Gradually, they became for Pollard a wooded glen, a meandering pathway leading through forests deciduous and evergreen, through ferns that opened themselves to the light, across rock-clinging mosses and strewn-about boulders lined with veins of obsidian and shining silver, the light itself filtered by the trees, glimmering between them in narrow shafts, through which beacon-like bugs floated and twirled, bringing the light to further light as they passed.

All the goats were chewing and, were it not so silent, you would think that they were talking, although not in a babble of amused, crazy monologues. Rather, they were conversing, asking questions, and pursuing suggestions. A charm of goldfinches fluttered about, above which a kettle of soaring hawks kept watch. Were there an ocean in view, Pollard would have expected to see a fluther of jellyfish or a shoal of mackerel. But in fact he noticed friendly swarms and flights of every kind of bright insect, a fleet of mud hens, a parliament of owls, and many others, all of them back and forth, talking, discoursing.

He felt Cassandra's hand caressing his. "Pollard...love." Together, they listened to it all. Raúl listened too. Talk of birth. Shades and phantasms. Rain falling. The bird rising. Who the gods were, so many of them, so diverse, yet all of them telling tales of the beginning of life and its end, of children supplanting their parents, the living and the dead, of humans changed to celestial creatures...the raven, the fox, the coyote, the leaf off the tree.

BLAZES

Riding with Leo in a taxi on Forty-second Street, Blazes felt that he should keep his eyes averted. He was, after all, about to sleep with Leo's wife, Molly. So he stared at his fingernails. They revealed little, especially with regard to Blazes's character and the depth of his feelings. There wasn't much depth, generally. But at the moment he felt strangely odd, being able to take such advantage of Leo. He liked Leo quite a bit.

"There's nothing like a day in New York, is there, Blazes? When the weather's..." Leo pointed out into the heat. "Jesus, like this."

The blacktop, cars, trucks, and pedestrians all appeared to have been brought from a kiln. Sunshine sprayed the back seat of the taxi in which they rode. The June humidity had caused their suits to become damp and itchy, irritating. Standing out in it, as the two men had been on a Times Square corner a few minutes before, had been like being immersed in a tall, hot puddle.

Blazes and Leo had attended Columbia University together some years before. Blazes (or Hugh, as he had been known then) had a degree in dramatic arts, but he had not gone very far with it. Hugh Boylan had been an actor who had just missed out on certain productions, who should have been cast in commercials, TV shows, and movies, but whose agents had lacked the moxie to get him those certain plum parts. At least, that's what he thought for quite a while. But then, finally facing the fact that he was a second-rate thespian—indeed, always had been—he became an agent representing classical music singers. Hugh Boylan Arts, with an office on

Fifty-sixth behind Carnegie Hall. Molly Flowers was one of them. She was a very fine singer, but what Blazes really liked about her was that she imagined him a remarkable lover. She had told him so just yesterday, in his office, while he was admiring himself in a mirror before taking Molly out for lunch. The smile on her lips gave her away. Blazes suggested they meet again the next day, after a funeral Blazes had to attend, to talk about a new, better contract, and Molly agreed.

At the moment, the two men were going to the funeral in the Bronx. Paddy Dignam, a Dublin actor whom they had known at Columbia, had died in a motorcycle accident.

"He never knew how to ride that thing." Leo laid a hand on his own knee, still looking out the window. "I told him, but he wouldn't listen."

Paddy had expired at the corner of Broadway and 125th, run into by a taxi. Alcohol had blurred his attention that morning. Paddy's frequent difficulties as an actor had been similarly caused by his drinking, and, like Blazes, he had missed out on parts for which he otherwise had been a shoo-in, and had been fired from productions that had gone on to great success. Paddy even missed the appointment to have his caricature drawn by Al Hirschfeld. At the time, Paddy was watching the Knicks lose to the Celtics in a playoff game, shouting out obscenities during a double overtime, a Guinness in one hand, the TV wanger in the other. With the excitement of the basketball, he was oblivious to the two phone calls from Hirschfeld's assistant to Paddy's agent, and the agent's to him, wondering *Where's Paddy?*

Also like Blazes, Paddy blamed his failures as an actor on elements other than the absolute true one, which in his case was the Guinness. Unlike Blazes, however, Paddy won two Tonys for his performances in Beckett and Synge. A fine man…everyone thought so. Fun. Wistful. So intelligent an actor, the textures in his roles solely Paddy Dignam's and no one else's, and someone in whom you could confide. It was for those reasons that Leo, at least, was going to his funeral.

It was Molly who had given Blazes his nickname. When she first met him, she told him that "Hugh" was a nice name. A very nice name. But also she said that, because of the curls in his hair, the many hundreds of them, and its dark red-brown colors, she would call him Blazes. At first Molly was the only person who used the name, but Blazes wished that someone in his family in Boston had come up with the idea of "Blazes" as a nickname when he had been a little boy. That way, everyone now would refer to him as such. But especially, Blazes liked that Molly thought him Blazes. His sense of humor responded to the name in the way that he himself responded to Molly.

Some months ago at a dinner, Hugh had even told friends of his that, when he was a boy, his father called him Blazes, coming as he did from "the ferocity of my parents' loins, you see." Although a lie, the line brought a laugh from the others. His tone of voice carried a suggestion of ironic embarrassment, as though he really didn't want the comedy of the name's initiation known, as though it were a long-ago, humorous secret. Blazes got the response he silently wanted from his friends. They were mostly New Yorkers, so he could depend on their making of his ersatz stumble a mark of his very personality. They would make fun of him for it. The name would become a badge that Hugh Boylan would have to wear for the rest of his life. Thus it was that Hugh Boylan became Blazes Boylan, and now was called so by almost everyone he knew.

Leo Flowers had marketed the Krakatoa Tacos fast food empire into a household name in the U.S. But he was also that oddity in the advertising business, a contemplative man.

Krakatoa Tacos was in China now, with 1,700 stores to add to the 5,300 stores in the U.S., and Leo's comic marketing prowess had brought it all about. *(Surely it wasn't the goddamned tacos*, Leo thought privately.) He had even asked Bruce Springsteen's manager to ask Bruce to compose and sing the jingle, Leo's only failure in his enthusiastic building of the Krakatoa Tacos brand. So it came as a surprise to many, upon first meeting him, to learn that Leo was shy. He often seemed distracted in meetings with clients. Bored just by virtue of being there. Thinking about other things.

Just now, in the taxi, he was indeed thinking about something else. He grumbled to himself about how a woman of such humor and sensuous intensity as Molly could care for a guy like Blazes Boylan. Was it just his silly name, the wholly intended pun of it? Did Blazes make her laugh in ways that Leo could not?

He had found out about Blazes's plans for Molly from Paddy Dignam, who was privy to the theater scuttlebutt around town.

"You might want to pay a little more attention to your wife, boy-o," Paddy told Leo over coffee a few weeks before his accident.

"Why so?"

"Well, I…" Paddy, his face a gathering of long-lined angles below a windstorm of red hair, his eyes wide with the possibility of tension-scattering laughter, looked over his shoulder. They were seated at the counter of the Empire Diner, and Paddy, a Visa card in his hand, was looking for the waiter, Benny, a sometime actor who was a friend of both men. "I understand that Blazes has been runnin' about airin' his quiff, as me great-grandmother would say."

"What does that mean? It's Irish?"

"The phrase? Or the act of doing it?"

"The phrase."

"It means, it means…" Paddy's mouth turned down at the ends, as though pulled to it by some oddity of gravity. "What would you least like to see your wife doing, Leo, with a man who's got a glorious head of hair like Blazes Boylan's?"

Leo sighed. Blazes Boylan? That fool? Molly, in the very act of walking across a stage or rehearsing a scene with some notable tenor, moved with such subtle spectacle that many thought her an even better actress than she was a singer. Just now, though, he recalled how, years ago, she had lowered herself over him in her Chinese silk nightgown, like a grand sea-blue butterfly, on their wedding night, as though to envelop him soul and all. "I'm dying for it, Leo," she had said.

Yes. That was gone.

Thinking about all this in the taxi, Leo took a moment to survey Blazes's fine manner of dressing. The gray silk suit from Barney's, the Shanghai Tang tie and socks. The fingernails. Blazes's hair was just beginning to lighten, and this suggestion of age actually gave him more swagger than he had had as a younger man. Of all things, Blazes looked distinguished, and it pleased Leo to be able to observe, after so many years of acquaintance with him, that Blazes was really just a well-appointed clown. A blowhard with a very minor talent.

Paddy grimaced. "Airin' his quiff?" He beckoned to Benny for the check. "It means, it—"

"I think I get what it means."

"Displayin' himself, you might say. Hair and all."

They walked out of the Empire Diner and headed down Twenty-third Street toward the subway stop. Paddy seemed conflicted. He wished to tell Leo more. He was nervous, Leo knew. *And that's why he's such a friend. He's not afraid. He's telling me something about my own personal intimate failure, and he's taking the risk. He'll do it for my sake.*

"I know Blazes Boylan." Paddy's voice made the remark sound like a grand revelation from across the footlights. "And, forgive me, Leo, I know Molly."

Paddy, who had met Molly through Leo when they were first going out, was now her close friend as well. The three of them frequently talked about their years of camaraderie, especially in the long conversations in which the singer and the actor talked about different ways of doing a scene. The conversations bristled with professional advice and gossip. Laughing insults as well. Paddy's singing, Molly tittered, sounded like air escaping a balloon.

He often teased her for her looks, especially on stage, when she had the talent to simply embody what she was singing. "First time I ever heard a voice that looked so glamorous," Paddy once told her, a compliment that brought pleased laughter from both Molly and Leo.

As the two men approached the entrance to the subway station, Paddy buttoned his dark brown sport jacket. The white shirt he wore, wrinkled, and the wrinkled slacks gave a note of elegance to his scuffed wingtips. "I know the effect Molly has on men."

Leo took in a breath.

"So, God help us, I hope she's not in love with that idiot."

After their son died as an infant, Molly no longer cared much for Leo. Upon his birth, the boy had indeed become the love of her life, and that was actually a satisfaction to Leo, something to be expected, he thought. Things would even out. But then the boy just as suddenly passed away. The opening of the door to the end of love that little Rudy had provided did not close simply because of his death. Indeed, with his passing, the door opened wide.

Leo's very heart struggled with Rudy's death. An accident, everyone said. But in his sad reflections afterwards, he knew that he was the cause of it. Despite the baby having been born just eleven days before, Molly honored an invitation to sing at a friend's wedding. So it was Leo who put Rudy in his crib that night, tummy down; Leo who did not awaken when the boy somehow got caught up in the blanket; Leo who slept through the silent struggle of suffocation. When Molly returned from the wedding reception, she leaned over the crib to give the boy a kiss. "Sweet little Rudy...."

The boy's coffin, on a side altar at Saint Patrick's Cathedral, was two feet long. The priest that had baptized him a few days before now eulogized him. Molly wore a severe black dress to the funeral, and she refused any effort that Leo made to hold her hand. Thereafter, they slept separately.

But he well remembered, often, what it was like to make love to Molly. Her heart pounding, her shouting out of the single word *Yes* time and again as her entire body seemed, like her heart, to open itself and flow, to turn to flesh-borne unruly heat as she came...came again...and then slowly calmed, her arms around Leo, whispering how much she loved him, that she would never wish to live without him, that Leo held her happiness in one hand and her desire in another.

Rudy had come to be in such a moment, so long ago.

Blazes did like Leo, but he thought he was a fool to leave his wife out to dry like this. When Molly and he were first talking about representation, Blazes watched her from the wings at a production in the Koch Theater. Molly, playing Blanche DuBois in a concert version of André Previn's *A Streetcar Named Desire,* stood on stage with the other singers before the orchestra. It was the usual for a concert version, nothing special, no dramatic action. Her long red dress was a knock-off of a Balenciaga, never actually used, that a friend of hers had bought at a fire sale of old costumes from the Met. Molly sang. The others sang. An attentive, silent audience.

But music filled the place, and when the moment arrived in which Blanche was being taken away by the kindly doctor, Blazes felt that he could actually see Blanche's madness and the seductiveness of her walk just in the way that Molly sang. Her voice seized Blazes's heart. "The kindness of strangers," she sang. It seemed at the moment that Blanche DuBois surely must be heading from Stanley and Stella's apartment to the implosion of her own soul. But her wish for love—the desire for kindness—compelled her to go with the doctor. "Whoever you are," she sang, her voice suffused with gratitude and confused sorrow. Molly's voice carried all that, and Blazes took the edge of a leg curtain into his right hand, holding it tight as she sang, as though, without it—"Whoever you are."—he would simply disappear.

Molly told Leo that Billie Holiday was buried at Saint Raymond's Catholic Cemetery. "Maybe they'll lay Paddy down next to her." She hugged Leo goodbye. "She'd enjoy that." Molly could not go to the service herself, her rehearsal schedule preventing it. For her, Paddy Dignam's acting was one thing, but his singing (despite her kidding of him) was a talent of another order altogether. Over dinner the evening before, Molly, in tears, had repeated a thought that had often come to her over the years. "You know, with training, he could have been just as big an opera star. A voice like the one he had?"

Paddy was congratulated by critics for, among other things, his first moment in *Waiting for Godot*, in which he played Vladimir. Because Vladimir begins the second act with a song and sings once more later, Paddy intended Vladimir to be a kind of wrecked troubadour. He suggested to the director that he begin the first act singing, too…"The Lass of Aughrim," a favorite of Paddy's, whose mother had often sung it for him back in Dublin.

"O, the rain falls on my heavy locks
And the dew wets my skin,
My babe lies cold here in my arms,
And none will let me in."

No one ever saw a Vladimir like Paddy's. He took the show on to London and then to Dublin, where he was equally lionized, not least for the ironic, immediate wistfulness offered by the old Irish song's soul-destroying isolation.

Leo and Blazes joined other mourners as they walked up an incline toward an open plot among many gravestones. The priest waited with the coffin. Most of the mourners were dressed in black, and Leo recognized several: other actors, theater people of every sort, movie stars...Liam Neeson, Nathan Lane. Blazes knew a good many of these people personally, and he worked the crowd, shaking hands and offering hugs. Leo held back. He would have liked to say hello to some of them, but he was too intimidated by their very fame to do anything but watch as Blazes went about enjoying his own banter.

Leo worried that he was about to lose Molly. He often resented his own contemplativeness, for which his father, Rudolph Flowers, had chastised him as a teenager, telling him that he "had to face up to life. Take it in your hands, Leo, and live it!" A Catholic boy. A reader. "Always got your nose in a book." At sixteen, Leo's favorite was *Little Women,* a fact that he kept secret from his friends, whose preferred authors were more usually the Rolling Stones or Huey Lewis and the News. His father was not a cruel man, despite the frequency of his criticism. Even then, Leo settled for amiable forgiveness as the way to further the relationship with his father. Rudolph thought his son way too lost in his feelings. Leo had had little interest in fishing for trout and sailing on Sebago Lake in Maine, which, along with duck hunting in California, were Rudolph's favorite joys. Leo knew about fish that they were good to eat. He was a quiet boy capable of a quick turn of phrase and refined hilarity. Rudolph's beloved New York Giants, for whose football games he had season tickets for a quarter century, still bored Leo to this day.

Poor Leo, Molly thought, so hurt if I betrayed him. The strange manners they had toward each other, which Molly cherished, in which they held to each other and talked, when he oiled and massaged her feet after a performance or wore the white, light cotton shirts that she "loved on a man, especially on you, Leo," would be scuttled.

What Blazes offered was stunning, of course. An exceedingly good-looking man, funny, tall and straight. His eyes alone brought Molly to the contemplation of film sets in Morocco and nights spent on location, for love scenes on blue, moonlit beaches. Paris in the afternoon, her cries, muffled as always by the back of her right hand, filling the hotel room in the same way that the breeze from the river murmured through the curtains. She toyed with the whispered excitement that she and Blazes could indeed become lovers. But in the end, Blazes's laughter entertained in the way that a Toyota ad on television does. A sporty product sveltely designed and built for speed, but...so what?

Leo...Leo was feeling itself, Molly knew, especially in his deep mourning for Rudy. Some dolt without a brain in his head might think Leo ineffectual in the way he had simply acquiesced to her demand, after her Rudy had died, to cease all demands. But even before Rudy, there were actually no demands. Nothing so militant ever preceded their making love. She came to Leo and they rolled about, laughing, delighted, lost in the flurry of lips and fingers and liquid. Molly felt her heart even now, just thinking of it, padding about within her like a prisoner longing for the past.

But Rudy, and Molly's suspicion of her own responsibility for his death...her anguish.... She simply couldn't touch Leo the way she once had. She just couldn't.

A sure thing, Blazes thought. Molly came into his office and sat down on the couch once more. She wore red. Her smile took him.

"Blazes, I'm so glad we're going to talk."

"Me, too." He sat down near her. "It means a great deal to me that you're here." *But not too closely,* Blazes counseled himself. *Careful not to rush things.*

"I don't know how much you've been thinking about our business relationship."

Blazes crossed his legs and rested his elbow on the arm of the couch. Gazing at her, he knew that this nervousness of hers—*Our business relationship?*—was simple preliminary uncertainty. *She wants reassurance. She wants me, but she needs time.*

"What I need from you, Blazes, especially now, is time."

"For the two of us to—"

"To think things over about my...my..." Molly looked to the side, toward a window. A woman at a computer occupied one of the offices on the fourth floor across the street. She placed each hand by the side of her head, and was clearly furious with the computer, which would not respond to what she was telling it.

"Please, Molly, take all the time you need." Blazes, too, looked out across the way.

"...about my career."

Your career?

"And, you know...I know that the air sweetened a little between us yesterday."

"It was wonderful."

Molly shrugged. "And that even more could have happened."

Blazes nodded, leaning forward and turning toward Molly. He took her left hand into his right.

"But I need to tell you how that would make me feel, Blazes." Molly surveyed the hand and the gold ring she wore on her index finger. An Egyptian design of some sort, a molded snake rising up, a tiny gold cobra. "Intimate trust means everything to me."

Blazes moved closer. Molly seemed not to notice as she looked out the window once more. The woman across the way stormed from her office.

"The wish to care for one another, to take care."

"Of course." Blazes inclined toward Molly.

"For there to be more than just—"

He placed the fingers of his right hand gently against Molly's lips, as though to quiet her with their reassurance.

She turned toward him. "Blazes?" The fingers muffled his name.

"I love you." He kissed her.

She turned me down!

And she fired me! Jesus, talent like hers, where can I...? And Leo, does he know? Blazes figured he had better call Molly on her cell phone and apologize, recalling her words—"No, no!"—as she pushed him away. Blazes's heart was going like mad, but Molly seemed not to have noticed. "No."

"But Molly—"

"What? You? Love me?"

She paused at the open door to Blazes's office. A few other people walked by in the hall outside. "Good men are rare, Blazes Boylan." The door was headed for a slam when she uttered the second phrase. "And, sweet baby Jesus in heaven, you're not one of them."

Blazes stood up from the couch and walked to the window. Taxi traffic on Fifty-sixth Street below was, as always, cantankerous. The taxis resembled small yellow slugs, nudging one another up a mud burrow. He saw Molly pass onto the sidewalk from the front of the building. Her red dress stood out like a firebrand lighting up the hurried, confusing flow of the crowds all around her.

Leo lay in bed with Molly. Their embrace—Molly holding to him from behind, her head laying sideways against his back—was the most that she was willing to give him, and he had accepted it for years.

They often talked about their marriage. She said that she forgave him for Rudy, although Leo did not believe her. But they had known now for years where each stood, and Leo accepted that, too. Molly understood that Leo wanted her, that he missed the bumptious humor and sexual flights that they once had had, and that there would be no more of those.

Leo accepted it all, because he could not imagine living without Molly.

She put her arms around him. They lay still a few minutes. Leo, alert to her as always, felt her lips approach his left shoulder, slowly, with timorous whispers. She took his left hand in her right, and a kiss came to his shoulder. The first in years.

"Oh, Leo."

His eyes remained open in the darkness, fixed on the lace curtain over the window. He caressed Molly's hand. A second kiss invaded Leo's breathing. He remembered again what it had been like with her, years before. The sadness of the ending of their sensuous lives together now revealed itself once again to him. And its foolishness. Shame had become accommodation, acceptance, and finally simple defeat.

He turned to Molly and embraced her. His heart lurched against his ribs.

"Can you? Forgive me for Rudy, Leo. It was my fault."

"No, Molly, it wasn't. It—"

"He—"

Leo put the fingers of his left hand against her cheek. "Molly."

"I'm dying for you, Leo. More than ever. Oh, Leo. Please. Yes."

ANNIE CROSS

Ed descended the stairway from the Metropolitan Museum of Art, meandering through the few hundred visitors sitting on the steps and talking so vibrantly with each other that the clouds of steam emanating from their mouths flew about like conversant puffs of feathers. For a February morning, the cloudless sky had the clarity of springtime, as though really it would be a fine day for a swim were it not for all the ice in the streets.

Ed bundled the collar of his overcoat around his throat along with a knitted wool scarf, and secured his tote bag on a shoulder, excited on this, his very first day as a citizen of New York City. He set out across Fifth Avenue and up Eighty-second Street. The street itself was lined with well-tended, leafless trees and substantial brownstones, each of which shined with settled dignity and high regard for itself.

Halfway up the block, he pirouetted across a puddle of sidewalk ice and took flight.

"Oh my God! Are you all right?"

A woman had been getting her mail, and now hurried down the half-dozen steps of her brownstone and through the tiny front rose garden. She was about fifty, slim with a dancer's kind of body and very long, curly blonde hair. She had thrown on a wool sweater many sizes too large for her, over a pair of black tights, and had wrapped her shoulders in a wool scarf, yet still wore her slippers. There was ice on the pathway to the gate as well, which she negotiated. By the time she reached the gate, Ed was picking himself up, rubbing his knee. He had begun to recover.

"Are you hurt anywhere? I'm so sorry!" She laid her mittened hands on top of the gate and then took them away, startled by the cold that radiated from it. She crossed her arms, each hand sheltered in an armpit.

"No, I…I'm fine." Ed examined himself. "It was more…more a surprise than anything else. I was just at the museum." He pointed back toward Central Park. "There's an Edvard Munch show."

"Oh, it's wonderful, isn't it?"

"A little terrifying, maybe." For a moment, silence hung in the middle of the encounter. "The way he does women." He recognized her. *But where have I seen her?* He examined his scraped right palm. "Thank you for… I'm Ed Pensil. I just arrived yesterday."

"To the neighborhood?"

"No. To New York."

"Where from?"

"London."

The woman's mouth hurried to a smile.

"You know it?" Ed said.

"I do. I've danced there many times."

"Danced!"

"Yes, with the New York City Ballet. I loved it, London. So beautiful."

He cradled the shoulder bag between his arms, holding it against his chest. "May I ask your name?"

"Annie Cross."

That was it! He had seen a film in which she had appeared, *A Dance in New York,* on the BBC, in which she had talked about dancing for Jerome Robbins. She was a star for the New York City Ballet for many years, until she retired in 2001. She had a talent at the celestial level, noted particularly for her quite legendary performances as a very young dancer with Mikhail Baryshnikov. Ed even remembered an article by a *London Times* critic about those performances, in which the fellow wrote, "The American Annie Cross, still just a girl, seems able to deliver her heart entirely into the hands of the man with whom she is dancing, as though she herself has ceased to exist. It is the most loving disintegration I have ever witnessed."

"Oh…Miss Cross."

"Well...Annie." She pointed at the smear of ice on which Ed had slipped. "It's so embarrassing to have something like this happen to a tourist."

"No, I hope that, starting today, I'm local." He looked down at the ice. "You would think that I'd know what I'm doing."

Again there was unbidden silence. Each seemed to wish the conversation to continue.

"A cup of tea helps after a fall like that." Annie gestured toward her doorway. "And milk."

"Sugar?"

"Yes, I have that, too."

They talked in her kitchen over tea and cookies, where Ed explained that he had traveled to New York for medical conferences many times for a number of years.

"You're a doctor. So, when you fell down out there, right away you were your own best ambulance." The casual, good-hearted tone in Annie's American accent surprised Ed. She seemed hardly star-struck by herself in any way. "I could have used you on several occasions," she said.

"Maybe. But I'm not so good with bandages and splints. You know, blood scares me."

"How's that?"

"That's why I'm a psychiatrist."

Annie crossed her arms, and at first the gesture seemed a casual, welcoming one, an invitation to more conversation. But briefly her arms tightened and became barrier-like. She said nothing for several seconds.

"And I've written a couple books." Ed was unsure where the warmth of the conversation had so suddenly gone. "Henry James in England. Lucian Freud. " He added that he had always wished to live in Manhattan. "Coming here for just a few days at a time is too sparse, you know...too little."

"I felt the same when I got here from Chicago. I had wanted to come to New York forever."

"How old were you?"

"Fifteen. My mother was with me."

Annie told him that she had just this week completed a book of her own, the only one she had ever written, a memoir about touring China with Jerome Robbins's Chamber Dance Company in 1981, when she was twenty-one. "A marvelous man. Tough, though." The book was coming out in the spring. "Jerome was like a lot of men."

"How so?"

"They think they understand love."

Ed sensed what was coming. Men…their cluelessness…. He had heard it in his office from many women.

"Like in what I did for a living, and the art those men made for me… Jerome Robbins. Mr. B.…that they make for all the principal women dancers…. It perpetuates the dancers' lack of…lack of…."

"They type-cast you?"

"Lack of depth." Annie frowned. "Of course. One beautiful girl after another ushered into true love in those ballets by intrepid, handsome heroes." Annie took up a cookie and broke it in two, proffering one of the halves to Ed. "Since…I don't know…whenever ballet started." She brought her own half-cookie to her lips. "The trouble is, I love that role." Annie offered a smile. "In ballet, it's the greatest role of all, and any ballerina chosen to play it, who would turn it down, would be a fool." The cookie disappeared. "We spend our youth striving for it, thousands of girls, and only a few actually get it." She poured more tea. "Every young dancer's wish."

As Ed was bundling up to leave her apartment, thanking Annie for the tea, she asked him if he would like to visit the School of American Ballet. "I've been teaching there for ten years or so now."

"Love to. I've never been to such a place."

Annie smiled, as though dismissive of the remark. "Such a place?"

"Well, I mean—"

"Don't worry. I understand. Some people would be intimidated." She handed him his scarf. "The beauty of it." She opened the front door. Cold air rushed in. "But Ed, you might find it…" She smiled again, this time with more ease, more humor. "…worth analyzing."

The next morning, Ed walked through the Lincoln Center plaza, crossed Sixty-fifth Street, and entered the Rose building.

The escalator was awash with teenagers, boys and girls, all walking and gesturing with considerable gayety and delicacy. They were laden with backpacks, schoolbooks, and cell phones, the escalator's satin movement lifting them like unhurried, gesticulating birds in laughing conversation to the second floor lobby.

He walked into the studio to which Annie had directed him, and a dozen and a half young women sat sprawled like leggy starfish on the wooden floor. Stretching, they wore black leotards and white tights, woolen leg warmers of every color bunched below their knees, their hair uniformly done up in tight buns. They glanced at Ed, who smiled, stunned by so much athletically sleek beauty.

He realized that he must surely represent dumpy middle age to these students. He wondered what he would look like in a pair of pointe shoes. He often reminded new acquaintances of someone they had seen in the movies. "Can't quite remember who," the acquaintance would say. "Not Colin Firth... not Branagh... somebody else." He felt that really he reminded them of the fellow who at the end of the romantic comedy serves as Colin Firth's best man or, at the end of the Devonshire murder mystery, Kenneth Branagh's barrister sidekick. Handsome enough, but not the star of the show.

The ballerinas promptly forgot about him and returned to their stretching.

Annie stood by an upright piano in a corner of the room below its large windows, at the end of one of the fully mirrored studio walls. She, too, glanced at him, although she was in conversation in French with the pianist, a portly woman wearing red-framed thick glasses, a baggy wool coat, a black wig, and thick-soled brown walking shoes. Her makeup reminded Ed of a painting by Jackson Pollack. The two women were discussing some sheet music, and Annie spent a moment specifying which parts of what compositions she wanted the woman to play.

Annie was indeed tiny, a feature of her body that had actually drawn a lot of attention when she was on stage. Like all great performers, she appeared more grand when dancing than indeed she was, her singular talent multiplied by an astonishingly beautiful internal drive. But here, leaning over the sheet music on the piano, she appeared too small, too fragile ever to have done the things that she had been so famous for doing.

She turned from the piano.

"Hello, Ed. I..." She nodded toward the dancers. "Girls, please welcome Dr. Pensil. From England. He's here to..." Her hands gestured toward him. He recalled how the fingers, in the Robbins film, themselves expressed acquiescent, forgiving emotion. On camera, Robbins himself had congratulated her for it. A quick grin hurried across her face. "He's here to make sense of us."

Disinterest oozed from the students.

"So shall we get going?"

Ed sat down on a folding chair just inside the door.

The girls stood and positioned themselves in three rows before Annie. Each observed herself in the mirror. Disconcerted vanity overtook the few seconds before the piano began playing. Fluttering eyes. Adjusted hair. No smiles. Self-castigation. When the music began—a waltz from some Tchaikovsky ballet, Ed couldn't remember which—the dancers suddenly burst into motion.

Immediately Ed could see the differences between those girls who danced with special ability and those who did not, although not one of them could be said to be bad. Indeed even the worst was clearly terrific. Motion, flight, delicate landings, twirls, arms outspread like slim wings, hands shaped like oiled mist, lower backs curved into burnished clouds, the suggestion of sweat on their temples assuring the presence of the sensual, heart-demanding wish to do well...all this to the accompaniment of the slightly out of tune piano. Parts of it actually rattled as the woman at the keyboard played it with heavy gumption and occasional wrong notes.

"Too fast, Chelsea. Too fast." Annie followed one of the taller girls around for a moment. Chelsea hurried to make the adjustment and to slow down.

"That's it. Listen to that phrase again." Annie turned to the pianist. "Olga, hold on for a minute, please."

The piano tinkled in mid-phrase to a rough stop, as did the girls.

"Always listen to the music!" Chelsea, the principal recipient of this piece of advice, jammed her lips together. Annie turned and addressed the entire corps of dancers. "How long have you all been here? Do you know *how* to listen to music?"

Mixed with the few disappointed sighs of the girls was a good deal of wounded silence, especially on the part of Chelsea.

"All right. We'll do it again." Annie gestured toward the pianist, who began the sequence once more with the same level of bored-sounding inaccuracy.

Eventually, Annie brought the class to an end. The students passed before Ed and headed out of the room, several whispering behind their fingers to each other that Annie was a little rough today. Like, what more does she want? Like didn't we, like, do it right?

Ed especially admired how Annie sometimes would shape the dancers physically, laying a hand across the lower back of one and suggesting that it be more curved, more sensuous, or sculpting an outstretched hand so that the very fingers revealed the emotion in the dancer's pause. Ed envied the ability to do that so directly and precisely. In his own work, the arrival of such awareness on the part of a patient was far more elusive. Often the patient had no clue about what Ed wished him or her to discover, no measure for finding the difference between dismay and self-acceptance, or the confusing, difficult passage to actual happiness. So it seemed to Ed in this moment, in Annie's practice studio, that psychiatry was much less precise than the dance these girls were doing, and often, he sensed, more disappointing.

"You know, Ed, they're just sixteen and seventeen. Children, no matter how they look." The last of the students progressed down the hallway. "Talented. But kids." Annie turned toward him. "Do you have children?"

"A daughter. She works in Hollywood."

"An actress?"

"No, an aspiring agent."

"Where's her mother?"

"In London." Ed took up his shoulder bag. "We're divorced. What about you?"

"Oh, I was married too. Maybe you've heard of him. Jeremy Blackwell?"

"Blackwell Securities."

"That's right."

"Famous."

"He founded it."

"You were married for long?"

Annie took up a sweater from a bench beneath one of the windows. She put on the coat as though she were angry with it. "Seven or eight years."

"And what about…forgive me." Ed allowed a smile. "What about now?"

"No. Nothing."

"So Jeremy is no longer…no longer your—"

"No." Annie stepped toward the studio doorway, taking up a large white canvas shoulder bag printed with the words *New York City Ballet* in red. It contained a book and a small leather purse. "He broke my heart, and then moved into Trump Tower."

That night, Ed watched a YouTube of Annie with Mikhail Baryshnikov in 1980, a *pas de deux* from Balanchine's *Theme and Variations*. Annie swirled quickly through Tchaikovsky's music with such deftness, her feet and arms composed in such a way throughout that she appeared incapable of doubt. When she flew, she flew slowly, with the delicacy of air itself. She possessed the stage, or at least that part of it not occupied by the incredible Russian, with ethereal precision.

"I married Jeremy a few years after that," Annie explained the following evening over dinner at a bistro on Seventy-second Street. "It was worth it for a while. A life that most people would envy, I guess, even desire. A great deal of money. Parties." Annie looked out from the banquette at the other diners. "Notoriety." Many of them recognized her. She waved to one or two. "But he didn't spend a lot of time wooing me." Her eyes hovered over her glass of wine. "When he knew all along that that's what I wanted." Annie took up her fork. "Even though he knew I was crazy for him."

Ed waited, not knowing how to move from the moment's distress. He kept his eyes on Annie until she looked up at him and attempted a smile. She succeeded with it, although the warmth that usually accompanies a smile was replaced by the sense, Ed felt, that Annie suspected Ed himself… that he could be negotiating a way to betray her.

They went out together for several weeks. Ed worried about the relationship, not sure that he wanted to deepen it. He had learned that Annie was only occasionally willing to move past the surface of a conversation, and Ed suspected she felt that anything she had to say, especially about herself, was of little note. Despite what she explored in her dancing, she had little wish to examine unlighted corners in her conversation.

She had vast knowledge of the places in which she had danced and of the people she had met. Her descriptions of these people were often unusually inventive. The suit that the president of Iceland wore at the Ballet's premier in Reykjavik "had puckers in it, like black wounds." The Argentine ambassador to the United States, an economist, was "dangerously mild. His smile was like…well, like a sheet of sweet paste." Annie spoke eloquently of Florence, where she had stayed in a medieval palace in which the damask wallpaper of her room reminded her of "fields of blood-red, fresh-blooming, dying roses." Cleveland left her cold, "like the industrial weather there."

She once described her marriage as one filled with tender imbecilities. "Even though I did love him."

But Annie's eyes often fluttered whenever Ed asked her a question about her emotions, and when that happened she would skitter through her answers. She very frequently pondered an answer at considerable length, as though searching a way to reveal as little about herself as possible.

Ed suspected that she was simply afraid in the end of encountering her own depths, with all the mud and watery disintegration that he worried those profundities maybe contained. *But how am I to know?* he castigated himself. Especially when he watched the videos of Annie's dance, Ed wondered at the gulf between what she exhibited about her feelings so successfully *en pointe* and what she seemed so unwilling to explore in her kitchen. So…they went to movies. They walked in Central Park. They had lunch in her brownstone.

Ed dined alone one evening at a French place on Eighty-seventh. Sipping from a glass of Bordeaux, he turned the page of the novel he was reading, *The Great Gatsby*, a book he re-read every two years or so because of its fine writing and, he always hoped, of what it could teach him about

Americans. He realized that Gatsby was a fraud. But he also thought that most Americans who brought themselves up from nothing—which is to say, most rich Americans—were in some ways frauds. So often so little knowledge. Not much sense of the heart. Bludgeons in search of money.

Luxuriating once more in the wayward desperation of Gatsby's love for the empty, pretty Daisy Buchanan, he lifted the glass of wine to his lips and, sipping from it, saw Annie Cross and a very wealthy-looking middle-aged man enter the restaurant.

They were shown to a table in a corner, beneath a large lithograph showing a Folies Bergère dancing girl of the *Belle Époque.* In golden light, she raised her skirts, revealing many confused underskirts. Beneath her bonnet, her teeth gleamed brightly enough to appear to be flashing with light.

Annie was clearly upset, frowns scurrying across her face as the conversation between her and her companion so intently continued. As the waiter brought glasses of water, she extended her arms onto the table, emphasizing things with her fingers, jabbing the tabletop with an open right hand as she spoke. Her companion, in a black suit, a white dress shirt, and a flourishing purple necktie, was attempting self-control. But he, too, appeared to believe that he was being thoroughly wronged, to such a degree that some of the other diners in the room were now talking about the couple in the corner, wondering what could have sparked such an argument. The battle was quiet, without shouting, and virulent.

As the waiter served them their salads, Ed finished his chocolate mousse and awaited the bill. Annie, looking away from the continuing fight, spotted him. Surprise sputtered from her eyes. Ed nodded to her, although he was grateful for the waiter's bringing him the check and, so, blocking the view that Annie had of him.

"That was my husband." She had called him early the next morning and asked him to join her for coffee. "My ex-husband."

"I see, I—"

"I'm sorry you had to see that, Ed."

"There's nothing to be done about it, Annie. I just happened to be there."

"Yes, but you must think there's something terribly wrong with me."

"Why?"

"The way he was talking to me."

"But I don't know what he was saying."

"Couldn't you tell from the gestures? His indifference? The way he wouldn't listen?"

"No, I—"

"A psychiatrist like you? Aren't you supposed to discern things? I mean, the way people hold themselves, the shoulders, his tightened lips?"

"Tightened lips?"

"Yes. Aren't you supposed to figure out how people really feel?"

"Annie—"

"How I feel about him? How wrong he is?"

A week later she asked Ed to water her plants. "I'm going to Belgrade. To teach. I'll be gone for three weeks." He agreed, and as she hugged him on her front stoop, she told him how much she would miss him. "I love going places with you, Ed. I wish you'd come to Belgrade with me."

He gave her a return hug. Annie turned away, disappointed.

Ed often contemplated the troubles associated with creativity. It was the phenomenon that most interested him as a psychiatrist. He had counseled out-of-work artists, down-and-out musicians, the occasional complaining novelist. Men and women both. Many such, and his writing about them had found an audience.

He loved trying to understand what causes creativity in the truly creative, and now especially in Annie Cross. When he had been writing his book on Lucian Freud, he had met with the artist on a couple of occasions at the Saatchi Gallery in London. The conversations had been perfunctory. Lucian had appeared quite unused to displaying his feelings, at least to someone who was a certified psychiatrist. Given the fact of the identity of Lucian's grandfather, Ed found this amusing, and told the artist so.

"You'll have to figure it out, then, won't you, Ed? It's not my job to help you understand these things."

Luckily, Lucian had enjoyed Ed's book, especially his detailed descriptions of the mottled, rugged skin of so many of Lucian's nudes, the oily patches of it, the ugly turning-to-age that seemed to engulf so many of his subjects' bodies.

"That's where their personalities reside." Lucian pointed to his large painting of a corpulent nude woman lying on a mussed bed, her skin resembling a sun-bleached, crumpled plastic drop cloth. The gallery manager, a Londoner with a precise upper-class English accent, flitted about Lucian and Ed like a self-obsessed bird until he determined that Ed could not possibly afford any of the paintings in the gallery. "None of those people are happy," Lucien continued. "And you can tell it by the way I do their skin."

He congratulated Ed for the book. "Most of the writers, they're afraid to say things like what you said. They're afraid to be appalled." Lucian clapped Ed's shoulder. "But not you, mate!"

Annie had given him a key to the front door. He walked up the hallway, carrying the empty watering can that she had left for him. The dark walls were hung with numerous drawings and small paintings by Clyfford Still, David Park, Richard Diebenkorn, and others. In the living room, a piano held framed photographs of Annie performing, or arm-in-arm with George Balanchine (he smiling and explaining) or Michael Smuin (Annie clutching his arm and smiling for several clamorous photographers) and others, at this or that reception or party.

A noise came from the kitchen, and suddenly Jeremy Blackwell came into view. Dressed in black jeans, a blue patterned sport shirt, and loafers, he, too, carried a watering can in his hand.

"Oh...sorry," Ed said. "I'm a friend of Annie's. I—"

"How'd you get in?"

"She gave me the key." Ed hurried the key ring from his pants pocket. "Here. See?"

"Who are you?"

"I'm a friend. Ed Pensil. Sorry. From England."

"I gathered that."

"And you're Jeremy."

Jeremy put the water can on the kitchen table.

"I don't mean to intrude," Ed said.

"You're not intruding, pal. She told me about you." Jeremy took up a mug of coffee from the table and sipped from it. "You're the psychiatrist."

"That's right."

"What have you found out?"

Ed fingered the water can. Suddenly he didn't know what to do with it. "Found out?"

"Yes. Anything you can…" Jeremy sighed and sat down. "…tell me about her?"

Silence—the silence that occasionally accompanies astonishment—filled the kitchen. The far-away rumble of traffic outside formed a rough whisper.

"I don't understand."

Jeremy pushed a hand through his hair, which left it rumpled. "She says she's in love with you."

"She does?"

"And that she hopes you love her."

"She's never revealed that to me."

Jeremy's shirt hung out over his belt in back and, Ed noticed, was quite wrinkled, details so unlike those of the well dressed, composed tycoon who had been with Annie in the French place on Eighty-seventh.

Jeremy frowned. "You can't be much of a psychiatrist if you didn't notice that."

"But I—"

"I'll give you some advice, pal."

"Thank you, I don't—"

"You'll need it. Annie is changeable."

"I…" Ed glanced at Jeremy's watering can.

"You'll need to know that. She…" Jeremy leaned over the table, his lower lip folded between his teeth. Sadness fumed from him. His back seemed to buckle as he lowered his head. Ed was convinced, suddenly and without warning, that Jeremy was still quite in love with Annie. "She doesn't want what she has."

"Oh, I wouldn't know—"

"She says I treat her like some kind of pretty little crystal goblet."

"Beg your pardon?"

Jeremy sat down at the table. As he spoke, his dismay deepened. "With nothing in it. I'll bet you know about this."

Ed hunched his shoulders, turning away. "Look, I'm not sure I'm the person you should be talking to. I mean, this is something private to you and—"

"You're the psychiatrist. You're the one who can help."

"But—"

"Women write about this, see? Annie's made me read about it. The whole concept of...." Jeremy held up his right hand, the end of the thumb semi-surrounded by the ends of the other fingers. He stared at the fingers a moment. "'Woman,' as she calls it. The artistic ideal, see? I mean, some man's artistic ideal of a woman, emptiness jammed up with, well, with what men call love and, uh, and...." Jeremy looked up, lowering his hand. "Desire. You ever heard such a thing?" He sat forward, joining his hands on the table. "Annie used to lecture me a lot about that. Which was, you know, what her dancing required her to do. Exactly that!"

"And she didn't think you could provide her with—"

"Not for her heart." Jeremy ran a hand through his hair, and then placed the end of an index finger against his chest. "Not in here." Restless silence took the kitchen over. "Jesus. The way I loved her." Jeremy's hair hung down before his forehead, disturbed, like his thoughts. "And it angers her that she's so famous."

"For her dancing."

"Yes. But even more so, for the clarity of her emotions."

"In person?" Ed said.

"No!" Jeremy sat back, placing his left hand in a pants pocket. He examined his right, as though it were some sort of disappointing oracle. "On stage." He shook his head. "In those roles."

Three weeks later, Annie greeted Ed from her front steps. He was filled with questions about Belgrade, the students there, about the dignitaries she had met. Ed's cab pulled from the curb, and Annie came out to the gate. She had clearly been waiting for him. She hurried into Ed's arms, her breathing short with anxiety, her head resting against his chest. "Ed, darling."

He embraced her, and she escorted him into the brownstone. He smelled coffee.

Annie indicated a chair at the kitchen table. A plate with pieces of sliced coffeecake and a few cookies rested on it, with two cups on two saucers. A ceramic white sugar bowl and a similar creamer were arranged next to the cookie plate. There was no spoon. As Ed dropped his shoulder bag to the floor, Annie turned toward him and wrapped her fingers around the top of the second chair.

"You don't enjoy talking to me, do you, Ed?"

Ed, expecting more of a pleasantry, shrugged, looking toward the plants in the hallway.

"I don't know anything about you."

"Annie, I—"

"Nothing."

"But—"

"You haven't said one interesting thing to me since we met." Annie turned away, waving a hand above her head. "And you haven't told me the truth."

"About what?"

"Like what you were doing while I was in Belgrade."

"I was watering your ferns." Ed sat down at the table and awaited more of an explanation.

"One of the neighbors saw you here, with another woman."

"Me?"

"I didn't ask you to water so that you could..." She looked aside, her hands at first joined on the chair-back, then quickly separated as the thought continued. "Carry on some little affair you're having."

"Annie, I—"

"My neighbor saw you."

"What neighbor?"

"A friend. A woman I've known for years."

"I don't know any of your neighbors."

"That doesn't matter."

"Annie, I didn't. I wouldn't."

"And then..." Annie stepped toward a kitchen drawer, from which, noisily, she pulled several sheets of paper. "Look at this."

They were out of order and crinkled, having been balled up and then re-flattened. For a moment, there was no sense to them. Finally, when Ed had put them in order, he saw that they were monthly bank statements, and a letter from someone in the same bank.

"So?" Ed said.

"You got my bank information. My identity."

"Me!"

"Money was taken. It was clearly you who took it." She took the papers from his hand and placed them on the table. She sped through a search of them. "Here. See this?" An index finger pointed at a few columns of numbers, many numbers. Ed could not understand them. No context. No explanation. Just numbers. "It was you, Ed. And I trusted you."

Ed, hurrying to defend himself, moved to speak.

"You think I'm that foolish?" She pointed at her left temple with an index finger. "That I've got nothing going on in here?" She glared at him, although evidently not actually seeing him. Her hands, circling about each other, appeared like ruined twigs. She took up the papers again and thrust them back into the drawer. "I gave you the keys to my house."

"Annie, this can't be.... I didn't."

"I thought there could be something between us. I thought you cared for me."

"But—"

"You don't care for me?"

"Annie."

"You lied to me?"

"I did not."

"Manipulating, awful—"

"Annie!"

"You did, Ed. Don't try to tell me you didn't. You did. And now I want you out of here."

"But Annie—"

"Get out!"

The following morning, the stairway to the Metropolitan Museum was filled with seated, chatting visitors, passersby, lovers, students, and tourists. The frivolity of all the conversations brought a spirit of disorder to the phalanx-like arrangement of the meeting place. Ed had always enjoyed this phenomenon, the way the steps and the museum entrance were so formal and ordered, while the imaginative, unruly crowd was like the art inside the building.

This time, he noticed especially one couple. Annie was seated next to Jeremy. His gestures were animated, an accompaniment to what seemed loving regard on his part. He was trying to explain something to her. Annie nodded now and then, and finally Jeremy took her left hand into his hands, to caress it as he spoke. Her reply was heated, yet seemed to be making sense to Jeremy. She calmed, and then looked away. Jeremy remained silent until, suddenly, Annie leaned toward him and kissed him.

Jeremy hadn't expected it. But after a brief moment of surprise, he grabbed for her. Others around the couple witnessed their embrace, commenting on it with considerable affectionate humor, and joyfully envious of it. Ed, though, noticed the rigidity with which Annie endured the return kiss.

Not a chance, he thought, immediately angry with himself. Annie retreated from Jeremy's affection, as though she were miffed by it. She looked away from him. Jeremy, surprised by her reticence, reached again for her hand, as though pleading with her to allow his touch.

As Ed walked from the museum steps, indeed he *didn't* think that Jeremy and Annie stood a chance. Jeremy—*like you,* Ed thought of himself—was not up to it.

That evening, he watched a silent, amateur black-and-white YouTube of Annie warming up. She was about thirty in the film. The room looked like an old warehouse, with internal columns providing the support for the roof. The floor was clearly made of the right kind of wood and appeared to be sprung. A few other dancers, men and women, sat around the edges of the room, leaning against the walls and watching. Jeremy was there as well, seated in a folding chair. He was casually dressed and, of course, much younger than he was now. Less harried looking. When the camera passed by him, Annie swirling along in the frame, Ed could see that Jeremy was amazed by his wife and what she could do. Along with everyone else in the room, he appeared spellbound.

Ed fumbled with the empty wine glass in his hands. He still was hurting from Annie's accusation of him.

In the video, Annie turned about with such languid feeling—made more so by the slow motion of the film—that she appeared to be readying herself for some kind of assignation, a meeting with a maddening lover, with someone she clearly adored. She glanced at Jeremy once as she passed him by. When she landed on one or the other foot, her entire body softened like a passage of exhaled breath, heart-strewn and silent. She continued on, playing the role beautifully, a display of the heart, her acting so fine and tender, a woman more and more innocent, more and more smitten, more and more in love.

ANDREA'S HAND

Declan met Andrea in the Conservatory Garden in Central Park, on a very hot June morning. She sat on a bench beneath some trees near the Burnett Fountain. The two children depicted in the fountain have obvious affection for each other, Victorian England at its childhood best, in which no unhappy secret need ruin the afternoon. The reclining pastoral boy plays his flute for the small Central Park birds flitting around the standing girl, who holds a large bowl that doubles for the birds as a bath. Declan frequently visited this fine-hearted bronze because, of all people, his father, Ben, a Montana rancher, big game hunter, and fisherman, had loved *The Secret Garden,* the book to which the fountain is a tribute. Ben Morris read the book to Declan many times throughout the boy's early childhood. Now a freelance political writer, Declan wasn't much of a cattle man, which came as a disappointment to Ben, who had wanted his son to go into the ranching operation once he got out of NYU. But Ben had the kindness to realize that Whitefish, Montana, isn't for everyone.

Declan had just returned from the Middle East. He carried a cloth bag from his shoulder, which contained notes for a series he was doing on the war in Syria...ISIS, the Americans, the Kurds, Bashar al-Assad, et al. The Russians. What Declan labeled as "the whole confusion." He particularly sought stories about how the different factions could possibly find ways to work together, and he understood that this was a very stiff reportorial challenge. But the difficulty interested Declan anyway: how to resolve the effects of intractable cruelty.

Andrea, a closed book turned face down on her lap, contemplated the water lilies in the pool. She wore a light, short white dress and sandals. He glanced at her as he approached the sculpture. She noticed the movement of his eyes, and Declan gathered himself, feeling that too much of a second glance would ruin his chances to speak with her. But he knew immediately that he would attempt a conversation.

She was from Spain originally, she told him. An artist. "My parents brought me here when I was two."

"So you're Catholic. So am—"

"No, I'm Jewish." She ran a hand through her hair. Her fingers curved and turned about each other with almost composed softness.

"Oh, I—"

"Yes, we were pushed out in 1492." She turned the book over on her lap. "But now and then a few of us have trickled back." She cradled the book in the crook of her right elbow. "The light is special in Andalucía." Andrea laughed. "Or at least it used to be, before the Inquisition."

"And there are other famous artists named Villalta?"

Andrea's grin remained. "A few. But I'm the only one, just now, in Central Park." The feel of her very slight accent, and the laughter that so complimented it—water purling in the sun from a Spanish fountain and flowing carelessly to a pool below—caused Declan himself to relax, a smile on his face.

He asked her to walk around the garden, which they did for half an hour, stopping to talk, sitting on benches in the shade, laughing.

"I'm going to the Met," he said finally. "Would you like to join me?"

Declan met her again a few nights later at the opening of an exhibition of her own work in Chelsea. "Three" was a ground floor gallery with large windows in front, spotless white walls, deferential silence all around, and the usual beautiful young gallery assistant positioned to welcome the guests. Eight large paintings hung on the walls. For Declan, each made up a flash of light, a lightning strike.

Declan, who had been looking forward to seeing her again, realized that Andrea was preoccupied, seated on a folding metal chair observing each of the paintings. She appeared barely to be breathing as her elbows rested on her knees, her hands intertwined. Her seated posture reminded Declan of one of Degas's ballerinas checking her pointe shoes. Her feet were splayed, a few feet apart, and she had let her hair down so that it hung below her shoulders, slightly hiding her eyes.

"Andrea."

Declan felt from her a sigh of unrest. Her eyes seemed uncertain of what they were observing.

"I'm glad you came early." She held out her right hand to him.

He took it into his, and she allowed him to hold it a moment before taking it away. Turning once again toward one of the paintings, she bent the fingers and then straightened them.

"What's wrong?"

Andrea slouched forward and dropped the palm of the hand to a knee. "I worry about these." She gestured around the room. "All these." She looked out the windows to the street. "Everything I do."

Declan stood at her side.

"I don't trust them." She shook her head. "They *should* give me—"

"They're hiding something?" Declan looked over the painting before him.

For Declan, there were breezes in each of Andrea's blue-black surges of emotion, and the soft touch of cold dusk air. This painting had considerable brightness, a light touch in the passages between one major setting of layered color and another. Declan searched, though, for Andrea's humor in the painting, and it seemed not to make an appearance, even though the subtleties of color in each of the large figures contained so much heart, he felt, and such determination to be cared for.

Andrea's eyes raced across the painting, quick, pain-laden unhappiness in each hurried pause and in each hurrying to the next pause.

She was thinking about her father, and what he would say. She had not seen him for more than fifteen years, and had no contact with him.

Hector Villalta scattered his way through each day, a disorganized, demonstrative, and unhappy man. A historian, he brought his wife and little daughter from Spain to New York, where he would be teaching at Barnard and writing. No one described so harrowingly as he did the worries of the Spanish Jews during the Spanish Civil War. Even more, he wrote about the Jews in the French concentration camps set up to hold Republican Spaniards escaping Franco in 1939. The camp at Argelès-sur-Mer, on the unprotected Mediterranean shore just north of the border, and now mostly forgotten by French history, was a particularly cruel place for Jews, and Hector wrote about it with great distinction. They were savaged there. Few were able to escape further into France. Many died, and it was all at the hands of the French authorities.

Hector himself was born at Argelès, struggling for breath in his mother's arms at two a.m., buffeted by winds on a ripped blanket on a beach.

When Andrea was eight, her father was already fifty, and she recalled his back as he sat at a living room table, writing. He was a large man, and his clothing was seldom neat. The way a coat bunched up around him, or the tail of his wrinkled shirt hung unbound from his belt, or a sweater wrapped about his shoulders fell from them to the floor while he beat at the keyboard of his computer. She would sometimes sit across from him in the living room and watch him work. Fascinated, she loved observing his hands, which with meaty, fumbling industry hurried the words onto the screen.

As a little girl, she enjoyed playing in Damrosch Park, across Sixty-second Street from their apartment. But Hector seldom asked her if he could accompany her to the park. Walks made him nervous, he said. Playing irritated him. They had Andrea's mother, Matilde, for that. Matilde, so retiring and frightened a woman that she rarely interceded in her husband's frequent losses of composure and eruptions of rage, provided little protection for her daughter *other* than taking her for walks. Hector ruled the apartment, and everyone else there simply had to acquiesce to him. So Andrea grew to think of her mother as a weakling who refused to come to the girl's aid when Andrea's wishes were being upbraided by the one man whom she had always loved more than anyone.

Andrea adored his heartbeat. As a very little girl, she knew that her father cared for her simply because of the sound of it. She leaned her head close to his chest and reveled in the strumming that came through the skin, at the feeling the skin gave to her as it throbbed against her closely held ear. There was no other experience like it for her as a five year-old. Even as, later, his feelings ("Keep quiet when I'm working." "You don't deserve anything from me.") roiled with disenchantment and the mysteries of his disapproval, she recalled the heart's beating. His breathing alone, as he worked, or in the less and less frequent moments when he held her in his arms, hummed through the girl's feelings.

Throughout the opening at Three, Andrea held a single glass of wine in her hand, bright humor coloring her conversations with friends and gallery patrons, from whom high praise and congratulation hurried with stunned admiration. All of the paintings sold. She did not answer Declan's question, though. The paintings indeed were hiding something, but the explanation of it was too shocking. She didn't know him well enough. Even now, Hector's behaviors radiated from the house he lived in, in Sevilla. Of course she could not see them, but she felt every jealous expression that surely must still be coming from her father, each threat against her that she knew he was still making, so many years later and so far away from her.

When she had been fifteen, Hector had attacked her, and he had then been served with a court order, removing him from Andrea and her mother.

The exhibition came down after six weeks. Declan had met Andrea at Three several more times, and the affection of their first conversations had slowly deepened. She found that she cared for him. A lot. Declan was a sweet man sometimes conflicted, despairing of the difficulties he witnessed for his profession. He told her one evening, "What I want to write about is brave humanitarian generosity." The ironic laughter that came along with this from Declan surprised her, because it accompanied a look of near defeat as well. "But I have to content myself with plain war, since that's what I usually witness."

He sometimes seemed beset by the very descriptions of what he had seen, especially during the afternoon in her apartment when he described for Andrea his research for a piece that had been published a year before, on Yazidi refugees, chased up Mount Sinjar in Syria. They had been caught without protection, hounded into the August mountain heat by ISIS fighters intent on killing them all. Kurdish troops rescued them, and as the refugees descended the mountain—"the cataract," Declan called it—he began talking with them. He learned that thousands had been executed by ISIS, the reason they had fled to the mountains.

Andrea did not speak as he described all this. She was especially quiet when Declan told of the children suffering from the heat in the trek to Turkey, and the isolation of so many of them, those alone, those orphaned. She took Declan's hands into hers and held them, caressing them.

Declan himself was filled with questions about how Andrea had come to the United States, whether her family visited her now and whether she visited them in Spain. Only some of her responses were truthful, especially the stories of her childhood art classes at the Heschel School on the West Side, and how they had thrilled her in ways that few of the other subjects in school could. She sweetened other anecdotes, though, intentionally cleansing them of elements that were too private to be shared with him.

Andrea felt that the conditions of her father's infancy had formed what eventually ruined him. Over the years, her mother told the girl about them, how one night Hector's mother carried him out of the camp at Argelès, a baby so sick he could barely cry. The French were forcing many of the Spaniards, all of them escaped Republicans, to return to Spain. Hector's father had been killed in the retreat north from Franco's forces. Only because a French doctor had the task of clearing the paperwork for each of the Jews that they were sending back was his mother able to get some respite for her baby to recover. The doctor sent her to a clinic set up in a tent just outside the camp. A few chairs. A few beds. Filth, basically. But the undernourished and dehydrated baby recovered after two weeks there, and his mother was able to carry Hector from the tent unnoticed. It seemed the French had forgotten about her and the baby. She walked from the camp and away from the trains heading back to Spain.

When the French police caught her, they took her and the baby in the back of a truck to the border at Le Perthus, and made her walk across with several others. Hector whimpered in his blanket. His mother, trying to protect him from heavy rain, cried out for forgiveness from the French policemen, knowing she would not find it in Spain. Under Franco's reign, she never did.

Their friendship turned to love.

In her apartment one afternoon, Andrea made iced tea. The lemons in the tea, quartered so that each slice was a size similar to that of the snow-like ice cubes with which they were mixed, moved about the crystal jug like sequestered suns. As she turned toward him, Declan touched the small of her back with his left hand. The cloth of her dress was slightly damp.

"Declan, I…"

Andrea leaned forward and took his head between her hands, then coaxed him toward her. He caressed her hips, kissed the front of her belly, and then laid his head against it. Her hand slipped into his hair.

Eventually, as the moon rose an hour and a half later, they drank the tea.

She brought him into her studio, the second bedroom in her apartment, the same apartment in which she had lived with her parents.

"This was where my parents slept."

The windows looked down on the park, and as she showed him around, traffic noise came in from outside, chaotic rumblings to accompany the rambling mess of the studio. The studio was the very opposite of the rest of her apartment. Squashed tubes of paint, oils and temperas alike, about a hundred brushes piled up on the stand next to the empty easel. Newspapers, folded towels, half-finished abstract canvases lined up against the walls, color and abrupt decision everywhere in every one of them, and two smocks, each indistinguishable from the other, each looking like it had survived a bloody automobile crash or maybe a hard-fought civil war.

She took up a large cleaned brush and held it between the index and middle fingers of her right hand, supported by her thumb. A grimace came to her lips. "I'm right-handed…." She held it out before her. The brush handle, spotted with every color of paint, seemed to Declan a kind of journal in which notes about Andrea's art—maybe about her entire past, he mused—were kept. "So there's pain whenever I hold the brush. In the fingers." She daubed the palm of her left hand with the end of the brush. "They were broken once."

"How?"

Andrea took the brush into her left hand, and surveyed its paint-mottled shaft. "I'd rather not tell you."

If her affection for him was an indication of how she really felt about him, Declan knew that she would tell him eventually. He was already far lost in love with Andrea Villalta. He reached out and took her hand, the brush cradled in the touch of each other's fingers.

Several days later, Andrea sat on the couch looking out on Damrosch Park, her hands folded in her lap. All the windows were open, the late-August heat turning her apartment into a kind of bath, wet but without actual water. A very occasional breeze did come up from the river, light-footed chicanery dispersing soon. She wore a cotton blouse and a light cotton skirt, both intended to allow as much air as possible to flow around her.

She had told Declan that, unlike most New Yorkers, she enjoyed summers in Manhattan, even as they immersed the place in humidity that made most citizens feel wrapped in plastic and tossed into an equatorial pit. Heat energized Andrea. She walked about the Lincoln Center neighborhood, past the Heschel School, up to Harlem and the far north reaches of Central Park, around the Battery and to all the museums up Fifth Avenue and the galleries on Fifty-seventh Street, not so much defying the heat, rather gathering it around her and celebrating the life that it offered her. Declan thought of her as the sort of Mediterranean flower that clings to sandstone walls and beckons to the summer sun.

But she had just told him about her father.

"And the way I feel about you, Declan...there are just such problems."

Declan tapped his fingers on the top of the table. "I don't understand. What have I got to do with him?"

The way he held his head, inclined a bit to the left as he studied the cup of coffee before him, brought Andrea to a kind of sympathy for him. Just a *kind* of sympathy, though. She knew that Declan loved her, and that his question was actually an expression of that love. He only wanted an explanation that he could live with. It was okay for Andrea to have troubles. Declan's single wish, she sensed, was that she allow him to be sympathetic with her.

"You don't have to visit his cruelty on me," he said.

Indeed she felt the flickering of personal cruelty—perhaps revenge—in her heart. She *was* using her father against Declan, and not admitting it to him. She was shamed by this, although it was not new. Indeed Andrea felt she was a failure at love because of it. She had punished her husband similarly before they had split up after just a year and a half, as well as the artist she had lived with, before he had left her. She had embraced the shame on those occasions, a foregone conclusion. But this with Declan was different because she felt so much more for him than she had for the others. Yet here was the intended cruelty once more, the joy it brought to her, and the shame.

The day of her fifteenth birthday, Hector had argued with Andrea about her schooling. He told her that he wouldn't pay for it if she insisted on this art tripe.

"Just another wrong-headed thing, like everything you do." He turned his back on her and walked toward the window. "You don't want to study science. You don't care about what I want, what your mother wants. All you want is to make those watery pictures." His Spanish was percussive and quick. He turned from the window and held his arms out. "Don't you realize how much I've sacrificed for you?"

He took her right hand into his. Two small paintings remained on the floor, propped up against the couch. She had told him that, yes, she did want to draw. She did want to paint. "So leave me alone, Daddy!"

It was a warm spring day, and Andrea was wearing the same jeans, T-shirt, and paint-speckled tennis shoes in which she had been painting at school. She had just shown Hector the two little oils she had completed the previous day. One, a pear and a peach in a red bowl, radiated spectral yellows and reds. The other, a view of the sunset over the river incarcerated by the elevated railroad tracks at the end of West Sixteenth Street, portrayed striated, brightening light in curved lines falling to the water. Andrea's knapsack rested on a living room chair.

"Don't argue with me." Hector tightened his grip on her hand.

"Daddy!"

"You're a Jew!"

"What does that matter?"

"They kill Jews, especially the ones like you, that don't realize they're Jews."

"Daddy, let go."

"Look what they did to me!"

"Please!"

"I said, don't argue." He secured the hand very tightly, crushing the fingers together. Andrea tried to pull away, which only increased Hector's outrage. He took her hand in both of his and twisted it. Like crumpling sticks, the index and middle fingers cracked.

"Daddy!"

Hector would not let go. When he finally released her, his voice in a sudden burst of anguish as he realized what he had done, she saw that the two fingers now surged at crazy angles from each other. The bone below the knuckle of her index finger half-protruded from the skin, blood smearing the front of Andrea's T-shirt as she scurried, weeping, to the couch, her left hand holding the right, cradling it.

She hunched forward, her breathing wet and strained, as her father hurried to the bathroom for towels, Kleenex, and water.

Sitting on the couch and listening to this story, Declan appeared flustered, unable to understand. "You've got to work this out. You worry more about him..." He pointed to her hand. "...and that than about me."

It was not true, and he hated the smallness of his remark. But he did not take it back. Hurt, Andrea sat back and brought her legs up beneath her.

"Did your mother do anything?"

Andrea grimaced. To her enormous surprise, her mother had taken the girl away from her father, the two of them moving into a small apartment below West Fourth Street, far downtown from Hector. She obtained a restraining order and hired a lawyer. She told Andrea that she was going to lodge a formal complaint in court against her husband, that he had attacked and injured his own daughter.

Her heart in nervous disorder that she could barely withstand, Andrea rehearsed her testimony with the lawyer, a Hispanic woman from some Central American country, Andrea guessed, who affected the same kind of dignity-ridden reserve that her mother always used as a defense against her husband's actions. The difference between Alicia Matamoros and Matilde was that the lawyer's questions were driven by precision for the truth and considerable kindness. She listened to Andrea's answers as the girl explained what had happened, as she told Alicia that she was terrified by her father, and that she feared he would kill her if she were not permanently separated from him.

Andrea imagined Hector in court, seeing in his conciliatory smile and his lowered gaze that, were he not seated in this courtroom, were he alone with Andrea, if he could only get her alone, he would attack once more. She continued answering the lawyer's questions, over and over.

The day before the court appearance, Matilde and Andrea sat at the kitchen table of their apartment, Andrea's hand in a cast and sling hanging from her neck. She sipped from the cup of tea Matilde had made for her. Andrea, having rehearsed so well what she would say, remained struck with fear of her father. She worried that even the guards at the courthouse would be unable to protect her. But Matilde and the lawyer had prepared her, and Andrea took comfort from her mother's courage. She had never seen such a display from her mother, and she determined that she would continue on through the quivering of terror that now took her heart.

At the table, Matilde's hands hurried about one another. Her now graying hair was done up in a bun, held there by a barrette. Friends often complimented Andrea on her eyes, and she knew she had gotten them from her mother. Matilde's eyes shined with lustrous night depth, enveloping Andrea. She had also once had the kind of slimness that now distinguished her daughter's beauty. She was shorter than Andrea, and at fifty wore the plain black dresses and low-heeled shoes that Andrea had seen women of a certain age in Sevilla wearing to market.

"Please don't do this, *mi'ja*." Matilde took the girl's free hand into her own and caressed it. "Don't testify against your father."

"Mother, I—"

"Do you love him?"

"Of course, but—"

"Then please don't."

"Mother!"

"I can't leave him." Matilde hung her head.

"But you told me that—"

"It will ruin the family, Andrea."

"But you told me..."

Matilde's eyes glistened as she leaned close. They caused Andrea's breathing to cease. "I love him, Andrea. Can't you see that?"

A week after the hearing was canceled, Hector left for Sevilla, with no notice. Once Andrea had passed her second year at Barnard, Matilde joined him there.

"So he ran away," Declan said.

"Yes."

"He's in Andalucía."

"Yes."

"And he's a monster, Andrea." The words hung between them, unspoken to this moment, and so much the truth that Declan wished for a moment to deny having spoken them. But it was the truth. "You know that, don't you?" Too much truth. He raised Andrea's hand to his lips once more.

The sun lowered behind the buildings across the river. She kissed him. She told Declan that she so believed that love existed that she had ventured in search of it even when she had been told that she did not deserve it. "I even worry that love...that love ruined...." Andrea lowered her eyes. "Even though I've always wanted it." She took Declan's hand. "He never understood how much I wanted to love him. But then, I..." She paused. "I thought it was a secret that he couldn't figure out, that I loved him so much. But then, outside the courtroom...my mother standing there, our attorney, a bailiff.... To protect us, you know. My father told me that day that my love for him was a sea that was drowning him." Her voice softened. "But my own love, too, Declan, was drowning. In the sea...gone...." She took her hand from Declan's.

"He's thousands of miles away, Andrea. How can he still rule you?"

"I—"

"How is it possible?"

She looked toward her hand. The clouds above the horizon turned to a blood-laced raggedy glow. *Like rage itself,* Declan thought, as he followed her glance out the window.

Andrea's cell phone rang early the following morning. She rose from the bed, shifting the phone from one hand to the next as she put on a silk wrap and walked to the window.

"¿Mamá? ¿Donde estáis?"

Declan understood none of the conversation, except for the clarity of nervous resistance in Andrea's voice and gestures, her resistance to having the conversation with her mother at all. Her Spanish was very rapid, her voice rising and falling in immediate turns of anxious anger. She stood by the window, looking out, through a few long silences during which Declan could hear occasional outbursts from her mother, what sounded like weeping, insistent interruptions of whatever Andrea was saying.

Andrea returned to the bed and sat down, the phone still at her ear. She reached behind her to take Declan's hand. The conversation continued until finally, reluctantly—*"¡Mamá! ¿Por qué?"*—she turned off the phone and put it down on the blanket.

Lying next to Declan, she sought his embrace. "He's dying."

They talked later over coffee. Andrea fell into silence, and Declan wished to offer some sort of solace. He pointed out the window to Sixty-second Street, at the stream of pedestrians passing up and down. They were going to work or doing errands or something. But just now they seemed to him like a migrating crowd being hurried to some unknown degradation. He was reminded of the arrivals he had witnessed in this or that camp. Refugees...always so much the same, from one vast group to the next, no matter what languages they spoke, deities they worshipped, or customs of dress they practiced. Always defeated, always incapable of revenge.

He studied Andrea's silence. "And you want me—"

"Please. She wants me to speak with him...but...so many years...." Andrea placed her chin on her gathered hands.

"Why?"

Andrea grimaced. "It's for him."

"Him!"

"She says he wants forgiveness."

Declan lowered his head.

"She used both Spanish words. *Perdón* and *absolución*."

"He wants to be absolved too?"

Andrea slumped forward. "Please, Declan. Help me." She laid her right cheek against her folded hands.

Declan, watching her diminishing calm, knew that he would.

An hour later, Matilde appeared on the computer screen. It was the first time Declan had actually seen Andrea's mother, except for the single photograph that rested in a frame on the dresser in Andrea's bedroom. Speaking in hurrying Spanish, Matilde was a small, round, gray-haired woman dressed in black, appearing quite rattled. Andrea's responses were precise and short. To Declan, she seemed intent on the setting up of perimeters. She mentioned Declan's name twice.

The two women continued speaking in Spanish until, in answer to a question from Matilde, Andrea brought Declan's chair close to her so that he, too, could be seen by her mother.

"Hello, Declan. Nice to meet you."

Matilde's accent was quite pronounced, but Andrea had told him that her English was fluent, all those years in New York having given her an accent humorous to Andrea herself, the Spanish inflections in her English colored by some that were of clear Manhattan origin. Matilde smiled at him, but Declan knew that she was very nervous about his intrusion. He thought a moment about excusing himself, but he could feel Andrea's own tense wish that he not abandon her.

"Your father is here." Matilde leaned forward, to change the position of the laptop before which she was seated. As the laptop bumped through a pair of quick placements, the large, white-haired visage of Hector Villalta came into view.

"Buenos días, papí."

Hector barely moved. His head inclined to the left, his eyes lowered, he seemed unaware of the computer before him.

"Do you see her, Hector?" Matilde's voice made no impression on him. Her hand holding a Kleenex appeared below his chin, and moved briefly to his lips, to remove a glimmer of saliva. When she removed the Kleenex, the same expression remained on Hector's face. It was immobile and incapable of expressing interest.

"You see, Andrea?"

Andrea's hand, in Declan's, trembled on her knee. Her eyes remained fixed on the image of her father. "And he doesn't hear?"

"We think he does, yes."

"But no speaking."

"No."

"O, mamá."

Andrea was herself almost expressionless. Declan awaited sympathy for Hector and her mother… anger with him….an outburst…. But there was only seeming clinical interest, Andrea watching the motionlessness of Hector's face, and awaiting something from *him.*

"Has he talked about me?"

"No, not now."

"But…ever?"

A sigh came from Matilde, off-camera and distant. "No." A silence followed, interrupted for Declan only by the sound of Andrea's carefully controlled breathing. "Seldom."

Andrea stood and walked from the computer, her hands on her waist. Declan excused himself to Matilde. He went to Andrea's side, where she stood at a window.

"What are you feeling?"

"Dismissal! What do you think?""

"What are you going to—"

"Hate."

"Are you going to tell him? He can hear, she says."

Andrea leaned her head against Declan's chest. Sighing, she turned with him toward the table and the computer.

Her father's visage loomed on the screen like sculpted granite. His only expression was one of uncomprehending distance. His current surroundings made no impression on him. Perhaps he didn't know that there *were* current surroundings. His white hair was combed straight back. His eyes seemed surrounded by a thin membrane through which a sliver-like line of bright liquid rested motionless. His lower lip gleamed, curved outwards.

"Hector?" Matilde's voice, off-camera, made no impression on him. "So...you see, *querida?*"

Declan turned toward Andrea. He thought of his work...his idea of "intractable cruelty." Surveying Andrea, he realized that he had little idea of how to help her. She stared at the screen, seeming on the verge of shouting at it. But nothing came. Hector's power over her seemed to Declan to remain, despite his current personal ruin. In Andrea's silence, Declan hoped he recognized an acceptance of whatever freedom her father's death would give her. But he suspected that the freedom, liberating as it would be, would also do nothing to relieve the pain of the affection Andrea had always offered her father. He had punished her terribly. For Declan, as she continued staring at the screen and at Hector's isolated incoherence, Andrea appeared resolved to prolong her yearning for her father's love, although that love would soon exist in her heart alone.

THE STAR OF DAVID

Mike Boyle (a Jesuit priest, therefore having paid close attention to the election of the new Pope Francis) headed for The Star of David. He hoped that this fellow Bergoglio would do well. Of course since he's a Jesuit, Mike grinned, he probably will. Muttering quietly about his own disrespect of certain papal traditions, Mike had noticed that Francis had refused to wear the gold cross that was the preferred frill of recent pontiffs. Instead he wore the old iron one that he had used for years in Argentina, as well as his regular black shoes. That was a good sign, Mike thought. No more pretty jewelry. No more red slippers. No more fashion shows.

An even better sign was Francis's washing of the feet of a dozen teenage criminals on his first Holy Thursday, at a prison in Rome. Usually a papal photo-op with twelve other priests (who barely need such succor, Mike muttered to himself), the event is intended to show the Holy Father's priestly humility. Mike, a scholar of the history of the Church and an attorney, knew from his studies that, well, there are popes, and then there are popes. He suspected that the hearts of a number of them had been peevishly chilled by the need to touch even the laundered feet of other priests, much less the weathered, scabbed and greasy toes of poor, beat-up kids.

But Francis not only had performed the ablution, but also had included the feet of two women, one of them a Muslim. This had never taken place in the history of the Church, and Francis was already getting miffed responses from offended Catholic potentates. For Mike, the gesture was a transforming surprise. He went over the *Newsweek* article about it several times, astonished by its revelations. "This guy's okay."

Mike knew that Nathan Feder would have something to say about Francis, the odd secrecies of Catholicism being a frequent subject of Nathan's quick mind and humor. Also, Mike enjoyed being kidded by Nathan for being a priest, because it allowed him to kid Nathan back for being a representative—though not a very devout one—of a belief that was even older than the Catholic one. Centuries older, millennia, and therefore of crotchety mind and forgetfulness, troubles that Nathan himself, of course, did not have at all. The back and forth between them was a constant source of enjoyment for the two men, and just now three pairs of Mike's black clerical slacks needed to be taken in, and he also wanted to get his shoes shined. So, dressed for the afternoon in Levi's, a sport shirt, and a dark gray sport jacket, unbuttoned, he headed down Thirty-sixth Street from Eighth Avenue, spying the neatly painted sign in the window of The Star of David Tailors and Shine.

One of the other reasons that Mike frequented the shop was that it reminded him of the old days in the garment district, when he was a student at Stuyvesant High School and had a part-time job pushing carts up and down these same streets. Mike recalled how the other boys at Stuy kidded him so much for it. Bolts of cloth? Clothes on hangers? Thread? Mike was smart, one of the best students at Stuy. *So what are you doing on a schlep job like that?* his friends would ask. *You'll never get into Notre Dame, Mike, pushing those dresses around.*

But Mike enjoyed the action on the streets, especially the shouting and conversation between all the people who worked the trade, the laughter and rough friendliness of it. Everything was funny walking in and out of those narrow passageways, and it was there that Mike actually discovered his interest in becoming a priest. He enjoyed the prattle and fellow feeling, and especially liked learning about where all these people came from. Africans jostled Arabs, who pushed Jews around, even as the Jews made fun of the Irish, who needled the Puerto Ricans and Mexicans. And vice versa. The Tower of Babel, Mike mused, was monoglot by comparison to the rag trade in New York.

A Catholic boy with midtown West Side Irish grandparents and a businessman father devoted to the Knights of Columbus and raising money for the Church, Mike had yet been the only person among all his cousins—Irish and Italians mostly—who had showed an interest in the priesthood. That interest came from his time pushing the carts and listening to the difficulties of so many of the people working there, difficulties with their girlfriends and husbands, their kids, the English language, the colors of their skins, the lousy pay, how not to get fired.

His faith was involved in Mike's decision to become a priest. But his interest came equally from the fact that he loved these people, and he went into the priesthood so that he could find ways to assist them. He did go to Notre Dame, became a priest, got a Ph.D. in the history of the papacy, and then became an attorney. He now was a legal counsel to the Jesuit order and taught immigration law at Fordham.

He remembered the news kiosk at Ninth and Thirty-fourth where his father bought his paper every morning, his father's local Keen's Steakhouse on Thirty-sixth, the men's haberdasheries all around the garment district, Arnold Hatters on Eighth Avenue, Nat Sherman's cigar store at Broadway and Eighth, and Horn and Hardart, especially the one at Broadway and Fourteenth that featured psychedelic posters of the Beatles, the Rolling Stones, and Bob Dylan. Mike's favorite dish at the automat was the Salisbury steak with mashed potatoes, which he still bought now and then as take-away from Zabar's.

Mike sometimes lamented that 2013 wasn't more like 1963, when he had been a freshman at Stuy. Pope Francis I was no John XXIII…at least not yet. Pope John, Mike recalled, had been a kindly man apparently voted into office by the cardinals as a kind of interim place setting until someone of a more steely ability could be brought along. But John surprised them all, convening the Second Vatican Council in 1962, which opened the door to liberalisms in the Church that no one could have expected the day he was elected pope. Liberation theology itself, for God's sake!

At The Star of David, just inside the door on the left, the shoeshine guys Pepito and Ángel manned the two chairs next to each other on a stand. Mike carried a couple pairs of shoes in a paper sack, which he gave to Pepito. Mike knew that his six dollars and the two-dollar tip were going to someone who could make good use of the money, Pepito's wife being pregnant yet again with a third child. Amalia clerked at the CVS Pharmacy in Williamsburg. But the baby was coming, and Mike knew that Amalia was still illegal. So who knew what would happen after the baby got here?

Ángel, the bachelor shoeshine guy, was a noted salsa dancer and usually dressed in a more dapper way than did Pepito. Mike kidded him for his svelte manners and perfect hair. He had never seen Ángel dance, but he understood that the kid was a natural. Ángel himself didn't care about not getting Mike's business. He had other sources of income anyway—Pepito refrained from telling Mike what those sources were, usually smiling as he kept the secret—so a couple dollars this way or that didn't really matter to him.

Both men greeted Mike when he entered the shop, both glad to see him. He handed the sack over to Pepito and told him he would wait for the shoes. He looked beyond the counter at the few racks of mended, altered, and refurbished suits, shirts, jackets, pants, dresses, and skirts. "Is Nathan here?"

"No, Father. But he'll be back." Ángel's accent was pronounced, but he had the English down pat. He wore a pair of tight, kelly green Levi's, a white cloth belt, a lemon yellow short-sleeved sport shirt (the sleeves further rolled up) and black loafers without socks. Mike knew that Ángel would be going to the Copacabana later, for Salsa Tuesday, a special party where the women got in free. Ángel had frequently bragged about how beautiful the women were there—"*Real* pretty. You know, Father, still dressed for work. So, wool suits, black shoes. But like every Latina, man, Father, can they dance!"—and how they all wanted to dance with him. His features reminded Mike of some dark-skinned bullfighter whose looks made the ladies in the stands breathe with combative desire and delicacy. His clothing was spotless, although his hands appeared bruised with shoe polish.

Ángel was twenty-six years old, from Puebla, Mexico. He had come to New York seven years earlier, illegally, to sell cut flowers from a stand outside a Korean market on Third Avenue. A bright kid, he had learned quickly that the wages at the flower stand were low, and that he could get tips shining shoes. Nathan had hired him because he had known about the boy's ability for languages—he was a quick learner of English—and his constant interest in getting into the building trades. He now attended a technical college in Long Island City and was on the cusp of getting his contractor's license. "I want to do skyscrapers," Ángel had once admitted, grinning with only half-serious levity. "The new Manhattan!"

Neither Nathan nor Mike had any doubts that within just a few more years, he would get there. "That boy, he's like me," Nathan had once confided in Mike. "He's a prize. Real smart."

"Will Nathan be back?" Mike said.

"Jeez, *Padre,* I don't know." Pepito replaced the cap on a bottle of cordovan polish. "He pretty mad."

Silently, Ángel turned back toward his chair. He laid the polishing rag in his right hand across one of the shoe stirrups.

"At what?"

"Avigail." Pepito shook his head, replacing the bottle in a rack on the stand. As always, he was confused by Mike's casual dress, as though a priest really ought not to be seen in a sport shirt. But especially now, Pepito appeared not to know how to respond to Mike's question. Finally, he placed his thumbs in the pockets of his baggy work pants, keeping his eyes on the floor. His head hung left to right, back and forth. "Avigail... *¿Qué sé yo, Padre?* What do I know?"

Avigail, Nathan's twenty-year-old daughter, made her father's life into a true, suffering labor.

A half hour later, Nathan, seated on an old wooden stool at the back of the shop, formed a tuck in the back waist of one of Mike's pairs of slacks. "Twelve pounds, you say, Father?"

"Fourteen."

"How'd you do it?" The pincushion attached to his wrist held several dozen straight pins. He held a pin by his thumb and index finger as he drew a triangle with a flat piece of chalk on the back of the slacks, from which he would cut the now overly expansive cloth.

"Diet. Exercise. Prayer."

"Not worry?"

"No, Nathan. What have I got to worry about?"

"Well, I know you haven't got a daughter, that's for sure."

Mike shrugged—"Never been in the cards for me, God knows."—not catching at first the tone of resignation in Nathan's voice.

Nathan had been born on the Lower East Side, although his parents, an orthodox rabbi and his schoolteacher wife, had taken him to Jerusalem as a boy, in 1967, to help defend the faith against the Arab infidels that surrounded it on all sides. Nathan considered himself Israeli, and had served in the army during the Lebanon war in 1982.

"I wasn't much of a soldier," he had told Mike. "What do I know from land mines? I never hurt anybody."

Now fifty-one years old and, as he called himself, "a lapsed Jew," he had owned The Star of David for twenty years. Nathan was not a tall man, nor was he thin. The way he carried his weight, though, gave him an authoritative, quiet sincerity that was attractive in him. He was a very accommodating man, made so, he often said, "by the kind of people who come into this place." That was intended as a joke, because Nathan's complaints about his customers usually proved how much he liked them. Hundreds of them, who had been coming to The Star of David for years. "You can't keep a customer if you treat him like...well, you know, Father. If they go away, they're not coming back, right?"

"That's what I've found, yes."

"What, a priest has customers?"

"Of course."

"They pay on time?"

"Sure."

"After Confession? Or up front?"

In Jerusalem, Nathan had learned that he didn't have the faith that his parents had, even as they battled against him, to turn him back in the right direction to orthodoxy and prayer. Nathan wanted to do business. He schmoozed. He liked dancing with girls. All that study in yeshiva, all that debate...he didn't want that. His father grimaced whenever Nathan shrugged his shoulders and talked back disrespectfully. But in the end, when Nathan defied his father's orders and freely entered the Israeli army, the young man rejoiced, even though he realized that he might come back to the Mea Shearim neighborhood in a body bag. He had to do it. He had to get away.

"Hurting people, I never wanted that."

"But what if you had run into Arafat one day?" Mike said. "You know, in a tea shop or somewhere, in the old town."

"Arafat?" Nathan had pursed his lips, nodding his head to one side. "That schmuck?" He had not completed the response.

"I'll have to hold off having a daughter until my next life." Mike looked out the window of the shop as Nathan pinned the cloth securely at the back of the slacks. "How is Avigail?"

"I think the last time she was nice to me was when you suggested that, if I didn't mind, you could baptize her Catholic."

That had been when Avigail was a couple of months old and Nathan's wife, Tamara, had brought the baby to the shop so that he could show her off to his customers. Mike's joke caused big laughter among the other visitors to the shop, most of them Jews. Mike, used to being with infants because of his many nieces and nephews, took the little girl into his arms and, in his socks (his shoes being shined that day by Cornell Jackson, an elderly black man and a vociferous fan of the Black Panthers, who himself wore a black beret every day)… Mike allowed Avigail to take firm hold of his right index finger. Even then, she had the black curls that now so peopled her long hair, and the enrapturing dark brown eyes for which she had been known all her life so far.

Mike well remembered the divorce between Nathan and Tamara, when Avigail was ten. It was notable for its cantankerous pain. The girl required a couple of years to even speak civilly with her father again, even though he had custody of her, and even though Tamara had moved to White Plains with a new boyfriend, a Protestant from Cleveland who worked for Air Emirates.

"Take 'em off." Nathan put the chalk aside, and Mike removed the pair of trousers. "The other pairs are the same size?"

"Yes."

"Same brand?"

"Yes."

"Okay. No problem."

Mike put on his Levi's and slid his arms into the sleeves of his sport jacket. "But what about Avigail?"

"Ah! She's got big plans. You know, always."

"That's bad?"

Nathan stood up from the stool, folding the pairs of pants and placing them on the counter next to a sewing machine. "In this case, yes."

"What is it? She wants to go to Israel?"

"Not in her condition, Father."

"What condition?"

"She's pregnant."

Mike bowed his head. At first he did not respond, wanting to assess Nathan's very sudden, obvious turn to regret. For the moment he seemed lost, oblivious to Mike's silence.

"God will forgive us," Nathan said. "But…a baby?"

"When did you find out?"

"This morning."

"Well…do you know who…who—"

"The father?"

"Yes."

Nathan removed the pincushion from his wrist and tossed it into an old cigar box on the same table. The tape measure remained hanging around his neck. For Mike, its numbers and lined divisions seemed too cool, too organized and therefore coldly impervious to the tailor's chagrin. Each individual number turned its back on Nathan, ignoring him. Nathan hurried the measure from his neck, crumpled it up between his hands, and threw it at the box. Only part of the tape made it into the box, the majority of it strewn like a disdainful utterance across the surface of the table. Nathan stood a moment staring at it, his eyes wavering back and forth as though he were singularly outraged by it.

"No, I don't know who the guy is." Nathan sat down once more on the stool and lowered his forehead onto the fingers of his open right hand.

"She's crazy about him, she says." Clearly his thoughts were battling each other for attention. "I mentioned an abortion." Nathan, suddenly recalling the profession of the man with whom he was speaking, swallowed. "Excuse me, Father, I don't mean any dis—"

"Keep going, Nathan. Please."

"She says that she loves the baby. She wants to keep it." Nathan frowned, seeking Mike's commiseration. "Abortion's out, she says." Nathan scratched the top of his head. "What would you do if you were me?"

"I guess I'd ask who the guy is."

"I did! And she told me to…well, you know, Father, she told me to go…you know, do something bad to myself." Nathan shrugged. "Although she did put the word 'Daddy' at the end of it."

"Was she crying?"

"She's worried." Nathan sat up straight. Mike now leaned back against the table, his arms folded. Nathan's face had thickened in the last few moments, his eyes glistening. He removed his glasses and wiped his eyes with the fingers of one hand. "She knows what this means, a little baby." Resting his hands on his knees, the glasses remaining in one of them, he let out an exhalation. "She never used language like that with me, Father." Slowly he put the glasses on once more, as though they were some new form of suffering. "Never." He looked through the doorway into the outer shop. "Jesus, I only hope he's a Jew."

The door to the shop opened with a sudden bang, and Avigail burst in. She glanced at the shoeshine guys, but did not greet either of them, and then hurried into the back of the shop. Though surprised to see Mike, she brushed the priest aside as she confronted her father.

"Daddy, please don't hate me."

"No, honey, I—"

"You do, too! I know you do."

Avigail was a student at the Fashion Institute. Once, Mike had asked her whether she wanted to design dresses or jewelry, and she had replied, "Father Mike, I'm into international trade marketing." Her wish was to found a brand that would nail the world. She would hire the designers, she said. She once told Mike that the thing she really valued in her father was that he was a tailor. "He always told me that everything starts with the needle and thread." Unfortunately, she made the remark as though it were a disinterested dismissal...although Mike detected a shading of smug approval in the turn of phrase. When Mike replied that her father was one of the kindest men he had ever met, Avigail shrugged and took a sip from her lemonade, her attention suddenly riveted by the ice in the glass.

"Honey, let's just talk about this," Nathan said now. He took up the tape measure and began rolling it. Mike glanced into the shop and saw that Ángel was leaving, closing the door quietly behind him. He turned up Thirty-sixth Street toward Eighth.

"Daddy!"

Avigail glanced at Mike once more, wishing him gone. She then turned back to her father and began speaking with him in Hebrew. Nathan's lowered shoulders suggested defeat, and Mike, offering a goodbye to father and daughter, excused himself. He headed back into the shop. Pepito handed him the paper bag that contained his shined shoes. Both men looked into the back.

"Daddy, I did it because I wanted to."

Avigail's eyes, like riveting black stars, fixed upon her father's. Nathan stepped back, placing the palm of his right hand against the back of his head. Pepito offered little help to Mike. He looked away, out the window. Nathan was, after all, Pepito's employer, and Pepito was embarrassed. Clearly this moment in the shop had little to do with the shop, and a great deal to do with the fact that Avigail was Nathan's resentful daughter, and was venting her rage in order to scald him.

Nathan himself frowned at Mike with embarrassment, conveying to the priest that there was very little solace that Mike could offer him. Mike wasn't an actual father, which put him out of the conversation entirely. And then it became even more than usually obvious that Mike also was not a Jew, which was worse. Maybe a priest would have something to say about a pregnant daughter. But what could he say—a Catholic, for Christ's sake!—about a Jewish pregnant daughter, or for that matter anything of such importance in The Star of David?

Avigail began weeping and shouted at her father again in language that neither of the other men understood, but in a pleading tone that both realized came from the girl's mortification. She was screaming for forgiveness, yet confronting her father with his own irresponsibility and ineptitude. Mike put an index finger to his lips, slipped a ten to Pepito, nodded to him and left.

He walked back up to Eighth Avenue, deciding to take the long trek to the Fordham campus, where he had some things to pick up from his office before taking the subway home to Spellman Hall in the Bronx. As usual in mid-afternoon, the traffic on Eighth Avenue was hobbled and barely moving. The sidewalk rumbled with pedestrian conflict. Mike moved quickly and saw Ángel up ahead, his hands in the pockets of his green Levi's. His head had lowered, his eyes stuck staring at the sidewalk. His walking, though slow, seemed driven. He was beset by troubles.

After several blocks, Ángel turned down Forty-seventh Street and headed for the entry to the Copacabana.

Mike paid the ten-dollar entry and walked into the club, having waited outside for several minutes to avoid Ángel's notice. The place was packed, and Mike realized right away that Ángel's assessment of the ladies had been a correct one. Many of them appeared to be lawyers or bankers, women dressed in dull office-dictated fashion that, really, did little for them. But they did not dance dowdily. Their movement was, always, soulfully celebratory, and the ocean-like, stormy flow of all the dancers, men and women, the multiple rhythms of the music determining the intensities of happiness and love, made the entire club a garden of joyous exchange. Even Mike, briefly putting aside his Jesuit vows, could enjoy that.

He spotted Ángel by himself in a half-round banquette, with some sort of drink decorated with a little paper umbrella. He was not savoring the drink. Rather he spent a lot of time staring into it, slouched over it, its dusky darkness seeming to reflect Ángel's own pensiveness. His hands were wrapped about the glass, and he appeared in thoughtful conversation with the surface of the liquid. His yellow shirt and, now, the black sport jacket he had put on gave off the same kind of fashion confidence with which Ángel always carried himself. But his isolation put all that aside.

Mike ordered a *cuba libre* at the bar and stood apart from it, leaning against a wall, a pillar partially hiding him from Ángel's line of vision. It was clear to him that Ángel didn't want to dance. Indeed he paid almost no attention to the music. A few women approached him—heart-stopping, although clad in business gray or blue—clearly asking him if he wished to dance, and he turned them down. His hands returned to the glass. He barely moved, except to look up now and then toward the entryway to the club.

A few minutes later, Avigail entered the Copacabana. Many of the dancers knew her, and hailed her as she passed around the perimeter of the floor. She was dressed as Mike imagined the women more usually dressed in the Copacabana. The same short dark brown dress she had been wearing at The Star of David, a light leather Eisenhower jacket in burgundy, a pair of ankle-length brown suede boots with a short heel, and a silk scarf in mustard yellow, covered over with stylized flowers and renderings of butterflies in every color.

The one person intent upon not noticing Avigail was Ángel.

Mike ordered a second *cuba libre*.

When she addressed Ángel, he looked up from the glass before him with an immediate look of chagrin. Defeat, even. Avigail pleaded with him, her need for talk made clear by the movement of her hands against the front of her jacket, like flowered creepers surging up a delicate wall.

After a moment, Ángel gestured toward the seat across the table from him. Avigail sat down, hurriedly unzipping the jacket and, with the scarf, crumpling it over the back of the banquette. For the next several minutes, their conversation was one-sided, Avigail's eyes unwaveringly centered upon Ángel's—on the few occasions when he looked up at her—or on his hands. Ángel barely spoke, despite Avigail's clear remonstrations that he do so. Mike worried that Ángel was merely waiting until Avigail stopped talking, so that then he could be rid of her.

Finally, Avigail leaned far over the table and—Mike could tell from the movement of her lips—called his name, several times. "Ángel!" A number of the people at other tables turned their heads toward the couple. "Ángel, look at me!" Their attention was taken by Avigail's quite evident sadness. Finally Ángel stood, took the few steps to the other side of the table, and slid in next to Avigail, putting his arm around her and pulling her close. She crumpled into his embrace, relief—and love—flowing from her with fresh tears. Ángel whispered into her hair, took up one of her hands, and spoke with her, placing the fingers of his other hand against her cheeks as he attempted wiping the tears from them. The tears became a flat sheen against her skin, Ángel's effort resulting actually in more tears, a tide of suffering and gratitude.

The following morning, Mike waited in the Starbucks across the street from The Star of David. He felt he had priestly duties to perform, and so wore his clerical suit and collar. He had taken a table by the window, in order to look up and down Thirty-sixth in both directions. He spotted Ángel, dressed in a pair of black slacks, a pressed white dress shirt, and a black leather jacket. Hurrying to the door of the café, Mike hailed Ángel who, surprised to see the priest and as always very respectful of him, accepted Mike's invitation for a cup of coffee.

"Okay, Ángel, what's happening?"

Ángel fingered the blueberry muffin before him.

Mike continued. "Avigail's pregnant."

Ángel's head jerked upward. He stared into Mike's eyes.

"And you're the father."

Ángel lowered his head and slowly broke the muffin in two.

"It's true, isn't it?"

Ángel lifted a portion of the muffin to his lips and took a bite from it.

"Listen, what are you going to do?"

"I love her, Father." He took up the cup of coffee and sipped from it. "I love her and our baby."

"Yeah, but what are you going to do?"

"Marry her!"

For the moment, Mike took in the news. "That may not be enough."

Ángel's brow rose up.

"Her father may not act like it, Ángel, but he was raised in an orthodox household."

Ángel's hands came to rest on either side of the plate. The muffin lay before him in pebbled bits. "What's that?"

"Orthodox?"

"Yes, Father."

Mike sighed. "Your parents, they're Catholic, no?"

"Yes. In Mexico, you know, they all—"

"They're all Catholic."

"Yes, Father."

"But there are different kinds, no?"

"You mean, like ones that go to church and the ones that don't?"

"Yes, but even more, Ángel."

Mike took up a piece of muffin, raised it above the plate and, with a glance, sought Ángel's permission to eat it. Ángel assented.

"There are those that just go to church, and then there are others who spend all their time in church and read the Bible all day long, crawl on their knees toward the statue of the Virgin Mary, and always think of the priests and nuns as the most holy people in the world, right?"

Ángel waved a hand before his eyes. "Yes, Father. My father."

"He's like that?"

"Always. He's a farmer. Comes into Puebla to sell his vegetables every Wednesday and Saturday, and the first place he goes is the church."

"To pray?"

"No…first, to give the priests some vegetables, then to pray."

"When does he go to the market?"

"After he prays." Ángel placed his forehead on the palm of his right hand. "In the church. You know, at the…" He splayed the fingers of his hand, searching for the word. "The glass box with the dead Jesús… The sarc…sarc—"

"Sarcophagus."

"That's the English?"

"Yeah."

"Same word in Spanish." Ángel took up a smaller piece of the muffin. "Almost."

"So…your father's orthodox."

"I guess so. That's why I had to get out of there. And we didn't have any money, too." Ángel pushed the bit of muffin into his mouth. "Another good reason to cross the border, no?"

"Yes."

"And *Señor* Nathan?"

"His family's really orthodox."

"But he…he told me once that he doesn't believe in all that stuff."

"Maybe so. But it matters to him that Avigail marry a Jew, and that her children be Jewish."

For a moment, Mike glanced up toward the café ceiling. Without knowing it, he had come up with a piece of advice for Ángel. But it was one that would come as a surprise to his compatriots. He considered the history of the Catholic Church. For two thousand years it had maintained itself, especially in the beginning, through proselytization, convincing others to come in. *I mean the Jesuits, Lord help us!* he thought. *What* was *Francis Xavier doing all those years out there in Japan and India?*

Mike searched the ceiling, hoping for a vision of John XXIII, that the pontiff would look down upon him and, patting Mike's back, calm his sudden, conflicted nerves. But there was only the ceiling, its white paint frayed here and there, yellowed here and there.

"You love her, eh?"

"Yes, Father."

"Does it matter to you that you're Catholic?"

Ángel's brow furrowed once more. "Sure, I guess."

"You guess."

"Well, Jeez, Father, I mean, I don't…" Ángel pointed to Mike, "I don't disrespect, Father, you know, you. But…I don't know."

"And you love Avigail."

"I do."

"You want to marry her."

"I do."

Mike looked up toward the ceiling once more, hoping again for the shade of John XXIII. When the pope did not materialize, not even as a slim gray suggestion of a ghost or some kind of oracular shadow smoothing the scuffed paint of the café ceiling, Mike did recall for a moment the riveting photo in *Newsweek* a couple days ago. Francis's hands had caressed the female feet of the young Muslim thief. Mike decided that he would have to go it alone.

"Could you become a Jew?"

Surprise rushed across Ángel's face. The fingers of his right hand rested against the muffin. "I'll do whatever she wants."

"You do want that baby."

Ángel smiled and ran a hand through his hair, which, for the first time since Mike had met him five years before, appeared messed and confused. "The baby is my life."

The dishevelment pleased Mike because Ángel's looks were suddenly those of a young man who may not have known himself very well until Avigail had come along, but who now, his heart having opened, had real regard for himself and what he planned to do.

"So you'll love your baby."

"As long as I get to save some for Avigail."

"All right. You wait here, and I'll see what I can arrange."

The Star of David was not yet open, and Mike had to knock at the door.

Nathan, coming from the room in back, waved, casting a mock-admiring look at Mike's sacerdotal finery. He unlocked the door. "Father Mike! You're all dressed up."

Mike took Nathan's hand, enjoying, even under the pressure of his mission, the circumstance of Nathan's humor. "Well, yes, you know, now and then I—"

"But your pants aren't ready yet."

"Yeah, I know. But listen, Nathan, can we talk?"

The shop was empty. Nathan stepped away from the door. "Sure. Come in, come in."

Mike followed Nathan to the back of the shop, and accepted the offer of a cup of tea. The two men sat down on stools at the counter that held Nathan's sewing machine.

"I've got some information about Avigail." Mike leaned forward over the tea, his elbows on the counter. Steam rose up, warming his fingers, which were gathered together above the mug,

Nathan appeared puzzled. He waited, silent.

"Ángel's the father."

Nathan said nothing. He blinked his eyes twice. Seeming surprise appeared in them, and Mike worried that he perhaps should have been less direct with this news.

"You think I don't know that?" Nathan frowned. "She told me last night."

"And what did you say?"

Nathan sat back on the stool, placing his hands on his knees. "Listen, Father Mike. I don't mean you any disrespect. But are you sure this has…" He shrugged. "This has anything to do with you?"

Mike knew that indeed it *wasn't* any of his business, and he brought the cup of tea to his lips as he nodded to Nathan's question.

"I mean, it's nice of you to care." Nathan frowned. "But, you know, when she told me…. She spoke with me like she hasn't spoken to me in years."

"You mean—"

"With kindness, and…you know…." Nathan's head turned to the left and right, his eyes watching the counter top. "Understanding." His shoulders sloped forward. "Imagine that."

"But do you understand?"

"No." Nathan stood and walked around the counter. Worry emanated from him. "I mean...Ángel?"

The two men seemed for the moment to be jousting in embarrassed silence.

"He's a Catholic boy." Nathan put his hands on his waist, then raised them a short moment above his head, the fingers splayed. "How do you expect me to feel?"

Mike nodded. "Pretty badly. But—"

"I mean, what are Avigail and me gonna do when the little kid is up there takin' Communion?"

At first, Mike took the remark as a note of Nathan's unhappiness. But when he looked to Nathan, he saw that the tailor was actually having a bit of fun. This did not make sense to Mike. But maybe it was just one more of Nathan's usual jabs at Catholicism, Nathan making fun of Mike as he so often did. Mike saw an opening. He took in a breath. "Would you be willing to talk with him?"

"No, Father Mike. I just don't see how this can work."

"How often have you talked with Ángel? You know, about important, important—"

"A lot. I like the kid."

"And this, this is—"

"Important. I know." Nathan turned his head toward the floor, where a small piece of gray cotton, a throwaway, a tiny remnant, lay partially folded beside one corner of the counter. He took it up and examined it, first one side, then the other, before dropping it to the countertop. "Believe me. I know."

"Nathan." Mike took up the cloth. "Please. Can I ask you just to talk with him? I mean...." He folded the cloth. "You never know...." He pushed it back toward Nathan. "It might be that I'll be attending the kid's bar mitzvah."

An hour later, Pepito applied the polish, his right hand spreading the goop quickly across the surface of Mike's shoes. Both men glanced repeatedly out the window, watching Nathan, Avigail, and Ángel, who sat at a window table in the Starbucks, over coffee. At first Nathan did all the talking, and his unhappiness gleamed through the window. His head plunged forward and back, like a small axe hovering over a chopping block. Avigail and Ángel's hands were intertwined on the tabletop, Avigail weeping. Ángel, calm and negotiating, explained himself. He was still dressed as the lady-killer *salsero.* He re-adjusted his hair from time to time, as Elvis might have. But his responses were serious, and with time Nathan seemed to realize that. He calmed, then calmed even more. Avigail leaned her head against Ángel's shoulder.

Nathan and Ángel continued talking, and even though Pepito tapped the toe of Mike's left shoe—the traditional indicator that the once-scuffed leather now shined again with fresh, gleaming authority—Mike told him to keep polishing. Pepito applied the cloth to the shoes again, something he did for several more minutes as the two men continued stealing glances out the window at the Starbucks.

When Ángel extended his right hand across the table to Nathan, Pepito finally retired the cloth from its duty. But even the cloth seemed to Mike to want to watch the scene across the street. After a worrisome pause of several seconds, Nathan took Ángel's extended hand into both his and shook it warmly.

On the A train to Fordham later that morning, Mike took the few-days-old copy of *Newsweek* from his briefcase. The photo showed Pope Francis on his knees, washing the foot of a prisoner, with loving respect for her. Appearing shy and moved by what was happening, she extended her bare foot to the pope's touch. Mike peered at the picture, fearful that never again in his life would he see such a thing. The silvery glint of fresh water flowed from the pontiff's hands. "It's about time!" He only hoped it was for real.

WILFREDO'S DEBUSSY

"May I ask you a question?" The man's coal-dark skin had a sheen around the eyes. He wore black-rimmed spectacles, and Monk sensed reserved self-acceptance in him simply in the way he leaned toward the piano as though it were a lectern. His puffy double-breasted brown suit was too large even for his enormous frame. The necktie seemed to have been tied just once, then loosened, removed and put back on, over and over again for years. His black shoes had quite thick soles and heels, the kind of footwear worn by security guards, so that what they give to the wearer in comfort, they lose in style. He also carried a large Trader Joe's paper bag that contained a number of sheet music scores, the covers of which, Monk could see, were faded badly or scuffed along the edges.

Monk had been admiring an old Bechstein grand piano for the past few months, jealous that such a fine instrument, from 1900 or so, made of rosewood with carefully hand-tooled mounts and other fixtures, and perfectly tuned, could be sitting alone—music itself, as it were, waiting to be played—on the showroom floor.

His jealousy was restrained, though, because he was also very glad that the piano store, called Debussy, on West Fifty-eighth Street, had the good sense to display this instrument for all to see. It had been sold back to the store recently. The refined beauty of its finishing, its general appearance so dignified and perfectly varnished in warm tans and browns, was matched—overwhelmed actually—by its somber tone. This piano played intimately, yet with a heartfelt resonance that made the delicacy of feel in its keyboard seem a miracle to Monk. He was thrilled to be able to come into the store and, watched always by the salesman Sándor, play one or two things.

They had become friends. One of Sándor's duties was to protect the pianos from amateurs, unless of course some amateur had just bought one of them and the bank had transferred the funds. He had learned though that Monk knew a good deal about what he was doing, even though he was not doing, say, Mozart. More often Monk did Bill Evans or Duke Ellington. That was fine with Sándor, since Monk seemed to understand those fellows quite well.

Monk himself knew that his own talent was only so-so. He recalled how his father had supported his playing, even as Monk had struggled through his high school years, wishing eventually to go professional. He had never been able to get his fingers to work with the proper complicated authority, though, when it came to imitating solos he had heard on records by people like Teddy Wilson or Nat Cole. He was always just Monk, he felt. Good enough. Not bad. While those guys were celestials.

Monk looked up from the piano bench. "A question?"

He had seen this man in the store on several occasions. He, too, appeared to savor the pianos...particularly the Bechstein. He walked around studying it, always with the bag of sheet music hanging from one hand. Monk had never seen him play, and had even asked Sándor about him.

"I've asked him if he wanted to try any of the instruments." Sándor had come to New York as an infant, after the 1956 uprising in Hungary. He had, he often said, difficulty selling an instrument to anyone who resembled Nikita Khrushchev. Sándor played piano well, but his real talent lay in understanding the workings inside the instrument. He had perfect pitch and could fix almost anything that had been broken, for whatever reason. Quite thin, he moved about with lax, slow moving angularity, even though he thrived on hearing and then repairing the least noticeable of problems in a piano. Indeed, he seemed to rage within himself in search of such things.

"But he's only done it once," Sándor said. "I always figured he understands the music, the way he talks about the pianos. And all that sheet music he has. He finds it in second-hand shops. He even has a copy of a Mozart sonata signed by Rubinstein." Sándor placed a hand in the pocket of his suit coat and brought out a pipe, which he tapped against the palm of his left hand. "But, play? Just once, and not for very long."

"How good is he?"

"Very, if you can judge it from listening to him for just two minutes, part of an Erik Satie piece, and then only when we were alone in the store, after closing."

"When was that?"

"Ten years ago. I almost had to force him to play." Sándor was fingering the keyboard of the Bechstein, and suddenly frowned, as though there were something wrong with it. Monk hadn't thought there was. "I just wanted to know whether he could."

"But he didn't finish the Satie."

"No. He stood up from the piano, thanked me, and left. In a hurry."

Now, the man dropped the shopping bag to the floor. "Yes. A small question." He ran his right index finger along the surface of the Bechstein. "It's just that I think you are not American." His accent was Hispanic, Monk guessed.

"How so?"

A large grin appeared. "For one, you say things like 'Good morning' and 'How are you?'"

Monk extended his hand. "Aren't you talking more about someone who isn't from New York?"

"Maybe that's it."

"Because I'm not from New York." Monk took the man's hand into his. "I'm Monk Samuels."

"Thank you. And I am Rodney Echeverría."

"Puerto Rico?"

Rodney's left shoulder dropped, a bit of despondency. "No. Cuba."

"I'm from California," Monk said.

"Ah, that explains it."

"Explains what?"

"Your seeming so foreign."

Rodney invited Monk for coffee at the Europa Café, on Fifty-seventh, across the street from Carnegie Hall. It was there that Monk explained to him why he was named Monk.

"Thelonious."

"The great one, who played so out of tune."

"Yes. My father was a fan."

"As is my wife, Marta." Thoughtful enjoyment flowed through a sigh from Rodney. "I never much approved." The jab at Thelonious and Marta, offered with kindness, made Monk laugh. "But she has a right to her own taste."

"She's a musician?"

"No...a nurse...a therapist. Musculature. Movement, all that." Rodney leaned forward. "He was a musician, your father?"

"No, he helped fund companies. Apple Computer and so on. Cisco Systems. He was very successful."

"Unlike my father...." Rodney made a circle with his right index finger on the tabletop. "Who, as I do, taught piano for an hourly fee."

"Mine loved Thelonious Monk because he played so many bad notes. He knew it was intentional on Thelonious's part. He loved the comedy of it."

"Just the comedy?"

"No. He also felt that Thelonious played with more...he called it 'emotional courage' than almost any of the other guys." Monk paused a moment, reflecting on his father's musical opinions and the thoughtfulness that went into them. "The sorrow in all that discord." His eyes blinked as the memory of his father took him for a moment. Mel Samuels had been a far better venture capitalist than musician, but he had known, somehow, who played well and who didn't. "Thelonious Monk was a very great man."

"He's gone, your father."

"A few years ago, yes."

"And he enjoyed your playing."

Monk swallowed, studying his coffee. He recalled his father sitting on the living room couch of their home in Woodside, listening to Monk essay a new piece from Oscar Peterson or someone. A country community near

Palo Alto, Woodside was where his parents, suddenly enjoying the benefits of Mel's extraordinary venture capital decisions, had built their estate. The large two-story house resided on several acres of a partially wooded slope, and was surrounded by a very large English garden, a product of his mother's expertise. As a teenager, Monk felt that his parents' conservative decorum didn't fit very well with his own wishes for improvisation and fun. But his father especially had allowed that fun…even encouraged it. "I think he enjoyed my music. But he didn't take it too seriously."

Rodney extended his lower lip. "I'm sorry."

"Oh, he was right. When the time came for me to give up my professional…aspirations, I guess you'd call them, he still asked me to play for him."

"That's good."

"By that time I'd decided to go to Berkeley."

"What did you study?"

"Finance. A minor in music history."

"Didn't want to lose touch."

"That's right." Monk shrugged. His coffee was too hot, and he stirred it with a small spoon, hoping that the infusion of air would allow him finally to enjoy it the way Rodney was so clearly enjoying his. "I was at least a better piano player than my father was."

"And you're as good an investor?"

Monk's eyes brightened. "No. My father was an amazement when it came to money." Finally, he brought the cup to his lips. The coffee was now full and warm, the compliment to the cinnamon toast and butter that rested on the plate before him. "But I do fine."

"You're looking at that Bechstein?"

"Yes."

"Then I would say you're doing quite fine." Rodney took up one of the three macaroons he had ordered.

Monk gestured toward the Trader Joe's paper bag that was now resting on the floor next to their table. "But why do you go to Debussy?"

"It's that Bechstein, Monk. My father brought it with us from Cuba. You know, Fidel and Che and so on. We had lost everything except for that piano. Imagine trying to get an instrument like that out of danger when danger is everywhere." Rodney tightened his lips, the memory of the revolution still clearly a frightful unhappiness. "Our escape took all his money. But then he had to give up the piano itself because eventually we still had no money."

"He sold it."

"Yes. Here. To Debussy. I was in the first grade when it happened. Like Sándor. Another escapee." Rodney hid a smile behind his right hand. "There are a few differences between us, of course. I'm a black *caribeño,* and he's…he's…" Rodney looked over his shoulder. "He's an eastern European white boy. The Communists put down the rebels in his country."

"And in yours, the rebels won."

Rodney's shoulders drooped. "Yes, sadly."

"How long have you been coming to Debussy, Rodney?"

"Fifty years."

"And the piano's been there—"

"It's been in the store, off and on, since that first time that my father brought me." Rodney stirred some sugar into his coffee. "They would sell it and it would be gone for a while. But then it would come back. The most recent owner had died or bet wrong on the market or something. And then my father would come back. I played it once."

"Why not more often?"

Rodney gave Monk a look of hurt and even, briefly, dismay. "You would ask me to betray my father?"

"No. Rodney, I—"

"The piano's been in prison, don't you see?"

Monk searched Rodney's eyes, a petition for forgiveness. "What was your father's name?"

"Wilfredo Echeverría Bourbón."

"What did he do that first day he brought you to the store?"

Rodney remained silent a moment. "He, too, was heavy, like me. He breathed with difficulty, a raspy sound that he had to quell when he was playing. He often said to me that he was afraid the children he taught would think him a ghost, a *fantasma,* as we say."

He spoke haltingly, as if a wound had seeped open.

"With chains running around his lungs. That day, he stared at the piano a long while."

"That's all?"

The wound flowed, and Rodney considered his reply. "No. He placed his right hand on the keyboard and played a few chords."

"Do you remember which ones?"

"Schubert."

"Anything else?"

"Brahms. And Beethoven, of course." Rodney lowered his voice, almost to a whisper. "Before the revolution, my father had been considering a concert career. Even though he was black, he had been arranging for his first appearances in Europe, but…" Rodney took in a breath. "Fidel didn't think much of that idea." Rodney replaced the cup on the table, brought his fingers across a second macaroon…his favorite cookie, he had told Monk…as he considered what next to say. "A career extinguished before it could even get started." He brought the cookie to his lips. "My father loved Brahms. But he often told me that he could barely speak of Brahms in the same breath with Beethoven."

"And he couldn't afford to buy the piano back."

"Never." Rodney lowered the macaroon to the tabletop. "He played on all kinds of other instruments. Friends' pianos. Pianos in the public schools where he taught. Tinny, elderly pianos. Out of tune, exhausted pianos. His students' pianos when their mothers would allow a black man like him to come into their apartments. But that Bechstein…he called it 'my Debussy.' And finally, of course, he died."

Rodney suffered a passage of silence.

"The loss of that piano broke my father, Monk, almost as much as the revolution did." He exhaled, a bit of gravel in his own breathing. "I've been saving up for years, to try to buy it back. But every time it comes into the store again, it's almost double the previous price."

"I see. And of course the price now is—"

"A hundred thousand." Rodney looked aside, out the window to Fifty-seventh Street. "Losing that piano…it broke his heart."

The next time Monk met Rodney in the store, the Bechstein was gone. He had told Sándor about Rodney's caring for the piano's welfare. Sándor had sensed it through the years but had not understood the full story, as Monk had related it to him.

But now....

"Sándor, I—"

"He's a cherished customer, Monk." Sándor had come from the repair area at the back of the store, hurried from it by Monk's clear upset. Rodney, holding his wife's hand, put his left hand to his chest. Marta, a small woman in a burgundy-colored dress, her very black hair detailed with a white gardenia, brought her two hands together, enfolding Rodney's right and coddling it. "Somebody we've been working with for years," Sándor said.

"But—"

"I know you were looking at it, Monk." He turned to Rodney. "I know. But Joe came in with a small suitcase that contained the...the—"

"Hundred thousand," Rodney said.

"A hundred and five, actually." Sándor scratched the back of his head. "He had asked us to hold the piano for two days while he cleared up a problem with the money, and he threw in the five thousand as a thank you gift."

Monk surveyed the space on the show room floor in which the piano had resided.

"A service fee, I guess," Sándor said.

Monk felt he could still make out the instrument, although the view was actually just a chimera, like an imagined drawing on a deteriorating, dust-ridden scrim.

"But you knew that I was—"

"Monk, he had the money in hand. I'm sorry. It was Joe Saxon."

"The dry goods guy?"

Rodney leaned forward. "Who?"

Sándor also examined the empty space. "Born in New York. A retailer. Made millions." The wooden floor revealed a few scuffs where the legs of the piano had met it. Small scars. "Not the first thing he's ever bought from us." Sándor offered a consoling smile. "A good man."

Rodney groaned. "But—"

"Rodney, I've known him since I was a kid. Joe and his wife, Delphine..."

Rodney and Marta glanced at each other. He swallowed. "Saxon?"

"That's right.

"Delphine Saxon?"

"You've heard of her, of course," Sándor said.

"Heard of her!" Rodney nodded toward Marta. "Oh, my love...."

Marta had remained silent through the conversation. But now she patted Rodney's hand. "We saw her perform."

Monk, at a loss, looked on.

"Carnegie Hall," Marta said.

Sándor shrugged. "I'm sorry, Rodney."

Monk went with Rodney and Marta to the Europa, where they sat down at a window table. Carnegie Hall rose up from the sidewalk like an arriving ocean liner across the way. Monk had ordered a cappuccino, but let it rest as he contemplated the hall. For a while, no one said anything. It was true; Monk had wished to buy the piano, even though it would be overkill, he had realized, given his questionable talent as a pianist. But the thing was so beautiful.

"My father," Rodney whispered.

Marta took up his right hand.

"Look, the piano isn't dead," Monk said.

She examined the hand, and then began massaging it, a combination of caresses.

"It might as well be." Rodney closed his eyes, grateful for Marta's attention.

"But you can—"

"I may never see it again, Monk."

Marta laid her head against Rodney's upper arm. She raised a hand to the back of his neck and massaged it.

"This is like death itself." Rodney leaned back, closing his eyes, accepting once more Marta's salving touch. "Again."

At home in his apartment on Riverside Drive, Monk went online, to read about Joe Saxon. But indeed it was Delphine who interested him more. She had been a concert pianist, raised in Paris, who as a teenager had embarked upon her professional career. She had been thought of as a notable for the future, a pianist who would take the world. But Delphine was afflicted at the age of thirty-two with multiple sclerosis and suddenly had to retire. Her husband, Joe, was fifty-seven at the time. After a business career that had been played out on the pages of *Women's Wear Daily* and *Vogue, Elle* and *Harper's Bazaar,* he had retired and given himself over to care for his wife. The years of silence that followed diminished the society pages' memory of Joe and Delphine Saxon. He now was known as the elderly, plainspoken businessman and devoted escort of his wife, while she was the luckless genius.

Monk went back to Debussy a few times during the next weeks, and Sándor told him that Rodney had not come in. Midsummer was blazing, and Rodney suffered from the heat. He had been staying at home.

"It's his weight, I think. I worry about him every year," Sándor said.

Monk knew, though, that no matter the weather or Rodney's heft, the absence of the Bechstein was what pulled at his heart. He remembered having asked Rodney at the Europa how many times the piano had been sold since his father had lost it.

"Nine."

Having witnessed this latest disappearance of Wilfredo's Debussy, Monk could well imagine how each of those had hurt Wilfredo and, to be sure, Wilfredo's son.

A few days later, he entered the store again and heard a male voice from the repair room, wavering, hesitant as it voiced a complaint. "It's the Bechstein's D key, Sándor."

Monk was able to visualize the key, knowing the sound it should make.

"It's off."

Monk placed his shoulder bag on the counter outside the repair room. As he waited, he heard Sándor's acknowledgment of the key, and his guesses about what had gone wrong with it.

"But can you fix it?" The voice was broken up here and there by the effects of age. "It's such a disappointment. She's in mid-passage, and then *that* happens."

Monk looked to the side. *She?* He hurried a glance into the back room. Sándor sat at a desk, his shirt sleeves rolled up. His gray hair was mussed, and Monk could tell from his demeanor that his puzzlement over the sprung key was genuine, as though an unbelievable, disastrous truth suddenly had been revealed to him.

"I'll look at it, Joe. Of course." The sound of Sándor's breathing intensified as responsibility for the Bechstein's breakdown hounded him.

"When?"

"Tomorrow?"

Monk attempted a look at the other person in the back room. He knew who it was. Through the narrow slit between the edge of the curtain and the doorjamb, he could see only a pair of forearms encased in the sleeves of a linen suit coat, a pair of emerald French cufflinks, and wrinkled, ivory-white hands that held a slip of paper. The hands reminded Monk of his father's hands when he had been lying in his bed in Woodside, the day he had died. Covered with dry, wrinkled skin and age spots here and there, Mel's hands had maintained a kind of spirited gracefulness in their gestures even as recently as the month before. His mother had occasionally told Monk that his hands were like his father's in this respect. Monk had sat by the bed waiting until, a few hours into the afternoon, his father, seeking yet one more breath, had gone.

"What time?" Joe said.

Sándor checked his cellphone. "Two?"

"Fine."

The hands folded the slip of paper and then disappeared from Monk's view. Sándor stood and motioned toward the show room. Monk stepped away from the counter, not wanting to reveal that he was spying on the conversation.

The curtain parted, and a small elderly man presented himself to Monk, surprised by him.

"Oh…."

Monk smiled. "Excuse me. I—"

Sándor emerged from the back room as well. "Ah, Monk. I'm glad you're here."

"I can wait."

Sándor shook his head. "But I want you to meet Joe Saxon."

Joe appeared scattered for a moment. Indeed he was very old. The whiteness of his hair was like fresh, though sparse, snow. Even his eyes appeared frail, helped to sight by the thick rimless lenses of his glasses. He stood nonetheless straight, and Monk noticed that his demeanor intensified right away after his moment of early surprise.

Sándor touched Joe's elbow. "Joe. This is Monk Samuels. Another friend."

Joe nodded, his eyebrows raised as he pondered Monk's chest. "How do you do?" He did not offer his hand.

"Monk was looking at the Bechstein too," Sándor said.

Surprised by Sándor's admission and this wish for chumminess between the two competitors, Monk frowned with unease.

"Ah." Joe extended his hand. "You understand pianos!"

They walked to the Europa. Joe's footsteps were tentative with age, and Sándor took his arm. The heat had not subsided, and Sándor remained dressed in shirtsleeves and slacks. When they sat down at a table, awaiting the waiter, Joe leaned toward Sándor.

"Have you told Monk about Delphine?"

"No, I—"

"Sándor did mention her name to me." Monk nodded. "And I did a little reading."

Sándor sat back in his chair and remained quiet.

"Then you know about her career," Joe said.

"I do."

"And you know what happened to her."

"Yes."

Joe sat up straight. The curved wooden back of the chair framed him so well that Monk felt compelled to sit up himself, in order to offer precise answers to what Joe may ask of him.

"Can you imagine what that must mean to her?" Joe said.

Sándor slouched in his chair, suddenly looking away, his arms folded as he listened.

"A disaster," Monk said.

Joe reached for his wallet. "Sándor's coming over to fix the Bechstein tomorrow." He took out a fifty and gestured to the waiter. "You love that piano, too, I gather."

Monk nodded.

"Why don't you come with him? He and Delphine are pals. I'd like you to meet her."

When Monk arrived at the Saxons' apartment, he heard piano music through the door. It was something by Mozart or Haydn, someone like that. But Monk couldn't tell because the music was being played so badly. He knocked at the door. The piano stopped, a few notes scattered about.

The door opened and Joe greeted Monk. Beyond Joe, in a large living room that had a view of Central Park and the Ramble, a hunched-over, rigidly still, gray woman sat at the Bechstein. Dressed in an ankle-length black smock, she wore her hair up in a bun, a black silk cloth across her forehead and tied in back. She wore a pair of green jade earrings, carved as swans. When she turned her head, with noticeable slowness, toward Monk and Joe, the right earring swayed back and forth like a bell hung from a slim ray of light.

"Delphine, this is Monk Samuels."

"Hello." Delphine's voice was not constricted by her condition, as most of her body so obviously was. The single word glowed. "Sit down, Monk." Her French accent accentuated its clarity.

Sándor arrived a moment later and, after a few moments' conversation, set about to repair the Bechstein. At first, Delphine seemed peeved with him. She pointed at the keyboard. "It's this one." But Monk discerned, as Sándor himself helped her stand up from the bench and assisted her to an armchair, that it was only the key with which she was miffed, not Sándor.

Sándor leaned over her in a moment of affection. "Don't worry. I'll get it." Returning to the piano, he lifted his tool case to the bench and pressed the offending key for a moment. Delphine winced as the sound came from the instrument. "Yes, I see," Sándor said, and he began inspecting the innards of the piano.

Delphine attempted a smile. "He's darling." It was an effort to do so. Monk sat down in another armchair. "Sándor has shepherded every practice instrument I've ever had. I referred him to all my colleagues."

Joe poured tea for everyone. "But it's a shame, isn't it, that so few of them come to play for you any longer."

"Well…." She had not wanted tea, and waited as the others sipped theirs. "It would be lovely to hear this instrument played by someone…." Delphine looked to the side. "Other than me."

Sándor, seated on the bench, slowed his work on the piano as he listened to the conversation.

"Someone…." Delphine sighed. She leaned toward Monk. "I suppose you heard me out in the hallway."

"I did."

"That's what it's become." Delphine sat so still, so rigidly, her hands folded on her lap, that movement seemed almost an impossibility. "I don't much enjoy the people who come here to help me. The nurses and so on. They're nice enough." She lifted a hand to her cheek. The effort to caress the cheek caused her pain. "But they don't…they lack…." The hand returned to her lap. "They don't have the music." She frowned. "They move me around, which is painful enough. But they don't understand the music, which is worse."

She made the complaint with such tenderness that her face actually softened. Until now it had seemed to Monk that even those muscles had grown rigid from her affliction. He now mused that the stoniness in her face was actually a sign of simple dismay. Outrage, maybe. Sorrow.

Monk sought Rodney's permission, and then asked Marta to meet him and Sándor at Debussy the next day. They sat alone in the repair room and talked the situation over. Marta defined her hands as "soft, Monk," "loving," and "a little sensuous, even. In the right way, of course." When Monk had explained to her Delphine's problems, she had raised her shoulders, unconcerned. "I can help her."

Monk turned to Sándor.

"I'll call them," Sándor said.

A few days later, though, Marta called Monk. She had been interviewed by Joe and Delphine. "I massaged her hands while they were talking with me," she explained to Monk. "That helped me get the job." But Rodney had not wanted Marta to return to the Saxons' apartment. Forming a relationship with them—as sought after as such a relationship would have been prior to Joe's purchase of the Bechstein—was now too painful a prospect for Rodney.

"He so admires her, Monk. But...."

Monk was about to ask Marta if he could speak with Rodney, when Marta spoke once more.

"I told him I wanted to keep going, that maybe I could arrange for a visit for Rodney now and then." She had pointed out to Rodney that it was not as if the piano were in solitary confinement. It seemed that it was in the hands of a kindly regime. "I mean, Miss Delphine *asked* me to ask him over."

"But does she know—"

"I told her. Cuba. That idiot *singao* Fidel. The revolution. All of it. And you know, Monk, she...she sounded heartbroken."

A week later, at Delphine's request, Monk sat down at the Bechstein to play a version of "I Got It Bad (and That Ain't Good)." Joe sat on a folding chair next to Delphine's armchair and held her hand. In their affectionate motionlessness, the couple resembled faded porcelain. The lilt and frivolity of the tune made everyone in the room smile, especially when Monk played part of it in the style of Thelonious Monk himself. Like Thelonious, Monk intentionally missed notes, came up short on the chords, or played chords that were heavily discordant. He did not know whether Sándor or Delphine could imagine the fruitlessness of such a task, since Thelonious's playful clumsiness had been so much more an issue of genius than Monk's could ever be. As a kid, Monk had known that he had some talent as a pianist, but not talent like that.

Nonetheless, as the lowering sun cast shadows across Central Park, Monk also knew that this was Delphine and Wilfredo's Debussy and, as such, could make any kind of playing sound better than it would have on some other instrument…even that of the immortal Thelonious Monk himself.

"Bravo." Amused cheers broke from everyone as Monk came to the end of the tune.

Marta had insisted on making coffee, and when she brought it into the living room, Rodney sat forward in an armchair, watching her arrival. "My wife makes the very best coffee in the world."

"Well, she is Cuban, after all," Delphine said. She was able to smile. "So you would expect such excellence, wouldn't you?"

Marta went back to the kitchen. She had found the paper bag with the dozen fresh coconut macaroons that Monk had bought earlier, and now brought them into the living room on a blue porcelain dish.

"Well, Rodney?" Monk returned to his armchair. He had taken great care with his appearance on this afternoon, making sure that the double-breasted black suit he wore fit him well, was properly pressed, and formed a formal, modest witness, with the deep blue silk tie and paisley green kerchief, to what it was about to hear.

Rodney stood and examined the Bechstein. "Thank you, Joe." He walked toward the piano. "Monk. Sándor." He ran a hand across the brown lacquer. "And especially Delphine. Thank you." He strummed the strings inside the instrument. Monk listened to the buzz-like response that resulted, a sound that had always reminded him of some sort of laughing threnody. He loved the sound, the shimmering anguish of it.

Rodney sat on the bench and removed his glasses. He placed them in the chest pocket of his suit jacket. No sheet music lay on the music back. He leaned over the keyboard and, after a moment's contemplation, turned to Delphine.

"Mozart. Köchel 397. Fantasia in D minor."

"Oh, Rodney." Delphine took a handkerchief into her right hand. She turned to Joe and, with some labor, brought it to her eyes. After a moment's quiet, she returned the handkerchief to her lap.

"She recorded this," Joe said to Monk.

Rodney laid the fingers of both hands on the keyboard. He appeared to hesitate, as though worried he had stumbled into some lapse in taste.

A breach of the Saxons' hospitality, maybe.

"Rodney, please," Delphine said. "Please continue."

Marta stood silently in the doorway to the kitchen, her right hand resting against her right cheek, as she watched her husband. After another moment, he began playing. The music moved with unsettling slowness. His head hung over the keyboard, almost motionlessly, while tenderness riffled from the instrument. Rodney's very large fingers made the lightest of impressions on the keys. For Monk, the music formed a stream of utterances and long silences, as though Mozart and Rodney—in writing the piece and performing it for Delphine, Joe, Sándor, Marta, and, to be sure, Wilfredo—were seeking explanations in the silences, for why there was such disappointment in the wish for beauty, for why revolutions can sometimes further the gift of contemplation, why dawn fills with slowly warming light and dusk takes it away, and why dreams are so often destroyed. It was a sad, violent memory brightly recalled, played so lightly that the lightness itself became an elegiac expression of true mourning.

MY BEAUTIFUL FRANCISCO

The voice came through the window, with the sunlight. A whisper. "Isabelita."

Oh, Francisco, Elizabeth sighed. She awoke, grateful for the interruption. *Darling Francisco.*

She couldn't move, but did not call Glorieta to come help her. The voice persisted. Francisco took her hand in his and kissed it, so sensuous, his hand like muscled silk, its fingers the very avenue to lovemaking. Francisco's hair was the blackest she had ever seen…or, more to the point, ever touched. When he had not responded to her letter, she had wept as she realized that she would no longer have that hair in which to entangle her fingers.

As usual when Elizabeth thought of Francisco, she wondered why he left her. But she knew why.

At the Spence School, all the girls loved Elizabeth Ryan. Funny. Noisy. So beautiful. And so it had always been, so that now, when some item appeared about her in the newspaper or online, the occasion of a major opening at MOMA or the Whitney, the photo caption always identified her as something like "the vivacious" or "the exotic" Elizabeth Schuyler. The plaque on the wall of the new Islamic wing at the Met carried the names of a dozen major donors, among them Edwin and Elizabeth Schuyler. The information was not entirely accurate, since Elizabeth's husband had died in the late 1980s. But she always included his name in any donation she made to whatever foundation, museum, or orchestra because, even though she had inherited a fortune from her father and grandfather's business successes, and had her own money from her investment firm—the Schuyler Funds, one of the first ever founded by a woman—Edwin Schuyler had made a tremendous amount of money all by himself.

Edwin often said to her that he had done that in order to show her father that he was not the Protestant bounder that Harry Ryan had thought he was. Her father thought so simply because Edwin's family was Episcopalian, and because of the circumstances of their marriage. "What's wrong with the Catholic boys up there at Yale?" he often asked her before Edwin popped the question. Elizabeth, who loved her father, knew that he was quite wrong about the boy that she would eventually marry—despite her father's disgruntlement—in 1942. With time, she also came to love Edwin.

She had to marry him, of course, but that was another story. Edwin had just graduated from Yale, and after their honeymoon in Maine, he volunteered for the army. When he returned home on leave from England a year later, Elizabeth presented him with the little boy—Franco—with whom she was pregnant on their wedding day.

An artillery captain, Edwin eventually fought in the Battle of the Bulge, for which reason, he said for the rest of his life, he hated being cold. So their summer home in East Hampton, and the other one in Augusta, Georgia, where he enjoyed playing golf at the club, were essential to Edwin's happiness. He once even played a round there with Arnold Palmer, a signal event in Edwin's life.

Now ninety, Elizabeth was confined to a wheelchair, her body having, as she put it, "preceded my soul, rigidly, to the grave." Franco had also preceded her there, a helicopter pilot killed in the Ia Drang Valley in Vietnam so long ago. Elizabeth remembered him as though the last time she had seen him were moments before. She recalled every movement in his face, his black hair so entangled, especially when he would come out of the East Hampton sea, all tan and salt and affection. The day he got his degree at Columbia, his future, his business acumen, and his intelligence were clear to everyone. She especially remembered Franco's hands, so like his father's in the way his right took Elizabeth's left—the firm touch of his hand—to escort her up the beach.

Despite his mother's tears, Franco insisted on Vietnam. "My dad went, Mom. I can go." In Elizabeth's office, he told her about his plan to enlist. The office was a library study in the Sutton Place apartment in which the boy had grown up and in which Elizabeth lived to this day. Franco entered the room despite his and Edwin's respect for her working hours, eight to twelve every morning. She was working on an idea for investing in movies, a script about a New York City romance between a wealthy art patron and a dashing but dastardly businessman. The eventual film starred Steve McQueen, although Elizabeth had hoped for Cary Grant, principally because she wished to meet him. "Too old," the producer told her. The movie was a dog at the box office, and Elizabeth therewith shelved her plan to become a Hollywood mogul with others that she felt were equally screwy, like private space exploration and Argentine government bonds.

The tone of certainty in Franco's voice, also like his father's, nonetheless still allowed for the laughter that everyone enjoyed in him, even when he bragged about how not to worry about those damned Viet Cong. She often imagined what he must have looked like that day, the helicopter's wreckage everywhere. The blackness of the smoke and even of the flames, his fire-rupturing lips, the already destroyed eyes swept up in the conflagration.... She could return to peacefulness only through an insistent intervention by her heart upon these images. The word *yes,* the word *Franco,* the word *love,* repeated over and over again by her, on purpose, unimpeded, as she would also recall the glimmer of good humor in most of what her boy had ever said, those walks up the beach, which they both had looked forward to, the way he had assured her—"It's okay, Mom. I love you. Don't worry."—the day he had shipped out, the last time she had seen him, forty-seven years ago.

Although she could barely move now, and had to be helped in every endeavor, she still loved going for walks, with Glorieta.

Glorieta would dress Elizabeth and do her makeup, so that, although Elizabeth was stuck in what she called "the Cadillac," she looked—as Edwin had so often said about her—like a million bucks. "The Cadillac" was a luxury adjustable wheel chair, on which she reclined rather than sat, sitting completely upright no longer a possibility. Elizabeth's preferred clothing came from Bergdorf Goodman. Her personal shopper there, Cecily Townsend, knew her tastes very well, and once Elizabeth had given her a call and made an appointment, she could depend upon Cecily's foraging for different surprises...everything with the stylish, considered flair with which Elizabeth so loved to present herself.

Just because she was ninety was no reason not to look her best, and she didn't see why her confinement with this stupid, awful spinal condition should keep her down. Always in a kind of rattling pain up and down her back, her spine was now her lover, as she put it, a distant—and of course male—acquaintance that she had ignored all her life but to whose insistent disapproval she now felt compelled to pay attention. Glorieta had such talent getting Elizabeth ready for their walks that when they finally did get outside, for a sojourn around Sutton Place to go look at the river, or over to Madison Avenue or for a visit to the public library on Fifth Avenue for a lecture—in Elizabeth's specially outfitted Mercedes delivery van—Elizabeth could be sure that the only thing she was missing that morning was, arthritis, the Cadillac, and all, an invitation from someone like Helmut Newton to do a fashion shoot.

And of course, Elizabeth mused, Glorieta was no slouch herself. From Mexico, she had lived in New York City for twenty-five years, and now served as Elizabeth's principal assistant and helpmate. The adopted daughter of an Hermosillo businessman, she had married an American from whom she was now divorced. Her two children attended the Cristo Rey High School on East 106th. Elizabeth had found her as a referral from a friend for whom Glorieta had been a personal teacher of Spanish.

Glorieta did everything. She could get Elizabeth into and out of bed in ways that previous assistants hadn't understood, so that Elizabeth was no longer shy about suggesting an afternoon nap for herself in bed rather than in the Cadillac. Glorieta wrote the letters dictated by Elizabeth to her nieces and nephews and the thank-you notes to her friends and the questions about investments to the fellow at Charles Schwab and the changes in her documents to Elizabeth's attorney. Glorieta could mend anything, and she read to Elizabeth, her lovely Mexican accent rendering the English of the nineteenth-century novels that Elizabeth so enjoyed somehow more romantic even than the author may have intended. Glorieta herself particularly liked Edith Wharton because Wharton wrote so much about old New York. Elizabeth—who had adored Edith Wharton since her days at Vassar—told Glorieta that if she wanted to understand where those mansions on Fifth Avenue had come from, or all that art at the Frick, or Central Park itself, she would have to read Edith.

For some reason, though, Glorieta had a faulty memory about certain kinds of merchandise that Elizabeth would want from Bergdorf Goodman: a particular brand of hand lotion, for example, or the nylons that Elizabeth so preferred. Glorieta forgot things, as though she were wandering through interruptive thoughts of her own that had suddenly come upon her. Elizabeth would chide her at such moments for not being attentive enough, for not attempting to control such rushes of...whatever it was. Her chiding was patient, though, because Glorieta's virtues were so special.

Most important, Glorieta listened when Elizabeth was explaining something she cherished about Franco, about the days of suffering after he died, and about the generosity of Elizabeth's husband's own mourning, and how he took such care of Elizabeth during the worst of it. Edwin's caresses and sweet whisperings were intended for Elizabeth alone in her anguish, even as he, too, was suffering so badly. When she talked with Glorieta about Franco, Elizabeth actually recognized some dark form of sadness in Glorieta herself. As she listened, the occasional sigh that came from Glorieta indicated that death, profound disappointment, or something very like those, had been part of her childhood or her family's fortunes. Glorieta kept it to herself. But Elizabeth knew nonetheless that, whatever it was, it was there.

Glorieta was named for the Battle of Glorieta Pass, a not much acknowledged event in the American Civil War. It was fought in the Sangre de Cristo Mountains in New Mexico in 1862 and, according to Glorieta herself, was the Confederate loss that lead to the loss of the western Confederate states by the rebel government and then, eventually, to the loss of every Confederate state.

"How do you know about all that?" Elizabeth asked a few months after hiring her.

Glorieta spoke English in a stately manner in which every word was carefully pronounced. "Because of my great-great-great-great grandfather, who would like to have been part of it. He was in the Mexican-American War—you know, in 1846—an officer in the San Patricio battalion." Glorieta was repairing a blouse as she spoke, re-sewing a collar that somehow had come partially loose from the rest of the blouse. Elizabeth had complained that they could return it to Cecily Townsend. But Glorieta had said that she could mend the blouse to a state better than any replacement blouse would have. "And then, those will be my stitches resting softly against your neck, Ms. Schuyler, and you won't have to worry about the blouse coming apart ever again."

Elizabeth grinned. She had asked Glorieta early in her employment to call her Elizabeth. In public, though, Glorieta always referred to Elizabeth as "Ms. Schuyler", and Elizabeth loved it. The term had been around for at least forty years, but no one ever used it for Elizabeth. Maybe everyone thought her too grand, Elizabeth chortled. *If they only knew!* "Ms." still sounded so modern to her that Glorieta's use of it made her feel a little like a feminist revolutionary, and at her age! Her childhood friends from Spence, now dead so many of them, would have silently approved...Becky Maynard, the true blonde who had finally gotten rid of that awful Wall Street idiot husband of hers who had gone to prison; Quentin Rose, with such beautiful skin, who really had been Italian with very handsome parents. She had left her husband, too, only in this case for a fashion designer named Mariela Assisi; and little Electra Severance.... Well, Elizabeth thought, at least some of them would have approved. Maybe not Electra, who was so tiresome with her Daughters of the American Revolution silliness and, just before she died, the Tea Party silliness of her husband, Marshall. Elizabeth recalled how Electra had gotten knocked up in her junior year at Spence. Elizabeth and the other girls surmised that to be so, with no proof of any kind while Electra was absent from school. Electra herself finally admitted it to Elizabeth at Franco's memorial service, twenty-eight years later, in 1967.

"Does Marshall know?" Elizabeth asked.

"Of course he does!" Electra replied, giggling. "He's Joey's father, isn't he?"

At the time, Joey was in western Borneo with the Peace Corps.

"You mean, Joey is—"

"Yes! I got him back when he was six, and by then we were...well..." Electra's grin contained a kind of conspiring, ditsy insouciance. "By that time, we were a loving man and his sweet-hearted wife."

Poor, dumb Electra.

Elizabeth did not know about the San Patricio Battalion, and Glorieta explained that they were disenchanted Americans who fought for the Mexicans against the Americans in the 1846 war. A great many of them were Irishmen from New York, Glorieta knew, Catholics enraged by the treatment they got in that city from its Protestants. She understood that Elizabeth herself was a Catholic, and so felt safe in her assertions.

"Oh, but my husband was a Protestant." A warm smile of pleased affection came to Elizabeth's lips. "Episcopalian in every respect."

"Sorry, Elizabeth, I meant no offense."

"Of course not, dear. I know that. But even my father, who would have made an excellent pope, and the very first Irish one, you know, would not have approved of those San Patricio men."

Glorieta told how her parents had revered the name of Zoilo Enrique Gomez, her antecedent who had fought in that war against the Americans and survived, and gone on to business success in his native Sonora. He had been fascinated by the American Civil War too, finding it odd that there had been just one, while in Mexico there had been so many. "'Only a *gringo*...'" Glorieta quoted him to Elizabeth, looking over her shoulder as though Zoilo might actually be in the room. "'Only a *gringo* would have just one civil war.'" As a very old man, almost a centenarian, Zoilo had helped fund the efforts of Pancho Villa, but had died just before Villa had attacked New Mexico in 1916 and then escaped the American General Pershing. "Better left dead, sad old Zoilo," Glorieta whispered, to Elizabeth's amusement. "Villa was a crook, you know."

Weather permitting, the two women went out for a walk every

day during the week, and they were well known in the neighborhood. Elizabeth—her hair usually covered with a fashionable Hermès silk scarf—resembled a once-fabulous, still formidably beautiful and beautifully dressed movie star, down to even the Louis Vuitton Petit Soupçon Cat-Eye sunglasses and, in the warmer months, the Jimmy Choo pumps. Glorieta, less fashionable, maybe, but elegantly lush nonetheless, also always wore Louis Vuittons, a gift from Elizabeth.

On a late April day, Elizabeth's driver Mahmoud drove them to Central Park, where Glorieta wheeled Elizabeth once up the Mall and then back, before they were to lunch at the Carlyle Restaurant.

They paused near the statue of Fitz-Greene Halleck.

Much ardent sculpture has been placed in Central Park, some of the very worst of it, in Elizabeth's opinion, in the Mall. "Ardent" in the sense of the sculptor's wish to lay bare his seething post-Romantic emotions. A statue of Robert Burns looks off into the distance, his robes flowing about him like leaden lava. The one of Fitz-Greene Halleck also looks off into the distance, a pen in his right hand hovering over the ground, the hand hanging down from his chair as though waiting for some divine intervention to make it move. Elizabeth knew that Halleck was as well known as Burns in his own lifetime, and actually wrote about Burns:

> "Such graves as his are pilgrim shrines,
> Shrines to no code or creed confined—
> The Delphian vales, the Palestines,
> The Meccas of the mind."

Halleck knew about where he lived, referring in a poem called "Alnwick Castle" to "this bank-note world."

"Well, it's New York City, isn't it?" Elizabeth's teacher Miss Hadwell had muttered to the class at Spence. Pretty, with somewhat bland, Midwestern girth and big ears, Miss Hadwell was generally hated by her students. "He was John Jacob Astor's secretary, girls," she sniffed, looking at the students in their school uniforms as though each girl were an unseemly embarrassment. "And you would expect him to understand money."

But a look of transfixed, clueless puzzlement wears on the face of Fitz-Greene's statue in Central Park. Elizabeth worried, looking at him just now, that the ink would dribble from the quill in his hand to the earth below, so that when the light finally did flash into Fitz-Greene's mind, he wouldn't be able to write it down because the quill would be dry.

Sunlight dappled the statue. Elizabeth asked Glorieta to turn her toward the sun so that she could get its warmth on her face. Glorieta did so, also adjusting Elizabeth's long, dark brown skirt so that it flowed properly the length of her legs to her crossed ankles. She buttoned the embroidered Tyrolean jacket—Elizabeth's mother's—that Elizabeth had so cared for through the years that it still appeared almost new. Noting Glorieta's hands and the sweet manner in which they adjusted the skirt, Elizabeth realized that indeed she cared for Glorieta a great deal. Her hair was so beautiful, universe black. And that smile… She was like the daughter that Elizabeth would like to have had, so that she wouldn't have to bear poor Franco's death all alone.

"I've told you about Franco, haven't I?"

"Oh, yes. A terrible story. So sad."

Glorieta sat down on one of the benches, next to Elizabeth's chair. A young Russian family picnicked across the way, its two girls running about playing tag while their parents argued. Birds sported in the branches.

"I'm sorry, dear. " Elizabeth looked away. "I'm repeating myself."

"No, you're not. I love it when you talk about him. He must have been such a nice boy."

A nice boy. So like his father. Elizabeth brought her right hand to her forehead, as though to smooth the grief-stricken furrow that had suddenly formed.

She also remembered a party, when she was nineteen. She had come home from Vassar for a weekend, and her father, Harry, had asked her to accompany him to a reception for Manuel Ávila Camacho, who was president of Mexico. She had to break a date with her Edwin to do so, and it was a date that she had been looking forward to. She and Edwin had actually started a—Elizabeth had to settle her excitement a bit—an affair. During a weekend at Yale, they succeeded in eluding their chaperons and going to, of all places, a hotel. A friend of Edwin's was working there as a day desk clerk, and Edwin got Elizabeth in without anyone noticing. So, while Yale battled Harvard on the gridiron, Edwin and Elizabeth lost themselves in the activity that Elizabeth had dreamt about since she had been a little girl. The experience with Edwin was everything she had hoped for...everything, even though Edwin was a little embarrassed at first. Considerably embarrassed, and shy. But Elizabeth, with quite a bit of good humor, was able to relax him and, so, awaken his more manly intensities.

Now, in New York, her father, Harry, told her "Honey, to miss an opportunity to see the presidential suite at the Plaza is like missing life itself."

Elizabeth dressed in a Chanel gown that her mother, Peg, had bought a few years before the war, something that Peg told her would glorify "those shoulders of yours, Beth." Her mother could not attend the reception. So, on her father's arm, Elizabeth was greeted at the door of the suite by a tall black man dressed in black tie and tails who offered to take her wrap. The very size of the suite took Elizabeth's breath. She could actually feel her eyes widening, stretched and round so as to take in as much as possible. The two chandeliers in the main room cast light across a hundred or so men, all of them grumbling with cheerful, self-accepting importance. There were women there, too, gloriously dressed and overlooked. A chunky man in a beautifully tailored black suit, with a green, white, and red sash displayed diagonally across his chest, shook hands and offered humorous greetings in Spanish and heavily accented English. More black men in tails served hors d'oeuvres and drinks, one being a rum punch of which her father allowed Elizabeth just one mint-garnished crystal cupful.

Elizabeth was thrilled by what she saw, never having been in such a place before, even in the Hamptons. This was statesmanlike splendor, and once she realized that the man wearing the sash was indeed the president of Mexico, Elizabeth felt that she had arrived—suddenly—at adulthood. Across the room, beneath another chandelier and above the enormous fireplace, a portrait of a formally dressed and disapproving John Pierpont Morgan stared at her. She enjoyed how the very materials in the portrait—the paint, Morgan's name engraved on the bronze plaque below the painting, even the gold-painted, carved wood frame—seemed as ruggedly pocked with age as Morgan's nose. Elizabeth also saw staring at her, from just below the portrait, the startling eyes of the most beautiful man she had ever seen. Ever.

He left the painting to its own devices, to approach Elizabeth. "*Señorita*, I am Francisco Herrera."

A polo team had come from Mexico to New York, to play a series of matches against an American team. President Ávila Camacho introduced the team, explaining that they intended the matches to help raise money for the American armed forces, reeling just at that moment from the attack on Pearl Harbor. The applause was grand with approval, and after the remarks, the team formed a reception line. Elizabeth, wishing to hear more of Francisco's lovely accent, joined her father in the queue of guests. Not all the players were handsome, and several spoke no English. But Elizabeth's father assured her that these men were the very best "in a country where upper class polo players seem to grow from trees. It's like Hollywood. You know, Douglas Fairbanks."

Elizabeth knew who Fairbanks had been. Her own mother had professed to have fallen in love with the movie star upon seeing *The Mark of Zorro* in 1920. "Especially the sword fight at the beginning, Beth. You never saw a man like that." She and Elizabeth were examining an old photo of Fairbanks in a movie magazine. "Of course that was before I married your father," her mother hurried on, to clarify the sigh that had escaped her. "And even then, I knew that a man like Doug Fairbanks could never be faithful." She looked up from the magazine. "Even to Mary Pickford, who was his wife, you know."

The photo showed him wearing a *gaucho* hat, a roughly folded, patterned cloth tied loosely around his neck—a good portion of which showed from his button-less open collar—and a gold earring in his left ear. He was smiling very broadly, his teeth shimmering from between the dashing mustache and the chin stubble, as though a beautiful *señorita* had just come into view. Someone not Mary Pickford, Elizabeth imagined.

Because he had already greeted her, Elizabeth knew that Francisco spoke English. Indeed his accent was so attractive that she imagined he was on his way to becoming some sort of diplomat or perhaps even president himself. Maybe thirty years old, he was taller than most of the other players. He had Fairbanks-like looks, although he was already so much more urbane than the movie star and so much better dressed that Elizabeth concluded that Francisco must also be rich. She disliked herself for this, her family's wealth being something for which she herself took no credit. The difference between Elizabeth's privilege and that of an Irish washerwoman in Hell's Kitchen had little to do, for Elizabeth, with the washerwoman's lack of nascent ability. That woman was stuck there because her family had arrived poor, while Elizabeth was greeting the president of Mexico because she herself had arrived on this earth rich. *I didn't have anything to do with it*, she thought.

She inched closer to Francisco.

His face had a lovely angularity that found its real beauty in his smile and the chin below it. The eyes, unquestionably, were one thing. But the smile was quite another. It was not large. It wouldn't cause you to stop breathing a moment were it to glitter from the silver screen. But it was imbued with outright kindness. Once seeing a smile like this, you had to conclude that kindness flowed from the man like blue Pacific waters wandering from the sea into a delicate, accepting inlet. It also did not appear to Elizabeth to be plastered on his face, the way President Ávila Camacho's smile was. No, Francisco's lovely good humor came and went as the occasion called for it...also like the Pacific. The smile was simply a natural result of his taste in conversation, his appreciation of beauty.

His chin supported it like a chiseled, humor-filled pedestal.

Elizabeth advanced even further along the reception line.

"Hello, Isabelita." Francisco took her hand in his.

Elizabeth sensed that her father, standing right behind her in line, flinched a bit when he saw Francisco. She didn't care.

"Hello, Francisco."

A moment later, as they re-joined the guests in the room, Harry leaned toward Elizabeth.

"Isabelita? What's all that?"

"It's the name he gave me."

"You'd met him already?"

"Yes, Daddy."

"When?"

"When you were talking with President Ávila Camacho."

Harry remained silent.

"Is the president nice?"

She didn't tell her father—yet—that Francisco had expressed the hope that Elizabeth would come to the polo match that following weekend at the Commodore Club in East Hampton. He would enjoy wearing a handkerchief from her around his neck, he said.

"I didn't care for you talking with that fellow," Harry said an hour later. He was driving their Packard up Madison Avenue, toward home.

"But Daddy!"

"He's Mexican."

"Oh, Daddy."

"You don't know where he's from or what kind of school he went to or—"

"But he's sweet."

Harry grumbled to himself.

"He's a national champion!"

"At what?"

"Polo!"

They drove in silence for several blocks.

"And I was there when you got tickets to the match, Daddy."

"I did, yes, but it's for the war. I hadn't much planned on going."

"I've never seen a polo match."

Two more blocks passed, with a long interruption at a traffic signal.

"Your mother won't like it."

"I'll bet she'll *want* me to go."

"Elizabeth… Honey, I want you to listen to me."

"I promise I won't do anything, Daddy. I'll behave." She looked down at the small handbag that rested on her lap, in which she kept her lipstick. "I always do."

On an exceptionally warm day on which Elizabeth wore a white summer dress, a pair of open-toed white pumps, and a large summer straw hat, horses surged up and down the polo field like heavy, muscled yachts. As they went from one end to the other, the ground beneath the shade tent from which Elizabeth and the others watched began trembling, then shook in earnest, and finally calmed itself until the horses came back in the other direction. The Americans wore white polo shirts; the Mexicans, black, and every one of the players seemed to be part of the horse on which he rode, an extension of the horse's hurtling grace and strength.

At one point, Francisco progressed the ball all the way up the field from before the Mexican goal toward the American one, his horse sometimes sprinting straight, with wildly nattering eyes, at other times meandering with nonetheless great speed through the opposing team's mounts, avoiding all of them. Elizabeth could see the skill with which Francisco guided his mare past the other animals, and defended her from them. The ball floated and bounced, seemingly flying along a path, the mallet a flying delicacy pursuing it. Elizabeth's handkerchief fluttered in the melee. When the mare and the man passed before the tent, the earth pounding as though it had a heart of its own, Francisco was able to flash a quick smile at Elizabeth. Her heart, she worried, would soon fail.

The Mexicans won, one to nil. The goal, of course, was scored by Francisco on that very play.

They sat on a covered porch swing outside the club ballroom. They had to be still so as not to alert the dancers inside or, Elizabeth worried, her parents.

"I would like you to have this ring." Francisco opened his hands. "As *un recuerdo.*" Elizabeth's handkerchief rested, roughly folded, within them. "A memento." It was soiled with sweat-mottled dust, and she took in a breath as she realized it had gotten so on the field of play, during the mayhem. "I don't know if we'll see each other again."

"We will." Elizabeth reached for the handkerchief with her right hand.

"I hope so. I wouldn't want—"

She undid it, her fingers pushing aside each fold.

"I wouldn't want to travel all this way to New York from my poor Mexico, and not come back to sit with you here again."

Elizabeth took in a quick breath. The ring gleamed from among the stains of sweat.

She allowed Francisco to caress her arm. A riveting shock went through her. *Love,* she thought. She felt a movement of sighs making its way through her legs and tummy, and everything in between. Would she succumb to a kiss? She hoped so. She wished for it. Francisco leaned toward her, and she waited for it. His fingers played with hers.

He kissed her arm. "*Mi* Isabelita." His lips were so golden and dark. Not like her boyfriend Edwin's, who was white beyond belief, in his lips and his ideas—a sweet, smart man with received ambitions. Wall Street awaited Edwin, while here, now, Isabelita awaited a kiss from Francisco Herrera.

He did kiss her. They kissed many times, and, as Isabelita ran her hands across both sides of his face, grasping for more kisses, she felt her blood rushing through her, swelling her. After several moments, Francisco stood, took her hand, and led her out toward the grove of Italian cypresses, in the darkness at the far end of the clubhouse lawns. She placed her head on the side of his left arm as they walked, both her hands wrapped around his left hand. The music behind them—the Ben Cutler orchestra—which seemed so cacophonous and rattling to her when they were dancing, now receded into the background, honey-like strings punctuated with youthful laughter. She felt that she could barely walk, she was so excited. The Atlantic Ocean, a ruffling sigh in the distance before them, seemed, in its immensity, to intend itself for just these two people.

They lay in the warmth of the evening on Francisco's smoking jacket, kissing, hidden beyond the trees. When, kneeling over her, he kissed her knee and then the inside of her left thigh, Elizabeth thought that now, finally, she would find what so many of her girlfriends talked about with her and wished for. What she would be able to tell them. How it was that real love made you feel so electrified.

"Do you see them, Elizabeth, across there?" Glorieta said.

The two little Russian girls raced up the Mall, while their arguing parents kept arguing. At the moment, the father was standing away from the bench, his hands in the pockets of his black slacks. His white shirt was wrinkled and sweaty, and hung out behind. Their incomprehensible Russian was filled with aspirated S's and Z's. The black tie resembled a slim rag. He was very angry with his wife and glowered at the walkway in silence as she berated him.

"It doesn't look good for them, does it?" Elizabeth turned back toward Glorieta. To her astonishment, Glorieta's lips were quivering.

Elizabeth took in a breath. "What's wrong, dear?"

Glorieta gathered her hands together on her lap. "Fathers...." She could not continue.

"What about them?"

"Fathers so often don't know what they're doing."

Elizabeth kept quiet, awaiting more. But Glorieta did not continue.

"But I'm sure yours did, didn't he? A pretty girl like...."

Glorieta inclined her head so closely toward Elizabeth that Elizabeth reached out to caress her hair. Its full softness felt like fine, dark silk.

"Please tell me what's wrong, dear."

Glorieta looked up at the couple across the way. "He doesn't realize the mistake he's making."

The argument continued, and the couple's daughters quieted as, their gayety and play turning to silence, they approached their parents once more. Uncertain. Looking to each other.

"He's thinking...look at him...he's thinking, right now, of how happy he'd be if he just left."

"I suppose so." Elizabeth glanced toward the couple. "But, with those two girls? Look what he'd lose."

"I know. That's the worst." Glorieta took in a breath, and then lowered her head once more. "The worst."

Elizabeth was pregnant. She had written to Francisco, to the address he had given her in Mexico City. She knew he would write back right away. The act of sending her letter to him, the very placing of the envelope in the mailbox slot, lessened the shocking fear that had seized her earlier that morning, before she had written it.

Now, she imagined his reading the letter, probably at first chagrined by the news. But Elizabeth concentrated more on picturing his consideration and integrity. His voice soothed her, the softness of the syllables "*Mi* Isabelita" bringing to Elizabeth a calming of her breathing, the certainty that Francisco's sincerity would immediately surface. He would take up pen and paper to write back to her, to describe for her how much he worshipped her.

For the moment, though, without that return letter, Elizabeth was too terrified to tell her mother. Getting pregnant was not part of the plan, and she knew that she would be tossed out of Vassar, too, if they found out. But once Francisco came back…once he arrived in New York and came with her to her parents' living room, when he asked for her hand, when he married her…. She knew that, then, she could withstand any sort of shame.

She sensed just now that she could feel her baby moving around, which he was probably doing, even though she knew it was way too early for that to be noticeable. When Francisco came back, there would be no anguish. She placed a few fingers on her lower tummy. Only happiness.

Is he there? My new little love? No letter of reply ever came. *My blood, my life?*

Edwin sat before her, in his parents' apartment on East Eighty-sixth. He wore a suit, in town for a cousin's wedding. His parents were at church, and would be picking up Edwin and Elizabeth in half an hour, to go to the wedding ceremony. As usual, Edwin's mother had embraced her, displaying the happiness with which she always greeted the girl. "Is there anyone who doesn't love you?" she asked. Elizabeth cared a great deal for Alice Schuyler too, and this morning, when she arrived at the apartment and Alice asked her that question, she looked away, embarrassed.

"Is something wrong, Elizabeth?"

"Oh, no. I…." Elizabeth brushed her hair back with her right hand. "Just tired."

"And happy to see Edwin."

"Oh, yes. Of course."

At first, Edwin barely responded when Elizabeth told him she was worried. He was tall and—always—quiet, a nice man whom Elizabeth felt that she could, someday, love.

"Because I have some news," she said

Edwin, putting on an overcoat, turned toward her. Serious and considerate, twenty-one, he always smiled in a way that pleased Elizabeth. She knew he cared for her, and just now she hoped that the sensitivity that that smile had represented to her ever since she had met him would see him through what she was about to say. She also worried, though, that Edwin might recoil from her, caught, angered by all this. Her reputation would be ruined. But his could be destroyed. Locked into a marriage he did not want.

Her chest hurt.

Elizabeth knew just one other girl who had become pregnant when she wasn't yet married: Electra Severance. Blonde, noted by all the girls at school for her cliché-ridden jollity, she had disappeared from school that day and had come back a year later, just as frivolous although slightly more guarded. She was in Europe, Electra explained. "I just love Venice!" she said.

Looking up at Edwin, Elizabeth gathered the words. "I'm…I'm going to…." She couldn't say it.

Edwin remained standing before her. "Have I done something wrong?"

"Oh, no. It's just…." Elizabeth leaned to the left, lowering her head so that her hair partially hid her face.

"Are you mad at me?"

Elizabeth cast her eyes down. She felt that mortification had stopped her heart. *The right kind of girl doesn't get pregnant. The Church…God…. They'll send me to Hell. Harry and Peg Ryan's daughter wouldn't get pregnant. What'll Daddy do?*

"Eddy, I'm going to have a baby." Elizabeth could not look up at him. She groaned. "Your baby."

When she did look up, Edwin's face appeared to her like weathered marble. Elizabeth knew that he was going to tell her to get out. He sat down on the couch next to her and leaned forward, his elbows on his knees. His hands were splayed, and he turned them palms up and down, studying them.

"Damn it, Elizabeth."

"Eddy, please."

"Christ!"

"Please."

"Well, we've got to get married." He rested his chin on the palm of his right hand. Elizabeth searched his face for the anger that she knew he must be feeling. The entrapment and the shame. But just now a smile appeared. Elizabeth sat in anguish on the couch next to him. But Edwin, sensitive to her worry, took up her hand and faced her. "I should say that a little differently. I mean...Elizabeth, will you marry me?"

The Russian couple did not make up. But they gathered their two girls together and made a semblance of agreement with each other. As the family proceeded up the Mall toward Seventy-second Street, Elizabeth and Glorieta watched, Glorieta still beset with the distraction with which she had first observed the family and, especially, the father. She held a handkerchief.

Elizabeth leaned back against the Cadillac's headrest. "Tell me about *your* father."

Glorieta leaned her head to the side as she examined her lap. "My real father?"

"Yes, I...I suppose so."

"I met him just once."

"Once."

"Yes. He had made my mother pregnant." Glorieta looked up, a grin appearing on her lips despite the liquid sheen of her eyes. "That's how I should say it in English, no?"

"It'll do, sweetheart."

"He made her pregnant."

"With—"

"With me." Glorieta's fingers hurried about one another.

"And then, he—"

"Yes. Then he left."

Elizabeth's heart tightened. "But you did know him."

"I met him."

"What was that like?"

Glorieta exhaled. She lifted a hand to her hair. "I was twenty or so."

"Where?"

"In Mexico City."

"What was he like?"

Glorieta groaned. "He was maybe sixty years old."

"What did he look like?"

"Defeat."

"How were you able to contact him?"

"Ruined. Gray." Glorieta swept her hair back, a fatigued gesture. "His overcoat was stained. His hair needed cutting. It was dirty." Glorieta's mouth turned down in an expression of revulsion. "He was wearing a suit and tie. But the suit was too big for him. He barely filled it." She wrung her hands once, finally looking up at Elizabeth and smiling for her, a clear wish to soften the revelation for Elizabeth, to relieve Elizabeth's own possible discomfort. "He was handsome, I guess...or at least he looked like he once had been."

"How did you find him?"

"He contacted me."

"How?"

"I don't know. I was a student at the Ciudad Universitaria...in poetry." Glorieta exhaled. "I guess I wanted to be a poet."

"And he sought you out."

"Yes."

Elizabeth's stomach quivered as though, to her chagrin, she herself were being sought out. "What did you think?"

"I didn't know what to think."

"What did he want?"

Glorieta's lips crumpled upon one another. "Money."

"Did your mother know?"

"Oh, no. This was just on an afternoon in Mexico City. My mother… my mother…." Glorieta took the handkerchief into the fingers of both hands. "This man…he betrayed my mother when she was just a girl. He left her…with me." She twisted the handkerchief around the fingers of her right hand, studying the way the fingers became incarcerated. "You know." Glorieta, pointed at her tummy. "Inside. And of course…." The handkerchief came unraveled.

"He left you." Elizabeth laid a hand on her own tummy. "With her."

"That's right."

Elizabeth knew how painful this recollection was to Glorieta. She wished to take Glorieta into her arms and comfort her. She wanted to alleviate the distress, suddenly loving Glorieta for being able to share such a story with her employer, who was an elderly cripple in a wheelchair. Elizabeth's own heart fell into a kind of grateful remorse. Her sympathy for Glorieta warmed it, even though Glorieta herself, in this moment, was too involved in the memory of her father to realize what might be happening in Elizabeth's comprehension of her. *It's so difficult for her,* Elizabeth thought. *And look at how long he kept her waiting, how long it took for him just to show up. A scoundrel. And look what she's giving to me.*

Elizabeth also worried, from the commiserative look that Glorieta now gave her, that the younger woman's story would come out even worse than the one that Elizabeth could tell her. Although she knew that she would not tell Glorieta the story, which had become a closely held personal grievance that nonetheless found its thread in the unrequited and absurd love she still felt for Francisco. That story would never come out, especially now, so long ago, so much examined and re-examined by Elizabeth for so many years.

"A playboy," Glorieta muttered.

"But not wealthy."

"No."

"A businessman, dear?"

"A *sinvergüenza,* we would call him."

"What's that?"

"A villain. A cheat."

"Did he have a job?"

"Played polo, my mother told me. She said that that was what made her fall in love with him at first. A fine Mexican man beautiful on a beautiful horse, the grace and strength—"

"The charm."

"Yes. My mother used that word too. '*¡Un guapo encantador, mi'ja!*' she said to me so often. "A handsome, entrancing man!"" Glorieta's mouth turned down. "She loved him…even though…even though he had abandoned—"

"What was his name?"

"Francisco." Glorieta lowered her eyes, now stricken, and compelled herself to stare at the crumpled handkerchief in her fingers. "Francisco Herrera."

"His name?" Elizabeth brought the fingers of her right hand to her cheek. "What?"

Glorieta, surprised, offered her a smile, not expecting the intensity in Elizabeth's voice. "Francisco. You know, it's nothing special. A common Spanish name."

"Yes, but…."

Elizabeth's thoughts careened against one another. Finally, she looked to the side, at the statue of foolish Fitz-Greene Halleck, the moony poet awaiting a word or two from the muse. After a moment, Elizabeth turned once more to Glorieta, whose unhappiness remained in the way she looked again toward the now far away, retreating little Russian girls.

Elizabeth floated into a reverie. She had so wondered about him, whether he had ever become the great Mexican statesman of which she had dreamed. She had looked for his name now and then, in the diplomatic news or the international gossip columns or the world polo news. But Francisco Herrera had disappeared, except in Elizabeth's dreams, in which Francisco kissed her time and again, took her hand in his and kissed it, caressed her hair with his lips. "His lips," she whispered to herself. His fingers…. Francisco Herrera, who had driven Elizabeth crazy when she was nineteen and who even now came to her from time to time, to help her to fall asleep, whispering "*Mi* Isabelita."

Franco's father.

Glorieta remained quiet. She lifted her eyes to Elizabeth's. There were no tears, although there was clear longing and regret. Glorieta's wish for her father's love, such as it could be.

She so reminded Elizabeth now of… *Oh, Glorieta. Of my beautiful Francisco.*

THE THREE-CORNERED HAT

Trevor thought it the perfect name for the place, a large room on the third floor of an old brick building on Hudson Street at Fourteenth. The structure bore a resemblance to the famous triangle Flatiron Building, in the sense that it was shaped like one of the paper airplanes that Trevor had enjoyed as a first-grader. Pointed at one end, wide at the other, the building would, were it not a nineteenth-century Manhattan ruin, soar from a little boy's fingers.

While the Flatiron is immortal, the Three-Cornered Hat building appeared sawed off at three floors, and to have been gathered into its present shape by machines pushing around large piles of rubble. It was layered above the sidewalk with the tatters of old paper flyers, and all its street level windows were barred with rusted iron. No sign identified the building. The only indication that the Three-Cornered Hat itself—a dancehall for Argentine tango—even existed in the building was its name handwritten in pencil on the back of somebody's business card, along with the detail "Third floor," with an upwardly directed arrow, also written in pencil. The card was taped to the front of a bank of mailboxes, half of which had no doors. Evidently, no other tenants occupied the building. The Hudson Street entrance was an implacable iron door with no window. It did, however, have a doorknob.

"Is this it?" Because he had never danced at the Three-Cornered Hat, Trevor stood outside the building looking up. Lights gleamed from the third floor, and he heard what sounded like faraway suggestions—perhaps emanating from an old crystal radio set—of very old Argentine tango.

He tried the door, which was locked. He pushed a doorbell button a half dozen times until, finally, a woman's voice murmured from the speaker box above the button.

"Yeah?"

"I'm here for tango."

A buzzer rang, and Trevor put a shoulder to the door, which eventually gave way. He hurried up the first three steps of the wooden stairway before the door shut, a bit like a sideways guillotine, Trevor mused. The stairs leaned to the right and left, here and there on the way up, covered with very old green linoleum. Various messages decorated the walls, rendered either in grease pencil or spray paint, or gouged. As he got closer to the door to the third floor, Trevor heard more and more tango, and his soul began to quiet. The music softened his misgivings. He heard laughter. Pushing aside a curtain, he entered the Three-Cornered Hat.

Trevor had once been a poet but had given that up as a loss-leader profession. He had then co-founded a start-up, marketing hand-made, original fashion collectibles—earrings, perfume bottles, silver cigarette cases—from a website that his friend Emilio had designed. After his market studies and focus groups, Trevor had determined that their customers—well, there were the gay men to consider, too—would all be women under thirty years old, a surprise to Trevor's mother, who owned a number of the kind of collectibles that he wanted to sell, and who couldn't imagine that "anyone would be interested in this old stuff any more, even though it's so beautiful." His mother was the principle source of funding for the company, having invested seventy-five hundred dollars. Trevor knew that the interest in his trinkets could be considerable, though, and he and Emilio, who came from Buenos Aires originally and, like Trevor, was a recent NYU MBA, had founded the company. All Trevor's models were girls from the Fashion Institute of Technology. His photographers, too. The company itself, Zowie Collectibles, wasn't going great guns just yet. Indeed, they hadn't really made a profit of any sort for Trevor's mother. But Trevor, who was ever insistent on possibilities and opportunities, knew that it was just a matter of time. Also, he and Emilio were only twenty-five, so he figured they had quite a lot of time.

"Trevor." Emilio held up a bottle. "How about a glass of wine?"

The Three-Cornered Hat filled a space about twice the size of Trevor's studio apartment. It had the same triangle shape as the building itself, with a wood dance floor and windows on the two angled sides of the room. Five slim iron pillars, placed in various parts of the dance floor, formed part of the building's support. They added an element of possible injury to the dancing. While normally the tango couples would dance in a circle around the perimeter of the floor, all in the same direction, at the Three-Cornered Hat they would have to weave and bob. As the evening progressed into early morning and the effects of wine were added to the beauties and intensities of the music, the pillars would very much come into play.

Emilio had brought the bottle of Malbec and two plastic glasses. He poured a bit of the wine into each, and handed a glass to Trevor. Both were dressed in Levi's and un-tucked sport shirts with rolled-up sleeves. Trevor felt particularly natty in his heavy black-rimmed glasses. Now and then, though, he wondered why it was that the young men who danced tango for the most part dressed this way—start-up slobs, really, he admitted—while the women clothed themselves with extraordinary attention to casual fashion. Even when they wore Levi's, the pants clung to them like fine, dark blue oil. But usually they wore dresses of the kind Trevor admired at Zara or the Anthropologie store in Chelsea Market. Their dresses brimmed with color, humor, and very successful attempts at sensuous beauty. While Trevor and Emilio's dance shoes always needed a shine, the stiletto-heeled shoes of most of the women at the Three-Cornered Hat were so carefully designed and shaped for elegant dance that a major subject of conversation among the women was their shoes. They modeled them for each other. They laughed, envious and appreciative of such romantically clad feet.

Music issued from speakers at one end of the room. Trevor and Emilio danced with a number of the women with whom they had danced at other *milongas*. The room filled, and suddenly...spectacularly...Marianita Miró walked through the curtain.

Trevor had seen her just once before, on the stage at Carnegie Hall. The Orpheus Chamber Orchestra was playing that night, a selection of modern concert music from South America. So a few Villa Lobos pieces, some *danzas criollas* of Alberto Ginastera, an arrangement of a tune by Violeta Parra. The orchestra devoted the rest of the concert to the Argentine Astor Piazzolla, and for several of the numbers, Marianita came on stage to dance. Her partner was an older man, a superb dancer, Trevor thought. But, in a moment of electrified bedazzlement, Trevor watched Marianita as though the old man were barely there. He figured she was no more than twenty-five years old herself. Yet she walked on stage with every suggestion of sensuality that had ever occurred to any woman. Her hair was close cut, like a flapper's, and shined like ebony lacquer. She had the look of the Middle East...Lebanese, Trevor thought, or Iranian, the Middle East done up as a Bollywood musical. He could see her black eyes even from the back balcony, and Trevor hoped that his watching her so glaringly formed the reason for those eyes' obvious glimmering. Slim, with small breasts enhanced by the Mediterranean marine-blue dress she wore, she nonetheless had a back and a backside that composed themselves so curvaceously, one above the other, that, when she moved in circles around the old man, still in his embrace, she yet looked free to Trevor, like a graceful cat of the African veldt finely sculpted by...by whom? Trevor wondered. By...? Yes, by the sun and the Iberian coast, by olive oil, the Spanish language, the Andes range and the mighty pampas, by the dark insistence of a young, fantastically talented *tanguera* in full possession of herself and her own wishes. At Carnegie Hall, in the back balcony, he pulled himself from his astonishment to look up her name in the program.

Marianita Miró.

Now, at the Three-Cornered Hat, she appeared impatiently perturbed.

"No!" She shook her head as she preceded the same old man into the room. "*¡Che dejáme en paz!*" The utterance was loud enough to be heard over the tango music in the room. Those who had not quickly turned their heads gaping at how she looked, now did so because of how she sounded.

"She's telling him to leave her alone," Emilio said. Somehow the tone of his translation also contained Emilio's amazed perusal of Marianita as she walked across the floor. "And, man, is she the answer!" His eyes sparkled blue in the reflected pink and blue light of the room.

"To what?" Trevor knew what Emilio would say. He didn't wait for it. "Who's the old guy?"

"Leopoldo Gaviota. But everyone just calls him Gaviota."

"He's Argentine."

"Of course! One of the greatest dancers of tango in the world. My grandmother Lela knew him many years ago. Before he became 'Gaviota,' she said. She danced with him when he was twenty."

"He was always a dancer?"

"She said he was a journalist back then. At least that's what he told her. But she never saw anything he wrote. When she knew him, he was a dish washer."

"What did she call him?"

"Poldito. Or '*hijo de puta*', depending on her mood." Emilio grinned. "My grandmother didn't like being mistreated."

Gaviota, dressed in a black long-sleeved shirt, black slacks, and black suede dance shoes, walked behind Marianita like a sleek gangster. A godfather, Trevor mused. He was also wearing a pair of large wraparound sunglasses, and as he pursued Marianita, he took a pack of cigarettes from the pocket of his shirt. He continued speaking to her in very rapid-fire Spanish, which Trevor did not understand, only to get a similar dismissive response from Marianita. "*¡No!*" He lit one of the cigarettes, tossed the blown-out match onto the dance floor, and turned away from her to approach the bar, where Trevor and Emilio were standing.

"Maestro..." Emilio extended a hand.

"How about a little of that red?" Gaviota grumbled in English. His sunglasses hid every aspect of his eyes, so that in the semi-darkness he resembled an attack helicopter.

"Of course." Emilio did not have a third glass, so he borrowed a paper cup from a small stack of cups on the bar. He poured out some Malbec and handed it to Gaviota, who turned away without another word.

"*Chau* Poldito...." Emilio whispered, toasting the retreating maestro with his own empty glass.

Trevor placed a hand on his partner's shoulder. "Yes, but he sure can dance."

"Hijo de puta." Emilio looked up toward the ceiling and, beyond, heaven. "No, Lela?"

Trevor determined to meet Marianita. He worried, though, about her outburst of temper, which seemed to be continuing as she removed her coat and turned to the immediate crowd of women dancers that had gathered to greet her. She knew some of them, and the flurry of loud kisses and congratulatory laughter, bubbling in two languages, did little to hide the grim glance that she gave Gaviota, who had stopped at the edge of the dance floor. Sipping from his wine, he reveled disdainfully in the attention he was getting from so many dancers himself. He had spotted one of the other women: Carla, an okay dancer, young, a little wooden in her movement on the floor. She wore a tempting red silk dress and three-inch red patent leather heels. A blonde from Brooklyn, Carla smiled when Gaviota greeted her, embarrassed to have been noticed by the great man. Her eyes darted about with self-conscious imprecision. Gaviota's eyes remained riveted on Carla.

Marianita's anger seemed to burnish her extraordinary beauty, so that now, close up like this, the very manner in which her lips moved as she spoke to the other women fired Trevor's imagination in ways that none of the other women ever did...or ever could. Trevor pondered the consequences of Marianita's someday being angry with him, and his success at overcoming that anger so that, in the end, she would wrap her arms about his shoulders and neck, incline her head back a little, accept his own now swelling lips, and kiss him with all the fury she could muster.

Should I ask her to dance? Trevor's own tango had been progressing well enough. He was frequently congratulated by his teachers and the women who danced with him for actually listening to, and understanding, the music. Without that, you're lost, Trevor felt. He was usually chagrined when he watched other men essay the tango. Few of them really could. They wobbled, lurched, or shuffled, while the dance requires a soul capable of being grabbed, wrestled with, shaped and freed with complete immediacy. It was the music that provided that kind of conflict. Love. Soul. Grace. Heart. Loss. Love again. The whole thing once more again.

But, dancing with Marianita Miró? Trevor grumbled to himself, a negative comeuppance. Fear took him.

Gaviota and Carla stood in a corner. He seemed to be murmuring at her, his sunglasses shimmering with sensuous intent. Carla smiled, but her eyes were now clouded with the uncertainty of her opportunity, and declared the wish for even more attention.

After a moment, Marianita strode onto the dance floor, and without any seeming contact between her and Gaviota, the maestro handed his empty paper cup to Carla and joined Marianita. They danced a very slow tango, an occasion that caused the other dancers in the room to hold back, to stand and watch. The change in Marianita's demeanor charged the atmosphere in the room. Suddenly, she was a woman being pursued, who wished it so. No longer waving a hand over her shoulder at the grasping Gaviota, Marianita now stood in his arms and walked with him intently, not retreating as he advanced, rather showing him that she would be moved only when she wished, and that she wished it so now. She appeared not just to be attracted to Gaviota, but to be driven toward him by the strength of his sensuality, yet challenging him with a sense of authority that was stronger even than his. She supplied the color, the movement, and the sense—Trevor swallowed—of time itself nearing its own desperate end.

He had some more wine.

But how could she possibly love a man like this Poldito? Hadn't she just been arguing with him? Yes, Gaviota was smooth. *Maybe no woman can resist him.* Carla herself was jealous, now standing next to Emilio, whose attempts at conversation with her were going nowhere. She pouted. *And surely Gaviota knows how to make Marianita feel watched,* Trevor thought, *wanted and excited.* But he also resembled the kind of man who shows up at his daughter's teenage birthday parties and schmoozes all the girls, toying with the frosting-filled spoon in his hand. Trevor recalled his mother's insistence upon manners being more important than anything. His mother…soft, warm, Midwestern and caring, Protestant, PTA.

Gaviota pursuing Marianita in this dance appeared to have no manners at all. He was sophisticated, yes. But his sense of himself took that sophistication and made it into a kind of Don Juan–like shining of dark lascivious suggestion. He moved as though Marianita would not dare turn him down, even though she obviously had done so earlier. His sunglasses spit back the light that reflected from them. He would have his way.

The tango came to an end, in which Gaviota took Marianita into his arms and embraced her. They reminded Trevor of one of those pillars in old Italian cathedrals, that swirl around themselves, earth to heaven in a spiraling gyre. He sighed as Marianita laid the fingers of her right hand delicately against the back of Gaviota's head.

Applause and shouting thundered through the Three-Cornered Hat. Trevor knew that he could never dance like that. So, rather than asking himself again how Marianita could possibly care for a guy like Gaviota, Trevor asked himself, without much hesitation, how could she possibly care for a guy like me?

"Go ahead." Emilio, a half hour later, urged Trevor to action. Carla had slowly begun speaking with him, and Trevor had the impression that, just now, Emilio wanted to continue that conversation with her alone. They had been watching Marianita's chatting with other women. No man had asked her to dance after what they had witnessed with Gaviota, who now sat quietly on a couch, alone, drinking wine. Trevor knew the reason for the men's shyness. He was one of the better dancers in the Three Cornered Hat, and was himself afraid of what would happen when Marianita slipped into his arms. He envisioned himself as the Tin Man in *The Wizard of Oz,* beset with rust. But unlike Judy Garland, who treats the Tin Man with such affectionate kindness and sympathy, Marianita Miró would leave Trevor struggling alone on the dance floor, the word *¡No!* rumbling from her mouth, her fingers spread out, sparkling, into a gesture of frustration at having her time so wasted.

He caught her eye and nodded to her, in the way that Emilio had taught him was done in Buenos Aires dance halls. Marianita nodded back, something Trevor had not imagined would be the response. Indeed, she wanted to dance with him, *and, so,* he wondered, *what'll I do now?*

They met on the floor. Trevor took her into his arms, and to his astonishment she immediately made him look better than he had ever looked. She could follow anything. She held to him as though he were the most handsome *compadre* in Buenos Aires, and she whispered, quietly, amorously, at him throughout the dance.

"Listen to the music, Trevor. Don't move your shoulders so much. Wait for me, wait for me."

It was a quick, dictatorial lesson in three and a half minutes. Nonetheless Trevor felt he was making immediate progress. He especially felt Gaviota surveying them, cigarette in hand, with a look of offended jealousy. He was standing by the side of the dance floor, ignoring Carla, who, it was clear, was suddenly disdainful herself. She was offended by Gaviota, because she had been cast aside. But now she had Emilio's attention, and Trevor knew that kindness was one of Emilio's true assets.

I'll dance this tango, Trevor thought. *Then a couple more. Then I'll ask Marianita out.*

He attempted remaining loose. Very difficult under the circumstances, when the fear-struck rigidity of every muscle in his arsenal fought against him. But judging from Marianita's not laughing at him or simply walking from the floor and leaving him out there, he figured he was doing okay. She even caressed the back of his neck. When she had done this with Gaviota on the stage of Carnegie Hall, a quite knowable sigh had come from many parts of the audience. A similar sigh came from Trevor just now, as measured as he could keep it so as not to make Marianita think he was losing control.

They danced a second tango, and Trevor felt himself improving even more. Then a third, during which he rehearsed how he would ask Marianita for a date.

Movement at the curtain distracted him. A boy, five years old with brown-black lashes of hair peeking out from beneath a Mets baseball cap, wearing a Spiderman T-shirt, Levi's, and small Nike running shoes, ran into the room, looking around, searching the floor.

"Bobby!" Marianita released herself from Trevor's arms and hurried across the floor toward the boy.

"¡Mami!"

A man followed Bobby into the room, causing almost as many heads to turn for him as had turned for Marianita. He paused, enjoying the embrace that Marianita now gave the little boy. In his forties, he wore a fine black suit, white shirt, and tie of such elegance that Trevor suddenly felt even more like a start-up slob. He retreated a few steps, doubt dizzying his thoughts. Had he seen this fellow somewhere…on television? Was he a star of stage and screen? Dark-skinned, very slim with Paris-seeming romantic male bravado, he walked toward Marianita as though she formed the very reason for living itself.

"¡Amir, *amorcito!*" Marianita embraced Amir.

"Daddy!" Bobby did, too.

Trevor turned toward the bar, where Emilio stood with Carla. A large sympathetic smile decorated Emilio's face.

Amir, Marianita, and Bobby danced together, a barely moving tango, during which Bobby, being held by both his parents, put his arms around Marianita's neck and lay his head on her left shoulder. The Mets baseball cap fell to the floor, and a few of the onlookers hurried to pick it up. Trevor was not one of them.

Moments later, he offered Amir, to whom Marianita had introduced him, a paper cup of Malbec. "Very good dancer," Marianita had said, pointing at Trevor with the thumb of her right hand. Bobby then led her back to the dance floor.

"What do you do besides tango?" Amir said as both men watched the dancing.

"I've got a start-up."

"What is it?"

Trevor gave a short description of Zowie Collectibles. He was suddenly embarrassed by it. A man of such elegance, evident wealth and confidence as Amir could hardly care about collectibles. But as the conversation progressed, Amir turned away from the dance floor to listen to Trevor. He wanted even more information, so that Trevor poured a bit more wine into his cup and continued talking.

"Sounds fascinating." Amir glanced occasionally toward the dance floor as Bobby, walking backward, led Marianita around by her hands.

"I hope so." Trevor smiled. "We're small. Just two of us."

"That's all right. Somebody funded Yves Saint Laurent in the beginning."

"Yes, but—"

"Whose initial designs in Algeria…you know, where he was born… were cute little hats for his mother." Amir held the paper cup up before him, in a kind of toast to Trevor. "Who's funding you?"

"Me."

"Just you?"

"No, *my* mother. And Emilio over there. My partner."

Amir put the cup aside, straightened his tie, and then took a billfold from his inside jacket pocket. "You'll probably need a couple million."

"What?"

"What are you doing tomorrow?"

"Uh… Well, I'm free."

"Here's my card. Come see me tomorrow afternoon. We'll talk some more." The card read "Tahlebi, Mortenson Venture Capital" with an address on Park Avenue and Amir Tahlebi's name. "Three o'clock?"

Jolted into silence, Trevor placed the card in his pocket.

"Bring your business plan." Amir smiled.

A few hours later, the dance floor was close to empty. Amir and Marianita had left, but not until Bobby had received a round of applause for his dancing and several kisses and hugs from the women watching. Emilio had left with Carla. A few couples danced about. The bar was cluttered with empty paper cups, stained plastic glasses, empty bottles, and crumpled-up paper napkins. The wood floor before the bar was sticky.

Trevor, seated on a couch at the end of the room, had had a little too much to drink. He sorrowed a bit at the love he had sought and lost, the love that little Bobby had won so easily, in which no doubt he was nestled at this very moment.

"You can dance, Trevor." Gaviota, too, reclined on the couch. He turned and gestured with both hands, open, palms up. The sunglasses lay folded in the palm of his right hand. "I was watching you." He tapped Trevor on the knee. "And don't let anyone," he slurred, "say something different." He sat back, the sunglasses hanging between his knees. "But there are a few things…"

Trevor sipped from his glass, listening.

"A few things. You give me an hour, and, *che,* I'll give you the tango."

"But what about Marianita?"

"No, *hermano,* she's happy where she is." Gaviota took in a long breath, and then let it out slowly, as the last couple on the floor finished the last tango of the early morning. *"Ay, dios mío,* I wish she wanted me…" He sighed once more. "The way she loves Amir. But that will never be. For me." He put on the sunglasses and turned toward Trevor. "Or you."

"For sure."

"*Bueno.* So you meet me here the day after tomorrow, and I'll show you a few things that will help you…maybe…with someone else who'll love you more than Marianita will ever love you. Or me. Or anyone else but Amir." Gaviota looked to the side, his hopes clearly dismayed. "That fortunate man."

WAR

"Why not just push the Brits back into the sea?" Martin held an empty fork over his dinner plate. He and his cousin Romero had been talking about the war in the Falkland Islands in which, at the moment, the British navy was ravaging the Argentine army. The reflection out the kitchen window, of the lowering sun glinting off the Hudson, was turning quickly from bright blue-green to gray. The river would soon turn dark.

Romero shoved the ravioli about his plate with so little enthusiasm that the ravioli itself appeared to have paled. A sickly little packet dripping with yellowing cream. His cheeks were flushed. He dressed with delicate care, so that his black suit, black vest, white shirt, and blood-red tie appeared made of smooth-glazed porcelain. Each strand of his composed hair was oiled in place, so that his head looked to have been enameled. His fingers gripped the fork with delicacy. They, too, looked sculpted. The nails were trimmed with military precision. The skin appeared to never once have been chewed upon.

Martin worried that the Argentine, with his imperfect English, had not understood the question.

Romero laid the fork on the plate in a small puddle of sauce. "I think..." He exuded personal grief. "That the English are our salvation."

Martin's lips tightened.

"That they will save us."

Martin leaned over his own plate of food. He wanted to take the lapels of Romero's banker's suit between his hands, to shake him. But he remained composed.

Romero looked up from his plate. "My family, I mean."

It had come as a surprise to Martin Heflin to learn that there were any Irish in Argentina at all. But evidently quite a few of them had emigrated there, and so the prospect of meeting one of them—a distant cousin of Martin's to boot—filled him with considerable excitement. What Martin knew about Argentina was limited to what he was told by his neighbor Oscar Benedetti, who sold pipeline to the Argentines and other South American governments, and who had lived in Manhattan for twenty-seven years.

"It's changed a lot since I left in 1955," Oscar would say. "And not for the better."

Martin enjoyed the humor of Oscar's pessimism. He had once said that the principal reason to live in New York was that there were so few Argentines there.

"And now, Martin, nobody can live in Buenos Aires." Sixty-five years old, with a gray, trimmed beard, Oscar laid a hand on his small paunch, giving off such disappointment in his exhalation that Martin realized that his friend missed the city of his birth very much, no matter what he said about it, its citizens, and, now, its government. "Perón was bad enough. But now we have the generals."

They were seated in the living room of Martin's one-bedroom apartment at the end of West Seventy-ninth Street, which Gerald Gargery had gotten for him. Gerald worked for an immigration law firm downtown, and he did what he could to help out itinerant IRA men when they were passing through New York. Martin was a special case, though. He had had to leave Derry quickly, pursued by soldiers for questioning in the bombing of a coal ship, the *Nellie M,* in Lough Foyle in January 1981. Martin, as a senior officer in the Provisional IRA and a former officer in the Royal Navy, had been working in hiding because the Brits had come to know who he was and how important he was. He was part of the planning of the attack and just barely escaped his cousin Mary's house when the British Army itself came to take him. It was difficult making his way to the west, to the border and into the Irish Republic, an escape in the middle of the night and in February, a lot of it on foot. They almost got him. But with the help of a heavy cloud cover on a sodden night across a number of mud-glutted fields, during which Martin contracted a mild case of pneumonia, he escaped.

Now, fifteen months later, the U.S. government was questioning Martin's visa, and he and Gerald Gargery knew that Immigration was keeping tabs on him. So he lived a life of proper comportment, and he invited his neighbor Oscar to his apartment from time to time for a glass of porter.

For the last two weeks, the principal subject of conversation had been the Falklands War, which the British had declared against Argentina in early April. Or as Oscar insisted, "in a year like this, 1982, when everyone should know where everything is and what the proper name is... those islands are called the Malvinas, Martin." The British had landed on the islands just a week ago, on May 21, several hundred miles into the Atlantic off the Argentine coast. They were offended that these bloody Argentines had the nerve to invade a proper British colony, just because it once belonged to Argentina. The war between the two countries, at the moment, raged across the islands.

Martin sifted through the mail every day, hoping for a letter from someone, anyone, about his cousin Mary Singleton and her husband, Cathal, with whom he was staying when the Brits arrived on their doorstep in Derry. He had escaped moments before, and the soldiers pretty much destroyed a large portion of the interior of Mary's home. They were now keeping a close eye on Mary, and Cathal, too, of course. The only letter he had received from Northern Ireland in the many months since his escape indeed came from Mary, in which she described the soldiers' arrival, the van parked in the midnight street before her house, and the terrible shouting and noise as the men ransacked the house, looking for Martin. Cathal, a stationery salesman, was away that week on business in Armagh. Mary wrote that she herself struggled with the soldiers, shouting at them to take their bloody Ulster politics somewhere else, to respect her privacy, to take their hands off her.

In reply, the army tore apart the two upstairs bedrooms and badly damaged the stairway down which they dragged Mary in order to stop her meddlesome, obstructive screaming at them. The Belgian wallpaper was scraped and dented by Mary's flails and the soldiers' banging against everything with boots and billy clubs. They knocked down half the pictures… *my mother's old painting of Pius X,* she wrote, *and that picture of you, Martin, that your mother sent to my mother so long ago, of your First Communion. All of them came down, so smashed and destroyed that it took me half the morning to sweep the broken glass out of the runner.*

Martin smiled, imagining Mary's foul bluster as they sat her down on the couch in her parlor and placed a guard before her…some diffident, heavily armed tosser from Edinburgh or Aberdeen…to keep her quiet. Martin had often visited Mary's house. She was a NORAID secret contact, and Martin knew that the British were being particularly tough in Derry on sympathizers of the American NORAID at the time, and the money that NORAID provided to the provisional IRA.

"People like me," Mary had once told him, "they think of us as Yanks... NORAID Yanks born on this side of the water." She had laughed. Mary—like her cousin Martin—had indeed been born in Derry and was an Irish Catholic through and through. Her husband, as well. She had never visited the States.

Ted Kennedy had recently said something in praise of NORAID, which his office later had to clarify by saying that Senator Kennedy was by no means endorsing the activities of the Irish Republican Army, and that he merely intended to acknowledge with his remarks that NORAID and others, like Sinn Féin, had a point of view that perhaps should be considered.

So Mary—not having been arrested that night because they didn't have a thing on her or her husband, no evidence, their clean slate marking them as model British citizens—would receive cash from the States, and in turn deliver it to the Derry Provisionals. The two cousins had not seen each other again because Martin had to get away in such a hurry. He left Derry that very night in the dark rain for County Donegal, and then went on to New York a few weeks after that.

"It's less a visit than it is..." Oscar looked over the letter. He had just come in from work downtown. "An escape."

He placed the letter on the coffee table, and Martin perused it a moment, its meaningless Spanish written in a large, loop-filled script.

The living room in Martin's furnished apartment had been done up some years before, and it appeared that little had been done, ever, to keep it up. The floor lamps had the look of the 1950s, including the lampshades themselves, which were brown-yellow with elderly cigarette smoke. Certainly the age of the lampshades accounted a good deal for the yellowish light that filtered through them and made the cream-colored walls appear smudged with darkness. The paint was cracked here and there below the plate rail, and underneath the bay window, where dampness had gotten in, the paint was discolored to dark brown. Martin's new cotton-lace curtains, which he had installed himself, were long enough to cover the blotchy darknesses. But he could see them nonetheless, and they added for him to the atmosphere in the room of run-down age.

An overstuffed sofa, the color of a tarnished dune in the far Sahara, with doilies on both arms, gave wan charm to the other furniture.

Unlike Martin, who had never married, Oscar was divorced, and his American wife had taken their children back to her hometown, San Francisco, the year before. He walked around in a kind of shrug all the time, weighed down missing his two teenage daughters. Oscar's beard and paunch gave him a look of settled working-class middle age, even though he was, as he stated that he had always been, a living, breathing capitalist. He had had to leave Argentina under difficult circumstances in 1955, the youngest ever vice-president of operations of a major shipping company, university-trained, badgered into exile by the first Perón regime for his anti-union sympathies. His insistence on a steak for dinner every evening and his love of tango music made him seem ordered and lushly romantic at the same moment. He was a capitalist in his talk and in his every action, and Martin enjoyed his bristling, humorous disrespect for just about everything working-class, even though Martin was a staunch union supporter in almost every way himself.

"Your cousin Romero is a banker, it says here." Oscar was translating Romero's letter to Martin. "That's good."

"Oh, ay. If you say so. But...Irish?"

"Yes, they came to Argentina during the nineteenth century. O'Leary. Maloney. O'Higgins. All those same names that you have here." Oscar laughed. "McGillicuddy? O'Shaughnessy? How does a man pronounce foolish words like that in Spanish?"

"And he's arriving in New York tomorrow?"

"That's what it says here, yes."

"Not a lot of notice, is it?"

Oscar perused the first page of the letter once again. "Well, you see, Martin, he's in considerable danger. Even his wife had to leave Buenos Aires. She went home to her mother in Chile."

"For what?"

Oscar cast his eyes down once more on the letter. His usual shrug became even more pronounced as he brought a hand to his cheek. "Their son is a priest."

"But that's no reason, is it?"

"No." Oscar swallowed. "Not on the face of it." He glanced up into Martin's eyes, and then looked away. He placed his hands in his pockets. "Their son, though, is an unusual priest." The change in one of the pockets rattled. "The government took him."

The new special laws in Northern Ireland were different from the old special laws. Someone arrested now would disappear into a police van with no charges and no acknowledgement. The police would have nothing to say about whoever it was. The person nabbed was suddenly a cypher...a rigorous, noisy memory who had been disappeared, as the current phrase had it, like those poor people Martin read about in South America. He could not imagine that the British would treat their political prisoners the way the Guatemalans did, or that fellow Pinochet in Chile. Martin could not bear the idea of being disappeared because really the phrase seemed so accurate a description of the way things were done these days. In years past, governments had had trials for sedition, and then sure they lined you up in front of a wall and gave you your last rites. Martin smiled a moment as he thought of poor revolutionary Pádraig Pearse breathing his last on May 3, 1916, in the shadow of the ruined Dublin Post Office building.

But at least in Pearse's case there was a process that everyone knew about. He made his choice, the English made theirs, and there you had it, out in front where everyone could see.

But now you got disappeared. Under the special laws, the Brits just took people away, and Martin lifted a hand to his lips as he imagined himself having been caught at Mary's house that night and then beaten into submission. They wouldn't have killed him, but there he would be, in some cold cement surrounding, no pictures, no window, dripping water coming down, poor light. An obliteration of his soul brought on by his inquisitors...two or three family men doing what they were employed to do by the British government before going home to dinner, and where's the harm in that? Martin would have disappeared into a cell, perhaps one day to be released. Perhaps not. There was no responsibility. No one had done it. You couldn't even be sure that it had happened at all. . .unless you were the poor sot being disappeared.

Romero Heflin arrived at the apartment the next day, and he hardly looked like an Irishman. For one he was tight-faced and prissy, dressed just as tightly in a suit and tie. He looked like a minor *mafioso.* Really, he resembled a jockey, as small as that, with the yellowed fingers of a man who smoked too much, and a strained smile. It turned out that he had been a jockey as a teenager. A fall from a poorly trained filly broke a collarbone, and Romero decided then to turn himself to his schooling. Discovering that he had ability as an accountant, and that his personal politics were quite conservative and anti-Peronist, he went to work for the Central Bank of Argentina.

By his fiftieth birthday, Romero was an economic analyst and a middle-level manager at the bank. He had studied in the U.K. and the United States, a year in each country, and had invested well in North American stocks. His wife, Dora, herself an economist, was now a professor at the University of Buenos Aires, and his son had been an honors student at the Catholic secondary school of Colegio Cardenal Newman before going to seminary and then getting lost—in Oscar's phrase, as he looked up from Romero's letter—in the *villas misérias.*

"What's that then?" Martin asked. "What is it, a *villa miséria?*"

"They are slums." Oscar surveyed the letter. "Big ones, in the middle of Buenos Aires. The *negritos* live there."

"Negritos?"

"Yes. The poor. Paraguayans. Bolivians. Poor Argentines."

Right away, Romero seemed to Martin to be isolated in personal squeamishness, as though his neat clothing and rigid face would protect him from unexpected circumstances...like laughter, for instance.

Martin suffered no such difficulties of expression. No shyness. He laughed and shouted. The Royal Navy had failed in its efforts to keep him neat. His clothing was occasionally wrinkled, occasionally soiled. The veins in his cheeks were broken, so that each cheek resembled a small terracotta cobblestone, and his graying hair flew about as though always in need of a cut. He felt that he looked disreputable, and he was proud of it. Too much order in one's personal appearance ruined life, he thought. It made you look English.

It quickly became clear to Martin that there was not enough room in the apartment for Romero. Martin had a bedroom, and he had installed Romero in the living room. It was there that Martin and Oscar had talked and listened to tango and the Beatles. But the room was quickly taken over entirely by Romero, and his nervous insistence on his own rights made the living room a separate, un-enterable domain.

Martin had never seen a slept-upon couch appear so neatly made-up every morning. Romero's clothes were hung in the living room closet with almost maid-like severity. When he pulled a suit from the closet, it appeared to not need ironing. He dusted the room the day he arrived. Also on that day, photos of his family were placed on the television set.

There were two. One showed Romero and his wife, obviously a studio photo. Dora had blonde hair and olive-colored skin. She sat next to her husband and, even seated, appeared taller than he. The background of the picture was made up of bookshelves, and Martin noticed that all the books had titles from the law and economics. The second photo was a vacation scene, with Romero and Dora and their son—maybe ten years old—in front of a Swiss chalet. The sign on the chalet was in Spanish, and identified it as being in Bariloche, Argentina, which Oscar told him was in the Andes. The boy Gustavo had hair to his shoulders, and appeared uncomfortable with his father's arm around his shoulder. In the picture, Romero smiled with somber festivity, in a sport shirt and slacks in bright sunlight.

One afternoon, when Romero was out, Martin went into the living room to look around. He took up the photo and studied it. The boy was indeed as dour as his father. Martin put the picture back on the television. Turning away, he realized that he had not put it in the exact place it had occupied before. A groove left by the frame in the doily on the TV set gave the secret away, and he adjusted the photo, to make sure it was right.

On a gray afternoon turning to gloom, in Central Park, Romero saw for the first time the large granite outcroppings and boulders that are everywhere there. The only thing that betrayed the presence of a city around him was the traffic noise coming from outside the park. Otherwise he was in solitude in the Manhattan forest.

It was a manufactured forest, he knew, made up by landscape architects. But the quality of mannered wildness that Central Park purveys was already special to him, reminding him—despite Central Park's enormity—of the far more intimate Thays Botanical Garden in Buenos Aires.

That park, equally surrounded by busy boulevards, allowed for personal peace and contemplation, and had done so for Romero many times, especially after his son Gustavo was ordained. Gustavo's calling was to help the poor, something about which Romero himself barely cared. But his son felt that the poor were the true children of Christ, and therefore needed priestly help in every way, spiritually, politically.... So now, at thirty years old, Padre Gustavo was hardly a priest at all, Romero thought, going around in old stained pants, a T-shirt, and sandals, scruffy and leftist, leading left-wing political demonstrations downtown every day, hardly the look of a man of God.

So Romero had spent much of his time on a bench in the Thays Botanical Garden, worrying about his son.

The dusk-ridden trees of Central Park were lined with the leavings of a light May rain, like watered bones. A monstrous, pot-bellied statue that rose up before him as he approached the West Seventy-second Street exit from the park looked lumpish and heavy in the delicate sheen of water that covered it. The statue appeared ready to launch into deeply considered speechifying, the subject's right hand planted with Napoleonic intensity inside his rumpled coat front. That much rectitude seemed inappropriate to the crystalline, liquid delicacy of the trees that made them appear so breakable, like darkening glass. The statue's bronze greatcoat and the heaviness of the fellow's left hand, which hung down as though held to his side by the weight and importance of what he was about to say, amused Romero. It was a comic touch made of oafish bronze in the slowly disappearing light. The granite boulders past which he had walked to get here floated beneath the light rain with much more graceful volume than did the grotesquely formed metal of this man's grand shoes.

Romero read the name of the fellow being immortalized. ¡Carajo! he thought. *Daniel Webster? Never heard of him.* But that was fair enough, he decided, since so few citizens of New York would have any knowledge of someone like, say, Domingo Faustino Sarmiento, a former president of Argentina who was often equally presented in self-important aplomb in parks in Buenos Aires.

Romero turned from Webster, who gave his worries no relief. The police had taken Gustavo in the night, from the little house in the violent and very poor Isla Maciel neighborhood of Buenos Aires, where he practiced his vocation, and he had not been seen for months. They then threatened Romero himself with imprisonment, as being hardly less villainous than his terrorist priest son, if only because he was that son of a bitch's father. That was all the authorities needed to terrorize Romero and his wife, along with one formal letter of investigative inquiry, and occasional visits. His wife, Dora, insisted to Romero that he was in jeopardy, too, and she recalled something that an Argentine relative of Romero's had told her, about a distant cousin in New York—"One of your Irish," she said—and suggested that Romero find out who he was and ask him for some help.

"So you think the British are there to save you, eh?" Martin asked. "You and your family?"

Romero poured some of the Argentine Malbec that he had brought as a gift into Martin's glass. "It would cause considerable disappointment to my fellow Argentines to hear me say this. After all, we're being attacked." He lifted his own glass to his lips, sipping from it. "But I hope so, yes."

"They're criminals, the Brits. They're invading your own bloody country."

Romero sighed and, replacing the bottle on the table, wrapped the fingers of both hands around its base. "But Martin—"

"Invading it!"

"My country...."

Martin, in his shirtsleeves, looked with apparent condemnation at the plate of ravioli before him. He halved one of them with his fork. Romero, dressed as always as though he were enjoying dinner at the Waldorf Astoria, barely moved, although he took up his own fork in his right hand.

"They will win in the Malvinas, Martin. Then the people will remove the generals and bring in a democracy, which is a good thing."

"Your own leaders? The people who would defend your sovereignty?"

Romero lowered the fork to his plate. He moved his chair back several inches from the table, crossed his legs, and folded his hands on his lap. "They murder."

"Your president?"

"Torture."

"Oh, come now."

"You do not know what you are talking about, Martin." Romero gripped the edge of the table with the fingers of his left hand. Suddenly, like lightning dressed for dinner, he was riveted with fury. *"Boludo."*

"The hell I don't! The British? I—"

"Maldito cafisho."

"What's that?"

"You have no right to speak to me like this."

"What did you say?"

Romero's face flushed, and he sat back, folding his hands once more and looking out a window toward the Hudson River. His black hair shined. "Nothing, Martin. I'm sorry, it's...." He lowered his eyes, and for a moment Martin sensed that Romero was about to weep. "It's nothing."

After two more weeks of battle, the British won The Falklands War.

Three weeks after that, though, Martin's original intention of being kind to his Argentine cousin, to wish him the best, was verging on ruin. Romero had taken the apartment over. He smiled, wishing to make up for their arguments, and accommodated his host. He brought Martin several more bottles of wine and a supply of porterhouse steaks. But he also brought to the apartment a continued pained uncomfortableness that made Martin, for one, feel that he himself had no privacy at all. Such withering politeness as Romero's could not be avoided.

Martin planned to speak to Oscar about the situation, when he received a letter from his cousin Mary.

I don't know how to tell you this, but I'm in real trouble. I've been the subject of a newspaper article here—in the Protestant press, of course—that makes me out to be some sort of American bomber, a terrorist, that sort of thing. I don't know what to do, and the British can do whatever they want. They haven't done anything to me yet, but I'm sick with worry, Martin.

He lay the letter down on the kitchen table. Romero was sitting in the living room reading a copy of an Argentine news magazine that Oscar received every week in the mail. The cover had a photograph of a military officer in full ceremonial dress, his white uniform crossed from right shoulder to left hip with a sash of double light-blue stripes. The shoulder boards resembled tightly framed omelets. He was a fellow of moderate girth who looked a bit like a generous-minded priest, his smile—expressing governmental kindness and sincere regard for the people—not quite in the same expressive league with the threatening phalanx of medals on his chest.

"His name's Galtieri," Oscar had explained to Martin the day the magazine had arrived. He tapped the military man's forehead with an index finger. "Argentina hasn't been at war for a hundred fifty years, so what are all the medals for?" He tossed the magazine onto the kitchen table, and then leaned over to look more carefully at the photo. "He was in charge for the Malvinas, but now he's disgraced. Another general's in, a schmuck named Bignone. Schmucks, both of them."

Martin, confused, surveyed the cover. "Schmucks? That's an American word, is it?"

Glancing once more at Mary's letter, he knew that the cigarette in Romero's right hand—a gold-tipped Dunhill—would be expelling its delicate smoke. Martin wanted his privacy back. He stood and walked into the hallway.

"Romero."

Romero turned from the magazine and surveyed Martin, who stood in the space between the two sliding wood doors that separated the living room from the hallway.

"You have to go."

"Go?"

Martin lowered his head. "Yes, I—"

"Leave?"

"Yes."

Romero remained very still. Smoke rose up his right sleeve. "But where shall I go, Martin?"

"I don't know. A hotel. Another apartment."

"But you've been so kind to me."

"I have not, Romero. I've felt invaded the whole time. I can't take your Limey sympathies. I can't move around in my own apartment. You don't understand the issues. You make the English out to be Salvation's own anointed—"

"I don't understand."

"You don't understand the politics of the situation, the pressure we're under."

"Martin, please."

"You live thousands of miles away from the Troubles, and you haven't an idea of what they even are."

Martin turned away.

"Or that they exist." He awaited a reply. But there was none. He held himself still a moment longer, feeling that, behind him, in the living room, he could hear the very smoke dribbling to the floor from Romero's Dunhill. He turned finally, and saw a look of dismay, even of despair, on

Romero's face, as though he were in black mourning for no one other than himself. Martin's rejection had muzzled him.

"I've read about your Ireland."

"So? What's that got to do—?"

"I know what you people have been through."

"How could you?" Martin shook his head. "How could you have any idea what really—"

"My son vanished."

Martin held up a moment.

"Many have vanished." Romero laid the cigarette in an ashtray. He fixed Martin with a sudden look of elegant hatred. "You think you've had it as bad as we?"

"Thousands have died. Eight hundred years of—"

"The same in my country. Six years. And it perturbs me, Martin, that I know so much about your foolish Ireland, and you apparently know nothing of my Argentina."

"Listen here."

"My son has vanished."

"Romero, I don't intend any—"

"Disappeared."

After a moment's silence, Martin's gaze fell solely on the Dunhill, which continued burning.

Romero crushed the cigarette in an ashtray. "When do you want me to leave?"

"Tomorrow."

Once Romero had left, Oscar seemed unwilling to talk with Martin. After several days, he agreed, reluctantly, to join Martin in the living room for a glass of porter.

"You're angry with me because I tossed him out, aren't you?" Martin had received another letter from Mary, apologizing for the previous one. Apparently, the British still had no evidence that she was involved with the Provisionals, and she went to her job teaching in a Catholic primary school every day, riding a tram to and fro, walking up and down her street unmolested and unharried. *When you wrote back to me,* the letter said, *I realized how much I must have worried you, Martin, and I apologize for that. I should have understood the circumstances better. It wasn't even an article in the paper. It was a letter from some bloke that I barely know, and I even got an apology from the editor, for Lord's sake. Imagine that! A Protestant asking a Catholic for forgiveness!*

"Yes," Oscar said. "Romero is a peevish man."

"Sure he's that."

"But he's a good man."

Martin sipped from his porter. "But even when he wasn't here, he was in the way."

Oscar placed his half-empty glass on the coffee table. "In the way of what, Martin?"

Martin sipped from his. "My living a life of privacy and no worry." He sipped again.

Oscar's eyes wavered to a look of disapproval.

"I don't have a right to that?"

Another letter arrived from Derry a few days later.

Dear Martin,

It's a little rough over here just now. The Brits came and took Mary last night, and we're not being allowed to visit her. We don't know where she is, really. No charges yet. No news. We don't know what to do. I hope you remember Willie Daly, who we went to school with. He's a solicitor now, and is trying to help us. But even he can't get to see her.

No bloody justice, eh?

I'll write again as soon as I know more.

I know she misses you, Martin. Take care of yourself.

Cathal

"He found his son." Oscar held an opened letter in his hand. Romero had returned to Buenos Aires rather than go to some hotel or otherwise acquiesce to Martin's dictatorial dismissals. Martin reminded him of General Galtieri, he had said. Oscar had also told Martin that Romero's wife was still in

Chile, too frightened to return to Argentina. "The mailman just left this."

"What happened?"

"Special delivery."

"What happened?"

Oscar looked down at the writing. "They dumped the boy into a river."

Martin lowered his head.

"The Riachuelo, it's called. It's famous. An industrial river. More oil and shit than water, Martin. It runs right through Buenos Aires, and many have been dumped into the Riachuelo in the last few centuries. Many." Oscar took in a breath and curled his lower lip between his teeth. "But they were murderers and criminals, most of them." He closed his mouth. The lips together resembled wrinkled straps. "This boy...this boy was just a Socialist, that's all. A priest. He carried placards. Hated the government. Loved his father."

"Read me the letter."

"Translate it?"

"Please."

Oscar laid the three sheets of paper out flat on the kitchen table and began, haltingly, to bring it into English. "I'll read the important parts. The parts about Gustavo." He placed an index finger at the beginning of a paragraph. As he read, the finger trailed beneath the writing.

"'I cannot imagine, Oscar, telling you what they told me. The Church, I mean.'"

Martin sat upright on a kitchen chair, his hands on his thighs.

"'Such dismissive disrespect. Or what I saw when I went to identify Gustavo.'"

Oscar paused. He did not look up as he read in silence. When he did look up, his eyes betrayed the wish to cease this conversation.

"Read it."

"'His clothing...it was muddied and ripped. He had no shoes. He had been in the water for...'" Oscar paused, keeping his eyes averted. He swallowed. "'For some many hours at least. He had no shoes. His skin was gray and he was very...very...' I don't know the word, Martin. *'Hinchado.'* It's like 'swollen' or something...'filled up.'"

"Bloated."

"Bloated. That's it. Bloated."

Martin put his right elbow on the table and placed his forehead against the fingers of his right hand.

"'He had been beaten, and then shot in the back of the head.'" Oscar stopped once more.

"Keep going."

"'And the odd thing was that there was no blood coming from the wound. I suppose...'" Oscar exhaled. "'I suppose that the Riachuelo water had cleaned his wound or sucked the blood from it or something. It was just a large hole in his skull, a bit of his hair annealed to its...its inside by the water.'"

Martin placed his forehead in both hands.

"'Imagine that filthy water, Oscar, washing a priest's wounds! He had no shoes.'"

"Romero."

Martin sat alone on the couch, looking out the window at the Hudson River. He cradled the telephone between his cheek and his right shoulder, and sipped from a glass of Malbec, the last of the wines Romero had donated to the apartment. It was a moonlit night, but the river formed a vast black emptiness upon which there were no lights, no distinguishing features, no movement. Just a long sightless hole.

"Oscar told me."

He imagined Romero sitting alone smoking a Dunhill. Every surface of his hair and the very skin on his head would appear laundered and pressed. This time, however, Martin was certain that the blood itself flowing through Romero was bruised with anguish. Martin could feel it emanating from the phone, from Romero's breathing. Besieged by thankless sorrow.

"I'm sorry to hear about your son."

"Yes, I know."

"You do?"

"Of course. You've been so solicitous of me. That's the right word in English, no? Solicitous?"

"I was more than rude, Romero. It was reprehensible, what I did to you."

"Yes, I thought so too. But not always." His breathing remained, the only thing Martin could hear for a moment. "But I knew you were concerned about me. About Gustavo. You offered me your apartment, after all. And now this phone call. And, of course, the...the similar story."

Martin looked to the river. His fingers held the wine glass as though its stem were that of a slim reed seeping blood. He knew that he had betrayed Romero.

Romero sighed. His almost whispering voice floated through the static of the telephone line. "Your worry, Martin, for your cousin Mary... the eight hundred years of...of the Irish island...Las Malvinas...of the British." Romero paused, as though scarcely able to breathe, and sickened by the requirement to do so. "You couldn't turn your back on your family, after all. You were at war."

THE SANDWICH

"Egypt?"

Muhammad's head nodded up and down over the grill. "Yes, the beginning of the universe." He surveyed the lamb, the onions, and the bread.

David recalled his one sojourn in Egypt, with his wife, Kitty, some years before. Sitting on a wooden deckchair on a boat going down the Nile, feeling like Somerset Maugham coming upon a disjointed colonial romance, he had luxuriated in one of the most spectacular scenic splendors he had ever seen. A thin sliver of green bordered each bank of the river, sometimes extending fifty yards from the bank, sometimes as much as a quarter mile. Beyond the green, desert of every shade of yellow and brown gave way to vast mountains similarly colored in the far distance. An ancient emptiness, it seemed, although David knew this could not be so. He imagined goatherds and camel drivers, caravans and dry, parchment-protecting caves, the wrecked evidence of centuries-old Napoleonic passings, shepherds, occasions of pharaonic glory and Muslim punishment, romance, Flaubert, T.E. Lawrence, Napoleon himself, Cleopatra, Mark Antony....

Every now and then, the boat would stop, and David and Kitty would go with a group of passengers to Karnak, the Valley of the Kings, or some other site, to view the antiquities. Here he felt indeed almost Napoleonically small. These great structures must have made the French Revolution appear to the emperor as an arriviste trinket. Were David to channel the pharaoh Hatshepsut and ask her what she thought of the effects of Paris 1789 on New York 2011, she would probably say that it was way too early to tell.

For David, the overall effect of the ruins of Karnak was one of drifting through a gargantuan dream delight that put aside for the moment anything of lesser importance, like the boat waiting back at the pier or his gallery on Fifty-seventh Street. He showed prints there by people like Kara Walker and Cy Twombly, and worried that those things were just moments of personal idiosyncrasy and slowly disintegrating paper, along with all the flatbed presses, silkscreens, lithograph stones, solvents, inks, and odd artist behaviors that, with time, would glimmer away to nothing. Ozymandias was right, David decided as he craned his neck to look up at the pillars of Karnak. "Look on my works, ye mighty—"

"I've been to your country."

"Where did you stay?" The large dollop of yogurt that Muhammad applied to the mixture of vegetables dripped through them like spiced, creamy snow. The pita bread in his right hand caught any that made it all the way through to the bottom.

"Cairo."

"Hmph." Muhammad shook his head, waving the plastic container that contained the yogurt in the air. "My nephew lives there."

"He enjoys it?"

"He's a student."

"What do you think of the place?"

"Eh! In Cairo, they are all bums!"

"Where are you from?"

Muhammad ladled a pile of lamb onto the pita. "Alexandria, my friend." He rolled the sandwich and wrapped it in tin foil. "I was trained for many years as a chef there." He took David's money. "My nephew's parents, my brother and his wife, they wish he would come back to Alexandria. They think he's in danger in Cairo."

"From what, the politics?" At the moment, a crowd of a hundred thousand people occupied Tahrir Square, despite the remonstrations of President Mubarak.

"No. The university girls." Muhammad tapped the griddle with his ladle. "They are pretty. He is handsome."

Mike's Lamb and Burgers stand was about seven feet long, four feet wide, made of metal, and seven feet high, plus an umbrella. It had a griddle for lamb and a grill for burgers and hot dogs. A small closed cabinet at one end of the stand contained soft drinks and water.

"Don't worry about the line," Kitty had told him. "It's always this way."

Mostly blue-collar people and office workers, they comprised the most patient long queue David had ever seen in Manhattan. He mused that this sanguine comportment was out of respect for Egypt and its antiquities.

"No, It's out of longing for the sandwiches." Kitty further told him that any New Yorker who did not come to this stand for a sandwich at least once in his life was condemning himself to the dismayed emptiness of a barren, joyless existence on a treeless plain.

Kitty carried herself with an air of elegant fashion, gleaned from her years working as an editor at *W.* Her clothing appeared, always, to have been taken from the pages of that journal, except that she was such an exceptional shopper that she usually ended up paying one third of what she would pay were she to go to the stores recommended by the magazine. Now, she wrote best-selling love novels for women, and she had explained to David that you had to supply such apocalyptic lines as that of the treeless plain at the end of each chapter, to keep the reader going. She was famous among her fans for that talent, and prided herself on it.

The stand, and Muhammad, had been here for years. He was a man of heavy proportions and casual dress, wearing a navy pea coat and a watch cap on this clear January day. His hair flew from beneath the cap in uneven curls, and his hands, whose thicknesses belied the speed with which they moved across the grill, appeared much larger than the rest of him would suggest. Indeed he operated the grill in the way that the organist at, say, Saint Patrick's Cathedral would essay the keyboards. The skin on his face appeared grainy, the result of so many years being surrounded by heat and smoke. He had a full set of teeth, and one of them, a lower one, was framed in gold. It flashed whenever he smiled.

Kitty had told David that she had bought her first food from Muhammad at least ten years ago. He was a maestro of the hot lamb sandwiches, the franks, the burgers, and all the accompanying accouterments to be found here: sliced onions, mulched tomatoes, shredded lettuce, and, in the case of the delight that David was about to consume, fresh pita bread and a yogurt sauce made with olive oil and various Middle Eastern spices. This was David's first time at the stand, and with regard to what was coming, he was a naïf.

Kitty had ordered a lamb sandwich, and while Muhammad had cooked, David had watched. He saw right away that the lamb was cut up into small pieces…a great pile of it on the grill, savory with spices that were, Muhammad assured David, a secret. David's attempt to eyeball the lamb more closely was foiled by the various depths of shadow cast by the exhaust flue just above. The tomatoes, lettuce, and yogurt were in plastic containers inside the counter. The pita bread was wrapped in plastic that was easy to access, so that Muhammad could grab one right away.

He was an authoritative man. When they had first arrived, David had read the menu on the side of the stand and determined that he wanted one of these lamb sandwiches. Muhammad's first question was, did he want it on pita or on a roll? David asked for it on a roll, and requested mustard and catsup. Muhammad glanced at him with only slightly muzzled disdain.

He then turned to Kitty. "The lady is always first, my friend." More knowledgeable than David, she ordered the lamb sandwich just as a lamb sandwich. She knew what she was getting and so made no special requests for things like catsup. Muhammad placed a pita bread on the grill, waited a few moments for it to warm, then began putting the sandwich together, a mixture of the lamb and all the other things, enormous amounts of each. He rolled the pita around the concoction and wrapped it in tin foil. This all happened very quickly, and he passed it hurriedly into Kitty's hands

He pointed at David with an index finger. "And you want what?"

Normally David carried himself with businesslike, slightly aging aplomb. He enjoyed being noted for his conservative stylishness. Just now, though, he realized that his request for catsup and mustard had marked him as a hick.

"The same as she got," he said.

Smiling, Muhammad gave David the thumbs up, and turned to his task.

A moment later, David and Kitty walked to Central Park, where, seated at a table near the zoo, in the dazzled cold, they devoured the sandwiches. David decided with the first bite that his sandwich had been prepared in the Garden of Eden, which was, he knew, also in the Middle East, probably not far from Alexandria.

He returned to Mike's three more times in the following week, always ordering a lamb sandwich. The first time, he got there early, hoping to avoid the line. But apparently there was always a line. When he arrived, Muhammad, grinning with falsely condemnatory glee, asked him if he wanted catsup. David responded, commandingly, that he did not. The next time, two days later, Muhammad offered his right hand in friendship, which David took. Of special meaning to David was Muhammad's touching his own hand to the front of his jacket—to his heart—after the handshake.

They talked as Muhammad prepared the sandwich.

"Have you heard from your nephew?"

"No."

"Are you still worried?"

"Yes."

"About the girls."

"Yes. Even though he's no fool, my nephew." Muhammad moved the lamb around the grill with a metal spatula. The odor of it rose to David's nose like a suggestion of sensuous whispering. "No politics or anything. Tahrir Square's not for him." He jostled the onions. "Politics are dangerous in Egypt. We all know that." Muhammad pursed his lips. "Look at Anwar Sadat!" He scraped the open grill with the edge of his ladle. "No, my nephew, he's a good boy. A good cook, too." A cloud of steam rose from the onions. "You watch. He's coming to New York this summer. He'll be cooking here, and it will be my great pleasure..." Muhammad slid the spatula beneath the lamb and hurried it onto its less-cooked side. "To introduce him to my new friend David."

"I've been watching television, though." David waited as Muhammad wrapped the sandwich. "The demonstrations."

Muhammad gave him the sandwich with one hand while he raised the other in a gesture of disdain. "Bums, that's what they are."

"Who?"

"Mubarak!" He glanced at David, his eyes centered, unmoving. "All of them. The politicians. The Brotherhood. The army." He shook his head. "No, you come to Alexandria, David. You'll enjoy it."

While David was shaving the next morning, Kitty called him back into the bedroom. She stood before the television, and turned toward David, a look of startled disbelief on her face.

"Look at this."

David held the ends of the long white towel, which he had wrapped around his neck, close to his foam-speckled cheeks. About fifty horses in some kind of charge hurtled through a large crowd in Tahrir Square. Armed with clubs and sticks, the riders attacked people in the square, and were in turn attacked themselves. Then camels arrived, at first appearing to be in a race, strange creatures so oddly shaped yet so graceful as they ran through the crowd. Their saddles and blankets were the same as those that David had seen in the books he had read, about Napoleon's conquest of Egypt and Lawrence of Arabia. Some of the men wore traditional Egyptian *galabeyas*. Others, the younger ones, were dressed in old pants and ragged shirts. They, too, pummeled people in the crowd, which scattered before the charge of each enormous animal. The attack from a camel—a much higher vantage point on a much larger animal—appeared safer for the riders than that of the horsemen. The camels turned through the crowd, separated from each other, their riders flailing at people with long sticks. Within just a few moments, the square fell into chaos.

A long shot from the roof of a building showed the panic that gripped the thousands gathered in the square. But it also revealed little pockets of return brutality. People pulled some of the men from their horses and beat them. Crowds surrounded them and clubbed them with merciless anger. The surviving horsemen turned to retreat, still pursued from behind by men hurling stones. The camels, too, ran for escape.

Kitty's eyes lowered with worry. "You'd better go see him."

David got dressed, put on an overcoat, grabbed an umbrella, and hurried out of the apartment building. He hailed a cab and told the driver to take him to the corner of Sixty-sixth and Madison Avenue, where, he knew, Muhammad would just be setting up for the day.

A freezing rain swept Madison Avenue, but the line nonetheless contained a half dozen people. The umbrella shielded the stand from the rain. Right away, David saw that Muhammad was not manning the grill. The new fellow was tall, having to bend beneath the exhaust flue over the grill. Another man was with him, both dressed against the cold and rain, speaking very loudly in a language David could not comprehend.

When he got to the head of the line, the tall man asked him what he wanted.

"Lamb sandwich."

"Pita or a roll?"

"Pita."

"Everything?"

"Yeah. But where's Muhammad?"

The man did not answer. David looked toward the companion, who turned away, not willing to speak.

"Will he be here later?"

Still, no answer came from either man.

"What's your name?" David asked.

"Mike."

"Alexandria?"

"No, I'm Greek. I own the stand."

"Is Muhammad OK?"

Mike stood up straight. Rain fell across his face as steam rose from the ladle in his hand. "Sir, he's—"

"Is he sick?"

"No, he… His nephew—"

"What about him?"

The two men exchanged glances. Mike spoke a moment with the other man in their own language. He appeared confused about what to say to David.

"Come on, what's wrong?"

"The nephew, he's dead." Mike wrapped the sandwich and passed it to David. "Muhammad was here earlier. He phoned me this morning, said he couldn't work. But he helped us anyway, to set up the stand."

"Do you know where he is now?"

Mike pointed down Sixty-sixth. "He headed for the park. But you know..." He put a hand to the back of his neck and shook his head. "He didn't seem to know where he was. He just took the sandwich I made.... I don't know if he had had anything to eat. So he took the sandwich and headed over there. I don't know where he is."

"How long ago was that?"

"A half hour."

"OK, I'll go look for him." David pulled some money from his pocket

Mike grinned, although chagrined himself. "Thanks, friend." He opened a side drawer and brought out a can of root beer. "For you, it's free."

David shoved the can into one overcoat pocket, the sandwich into the other.

"He's a good man, Muhammad," Mike said. "A valuable employee."

"Thanks." David turned away.

"If you find him, let me know how he's doin'. Please."

"Okay."

Very few people walked on the Mall, and only one person, at the farthest end, sat on a bench, slumped to the side as though asleep. David could barely see, the rain thick with cold and patches of condensed fog. Muhammad was nowhere in sight. The park remained gray, dark mists obscuring the leafless trees into the distance. The sandwich that Mike had made remained in David's left hand, in the pocket, its warmth passing quietly through his fingers. He stood below the Shakespeare statue, bowed before the cold rain and holding the umbrella tight in his right hand. Everywhere the park appeared beaten down, its green turned to gray and black, its growth snuffed out.

Will Shakespeare stood casually behind David, who looked around at him. The poet had paused on the marble pedestal in Elizabethan attire: short ballooning pantaloons, long stockings, a pair of leather shoes with buckles, a shirt with floppy sleeves that was open at the throat, and a vest, perhaps of leather. Also, a cape hung down his back from his shoulders. Will held a book in his right hand, clutched to his chest. He looked down at an angle, in a moment's thought, maybe a little despondently.

David had always felt that this was a major sculpture suffering a minor distraction. Will was looking for the homely moment in which to find his metaphor. He was seeking the proper collaboration of words. He was quizzical and self-involved, caught for the moment in private.

David could tell he was an actor because a lower portion of the cape was draped over his right arm, the arm holding the book. It was a jaunty thing he was doing there, a gesture to showmanship. But this man was also a working writer. He had little interest in having some flash of inspiration flood his eyes. Rather, he wished to find the right few words for his valiant, black military hero's increasing worry that this world is not a safe place for those who would protect good people. Simple as that. Will had a problem—how to get Othello from here to there, how to change his actor's mood—and he was trying to figure it out. Great international struggles had brought his hero to this moment, alone with Desdemona in her boudoir. Othello struggled with his private suspicions. Armies clashed far away. Children died. Whole cultures were destroyed, while this single man, home from the wars, worried that he was losing his mind, his will, and his love.

The world had come apart so far away, and here it was coming apart in Othello's heart.

The person seated at the far end of the Mall stood up. He walked a few steps from the bench, looked up into the sky, and, shaking his head as he fell forward to lean on the bench's back, sat down once again. It was Muhammad.

David hurried up the walk and sat down next to him. Muhammad's sandwich had grown cold, soaked with rainwater where it lay barely eaten on a piece of newspaper on the bench.

"Muhammad.... Mike told me. Your nephew...."

Muhammad could not speak. He took up the sandwich, but it remained between the fingers of both hands like a sagging, filthy towel.

"I'm sorry."

"Thank you."

"It's a terrible day. For you. For your people."

"What people?" Muhammad whispered.

"The Muslims."

"Muslims! What have I got to do with Muslims?"

"Well, your name, no?"

A flash of anger showed momentarily through Muhammad's mourning. "I'm a Coptic, David."

"Christian."

"Yes."

"But your name—"

"So what?" Muhammad slumped forward. "My father named me that. He wished that the Prophet had been a Coptic prophet, instead of…well, you know. But, who cares? What's in a name?" Muhammad frowned. Suddenly distracted, he turned away from David and looked down the Mall toward the Shakespeare statue. "It's like wanting it on pita or a roll." He laid his sandwich aside on the newspaper, leaned forward, and folded his hands together, placing his elbows on his knees. He studied his shoes. Sadness rolled through him so regretfully that David regretted immediately what he had said.

"My nephew's name…now, my nephew…his name…." Muhammad looked across the pathway at the empty benches. David waited. "His name was Mark. After the apostle." Muhammad's hands intertwined each other in nervous indecision.

David could feel the certitude of disaster that flowed from Muhammad's very inactivity. He was imagining the worst. Mark trampled by raging animals in the square. Crying out, his skull crushed by an iron-shod hoof. A face smashed into unrecognizable, flesh-flecked blood by the great stick of a Bedouin attacker. Worse.

David put his hand in a pocket. "Muhammad." As a few days before, with Kitty here in the park, the sandwich's warmth seemed more like proffered kindness than just a lot of yogurt, pita and lamb. But this heat now felt so insubstantial to David, so irrelevant to Muhammad's concern, that it seemed to dribble away, falling from his very fingers through the cloth of his coat. Both men waited in silence.

"Muhammad!" A high voice, that of an excited woman, came up the Mall. "Ay, Muhammad!" The woman, dressed in a thick black wool skirt and black stockings, wearing a puffy cold-weather parka, her black hair covered by a wool watch cap, hurried along the walkway. Her exposed brown face was exceptionally round, a pocket of fat below her chin. She wore rimless eyeglasses and a pair of old running shoes. She carried a large plastic bag from which the green heads of carrots and the end of a large bunch of celery appeared rattling back and forth as she ran.

Muhammad stood. His face, fallen now into unguarded fear, appeared many years older than it had even moments ago. He held his hand out to the woman, who approached him shrieking, her free hand waving in the air. During a long exchange of Arabic—David hoping for a translation of some kind—Muhammad asked numerous questions, his voice breaking with anger and distress. The woman hurried answers at him, shook her head "No!" a number times, "Yes!" even more often, more words hurrying from the couple like garbled water.

Muhammad grabbed the sides of his head with the palms of his hands, and then held his hands together close to his chest, beating against it. He sat down and laid his forehead into his palms, unable to gather himself as the woman continued shouting at him, the name "Muhammad," as though the woman were seeking to regain his attention and to calm him.

"Please..." David muttered, placing a hand on the other man's knee. "Can you tell me? What...what—"

"He's alive!"

The woman held her hands before her face, for the first time seeking David's attention. "Yes!" she said in English. "He is...he is...eh?" She searched the English word, her heavy accent revealing that she spoke very little of it. "Alive!"

"My brother..." Muhammad clasped his hands together. "He didn't realize. It was a neighbor boy, another Alexandria boy, a university friend of Mark's...killed. Horrible." He looked away. "They were attacked by the horses. But it was not Mark." He clenched his fists in a gesture of victory. "No, he lives."

He turned to the woman and asked a few questions in Arabic, then spoke again to David. "Wounded, yes. A broken leg. Blood. But..." He made the Sign of the Cross, muttering its language. "He lives." Lowering his head once again, he fell into anguish. "I know that other boy, though. I…I know his father."

After a moment, Muhammad started, suddenly remembering something. He gestured toward the woman. "My wife, David. Miriam." Miriam's hands remained in the pockets of her parka as she gazed at her husband. Her eyes, the skin around them thick with worry and the effects of tears, clearly conveyed how deeply she loved him.

The couple spoke with each other a moment more, until Miriam reached into the pocket of her parka and handed Muhammad a cellphone. He asked a question, and Miriam started feeding him numbers, in English. He punched them into the phone, many numbers, and then, after a moment's waiting, he spoke.

"Androus." Muhammad talked with the other person for more than ten minutes. The mood of the conversation went from a number of seemingly fiery, desperate questions to deep quiet and commiseration. Simply from the slope of Muhammad's shoulders and the way his free hand went from rapid, imploring gestures to tapping on his right knee to hanging almost motionlessly from the knee, David could feel the conversation's downward spiral to ultimate silence. Muhammad slumped, and still with the phone at his ear, his voice ruptured and broke up. "Androus…Androus…."

Miriam sat down next to him and put her arm around his shoulders, taking him close. Muhammad placed the phone in a pocket of his jacket and embraced her, hiding his face in the water-soaked roundnesses of her parka. He wept and wept and wept.

David put a hand on Muhammad's shoulder, waiting.

"God be praised, it was the other boy's father."

The following morning, David and Kitty arrived at the stand. As the line progressed, they saw how Muhammad's work was being hampered by the calls he was getting on his cell phone. His Arabic flew as, shifting the phone and the ladle from one hand to the next, laying the phone down momentarily so that he could wrap whatever he had prepared in tin foil, he yet kept up these multiple conversations.

"My father," Muhammad explained when Kitty and David arrived at the head of the line. "In Alexandria. My cousin Beshoy in San Francisco."

He shrugged. "Who would live in a dump like San Francisco, when you got New York, eh?" He turned the lamb about slowly and tended to a large hamburger on the grill. "Beshoy's mom in Cairo. My other brother, in Amsterdam. Everybody..."

Finally, he put the now silent phone into his jacket pocket. "Poor Egypt." Slowly, a sorrow-laden smile appeared on his lips. His face came to sad life. He turned to Kitty. "And you, pretty lady. Please. Pita? Or a roll?"

BOUQUET

"When does he get here?"

"A while."

"But when?"

Javier offered Bouquet a glass of water. "He's Gonzalo…so, who knows?"

His heavy fatigue jacket was ripped down one arm. He smelled of rotting smoke. "It's dangerous for him."

Javier's patchy facial hair reminded Bouquet of a couple of the actors whom she had helped prepare for Richard Avedon's shoots. But while theirs was made intentionally scruffy for whatever part they were playing at the moment, Javier's was gummy and caked from weeks of neglect. It smelled.

The water glass was an old one, thick and much scraped. Bouquet took a sip and placed the glass on a boulder next to the falling stream. The site was otherwise deserted, two one-room mountain huts made of rocks, with plain board roofs, across a road from each other. The dirt and gravel switchback, one of many in the road that ascended through a great Andean moraine from the forested canyon far below, was wide enough for a few trucks to pass each other, although slowly.

Bouquet hoped she could trust Javier. His wife, Yulitza, also a Sendero *subcomandante,* had been kind enough to secure a hammock for Bouquet inside one of the huts, out of the cold wind. This was largesse that Javier did not wish to offer Bouquet when she arrived. He had been told that she was okay. But how was he to know for sure? Yulitza recognized the photographer's bravery and the fact that she had been so careful in making the arrangements for this clandestine meeting, that she had struggled through the two-day hike to get here from down below (on purpose; they provided no transportation), and did so alone.

Also, Javier and Yulitza had a little boy, with whom Bouquet played during her four days' waiting, and she could not believe that they would do anything to jeopardize his safety.

It was well known that "Gonzalo" was the *nom de guerre* of Abimael Guzmán, the founder of the Sendero Luminoso. No one ever saw him, so Bouquet's opportunity was unique. As she awaited him, the stream hurtled past, a continuous rapids through the steep moraine, its clear morning spray riffling with light.

"And imagine," Mike said. "Along with everything else, her name is Bouquet."

"And she did all that?" Nora Diamond fingered the book before her. An indie film producer and screenwriter, she and Mike Levin had worked on a couple of movie projects for which he was the literary agent.

"She did." Mike lifted the pint of stout to his lips. The after-work crowd in McSorley's forced him to speak loudly. His eyes widened above the curve of the glass's rim. The familiar tan foam left by the stout shivered and popped.

"On her own?"

"By herself." Mike lowered the glass to the tabletop. The book was a thick coffee table volume, hardcover, of photos taken by Bouquet Alonso. Mike had placed it at Aperture, and the book had been taken up—indeed lionized—by the international press. Although now a fashion photographer, Bouquet's earliest pictures were actually taken in war, most famously in Peru with the Sendero Luminoso. With or without her notoriety, Mike would have continued representing her because he so loved how she looked at an object, no matter that it be the ruined corpse of Olegario Curitomay, a *senderista* commander killed and burned by peasants in 1983, or an Alexander McQueen gown modeled in the Japanese garden at the Brooklyn Botanical. He knew that the photo supplied the heat and the full heart of her feelings for what she was witnessing, no matter what it was. The very brief passage of light through the lens compelled her professional life, and the results always thrilled Mike. "It's a fever," she had told him.

"In the end, in Peru, it almost took more than she had." He pointed to the photo of a six year-old in the double page spread open on the table. "This was the last she ever took…of war, I mean." The boy was dressed in ragged sweat pants. "Manolo." He also wore a stained wool jacket and a black wool cap. A long cut above his right eye was scabbed over with fresh blood. Soot from some sort of fire or blast splotched his right cheek and temple. Seated on a wooden chair in what was clearly the doorway of a hut destroyed by fire, he held an empty glass in his right hand.

"And, of course, he's in New York now, too." Mike sipped once more from the glass of beer. "A photographer himself."

A few Peruvian soldiers stood several feet to the side, observing Bouquet as she took the photo. All but one were masked and so heavily armed that the child appeared as the only expression of possible kindness in a scene of brutish devastation. One would have thought that the soldiers were a danger to the boy himself, even though the photo caption explained that he had been saved in the battle that had killed his Sendero Luminoso *comandante* father. The soldiers apparently had pulled Manolo from the burning hut. His mother had also died in the firefight.

Nora surveyed the black-and-white picture. Sighs issued from her.

"Pulitzer Prize," Mike said.

A dead body laid a few feet from the chair, near the soldiers. One soiled bare foot extended from beneath a lumpy sheet of canvas. The canvas was torn and smeared with ragged swatches of dark color. Blood, clearly. The unmasked soldier laughed, preening for the photographer. Manolo was expressionless, yet accusing of the camera, as though it were out to hurt him even more than he already was hurt. A military helicopter surged through the air in the far distance, seemingly etched against one of the peaks, while smoke fumed from different charred objects around the chair, the most identifiable being a gnarled shoe on its side.

"And you say she wants to make a film?"

"She does. She says that this story…" Mike pointed once more at the picture. "That his story is *the* story."

"How so?"

"All the kids running away from war now. So many of them like him."

Nora flipped the pages of the book, toward the front. She stopped at the table of contents page. "But this picture was taken in 1988."

"So?"

"Twenty-six years ago. Times have changed."

"Depends. The Sendero is still in operation."

"They are? But I thought—"

"Just not everywhere in Peru, like it was back then. The country's better now. For kids in general, though, other countries are much worse."

Nora closed the book and turned it over, to look at the picture of Bouquet that took up the entire back cover. In color, it had been taken by Susan Meiselas, also in the 1980s. Bouquet leaned against the front of a badly dented army truck. She was in her mid-twenties and dressed in the kind of romance-laden casualness with which combat photographers often wish to portray themselves. The sleeves of an incredibly wrinkled khaki shirt were rolled up roughly with imprecise bravado. It had cotton epaulets, one of them unbuttoned. She carried a cloth shoulder bag, the repository of additional rolls of film, its strap across her chest. Her cotton pants and combat boots were scuffed and muddied. The red bandana, in which Bouquet had gathered her hair, held only some of it. The rest spilled from around the bandana in bunches of ragged black. She wore no makeup, and her eyes paused on the onlooker's eyes with such peacefulness that they belied the slight, fearful-seeming frown on her lips. Two brass earrings lay against her neck, each one askew as though they were intentionally mocking the two Nikons that hung before her.

"What was she doing?"

"Trying to photograph Abimael Guzmán."

Nora shivered. "The Shining Path guy."

"Yes, and it was difficult."

"Did she succeed?"

"No. Hardly anybody ever did, until they finally captured him. It was too dangerous."

"And Peru, up in the mountains..." Nora re-opened the book to the boy's picture. "That's where she found—"

"Manolo. Yes. She was able to rescue him after his parents were killed. He too is—"

The crowd noise lowered as a slim black-haired woman moved from the door of McSorley's toward Mike's table. She swept through the room, rather than simply walking through it. She seemed averse to noticing the bar crowd, almost all of whom turned to watch her. She treated their interest as though it were completely ignorable.

Dressed in black cargo pants, a red turtleneck sweater, and black tennis shoes, she wore her hair up, abundant, carbon dark, and very fine, secured by a red cotton kerchief. She carried a black leather camera case.

"I'd almost forgotten." Nora grinned as she, too, watched the approaching woman. "She's a fashion photographer."

"Now she is, yes. *Vogue. Harper's Bazaar.* But she told me once that she always felt more in charge of things out in the field."

"War, you mean."

"Right."

"In charge, you say?"

"Completely." Mike stood up, turning toward the approaching woman. "And always, as you'll soon see."

Bouquet was now fifty-four. As she approached, Nora pondered the quality that her face had of roughly achieved knowledge. Bouquet's looks had no Castilian or Mediterranean finesse, and her diminutive stature actually enhanced the way she took over the room as she passed through it. Many of the younger people in the bar muttered to each other in ways that Mike frequently saw, as they wondered, *Who is that...?* Nylon, *isn't that her? What movies...?* Bouquet's smile quieted the crowd.

"Michael."

"Bouquet. So lovely to see you." Mike took Bouquet into his arms. "Would you like a drink?"

Her entire demeanor turned to one of expected, and received, affection. "No, a glass of water, sweetheart. That's all." Nora noted the display. It was actorly, the sort of embrace given by a Hollywood diva receiving a prize for lifetime achievement. Scripted, phony, and self-serving. Hardly affectionate at all.

"And you must be Nora Diamond," Bouquet said.

Bouquet mentioned that she was having a party the following weekend for Mike, and she invited Nora. "A lot of friends. People I think you'll like."

As the elevator ascended to Bouquet's place on Christopher Street, noisy conversation and laughter came from above, closer and louder moment by moment. The elevator door opened directly into her fourth-floor apartment living room and an excited mob of guests. Nora was greeted right away by a waiter with a tray of flutes of champagne. She took one and, holding it carefully as she made her way through the crowd, she suddenly dropped it.

"Oh—"

"That's OK. Don't worry."

When Nora looked up to see who was speaking, she suddenly felt even more embarrassed. His obsidian hair was combed straight back, and he wore a shiny, slim dark brown suit. A small scar marred his forehead like a graceful kris. He took hold of Nora's arm and pulled her a step away from the broken glass. She stumbled and fell against him.

"I'll get it." He knelt, excusing himself to a few of the other guests, to pick up the broken flute, which luckily had not shattered. Its few pieces glittered from his fingers as he stood up. His eyes searched hers. "Stay here, please. I'll get you another."

"Oh, thank you, you don't need—"

He smiled, holding the glass with the very ends of his fingers, careful. "I'm glad to." He turned, but only slightly, thinking better of it for a moment. "What's your name?"

"Nora. What about yours?"

He paused a moment. A smile hurried to his lips. "Nora Diamond?"

"Yes, how did you know?"

"My mother told me about you."

"Oh, so you're—"

"Manolo," he said. "Yes, I'm Manolo."

"My mother." Manolo looked out the window of Nora's office. Combative cabs and delivery trucks glutted Fourteenth Street. A fire engine turned down Broadway, only partially clearing the lanes. It had to bluster its way through the intersection, its sirens and klaxons a pushy chaos. The usual crowd of NYU students and homeless people watched from the plaza before the Union Square subway entrance. "She's a refugee, too."

"From Peru?"

"No, no. Guatemala. She was three."

He took a couple quick portraits of Nora, despite her wish to at least brush her hair and freshen her makeup. Manolo complimented her hair. "The brown in it, the light, the intensities." Nora had been trained in acting at the Actors Studio. But she really preferred being behind the camera to being in front of it. Her self-consciousness before an audience made each attempt at a scene a misstep charged with worry. Her coaches had all thought she resembled Lauren Bacall and had said that her eyes would be her ticket to stardom in films. But it meant little to her in the end. She knew that, as actresses go, she was just way too nervous.

She did not know how to take Manolo's observation, since, his eyes aside, the visual pleasure of his mouth simply startled Nora. Manolo so flustered her with his insistence on taking her picture that she forgot he was in her office to advise her about the screen treatment she was supposed to write, and then, it was to be hoped, the script.

"Her father was the mayor of a little town near Lake Atitlán." Manolo knelt down on one knee across from Nora's desk. He looked through the viewfinder and did not like something in the image. He moved a few feet to his left, Nora's eyes following the camera. Finally, he muttered a profanity and stood up, dropping the Nikon to the couch opposite the office windows. "1963. He was disappeared."

"Who by?"

"The Guatemalan junta. They accused him of being a collaborator with the Indians who were fighting the civil war."

"Was he an Indian?"

"Yes. Tz'utujil. But his wife—Bouquet's mother—was a Ladina. Mixed race Guatemalan, but more Spanish than anything else." Manolo sat down across from Nora. "Bouquet's father was a kind of broker for farm goods."

"He didn't survive the war?"

Manolo frowned, his mouth downturned. "Of course not."

Nora was startled by the disapproval in his tone of voice. "That was a reasonable question."

Manolo was now startled himself. "Excuse me, it's just that—"

"What was so bad about it?"

"Bouquet never recovered. They never found him. He was just...gone."

"And how did she get here?"

"Undocumented. She and her mother crossed over in Arizona, which, fifty years ago, was just as usual as it is now, only not quite in such numbers as now." Manolo fingered the camera, studying it. "She told me that she had always wanted to find out what happened to her father. But, when you get disappeared...you disappear."

"And it's true that she was on her way to a whole career in fashion here in Manhattan before she went to Peru."

"That's right. She assisted everybody...Avedon, Herb Ritts."

"Right out of NYU."

"Yes. But the memory of her father...I mean, that's why she...you know, that's why she left New York back then. That's why she got a job as a stringer journalist. How she found me."

"But why didn't she go back to Guatemala?"

"Too dangerous. Or at least at first she thought so. The American daughter of a political enemy? With a camera in hand? In the eighties, though, the Guatemalan war was one thing, but the Sendero Luminoso was quite another." Manolo made a few adjustments to the camera. "She found the worst."

Manolo's face was seamed and weathered around the eyes. Nora knew why. Bouquet had told her at McSorley's about her adopted son, that he, too, was a photographer of pillage and war. Libya, early in his career, with the rebels hunting down Muammar Gaddafi. Gaza. Afghanistan. A freelancer on his own.

"I worry it was my influence on him," Bouquet told her at McSorley's.

With the utterance, her eyes turned toward the floor, the first sign of insecurity on her part that Nora was to see, although there would be many more later. "That, you know..." Bouquet fell silent a moment. "That he loves war because of me."

For Nora, Manolo's eyes indeed purveyed a fascination with violence. But she sensed that what he had seen had hurt him. He took up the camera once more and stood over her at the side of the desk, so that a partial view of Fourteenth Street out a window would form the backdrop to her portrait.

"I stopped a moment ago because the picture was going to be too formal."

"High school yearbook."

"That's right. Too composed."

Nora hurried to adjust her hair, caught out of balance. She was excited.

"You've got to let chance..." Manolo snapped the picture. "You know, luck. It's everything, and you've got to let it..." And then several more, very quickly. "Even though it can do you harm." With each exposure, Nora felt the more fevered intensity of his attention to her. He took another. "I remember that day, for instance, when she found me." And another.

"What happened?"

Manolo lowered the camera. "She got me out of there."

"She saved you."

"Yeah, well..." He fumbled with the camera, studying its surfaces. "Maybe."

"Does she think she saved you?"

"Yes."

"And you don't."

Manolo put the camera down on the couch and glanced out the window.

Nora recalled something that Mike Levin had told her the day after the party. Already her attraction to Manolo was overtaking her. Manolo had asked if she would meet him for dinner the following evening, and she had had to remember the true state of things, that this was to be a professional relationship, that there was much else at stake: a big story, a possible film.

She phoned Mike the next morning to ask him about it.

"I'm glad you called. He's known for…for…." Mike's voice lightened, in the way that Nora knew was the preamble to a joke or some humorous shared secret.

"What, Mike?"

"Women, they seem to—"

"To fall in love with him?"

Mike's silence—an assent—caused Nora to hurry her next question.

"Many women?"

"I don't know how many, but—"

"And how does he treat them?"

"Superbly, I understand. Superbly, for a while."

"Then what"

"Getty Images calls him, and he ends up in, in—"

"Somalia."

"Yes, or some other place just like it."

"And the girlfriend?"

"She does not accompany him to Somalia."

"I see."

Again there was silence. But this time, Nora sensed that Mike was about to ask her a question, and she knew what it would be.

"I care for him, Mike."

"Already?"

"Yes."

"Well, keep it buttoned up for a while, Nora…please." She heard his walking across the floor of his office, and sitting down at his desk. "Can you?"

Nora's mouth twitched as she tried putting aside her disappointment.

"It's business."

"I know, Mike. I just want to see if—"

"Try, Nora. Please."

Nora descended the station stairs to Queens Boulevard. This stretch of the 7 Line was the only thing she really cared for in Long Island City because the stations here were elevated, even though, during winter, they were subject to polar winds coming up from the East River. They were also uniformly rust-laden and so long ago painted that, standing on the platform of one of them, Nora felt that she had slipped back into the battered leavings of a previous New York's charm. She loved the rattle and shaking of the stations when the trains passed through.

Otherwise in Long Island City, the old warehouses and factories reminded her of aged aircraft carriers beached everywhere, one after the other. Now, at least, many of them were converted to uses other than those that vanished when industry left New York City fifty years ago. These days, instead of men in work clothes punching in and out of factories that manufactured Swingline staplers or Dentyne Chiclets gum, start-up software geeks, grubby artists and youthful filmmakers, independent publishers, electronic rock 'n' roll bands, and rising fashion designers formed the usual trade. A plaque among many others in the entry to one of these buildings read "Bouquet Alonso" and nothing else, except for the information that her studio was in number 3-56.

Nora ascended a wide wooden stairway, which she assumed was original to the building. A white hallway stretched the length of the third floor a hundred yards or so. Painted iron doors broke up the blank walls every fifty feet, each one with a sign identifying the business inside.

Bouquet was in the middle of a shoot when Nora arrived. She had been commissioned by *Nylon* to do the photography for a big piece on Williamsburg, Brooklyn. A half-dozen teenagers stood around in the studio, dressed in the intentionally beat-up clothing that was the standard for fashion among the youth at the moment. Two skateboards were stashed upright in a corner near the door. One of them had a stylish porkpie hat lodged on its front tip. Nora knew that the monosyllabic talk and similar rag-tag inelegance of all the photo subjects belied the fact that, for the very young crowd, some of them were no doubt quite famous for something. Feeling a little jaded and elderly despite the fact that she was only thirty-two, she said hello to everyone. She felt quite a bit out of it, guilty that she had been listening to one of her favorite Prince albums on the subway, rather than to one of the streamed, indecipherable indie cuts to which these kids had been listening. She set up her laptop on a worktable, to watch as Bouquet did the shoot.

Mike was right. Bouquet was inviolable in her orders to the kids who were modeling. The stylist—a young redhead named Marge, herself dressed in retro punk black and jewelry that appeared made for self-harming, who was clearly from somewhere in the South—Texas, maybe, Nora guessed—simply said "Okay" to every instruction from Bouquet and then did what she was told. She did venture an opinion now and again about how to place some object in a shot, but rarely got a consenting response. The hair guy, De'ron, whose name Nora recognized from other spreads that Bouquet had done, was a gay, twenty year-old Jamaican, quite beautiful, whose fingers working the hair between shots reminded Nora of tentacles hurried back and forth by nervous waters.

Bouquet, in black tights, a black T-shirt, and black boots, moved the models around in the same way that she moved objects around, expecting no more objection to her wishes than she got from the flowers or the lighting.

Two hours later, she placed a glass of water on the table next to the Aperture book, which was open to the photo of Manolo. The water glimmered, evanescent silver. Nora had many questions about the picture, although she was as interested in what Bouquet was doing at the moment as she was in the view of the little boy. Bouquet was curating the images of an actress named Winter. The exceptionally white dress that Winter was wearing, from Alexander Wang, reminded Nora of layered whipped cream.

At one point during the shoot, Winter had broken down, weeping.

"What's wrong with you, pretty?" Bouquet's hand rested on her waist. The Nikon hung from her neck, swinging back and forth across her stomach in a disapproving nod. Bouquet had been shooting quickly, a photo every few seconds. Riffling tears now glowed down Winter's cheeks. She wiped them away, but more came.

"Why can't you do it?"

"Bouquet! I can too do it!"

"You're not." Bouquet turned toward a worktable, shaking her head.

"Oh—"

"You're not! So, come on!"

The session continued for another hour, Winter's feelings hurt the whole time.

Two hours later, Nora sat next to Bouquet as the photographer hurried through the several hundred pictures of Winter that she had taken. The quick flashes of color from the computer screen were gone so quickly one to the next that Nora could barely concentrate on any individual image.

"Mike told me that you always like to be in charge."

Bouquet smiled, although not taking her eyes from the photos marching past.

"That you're the boss."

"He's right. Luck—you can't depend on luck."

"Why not?"

"Just because you happen to be there at the moment and can get the shot…there's no craft to that. No expertise. It's just a snapshot."

"Robert Capa at Normandy?"

"What about him?"

"That blurred shot of the soldier in the water?"

"A snapshot."

"Or his famous one, of Picasso, Françoise, and the umbrella on the beach?"

"Staged. Beautifully designed."

Nora shrugged, a personal acknowledgment of Bouquet's assertiveness. "But this picture of Manolo…" Nora pointed to the book. "It wasn't staged, was it?"

Bouquet, her attention interrupted, looked hurriedly at the boy who sat so calmly on the chair, and at the shoe. "It clearly was."

"But you wouldn't say that you manipulated *him,* would you?"

"Well, there were circumstances."

"What circumstances?"

"None of your business, Nora."

The procession of Winter photos started up again, now almost a blur. But Nora knew that she had Bouquet's attention. She felt it in the very mention of her own name, as Bouquet had pronounced it with considerable irritation. Nora also knew that eventually—now—she would insist that Bouquet cease this one-sided ordering of the conversation.

"We'll want to tell about those circumstances in the script."

Bouquet did not respond.

"Bouquet?"

Bristling, Bouquet busied herself, taking notes about one of the studio photos.

Nora waited, but only for a moment. "Does Manolo visit your studio?"

"Almost never." Bouquet lowered her head. The reflected white from Winter's Alexander Wang shined, the resplendence causing Bouquet's face to pale. "He thinks it's frivolous..." She shrugged and turned toward Nora. "...what I do." Bouquet's photographs of the young actress and her dress, even without any corrections, elevated the girl's disappointment-laden beauty so much that Nora could not imagine a senior editor passing her over for a cover shoot. "He thinks that *I'm* frivolous."

"What would he prefer that you do?"

Bouquet examined the photo of Manolo. "Once, a few years ago when I was worrying out loud to him about his going to...where was it? Fallujah... he told me about this picture, and what it means to him."

"What did he say?"

"That because of what happened here..." Bouquet caressed the photograph. "He could barely do anything else. He...he—"

"Loves the picture that much?" Nora adjusted the book before her, lowering her head over the image.

"He hates it."

Nora felt her heart turn, a tight fluttering, a discovery.

"Because of what happened there that day." Bouquet's lips tightened. "He said that what he does...his own work.... He used the English word. 'Exorcise.' You know that word...yes?"

Nora realized that the little boy in the photo had been crying. The tracks of dried tears formed flattened, obscured trails through the soot on his cheek. "But, he doesn't...he doesn't hate you."

"I—"

"I'm sure he hates what happened there that day."

"Of course. He wants it to be gone."

"But it wasn't your fault."

"Nora, I know something more about what happened that day than you do."

"What's that?"

Bouquet shook her head, took the mouse into her right hand and erased the picture of Winter from the screen. "The details. And that, as luck would have it, I caused it."

"But what's it like?" The glass of wine before Nora was motionless, the surface of the blood-red liquid reflecting the flames from the candles. She barely heard anything else in the room, a flourishing Manhattan bistro.

"You have to imagine what that kind of market looks like before the explosion," Manolo said. "People everywhere. Laughter. Sunlight. Noise."

He paused, searching the rest of his story.

"And especially the wares…all displayed under a cloth pavilion or cover, to protect them from the sun. Dolma. Falafel. Tomatoes. All piled up on tables, in perfect order. Olives. Spices. Pomegranates. Figs. Such display!" He grinned. "It's all celebration."

"And then—"

"The suicide idiot arrives, and—"

"Everything disappears."

"No. Not at all. But nothing is the same. It's all still there, but scattered by the blast. Sandals. Smoke. Screaming. Part of a head…an arm…." The intensity of Manolo's voice sharpened as he sipped from his wine. He frowned. "And I take the picture."

"What's that like?"

"The carnal instant. But when you actually see the market after one of those attacks, you see the continuance of life. Suddenly there are people everywhere. Survivors. The wounded."

Nora laid her hand on Manolo's across the table.

"Life is still moving, Nora," Manolo lowered his eyes, surveying their joined fingers. "Still terrifying…like always."

They had pulled him from the hut and, years later, all Manolo could remember from the inside of the building was his own screaming at his mother, Yulitza. She had hidden him across the hut from the doorway, in a corner, in a kind of close bunker that she had thrown together made up of the three mattresses on which the family had all been sleeping. She continued talking with him as she gathered clips of ammunition toward her, on the piece of canvas on which she lay against the interior front wall of the hut, peeking out the doorway. *"No te preocupas, mi Manolito, mi amor."* She waved a hand at him. "Stay down. Stay hidden." The noise of the firefight terrified him and, sheltered within the mattresses, he held two old pillows around his head. But after the explosion—the instantaneous burst—he heard no more from his mother. He struggled from between the mattresses, and despite the smoke's gagging him and the fire all around, he crawled to her on his hands and knees.

Yulitza lay still. Parts of her were on fire. Smoke buffeted him. Manolo now most clearly remembered the sound of his own voice then, the high shrill of it, and his coughing as he pleaded with his mother to wake up. He pounded his fists against her back, but she did not respond. One of the soldiers grabbed him by the collar of the jacket and dragged him out of the hut, into the cold. The woman with the camera was snapping pictures as he continued screaming, trying to pull himself from the soldier's grasp. Yulitza, so silent and motionless in the chaos and fire, remained in the hut as, moments later, its roof collapsed on her.

Manolo didn't know what had happened to his father.

A few minutes later, three of the soldiers picked their way through the ragged embers of the hut's interior, and pulled Manolo's mother from the wreckage by her ankles. Away from the wreckage, they tossed the piece of canvas over her. The canvas was splotched red, a large, shapeless swatch of it, gray with ash. They wouldn't let the boy approach it. When he tried to get away from them, they threatened him, telling him that his mother was dead. "Leave her alone, *chico. No se la puede ayudar, la puta."*

The vivid dream—the exacting dream, so accurate and precise a re-enactment of the flames and the cold—jolted from Manolo into the unlit bedroom. It was the dream he most often had. *No se la puede ayudar, la puta.* The utterance was a repeated thought, a few times a day, every day.

She can't be helped... *Mami. Despiértate mami...por favor.* The whore. Wake up, mommy, please. He struck out at the dream, and the unseen water glass on the table next to him, luckily empty, shattered against the wall behind the bed table.

Nora awoke, frightened. "Manolo. Manolo, please."

He couldn't answer, driven by the images of the fire, his mother's burning clothing, and the clicking of the camera shutter over and over, like tiny stabbings from an unsharpened pin.

"What's wrong?" Nora said.

He didn't speak, still surrounded. But when Nora took him into her arms, fully awakening him, he realized that he was safe and that she was with him. But others had been with him too, women who had been frightened by the dream...by his dreams. The dreams always intruded. He worried that he might actually put whoever was with him in danger, and attack her in his sleep, fearful that she was attacking him. Intimacy, especially the kind already being sought by Nora, would require that he suffer even more, that he share the dreams with her. But they drove him crazy, and Manolo didn't want to force those images on anyone else. Especially Nora. Fear like that...flesh like his mother's....

A few weeks before she headed into the higher Andes, Bouquet had lunch in Cuzco with a *Time* magazine reporter who was doing a story on the Sendero Luminoso. He wanted to speak with her because she was known to be having more success in talking with the terrorist group than almost any other journalist. The old Spanish colonial hotel in which they met, on Calle San Agustín, had a few tables in one corner of the covered walkway that surrounded the hotel garden. The place settings appeared to her to be from the nineteenth century. The tables and chairs were designed from hand-hewn wood with heavy Andes charm, while the fine white linen tablecloths and napkins, according to the waiter, were from Argentina, the glassware of contemporary Spanish crystal.

Bouquet avoided giving information to other journalists. She was lucky with her contacts in Peru, mainly, she knew, because she always made a point of telling them how she had lost her father. His having been disappeared was evidence to the Sendero that Bouquet might favor them, instead of the government, in this civil war.

The Sendero people were never easy to deal with. But because Bouquet was herself a victim of a raptor-like regime, they occasionally would at least talk with her.

Bouquet had almost no memory of her father. Two photos of him were in a cardboard box in storage in New York City. In one of them, Bouquet herself, a year old and dressed in white lace, sat on his lap. The posed picture, taken in a studio in Sololá, a town across Lake Atitlán from their own town, showed him as a small dark-skinned man in a black suit, white shirt and black tie. Bouquet's mother had told her that the picture wasn't a very good one because Aurelio had been so nervous in front of the camera. "He didn't like it staring at him like that, *mi'ja,*" she said. "Such a kind-hearted man." The straight hair had the same tone of black that his suit and tie had. "He was always so sweet to you, *querida.*" Bouquet's own pose had a similar stoicism, the white of the lace nonetheless a suggestion of happiness.

Otherwise, her father, Aurelio, did not exist for her. For Bouquet, his having been disappeared had led her into adulthood almost empty of wishes, except for those still granted to her in so kindly a way by her mother before she too died. Her mother had often told her that worry over Aurelio's fate caused the almost constant cruelty of her dreams. Both women shared a sensibility for destruction and absence.

The Sendero Luminoso expressed its political ideals through sabotage and assassination, so it seemed important to Bouquet that she operate alone. She did not want to endanger anyone else, but mostly she did not wish to jeopardize her own life. If the Sendero could trust her to always show up alone and never share her information with anyone, she could get the interview when her colleagues could not.

"But Abimael?" The *Time* correspondent—Joe Ackroyd—shook his head. He was long-boned and drooped, in his mid-forties, clearly no fun, his old forest-green shirt showing the evidence of spattered sauce or wine that had not come out in the wash. An American had been assassinated by the Sendero a few weeks before, the first such American. Constantin

Gregory was just twenty-five, working in agriculture with Peruvian farmers. Joe had approached the U.S. State Department for their reaction, the killing of Constantin being a "game changer," as he put it. He then came to Peru to interview some of the Sendero Luminoso.

Right away Bouquet knew that Joe would have little chance with the Sendero because he could barely speak Spanish, and had no Quechua at all. Your language condemned you, as far as the Sendero was concerned, and the Indian language was their usual. If you were Spanish-speaking only, and wanted to be a *senderista,* you had to learn Quechua. Those who did speak Spanish—even those like Bouquet who spoke it as their own native tongue—could dangle for months awaiting an interview, as she had dangled, held very far away by the Sendero's distrust of everyone. Bouquet had set out right away, the week a few years ago that she had arrived in Peru, to learn enough Quechua to get by with the Indians, and had succeeded...at least with those Indians who were not themselves *senderistas.*

Joe did not know much about the Sendero or, for that matter, Peru or South America. The first fifteen minutes over coffee was spent on his effort to figure out which journalists from which organizations he and Bouquet knew in common. But she didn't want Joe to know anything about her. She knew that he had spent time in the Vietnam War, and she had actually read a little of the one book he had written, that he had delivered to her hotel. His writing was notable for its straightforward plainness, which usually is okay in journalism. But Joe wrote the way he dressed, with scruffy carelessness. He had trouble with how to tell a story, even admitting to Bouquet, as though it were a badge of special favor, that "editors were put on this earth to clean up what I'm too busy to fix." In that book, he wrote about the Da Nang airport during the American abandonment of that city in March 1975. One of the last American journalists to be flown out, he was almost abandoned with the thousands of South Vietnamese who had fled to the airport, and then indeed *were* abandoned.

The one name that Bouquet should not have shared with him was that of Abimael Guzmán. Few people had seen Abimael during the previous decade. Bouquet, who did not have the cachet of a connection with an organization like *Time,* felt momentarily jealous of Joe's insistent name-dropping. He luxuriated for Bouquet over the various international correspondents he knew personally. She had met a few of them, and none had paid much attention to her.

She finally interrupted him to ask whether any of these had ever talked with Abimael.

"Have you?" Joe laid the *medialuna* that he had been eating, broken in half, in a basket on the table.

"I'm working on it."

He took up a dollop of honey in a small spoon and placed it in his mouth. Right away, Bouquet cursed herself for her admission. It had just broken away from her. She tightened her lips, fuming at the cup of coffee on the table before her.

Joe licked a splotch of honey from his thumb. "Tell me."

"No."

"You already did, though."

"You just have to forget about that, Joe."

"Forget it!" Joe broke out laughing, a noise that drew the attention of a few other people at other tables. "Abimael?"

A few weeks later, awaiting Abimael with Javier and Yulitza, Bouquet worried whether Joe had shared with anyone what she had blurted out to him. Her deepening suspicion, that he must have, besieged her.

Manolo went back to sleep. Nora lay awake. She had known him for just three weeks. Manolo had inherited from Bouquet the worldly irony with which she went about everything. He was humorous, very self-deprecating and funny when alone with Nora, well mannered with almost old-world reserve, and, to Nora's growing chagrin, distant. Nora worried that, for some reason, Manolo felt she couldn't be trusted. He greeted her with the same deference with which he greeted others. He was a companion, nice to be with, easy with conversation...and evasive, even, to her wonderment, after they became lovers.

A few days before, he had admitted that he was falling in love with her.

"Oh, Manolo. But please, we need—" The few patrons passing by them in the Café Sabarsky, at the Neue Gallerie, spoke in whispers, quietly respectful of the Viennese aplomb of the place, and generally stunned by the art they had just been viewing from one room to the next. “We need…” The electricity in her heart, the way that simply touching him took her breath, made her worry that she was already asking too much. It was way too soon, and she didn’t want to lose him. “Honesty…“ Her breathing stumbled.

“I’m dishonest?”

“Of course not. But I want to know what’s…” She laid a hand against his chest. “In here—”

“I’ve told you, haven’t I?”

“For me.”

“Nora.”

“More than that. I want to know what frightens you, Manolo. What your heart wishes for. Anything that stands in your way.”

“Nothing stands…. What are you talking about?”

Nora explained to him that she felt excluded from—

“Excluded!”

That she didn’t know much about this man who was now telling her he loved her. “I want to learn what I’m supposed to love in return?”

His anger brought the conversation to an end, and it took another hour, spent walking around in Central Park, for the couple to begin conversing once again. But the reserve returned. The kindness, the pleasantry…leaving Nora astonished by Manolo’s obvious intention to keep her out of his heart.

Now, though, with this dream of his, she felt she had found a way in. Manolo shivered as she held him. Still half-asleep and still half in the dream, he called out in Spanish, short bursts of words that Nora did not understood. The one English word was *stop.* Riven through with fear, he tried to pull away from her, until she was able to calm him.

The following morning, he left after a single cup of coffee, embracing Nora.

“But, Manolo, what was the dream?“

“I’ll call you later.”

“Manolo.”

“I’ll call you.”

In the brash, uninhibited light of the hallway, he glanced back at Nora, throwing on his jacket as he strode away, his eyes seeking commiseration even as he was in the midst of an escape.

Bouquet, covered over by a stained blanket, dozed in the hammock that Yulitza had given her. Her heavy jacket did little to ease the high mountain cold that enveloped her. Such cold—worsened by the thin air—made her ill, as though she had eaten long-ago sullied meat. Her stomach felt encased with fever.

Startled by the sound of breaking twigs, she glanced out the door of the hut. Javier—fear propelling him toward the road—ran from the other hut, an AK-47 held in his right hand. He was rocked back by automatic rifle fire from somewhere, his body flailing from the stone-filled footpath down which he had been running. Like a blood-spilling rag, he hurtled a few yards down the moraine slope. The rifle clattered across the rocks as well, leaving Javier silent and twisted, one leg bent beneath the other, face up. Rifle fire came from the hut, and Bouquet hurried from the hammock. She took up the two Nikons, flung their straps around her neck, and stepped toward the doorway, dropping to one knee. Ricocheting bullets scraped the other hut, and more answering automatic rifle fire burst from the doorway. Lying down, Bouquet started shooting pictures.

A masked soldier, bent over and scurrying along the front of the hut across the road, tossed a grenade through the doorway. He fell down and covered his ears. The grenade exploded, and thereafter no more rifle fire came from the hut. Immediately, Bouquet heard a child's high voice. Flames took the roof, and the anguish of the boy's outcries, so clear to Bouquet, caused her to crawl from the doorway where she was hiding herself. She rose to her knees, still shooting pictures.

"Mami, despiértate..." The voice formed a sharp seam in the noise of the flames.

"You!" From the end of her hut, a soldier shouted at Bouquet. He pointed his rifle at her.

"¡Soy prensa!" She held a camera in the air. *"¡Por favor!"*

"Don't care who you are, bitch. Stay down."

A moment later, the soldier, bent over as he approached her, grabbed the back of her jacket. "Get up." He pushed her toward the hut, which was now being approached by several other soldiers. Smoke swirled across the road. The soldier struck Bouquet from behind with the flat of his rifle stock. He was using her as a kind of shield. Two others stood a moment in silent apprehension outside the doorway, their backs to the stone facade. They were waiting, listening, and signaled finally to the others to approach.

The single voice continued. "*¡Mami!*"

"Press, eh?" The soldier nudged Bouquet. "Okay, get out the camera."

She did not respond.

"Get it out."

She stumbled as he pushed her forward. Bouquet ran a few steps toward the hut, taking up one of the Nikons. Two soldiers ran through the doorway. Bouquet realized that Yulitza's defense had been an attempt to protect her son. The child's voice rose up. Bouquet understood the foolishness of that return fire, and of Yulitza's desperation.

She knelt down and began shooting once more.

They pulled Manolo from the hut. A thick, empty water glass was in his hand. He looked back, trying to turn his body, turning his head, straining to see. "*¡Mami!*"

Bouquet lowered the camera. She wished to gather the boy into her arms.

"Take pictures."

She could not. She couldn't force the camera to her face. The boy's eyes shivered, savaged with fear.

"Take pictures!"

She did, terrified that the soldier would kill her if she refused. Another soldier brought a chair from the hut, and forced the boy to sit on it. He brought a few other things—a half-burnt pair of pants, a shoe—and threw them down to the ground next to the boy. Bouquet continued shooting, changing the rolls of film one after another.

"Hurry up."

She shot the shoe. She shot the glass. Stepping forward and back, going down on a knee, standing up, side to side, she could not stop shooting. They pulled Yulitza's body from the shack, its lower extremities broken and the source of smoke. Tossing her to the ground, they covered her with a piece of canvas also brought from the hut. Bouquet kept shooting. Even the soldier seemed surprised by the avidity with which she framed the photos of Yulitza in death, and tripped the shutter again and again. The very sound of the shutter excited her. She argued with herself over the correct angle, the set-up of each shot, the way to make each one unique.

"Nora?"

"Hello, Manolo."

"I want to see you."

For a moment, silence stifled the conversation.

"All right. When?"

Again, there was silence. Nora was hurt. Manolo had not called since he had had the dream, which had occurred a few nights before.

"How about now?" he said.

"Where?"

"My place."

When the lobby security guard phoned upstairs, Nora worried that Manolo would not allow her to come up. But then, when the man nodded to her and pointed to the elevator bank—"Fifth floor, Miss"—her anxiety actually worsened. How would he greet her?

His apartment, on Fifty-seventh Street near the Art Students League, was larger than Nora had expected. The furnishings were actually ordered and luxurious, a surprise to her when she considered the frightening stories he had told her about his work, in so plain spoken a way. One portion of the living room was furnished as an office. Several bookshelves met each other in a corner, and they sheltered a dark wood table on which Manolo's laptop, cell phone, iPad, and printer were accompanied by a few notebooks. A single photograph, a portrait of a young man that had clearly been taken a century before, rested framed on the table.

"Béla Bartók," Manolo said as Nora took up the framed picture to look at it. "He lived in this building."

"You know about him?"

Manolo smiled. "A little. Strange music."

"Then why—"

"He was brave…artistically, I mean. He wasn't intimidated." Manolo gestured at the rest of the living room. "Please look around. I'll bring coffee."

Nora circled the living room. This was the first time she had been here, and she was taken by Manolo's considerable taste. The room was of Mediterranean color in the drapes and furniture, filled with Spanish poppy reds, Provence yellows and browns, and sea-light sun-imbued blues. Two small David Hockney lithographs, of trees striving for light in an English park, formed the centerpiece tableau of a wall filled with photographs, all in color, all signed by Manolo Alonso. They showed scenes of families caught in desert strife, women—in what reminded Nora of medieval dress—running from war, men in a street declaiming for the camera, dirty children weeping, surprised by the camera…. For Nora, each photograph was notable for its almost Vermeer-like grace, surprising to her when she considered the violence to which, surely, all of the subjects were reacting.

Nora sat down on the sofa. The coffee table had books on it devoted to photos of war, by Gerda Taro and Sebastian Junger.

"I apologize," Manolo said as he brought Nora her cup of coffee. "I know we're not here to talk about Béla Bartók." He moved to sit down across the table.

"What about your fear, then?" Nora waited as he paused next to her, still standing. He remained silent. "What was the dream, Manolo?"

Manolo glanced at Nora with, as before, a look of having been captured. But he continued sitting down, fingering the cup of coffee and the saucer before him. Nora sensed with considerable worry that he was contemplating how, indeed, to continue his escape.

"All right. I'll show you." He stood and walked to the shelves. He brought out Bouquet's Aperture book and, leaning over the table, opened it to the picture. Nora had known, immediately, that that particular photo was the object of his thumbing through the volume. She had waited. The picture was one thing, and she had studied every object in it very closely, many times. But Nora hoped that Manolo's explanation of his feelings would finally explain the reality of the picture to her, in some way more than the image itself could possibly do.

"This is the dream."

"Just the moment, that particular—"

"Yes. The moment right here." Manolo tapped the image with an index finger. "The half-hour that preceded it, too...and that followed it."

"Yulitza's death."

"Yes, and my father's. The explosion." Manolo pointed to the ground next to the chair in which he was sitting. "His shoe. The hut, before...before it all.... The fire, and..." Manolo looked away, taking in a breath. "After."

"And the fear?"

"The camera. Bouquet right there in front of me. The sound of it." Manolo turned the corner of the page up, caressing it, before laying it back down. He studied the photograph. "I hated that sound."

"Even with everything else going on?"

He exhaled. "It's what I remember the most, that sound." He kept his eyes on the photo. Nora studied the fatigue and unhappiness with which he viewed it, the impatience. "And it's the one reality in that entire moment that's not in the picture itself."

Nora took in a breath. "Except for Bouquet."

"What?"

Nora passed the backs of the fingers of her left hand across the image. "She's not here."

"Of course not. She's taking the—"

"She's not in your dream."

Manolo's back seemed to buckle. He lowered his head. "I wouldn't... No, that's not—"

"Bouquet herself isn't anywhere." Nora exhaled.

"Yes, but I mean—"

"She isn't, Manolo. You've taken her out entirely. The shutter might be there, but you've edited Bouquet out." She took up the book from the table, leaned back on the sofa, and laid the book on her lap. "And that isn't fair."

Manolo sat back, his eyes in sudden commiserative surprise. "It's also not true, Nora." He ceased speaking. But his glance at Nora suggested to her that he was not about to leave for some place like Somalia without her, at least not right this minute. "She's everywhere in this picture. And what she got here…my whole life….” The promise of probable abandonment, of which his silence for the last days had convinced her, fell away. “Nora…” He leaned forward and placed his elbows on his knees, joining his hands together. “She got it all.” He looked up at her once more and took her hand. “Nora, I….”

“You don't know him well enough to love him.” Bouquet, in her studio later that same day, could feel the movement of her own eyes, the quick, annoyed wavering of them. “How much could you possibly love him?”

But right away, the tone of her voice eased. She knew that Nora was sympathetic with her worry for Manolo, and Bouquet welcomed the commiseration. But she also knew that she herself never got the kind of love from him that Nora was getting, judging from the way Nora's eyes brightened with the mention of his name.

“You don't know him. These children…” Bouquet grimaced. “Us.”

“Don't change the subject.”

“The subject of what?”

“This conversation. The subject is you, Bouquet. It's not me, or that I'm in love with Manolo. Or ‘us’, as you put it, some worldwide trek of ruined children. The subject is you.”

Bouquet swallowed.

“It is, isn't it?”

Bouquet strove for her usual emotional cover, the sturdiness of it. But she also knew, indeed had always known, that all that arrogance was just a playact. “I'm afraid, Nora. For him.” Bouquet took in a breath. *How many times has Nora seen the terror that still so surges through him?* “For his safety.”

Nora had told Bouquet about the nightmare and Manolo's retreat down the hallway the following morning. And her conversation with Manolo in his apartment. So Bouquet knew that Nora had seen the terror at least that one time, while it had appeared dozens of times in Bouquet's raising of the boy. Hundreds. And the wish for escape. Manolo owed Bouquet his life, and Bouquet felt that that responsibility caused him to flee from her.

“I've asked him so often to stop this.” The self-congratulation with which Bouquet had first entered McSorley's a month earlier had disappeared entirely. "Because of what happened to me. But he's obsessed." Bouquet reached forward and caressed Nora's cheek. "You are in love with him, aren't you?"

Nora nodded.

"That makes me happy, Nora."

Nora tried imagining the act of taking that picture in the Peruvian Andes. She didn't know which story of childhood escape she was more compelled to tell. For her, Bouquet's was—Nora was surprised to discover—the sadder of the two, especially in its silent isolation. The decision to go to Peru had been made from her wish to discover the kinds of conditions that had killed her father. But its method—pursuing the Shining Path—had been so dangerous that it seemed to Nora to have been in some way even suicidal.

Suicide that did not succeed.

At first, for Nora, the story in the photo had been conveyed entirely in the split second observance of the moment before the hut, in the painfulness of Manolo's stoical sitting on the chair. But she knew now that that was not the entire story. Manolo's plight in the picture was just one hint to what was forming in his heart. To who he was now. What Bouquet had been feeling was invisible to Nora, hidden within the shocking calm of the picture itself. So, sitting before Bouquet, Nora wanted to know what it was, from the image in the book, that would tell Bouquet's story.

At McSorley's, Bouquet had described for Mike and Nora how, when the soldiers brought Manolito from the hut, she wanted simply to run to him and hold him. To kiss him. She loved him already, and the brutality of what he had gone through a moment before allowed him now to take over her heart.

But Bouquet's further confession, that the pictures she was getting that day had been as important to her...in the midst of all the small arms fire, the grenade's explosion and the instantaneous silencing of Yulitza's love for her little boy.... When Bouquet so suddenly realized that she was ashamed of herself for memorializing what was taking place, she stopped shooting. The soldier, buffeting her back with the rifle stock, compelled her to keep going, and it was then that hatred for the pictures began driving her heart. But she continued, desire and mortification battling each other, all to the sound of her shutter clicking over and over.

"My heart was beating. I couldn't stop, Nora. He was there. His mother...gone. Violence everywhere. I felt enveloped by the...I had to keep going, you see, to take the pictures, to..." In the fever of the moment, Manolo himself was of little importance.

"Were you taking advantage of Manolo?"

"...to display the destruction."

"Were you?"

"Of course. And he's punished me for it."

"How?"

"He won't stop."

"Doing what?"

"Going out there and taking those pictures himself."

"I don't—"

"Doing what I did. I've told you what it was like when I found him."

"Not the entirety of it."

Bouquet grimaced. "It's difficult to hear."

Nora waited.

"Abimael never showed up, of course."

"But what happened?" Nora said. "How did the army know?"

"They just knew." Bouquet leaned forward, waving a hand before her. "Intelligence. Someone told them." She grimaced. "I don't know. The *Time* guy, maybe."

"The picture, *puta.*"

Manolo sat on the chair outside the destroyed hut. The soldier—the only one of the dozen who had attacked the site to be unmasked—prodded her with an index finger.

"Take it."

"No."

"Why not? You took plenty before." Despite his youth, the soldier's jowls were begrimed sacks. His teeth were brown and yellow. His left hand, which did not have a black glove on it, as did the other, was creased with dirt, the fingernails especially, which were broken. It gripped the stock of his M16, which was pointed at the ground.

"But what about Manolito?" Bouquet said.

"Who's that?"

She nodded toward the boy. "Him."

Manolo's right hand rested on the back of the chair as he looked to his right, at the crumpled ridges of the canvas that covered his mother.

Another of the soldiers called out. *"¡Eh, perucho!"* Bouquet recognized the term, one Peruvian man haling another, which in a pejorative tone could be a mild insult. Because this man was masked, she could not tell whether he meant the insult seriously or as a kind of joke. "Leave her be." Another soldier, equally masked, stood by, watching. Others wandered around the site, turning over old boards, looking into Bouquet's hut. The truck that had just arrived was still running, its driver watching the confrontation between the *perucho* and Bouquet. Unmasked, he too was amused by the conversation, as though Bouquet deserved disrespect, but was also undeserving of the other man's particularly gruff treatment.

Bouquet wondered, was there an officer anywhere? Was the *perucho* an officer? Was anyone in charge?

"Take a picture of the kid."

"No."

Perucho turned toward Manolo. "You. Boy. Look at her."

Manolo, confused and clearly terrified, did not know what to do. Perucho gestured toward Bouquet. "Look at her!"

Manolo did so, although with a look of deadening disinterest. There was no fear in his face. Bouquet sensed that he barely knew where he was.

"La foto, chica." Perucho reached for Bouquet's hair and grabbed it, pulling her back. "Do it now."

Bouquet lifted one of the Nikons to her eye and began the adjustments for the photo. Perucho held on to her hair, his clutching of it like pulling tough grass from dry ground.

"Don't touch me."

Perucho laughed. Lowering the camera, Bouquet saw that none of the others was going to intervene. Even the truck driver now stepped forward.

His eyes sparkled. Knowing she was surrounded, Bouquet took up the camera. She looked toward Manolo, whose eyes widened with renewed fear, even more so than when the soldiers had dragged him from the hut by his shirt. She offered the boy a pained smile, for a second or so, no longer. She could not tell whether Manolo actually saw it.

She adjusted the focus, framed the picture, and took it.

Perucho pulled at her hair again, then stripped the second camera from her neck, the strap breaking away. Holding on to it, he released her hair and reached for the front of her shirt, ripping a few of the buttons away, exposing the undershirt beneath.

Later, Bouquet, lying on the dirt floor of her hut, turned toward the wall, her eyes closed against the bloodied pain down her legs. She struggled with one hand to find her pants, which were strewn on the floor behind her. The smells of smoke and offal in the shack caused her to gag. The tears that flooded her cheeks felt enflamed. The severed strap of the Nikon that they had taken was caught around her neck, and she pulled it loose the better to breathe. Outside, the truck's motor turned over, blurring the soldiers' shouts as they tumbled into the back. She heard the cluttered noise of weapons tossed aside on the truck bed, the laughter from the soldiers, about her tight *conchita,* about the blood, man, did you see it? About her big tits, no? *"¡Epa chicos! ¡Qué perrita!"*

The truck pulled away, leaving the huts behind, the only sounds after a while coming from the far away, descending truck engine and the cold wind.

Bouquet wept. She hurt. The cuts and blows she had suffered. Her flayed back. Her bruised neck. Everything.

Footsteps stopped in the doorway. She cowered, her face still toward the wall. After a moment, the footsteps continued, three or four of them inside the hut, approaching her. Bouquet pressed her palms tightly against her temples, turning her face to the dirt floor.

Another....

She spotted the edge of a sandal, next to her head. A child's sandal. A foot with a dirty sock.

"*¿Señora?*" Manolo stood over her. Smoke twirled in the door of the shack. His face was strained and tight, like thick, flayed grease, his lips turned down. "You want some water?" He placed the glass on the dirt floor, just before her face. Smudged with wetted dust, the glass was scraped on one side. The liquid, at least, was clear. "Please, *señora?*"

THANK YOU, PIERRE-AUGUSTE

Renoir invaded Bud Bacon's sleep. In the dream, the Frenchman floated from a golden field of fine wheat, his beat-up straw hat the same color as the wheat itself. A smile flailed from his unkempt red beard. He had tied a portable easel and a stretched canvas to his back with rope, and as he turned up the dirt path, headed for a large oak in the distance, the distance suddenly changed.

Now Renoir was on a boat in the middle of the Seine, surrounded by working-class revelers drinking on the shaded deck. The women were so young and beautiful in their summer dresses that Bud was distracted quite a bit from the figure of Renoir himself, who sat on a stool, the canvas now set up on the easel, painting the scene. A young fellow in a boater hat and an open-collar white shirt sang to one of the girls. Another girl gazed out across the water, her hair and face mottled delicately with playful sunlight and light shadow. A strand of her dark hair floated in a breeze. She wore a fine pink dress, tight above the waist, and floating into a cloud of silk below it. The object of affection of an amusing young man with a black, well-trimmed beard and a dark slouch hat, she attempted ignoring him, but not successfully, if the caressing smile on her lips was in any way truthful.

Color splashed across the entire scene, lights and darks of every hue, swirling throughout the boat party. Every woman in the scene made up a kind of bouquet in her own right, her full flowering made loving by the laughter and fun that came from her.

Puzzled guilt seized Bud. *Have I wasted my life?* "Thank you, M. Renoir." He stood behind the artist.

"Pierre-Auguste, my friend."

"I'm sorry?"

"That's my name."

"Yes, of course. I know." Bud brought a hand to his chin and thought for a moment that, were he doing the painting, he would darken, just slightly, the pink of the girl's dress. This pink—Renoir's pink—was too pink, therefore unmindful of the shade being cast by the canvas pavilion that protected the revelers. But Bud decided that his objection would be frivolous and way too nervy.

"Thank you, Pierre-Auguste," he said instead.

Renoir took his pipe from the table next to him and puffed on it, studying the scene. After a few seconds, he nodded and grumped, raising the brush in his fingers toward the canvas.

The next morning, Bud decided, as he so often did, that his studio needed to be cleaned up. Badly so. But Bud Bacon had been working here for so many years, and the materials he used—steel, with an occasional nod to cast iron—dirtied everything so remarkably and so quickly that he had never really attempted to clean the place, much less organize it. So his studio looked more like a scrap-iron yard, inside and out. It was an old warehouse at the corner of North Eleventh and Berry Streets in Williamsburg, Brooklyn, and the only thing attractive about the building was the view from it. The East River slid by more or less constantly, and there were many sea birds. The property covered one-half of the city block. The galvanized tin studio itself rested on the back two-thirds of the lot, the front third—sequestered by a locked cyclone fence—being a gathering place for much of the work Bud had done that he had not been able to sell.

There was a lot of it. Mostly squares of steel or flat rectangles of steel an inch or two thick, which would grace the floor of whatever gallery or museum room that housed it. His pieces were famous for being huge. Generally, people just walked on them. The pieces resembled the kind of large steel plates that are placed over trenches in the road during the night, to cover ongoing sewer work. Many viewers sniffed at his steel squares, wondering *Does anyone actually think this is art?* But contemporary art curators around the world stumbled over themselves to show "Bud Bacons," as they were called, and Bud's market-driven insistence on doing them over and over again, with some inventive variation piece after piece, garnered him real fame in the art-critic press. His face had appeared three times on the cover of *Artforum* magazine, in one article of which his deep artistic vision was lauded as that of "the most complicated minimalist in contemporary art." He didn't do just squares and rectangles, of course. Now and then he did a triangle.

With the significant notoriety his work had gained over the decades, Bud Bacon—artistically the simplest—was now certainly the most famous minimalist in all of New York City.

The yard did contain some half-moon-shaped bars and slabs, Bud's effort ten years ago to ease himself from the boredom of straight angles. He had come to think that those squared-off structures had constricted his mind, and maybe his soul as well. So a few curves, he thought, would open him back up. He sold some of them, but none of the great museums around the world that now showed his monumental plates liked any of those curves. Curators suspected he had lost his intensity, that he had gone soft. "Just isn't, well, you know, just isn't Bud Bacon," the guy at PS 1 opined. Then the guy at Los Angeles MOCA told him that there wasn't the same level of feeling in the curves that had been so well expressed by the squares and rectangles. "Power, Bud, that's what those straight angles represent." The guy at the Venice Biennale, a New Yorker himself, expressed a similar opinion with the same kind of dismissive aggression that sparkles from so many citizens of Manhattan. Self-congratulation and the assumption that no one outside the storied island has any balls. "Those curves, man…Bud, they're schlock."

Bud supposed that he appreciated the straightforward intensity of the Venice Biennale guy, but the fact was, he was hurt by his words. It did turn out that few other museums and very few of Bud's galleries liked the new work either. So, after two years or so and about thirty curved pieces, he gave up and went back to the squares and rectangles. They immediately re-kindled interest, and Bud Bacon again returned to the kind of world-wide attention and *Artforum* notoriety that he had enjoyed for many years previously. Indeed, the latest *Artforum* cover article congratulated him for his return from "a failure of artistic nerve," as the writer called it. "Bud Bacon's coming back to automatic gesture and the meaning of line ensures that contemporary art is safe and in good hands." This was language that Bud had never much understood. He wondered how anyone ever could. But it was art-critic-speak, which meant that museum curators would pay attention. So, Bud was for it. The writer, who, like most such, was no artist himself, appreciated Bud's phone call to him, to thank him for his deep understanding of what Bud was trying to do.

So, to hell with cleaning up the studio.

He looked across the floor at his latest piece, delivered from the foundry the day before, titled *What's This?* It was made up of seven large, flat squares, abutted one to the other like dominoes. The resulting L-shaped darkness caused him, as always, to worry that this vision of his had taken over completely from more colorful ones, those that had filled his art school drawings and paintings. He had loved his student days at Carnegie Mellon in the early 1990s, when he had been a painter. He had begun making exotically colored metal sculptures there, even congratulated for them by Frank Stella, whom he then interned for in Stella's studio in the East Village. Bud made his first flat steel square—now a major installation in the main gallery of the Hamburger Bahnhof in Berlin—as a joke, shortly after having gotten his MFA. It was a sort of political anti-art statement, the kind that he made in the mid 1990s when he belonged to Less Is More, a commune of young Brooklyn artists who favored manifestos and sit-ins and things of that sort. The other communards had long since disappeared, who knew where? Among all of them, only Bud's artistic career was flourishing. But locked in by the immediate fame that had come to him and the refusal of the avant-garde establishment to welcome from him anything different (a common trait among the avant-garde), he had become stuck in the niche where he remained to this day. He was asked to appear at international conferences. Students came to his studio to marvel at all the pieces of steel that were strewn about. He drank. He opined. There were documentary films about him.

He took up his glass of wine and went outside, to sit down on the bench next to the galvanized tin door. The bench was made of wood, and had once been painted. The only evidence of remaining color resided in some of the sliver-like protuberances down the legs of the bench, which heralded a once bright-red structure. But Bud had never moved the bench inside the studio, leaving it outside for the previous fifteen years.

Someone once took a publicity photo of him sitting on the brand-new bench, when he was twenty-nine years old. Handsome, rugged in the way of a West Side Irish gangster, Bud's looks, like a slightly roughed up Marlon Brando's, had gotten him almost as much reaction wherever he had gone as had his art. Now, he still maintained his appealing manliness, still attractive to women who were moved to offer pleasure when encountering the extreme avant-garde. At forty-five, he felt a bit more wrecked than he had been at twenty-nine. Leaning toward slower movement. Scuffed here and there. But on the whole, Bud Bacon remained a fine-looking man.

The sun lowered gloriously behind Manhattan across the way. Bud had lived in New York for so many years now that one would think he would no longer be impressed by the sunsets here. But he loved the romance of the colors that the sun put out, the magisterial greens caressed by the shimmering blues and reds of Monet-imagined clouds roiling against one another, the pinks—so like Pierre-Auguste's pinks when he dressed those young women in silken gowns for flirtatious assignations—puffy silk of the finest sort, the star-blanched blues favored by Van Gogh turning in minutes to the somber Goya blacks in which so much is hidden, so alive with suggestions of death, all of it eventually populated by the necklace of Manhattan lights across the river, Georgia O'Keefe lights, the universe in the grainy lights, the only things man-made in all the sunset, the whole show to be repeated the next evening.

Later that night, Bud had a vision of apocalypse.

Mark Rothko sat on a stool in his studio, staring at the enormous canvas before him. The studio was dark, forbiddingly so, the walls lined along the floor with one stretched canvas after another leaned up against them confusedly, unkempt and unfinished. The floor itself, of wooden planks, had been glopped up with what seemed a very heavy storm of multicolored goo and oily splotches…*maybe blood,* Bud thought, the blood that had spurted from Rothko's mortal self-wounding. Rothko's pants and white undershirt were covered the same, as were his old leather shoes, and he gave off the smelly air of a man whose portly slovenliness is just the tip of the iceberg of how unhappy he is.

Bud turned over, trying to dismiss the dream. It would not go away.

Bud had read about Rothko's suicide, and he hoped that here, now, the artist would not re-enact it. He felt reasonably confident that that wouldn't happen, because of the painting at which Rothko was gazing. Tears came from beneath Rothko's glasses.

The painting was a sensuous, enormous cloud wishing to be touched. A square.

For a moment, Bud was comforted by Rothko's preference for squares. This fell away after a moment, as Bud marveled at the color in Rothko's piece. The square was blue. But this blue was not just one blue. Rather it was made of innumerable hues, the way the surface of the sea changes in its infinite detail in late sunlit afternoon. In the painting, reds were entwined with different shades of purple and blue—the sprite-filled blue of light silk, yellow-tinged sky blue—and others that had turned the blue more dark or more light as Rothko had paid such close sensual attention to placing it on the canvas. Love found in the touch, the senses complicated and fervid, ecstasy in the dark.

In the dream, Bud was enveloped by these colors as Rothko dissolved into the very tears that flowed from him.

"Hi, Bud." Paula Mardikian, who owned a bakery on Wythe Street called Muffin—Bud's first stop on his daily walks—waved as she approached the studio the following afternoon. She lived several blocks from Bud's studio, in a new apartment building at the foot of North First, with a view of Manhattan. Like Bud in her mid-forties, she had been married to an older lawyer for twenty years. Her two children were now in college, and their leaving home had brought about the unveiling of her bohemian desires. Tired of dinner parties on the Upper East Side with abrasive men (and their silenced wives) in dark suits who smoked cigars and argued, she had found that she preferred hand-making cookies and croissants, and talking seriously with artists about their art. She was divorced now, and she and Bud had been dating for six months.

She walked through the gate and approached Bud's bench. Paula's heart showed so clearly in her conversation that Bud had been attracted to it immediately upon meeting her. Attracted to it *and* to her. He learned quite a bit about her just from their frequent chats in the bakery. Muffin was the size of a small living room, with five wooden tables. The counter, on the left as you entered, was made up of two wood-framed glass cases that appeared to be from the 1940s. Inside the cases, the selection of baked things changed every day, warmth, chocolate, shards of fruit, honey, and delicious butter throughout everything. The oven was farther back in the shop, also very old, and constantly producing new croissants, muffins, breads, brioches, and cakes as the customers came and went.

The light in the always-crowded bakery reminded Bud of that of a Bonnard interior. It was bright and conflicted with brash color. His favorite item for breakfast was one of the simple croissants that Paula and her staff made, with a dollop of the blueberry jam that she concocted personally, and a dark cappuccino served in an antique English porcelain cup and saucer. Occasionally, the cup would be chipped, which only added to the charm of the café.

Paula sat down on the bench next to Bud. She wore the black pants and white double-breasted chef's smock that she wore every day at the bakery, and removed the black headscarf that she also wore there. This was very pleasing to Bud because Paula's long hair had a kind of deepening flourish in it that thrilled him. He loved touching her hair, and she loved it when he did. Paula's hands were extremely slim, gracefully belying the amount of physical work she had to do at the bakery, with sacks of flour, ten-pound squares of butter, flats of fresh strawberries and blueberries, sacks of sugar and coffee, gallon cans filled with honey, and huge slabs of chocolate. She had told him that, despite the labor of it all, she cared enough for her hands—which her mother had told her were the prettiest she had ever seen—to take extra care with them every day.

She had come to the studio because Bud had invited her to look at *What's This?* Paula usually maintained silence when viewing his work. He worried that she didn't care for it, even though she congratulated him for every new piece he showed her. But the lack of an actual description of her feelings when he exhibited his work to her worried Bud. She often seemed not to want to talk about those feelings.

He had asked her about it, and she had replied that she didn't feel qualified to talk to Bud Bacon—"Oh my God!"—about his work...Bud Bacon, so lionized an artist, famous everywhere. When he demurred and said to Paula, "Look, we're all just trying to make our way," she herself demurred, saying that if she wrote for *Art in America* or something, well, then, maybe she could tell him what she really thought. The smile that accompanied the remark disarmed him. But he still wondered, *Well, what does she think?*

He showed her into the tin building and pointed to the new piece that graced his studio floor. Late-afternoon light flowed through the windows. Paula stood quite still, her arms folded before her. She bent over the piece now and then, seeking out its details, such as they were. She walked around it once, staring at it, and then repeated the circuit in the opposite direction. Finally, she held a hand out before her, gesturing down at the sculpture.

"Bud, I don't see the heart in this."

"Heart?"

"Yes. You know, things like desire, flight, the soul's wish."

Bud swallowed. Here it was again. Was he revealing his deepest soul with *What's This?* or trying to make it to *Artforum*? Was he seeking the finest gift to give, or was he working on sales? Love or fame? Clarity or just...fame? Truth or fraud?

"Paula, the world's a dark place, and this...uh, this work...I think it shows that." Bud placed his hands in the pockets of his Levi's, shrugging. "Truth."

"Oh, Bud."

"Fate."

"Come on!" Paula's breathing filled the long silence that chilled the building. Eventually she turned toward Bud. "I..." She gestured toward the floor. "This doesn't... This—"

"Doesn't what?"

"I know you, Bud, and..." She lowered her head. "I'm embarrassed to say this."

"What?"

Paula gathered herself, straightening her shoulders. "These don't come from you."

"What do you mean they don't?"

"Bud, you laugh. You're fun." She pointed toward the tin door. "You care about those birds out there on the river." She glanced back at Bud. "I've sat on that bench with you and watched the sun go down. That's when you're happy. That's when you're looking at something you love."

"Love."

"Yes, and you don't love this…" She nodded toward Bud's piece on the floor. "This…" She turned briefly back toward him. "What's this?"

"Yes."

"What?"

"That's the name of it. *What's This?*"

"Oh…yeah."

Phlegm suddenly rose in Bud's throat. Anger, fueled by his unguarded worry that Paula had discovered the secret that his recent dreams…those goddamned, intrusive dreams…revealed to him.

"Listen, Paula, you leave my work to me."

"Bud."

"I'm successful. I know what I'm doing. It sells. What more do you want?"

"But, Bud, I—"

"This is what I do. What I'm famous for."

"Oh, Bud, what does that matter?"

"It's my work." Bud strode out onto *What's This?* and paused in it's very center, surrounded by ten feet of steel slab on all sides. He placed his hands on his hips and turned about, his eyes circling over the piece, his mouth tightly set and muscled.

"Bud, you don't have to—"

"Just keep your opinions to yourself."

At four o'clock the following morning, Juan de Pareja fixed Bud with his sad gaze, the same gaze with which he had posed for Velázquez. Paula had very abruptly left the afternoon before, a brisk profanity sparkling from her lips as she had slammed the tin door shut behind her. Juan de Pareja had been Velazquez's slave, the entire disappointment with his station in life made clear by the way Velázquez had painted his portrait. The irony that the master so understood the slave's sad resentment was not lost on Bud. A painter like this could see into everything, even the rank injustice of keeping sequestered a slave with such expressive personal beauty and artistic talent as Juan's, a fine painter in his own right. Of all the paintings about which Bud had been dreaming, this one came closest in its mix of colors to Bud's own work. It wasn't *very* close, to be sure. The browns and blacks that make up so much of Juan's portrait shimmer with somber light, while Bud's work seldom shimmered even a little bit.

"Don't lose her, Bud." Juan spoke English with a heavy Spanish accent. "She is the most glorious *señora* one could hope for." Now Juan's sadness took on the aspect of abandonment in love. It conveyed an entire life in danger of being lost. "Listen to her."

Bud did not go to Muffin the following morning, too mortified to do so. Finally he asked one of his studio assistants, Tupac, to deliver a note to Paula. Tupac was a talented sculptor, twenty-four years old, who had already had a solo gallery exhibition in Chelsea. From Bolivia, he had read about Bud and had showed up at the studio door one morning, an iPad filled with photos of his own work under his arm. The kid so loved working in Bud's studio that he had become indispensable to the famous artist just in the year that he had worked for him. Bud had noticed that Tupac's own work was awash in Andean color and splendor, moderate-sized wood structures hung with cloth, paper, and plastic, all colored so beautifully and humorously that his gallery show had sold out. No show of Bud's had ever sold out, even the ones that showed only one piece.

Tupac's profile resembled those Bud had seen on Aztec friezes and in paintings of Indians by Diego Rivera. His hair seemed to thrust itself from him in enormous black urges. He rode a fat-tire bike that had a straw basket on it in front and saddlebags on the back. The bike's name was *Las Alas de Tupac.* The red letters, which were surrounded by bougainvillea blossoms in purple and blue, had been painted by the artist himself on the hand-painted yellow front fender. The quotation marks at either end of the phrase were stylized angel's wings. Bud had noticed that many young women, dressed in arty clothing with nose rings and Texas Steer high-top yellow work boots and blue or green or orange hair, arrived at his studio unannounced, asking if Tupac were around. Tupac occasionally gave the greeted guest a ride home on *Las Alas.*

"*Señora* Paula, she said 'maybe.'" Tupac paused briefly before Bud's gate. He was on his way home. One of Paula's bakers—her name was Evelyn, Bud knew, from Queens—sat on the back of the bike, her arms secured around Tupac's waist. About twenty, she reminded Bud of whoever the model had been for Canova's amazing nude *Pauline Bonaparte as Venus Victrix,* even though Bud had never actually seen Evelyn outside of her own double-breasted chef's smock. She laid her right cheek against Tupac's back. "'Maybe tomorrow,' she said."

"Thanks, Tupac."

The couple wheeled into the distance.

That night, he dreamt about *Les Demoiselles d'Avignon,* a vision in which Picasso jumped wildly around as the painting hurriedly materialized in vectors and smears on the canvas. The artist's laughter jumped from him in immediate, high chuckles, while paint flew from his hands in every direction. The women looked down upon the maestro. They were amused and, it seemed, aroused. Bud reached across the sheet for Paula's hand. Sound asleep, she yet took his into hers and squeezed his fingers.

Because of their tiff, she was of course not actually there. So Bud incorporated her into the dream, putting her, suddenly bereft of her clothing, among the others in the painting. The dream continued.

Several of the *demoiselles* spoke with Bud. They gazed at him, all licentious, making suggestive murmurs and lascivious compliments. He thanked them. They talked about the soul. "Bud, it takes color like ours to excite the heart." He offered his gratitude to Picasso, who paid him no mind. "Bud, move like we do." The women resembled soft-whispering sirens. "Move your art the way the maestro moves us, Bud. You can do it."

The following morning, disturbed and conflicted, Bud hurried to Muffin. Wearing a navy blue pea coat and a wool scarf, he carried a paper-wrapped flat package in his right hand, a few feet by a few feet.

Paula stood behind the counter as he entered the bakery. She held a tray of fresh croissants, and frowned when he approached her. "Hello, Bud."

Remorse flooded Bud's confusion. He knew, of course, that he had badly insulted Paula. Just now, her salutation was spoken more to the croissants than to Bud himself. He immediately began an apology and, after distributing the croissants in a circle on a large platter inside the glass case, Paula seemed—almost—to accept it. He continued with the apology, very worried by how badly he had treated her. A few interested customers in line listened in. Evelyn was also behind the counter, and tried to maintain a look of busy inconsequence. But Bud could tell that she was listening closely. He guessed that Paula had told Evelyn about his behavior, and that maybe Evelyn had counseled Paula to get rid of him. That's what he would advise, were he not so intimately involved in what was happening. *Think of it! Such insults over a matter of heartfelt advice.* Paula was right to be so guarded.

"Bud, we'd better talk about it."

"All right. Yes."

"But some other time. Not here."

"Yes."

Paula put two croissants into a paper bag, with a small plastic container of blueberry jam, and handed them to Bud. As he pushed the small bag into the pocket of his pea coat, Paula gestured toward the door. "After work, Bud."

His hand fell to the doorknob. He looked back, having shifted the large wrapped package from his right hand to the left. A few of the customers glanced up at him from their newspapers...guardedly, not wanting to interrupt.

"My studio? On the bench?"

"Okay. But what's that you're carrying?"

Bud noticed that Evelyn, still engaged and busy in all the flour, butter, and heat, smiled surreptitiously to herself, her glee hidden in her dedication to the baked goods.

"I'll show you later," Bud said.

They sat on the bench together that evening. Each had a glass of cold white wine. A stretched, blank canvas leaned up against the bench, facing the river. Its pristine surface reflected—very dimly, only touched by them in a kind of glorious, disappearing fury—the hues of the sunset. Coming up Wythe Street, Tupac and Evelyn approached on *Las Alas*.

"He's very nice to her." Paula's cheeks tightened.

"I hope so."

"Nicer than you were to me." She wore a red and white kerchief, tied about her hair so that it fell messily—attractively, Bud realized—down her back.

"I'm very sorry, Paula. I so love you."

"I have trouble keeping my mouth shut when I—"

"I've thought a lot about what you said."

"When I believe something as deeply as what I felt the other day."

Las Alas arrived at the gate, and Tupac leaned toward the latch.

"I know, Paula. I…."

The gate opened. Tupac hurried the bike through the entry and then proceeded through the clutter in the lot before the studio, the unfinished steel and iron, the dark, disorganized, and sometimes rusted bric-a-brac. The bicycle came to a halt before Bud and Paula. Evelyn peered at the couple over Tupac's left shoulder, her eyes beaming and round with concern.

Bud exhaled, lowering his head. Then, glancing a moment toward the river and the sea birds, he turned to Tupac. "Can I borrow some of your oils?"

Paula turned her head toward him, surprised.

"And maybe a few tips, when you've got the time."

"Of course, maestro." Tupac leaned over the handlebars, looking to the bench and the canvas. "Tips about what?"

"Color."

"You mean you're going to…" Tupac pointed at the blank canvas. "You're going to—"

Bud took Paula's hand. His dreams whispered at him. "Yes, Tupac." The canvas appeared to him like a blank dream itself, ready to be filled.

"Oh, Bud," Paula whispered, fresh love brimming from her fingers into his.

"Yes, I am."

INTO THE MYSTIC

Mary Dalton's star had ascended. Quickly. Named in a *New York Times* magazine article as one of the dozen hottest executives of the year under thirty-five, she ran marketing for Hachette in the U.S., a senior vice president. In the cover photo, reclining on a leather couch, she gazed out the window at the passing pedestrians on the High Line. Her corner apartment was two floors above the level of the pathway itself, so that Mary could watch the strollers below, so many of them having such fun walking through the linear gardens. To the east, north, and south lay all Manhattan. The buildings rose in a great clutter of shapes and heights, one of the influences that had brought Mary to New York in the first place. The roar of the city filtered through the double windows, and was greatly subdued by them. It was a background whispering that she actually loved for its simple constancy. Indeed, though, she knew that, in Manhattan, she was being cradled by irrepressible change, even though she worried that that change—even the principle itself of change in this town—was too immediate and too dismissive of what had been inspiring, or even uncontrollably riveting, just a few days before.

New York was indeed, as Mystic had once told her, a lot of noise. Mary cherished the excitement of it but suspected now, since her phone conversation with him a few minutes earlier, that there was something far more profoundly ungovernable to be found elsewhere.

Ten years earlier, Mystic had been standing on the cement stairway leading down between the rocks at the Forty Foot in Sandycove, County Dublin. He was about to descend into the Irish Sea. Rain and wind the night before had stirred the sea up so much that its blue, green, and white skirmishes were indistinguishable one to the next, now muddied beneath the morning gray. Mystic stood on the last step. He turned to Mary, who sat waiting at the top of the stairway. He held his arms out to her, his skin pearlescent and shivering in contrast to the pair of black undershorts he wore.

Mine for the taking, Mary thought, *Lord help me.*

"Mary. Stay." He then continued into the waters themselves. Swimming out, he ignored Mary's cries to come back. But then he turned toward her. The swells lifted, buoying Mystic up and back. His hands fluttered at the surface, his treading balancing him despite the shove of the waters as they came and went.

"Mystic. Please."

He swam back to the stairway and ascended, his skin now turned pale blue. The élan with which he had been swimming through the Neptune swirl seized Mary's heart.

But once she helped him put on his pants, sweatshirt and jacket, and handed him his shoes, she took the lapels of that jacket in her hands and knelt before him, bringing her face close to his. "I'm goin' to New York, Mystic." She kissed him. "I'm sorry, but I'm goin'."

Dermot Cleary, an immigrant whose life had settled into its insistence on conservative carefulness the day he was born in Cashel, County Tipperary, sat across the table from Mary, at the Beatrice Inn in the West Village. "I don't understand." He was an investment banker, forty years old, whose company had hired him out of Harvard Business School. "Are you going to answer me?" Now, fifteen years later, he was an American citizen.

"The greatest adventure of me life," Dermot liked to say when it was important to him for some reason to admit that he was Irish. People already knew that about him, but Dermot felt that the importance of being an American was much greater. American humor, American speech, the New York Giants, the Knicks, and the Liberty Plaza Brooks Brothers store were first on his list of cultural priorities. A home in Greenwich, Connecticut, was his formal long-term goal. It would be the imprimatur—along with a membership in the Greenwich Country Club—that would certify his having made it, big time, in the States. Dermot espoused, silently and gratefully, the traditional ethics of the Republican Party. Money and place were everything to him…except for what, now, just in the last few months, Mary was bringing to his life.

They had met at the party celebrating Mary's appearance in the *Times*, to which one of Dermot's corporate senior officer friends had brought him. It took place at the White Horse Tavern, and Dermot was uncomfortable there. The portrait of Dylan Thomas, his drinking interrupted, looked down upon the festivities. Dermot and his colleague were the only men wearing suits and ties. The other celebrants wore jeans and hoodies, some of them fashion-conscious in hiking boots, others more casually attired in soiled running shoes without socks. There were many writers, the kind of people that made Dermot nervous. Seemingly with no financial sophistication—a lot of them actual anarchists, it seemed to him, crazy declaimers—they were notable for confused beer-driven speech and gossip riddled with professional jealousy and distrust.

Are all writers like this? he had asked himself. Mary had assured him they were not, although judging from the few authors of hers whom he had met on that evening, Dermot had concluded that she was wrong. They seemed to look upon him as they would an operative from the National Security Agency.

But he also met Mary that evening, which caused him to stay on at the party, even after his business friend left after twenty minutes. "Got to get back to the office," he said, equally flummoxed by the party guests.

Dermot had been watching Mary across the room. He recognized formal adventurousness in her that *did* fit in with the bohemian sloppiness of most of the other guests. She stood out from them, though, because of the kindness of her gestures and especially the way she spoke with others, her eyes directly on theirs and darkly noticing everything they were saying. Reacting to them. Listening…and then offering responses that seemed to Dermot, even this far away from her, to be filled with humor and joy.

Mary was not beautiful in the way that so many women in New York are—those involved in fashion, Broadway, or movies—whose looks are one of the few tools they've got. Hers were far more engaging—her black hair like deep evening itself, her eyes conveying so many considered, and considerate, ideas—and therefore more refined than the Photoshopped perfection common to the fashion press. Mary's eyes were also dark, her hands large for a woman as diminutive as she. Her smile opened the conversation even further. Authority flowed from it. It provoked responses.

She wore a leather coat, black, with long collars, over a pair of red silk pants and a black turtleneck sweater. A woven heart, made from thick red and black yarns, hung from a strand of black leather around her neck. She played with it from time to time, and Dermot noticed the precision of her dark red nails and the way that, when she gestured, her fingers seemed to be punctuating what she was saying. The three men with whom she was speaking were paying close attention. Dermot guessed they might be clients, and so, writers. While the others in the room were scattered about in slovenly conversations, these men were simply enthralled.

He made his way through the guests, and when he arrived at the conversation, obviously wanting to be part of it, Mary glanced at him with surprise.

Dermot was a big man whose face revealed the good-natured humor that blustering Irishmen often have. But he didn't drink, so that that particular cultural trait, often encountered among the Irish in New York—and, to be sure, the Irish in Ireland—was subdued in him. But he displayed wellbeing that came as a surprise to people who might think that being so large a conservative financial executive meant that you were also a bully. Dermot was not, but neither was he delicate. When he spoke, his American accent misled whoever was listening to him who may not have known of his origins. But once they discovered what those origins were, they would routinely ask him why, if he was from Tipperary, he talked like a New Englander.

Like Mary, Dermot was Catholic, but he had put an intentionally Northeastern Protestant spin on the way he spoke. There was little Irish in it, nor in his gestures, which were, at best, occasional and simple. He planned on people mistaking him for a reserved American blue blood... from Connecticut, to be sure, but he could accept being from Rhode Island as well, even from some parts of Massachusetts. All those states represented the kind of accepted self-regard that he knew was essential to his work. If he wanted to become a CFO or CEO of a Fortune 500 company, he would have to project the sort of personality that, driven by ambition, was also open to conversation, ever friendly (although from time to time politically judgmental), and interested in the things that others who spoke similarly would be interested in…so, golf in The Hamptons, boating on Long Island Sound, goddamned government interference, ROI….

Dermot was therefore a kind of fraud, personally. But his easy manner and conversational willingness allowed people to like him, and he was on the fast track at Citibank.

Mary's silence at the Beatrice Inn silenced Dermot for a long moment. They had been dating for a few months, and Mary had told him that she enjoyed her time with him. But Dermot sensed, with this conversation, that there was a new hesitation of some kind in her feelings for him. He declared himself to her. He loved her, there was no doubt about it.

He was hers, he said.

And when he uttered those words, Mary's soul seemed to pull away from him. He couldn't put his finger on it. The declaration brought about so subtle a change in Mary's treatment of Dermot that, at first, he barely noticed it. But after a few minutes, he began feeling isolated. She smiled. They talked. But Mary now held back, beginning with that very moment in which Dermot tried to put himself—himself alone—into her heart.

She had come back from Dublin a few weeks before, from a vacation visit to relatives with her mother, and Dermot wondered what else had happened there.

Dublin was no Manhattan. Just now the sky, the sidewalks, the architecture, and the Liffey itself seemed to Mary to be colored the same. Walking across O'Connell Bridge, she recalled how this much gray had been a major element in why she had left Dublin in the first place ten years ago.

Born in the Dublin suburb of Dalkey, she had remained a hometown girl, even spending a few months during her last year in graduate school at Trinity College as a bargirl at Finnegan's. She was already a fan of American writers, and had plans to go to the States. Just thinking about it thrilled her. Central Park. The Great White Way. Walt Whitman loafing on the grass. It was a glimmer for Mary, a dream, all of it.

It was in Finnegan's on her first night working there, in 2004, that she met Mystic, serving him a pint of Guinness at what she learned was his usual table in a corner. She recognized him right away. Though an American, he lived in Dalkey and, besides Maeve Binchy, was the pub's primary celebrity.

Mary loved Mystic Brennan's band The Yank's Laughter. She owned all six CDs. Who would have guessed that a fellow with an accent like his—"Hey, you know, PS 155," he had at first explained to Mary, "Up there in East Harlem."—would enjoy Dalkey?

"What's all that, then?" The number, the spare references, meant nothing to her, although Mystic had given her the information as though she, too, had grown up on the East Side of Manhattan.

"You don't know?"

"Haven't a clue, love." Removing the empty pint glass from the table, she left a fresh paper napkin next to the full pint glass.

"It's New York. What do you think?"

Mary, put off by the rough question, remained standing at the table. Just because this man was so famous a rock musician and actor didn't mean that she had to take this kind of guff, so barren of information and friendliness.

To her surprise, Mystic spoke again. Regard brimmed from a smile. "Sorry, Mary, there's no reason for you to know."

Mystic had all the world-weary bravado that immortal rock musicians are supposed to have. He slouched on the cushioned bench on which he sat, one hand extended onto the table, where it caressed the pint. His black leather jacket was unzipped, scruffy and darling. His dark eyes shone as though some recent happiness had awakened them to luminescence. He wore a Yankees baseball cap, from beneath which flowed, Mary noticed immediately, locks of ebony hair. About thirty, he had a dark complexion that pleased her quite a bit because of her own Black Irish antecedents. Her mother, who was from Connemara, had explained to Mary when she was a girl that "sometime way back, there was a trade route, Mary, that included a port over there somewhere… Killary Harbour, Leenane, probably...who knows? And there were Spaniards and the like...." She laughed, hiding her lips with the back of her hand. "Mohammedans, maybe..." She raised her eyebrows.

Mary had decided that one of those Mohammedans had spotted her medieval relative Ailish or Éirinn or some such, pretty and barefoot, waiting there on the rocks, and that was all he needed to know. Thus, with time, Mary's mother's flourishing black hair had come to be, as had Mary's.

But Mystic was no Irishman, and Mary wished to ask him why he liked Dalkey so much. He lived up on Killiney Hill, on Vico Road, and the barman Liam had told Mary that the wall that protected Mystic's estate was "more or less impregnable. You can't even see the place."

"Is he a hermit?"

"Mystic? A hermit?" Liam laughed. "He's a swashbuckler, Mary. Famous for it." He placed a couple of napkins on her tray. "Very famous."

A few days after they first met, Mystic came into the pub early and asked for a cup of tea. There were few customers. The place was almost silent, the conversation in the different dark wood-lined rooms being settled and close. Mary placed the pot of tea and the cup and saucer before Mystic. She offered him a warmed scone as well, with butter and jam. "It's on the house."

"Thank you."

Mary began turning away, but noticed that Mystic was observing her with what she surely mistook as...interest. *What does he see in me?* she asked herself before finally turning from him entirely.

"Mary."

She looked back.

"Please. Would you bring me some cream?"

As Dermot escorted Mary from the Beatrice Inn, they argued.

"I don't understand this wordlessness," he said again.

The next day, after he had hung up on her, he appeared in the lobby of her apartment building. The security man Julio announced his arrival. She did not reply, and the silence on the phone finally brought another question from Julio. "You still know this gentleman, Miss, don't you?"

"I do...yes...send him up please."

Dermot entered the apartment on the very verge of making a scene. But as he removed his overcoat and tossed it onto a chair, turning to Mary with his opened hands extended before him in a gesture of insistent declaration, he saw that she was weeping.

"What is it?"

"When I was in Dublin, Dermot—"

"In the company of your sainted mother."

The remark was rude, but she figured Dermot had a right to be angry. It was the only mean-hearted thing he had ever said to her.

"Dermot, I met someone I used to know."

"Used to know."

"That's right. Ten years ago."

"A classmate, then, eh? An old boyfriend."

"No. Hardly."

"Then who is it? Not an old girlfriend, I hope."

"Dermot. Please. He's just someone I knew."

As Dermot sat down on the couch—at the other, far, end of the couch—Mary continued feeling terrible. Dermot was hers. She had won him, she realized, almost the moment he had arrived at her side at the White Horse Tavern. The other men with whom she was talking, two Hachette marketing guys and Mary's assistant, immediately noticed his arrival, too, and the conversation turned a bit lumpish and unnerved, as though Dermot and his suit, his looks, and his serious executive comportment should be in some other bar somewhere. But he was also extremely handsome. (Her assistant, Brad, his hands gathered together breathlessly beneath his chin, exclaimed about it during the Uber ride home later.) Mary realized right away that Dermot was an Irishman, even before she began talking with him.

Dermot asked Mary out that very evening, and she accepted. He took her to dinner the next night at Jean George, and their romance proceeded apace. Thrillingly.

But now, in Mary's apartment, she realized that she had to tell him what had so thoroughly, abruptly happened in Dublin. "He's a musician."

Dermot's silence exuded disbelief. Mary knew he was not an adventurer. She admired the carefulness with which Dermot addressed his prospects and pursued them. His organization. *He's a lot like me,* she thought. *Came to New York looking for success. Found it. Loved New York. Loved me.*

"Plays with his flute, does he?" Dermot frowned, looking out the window.

"Please, I—"

"Mary, I wish you had let me know about this before you let me—"

"Dermot."

"Sweep you off your feet." The phrase came from him with real hurt.

"I didn't know."

"Then how did you find out?"

Mary wiped tears from her cheeks, and then she, too, looked out the window. "I guess…I guess I *did* know."

"When? The night we met?"

"Oh Dermot, no. It was years ago."

A few days after she brought him the scone, Mystic came into Finnegan's again and asked for a pint.

"But what's this PS 155?"

"It's the public school I went to when I was a kid. You know…" Mystic fondled the pint glass with both hands. "We all talk like this up there." He grinned. "All of us, no matter what color we are. Puerto Rican. Black. White. It doesn't matter."

Mary had had just a few exchanges with him, but with this one she realized that it wasn't just Robert De Niro and Harvey Keitel, whose movies she had seen and loved, that spoke this way. In New York, apparently, lots of people did. She walked from the table, her heart excited by the fact that Mystic Brennan was actually speaking with her.

He did once more the next night, and then the night after that.

Mystic explained that his mother was Puerto Rican, a third-generation New Yorker. "My father was Irish. I didn't know him."

"His name was Brennan."

"That's right. But from Philly, which is a ways from Ireland."

"I know. The Liberty Bell. I've seen it on the map."

It was early in the evening. Liam had also explained that Mystic had very respectfully asked the Finnegan's employees to respect his privacy. "Sometimes," Liam told her, "he'll have musician friends with him. You know, Keith Richards came in here with him one night. And, once, the hip-hop guy…what's his name? Jay-Z? Even Amy Winehouse, who shook the place up considerable, I can tell you." Liam, dressed as always in a white shirt, the sleeves rolled up, and a black wool vest buttoned in front, leaned forward over the bar, looking to his left, as though he were about to whisper. "But Mary, normally he doesn't want to be bothered. So, bring him his Guinness and leave him alone."

Mystic, though, welcomed Mary to his table. Employees were not to fraternize with customers except to service their request for another drink or a meal. Mystic liked the fish pie and the apple and blackberry crumble.

"Why the name?" she asked him, slipping the pie in its serving dish toward him.

"My mother. She was a fan of Van Morrison."

"Oh. 'Into the Mystic.'"

"Yeah. She was listening to it when she went into labor, she told me. She said that there was no other possible name for me. Boy or girl, it had to be Mystic."

"But weren't you ever embarrassed?"

Mystic fixed Mary with an amused gaze.

"By the name, I mean."

"Me?" He frowned, at first with comic quiet. She felt that she had asked a foolish question. He touched her hand. "Never." He removed his hand, taking up a fork with it and addressing the fish pie. "Not once, sweetheart." He laid the fork down a moment. "For her, the mystic was the other world, see? The place where you dream. Everything's chaos and experiment. Nothing's settled there."

"Chaos and…?"

"Dreams." Mystic unzipped his leather jacket, to reveal a T-shirt with the word "Manhattan" on it. His fingers traced the lettering that traversed his chest. "That's what they *think* they've got here."

Mary grinned. "They have your heart?"

"No, Mary…The heart was what my mother was talking about. In Manhattan, they just make a lot of noise about money—"

"That's all?"

" —and nothin'."

Dermot sent flowers. He wrote her a long love letter in which he spelled out what he had to offer to her.

You clearly don't understand, Mary. We both came here, and found what we were looking for. You're famous now. Mary Dalton. Came to the States and into her own, all on her own.

This was true. Everything. And there was more, as far as Dermot was concerned.

I would do anything for you. I love you. You don't realize how much I love you.

Mary disliked the harridan-like indifference that suddenly invaded her. But the words "I love you"…pronounced the way that kind Dermot pronounced them…. How many had uttered them since the formation of the earth, and meant them as true, not realizing that the words themselves were wooden, a cliché, an utterance more like everyday marketing than deep-felt yearning or the sighs of connection or sweat-laden embrace? She couldn't evade the fact that, although Dermot was ever considerate and, yes, loving, he was more affectionate with her than obsessed, more fine-tuned than rugged, more a man of the mind and of few words than a creature from the ocean whirled up and back from the Irish islands.

After her shift at Finnegan's one evening, Mary walked to the video store in Dalkey and rented Mystic's movies. On screen, he was a chameleon. He could play a Nantucket sailor drowned by a frustrated whale, a minor league center fielder in the Mexican leagues, a betrayed Mafia hit man dumped into the East River, even the romantic lead (electrifyingly so to Mary) in an L.A. drug thriller opposite Jennifer Lopez. Suave, lovely, idiosyncratic, and funny, Mystic was now as well known for his acting as he was for his music.

"Is acting part of that chaos you talked about?"

Mystic took up a helping of salad. "Sure it is. It's pure deception, you know. It's like fiction. You make it up as you go along. You lie. But you're not really the character. You're just playing the role, and the character arrives from…from—"

"The mystic."

Mystic pushed his fork around the plate. "I think so, yes."

"What your mother knew."

Mystic shrugged, looking away. Mary could tell, from the sincerity of his shyness, that he liked her.

After a few more weeks, over a plate of blackberry crumble, Mystic asked Mary to join him in Dublin. It was the fifteenth of June.

"Oh…I can't, Mystic. You know…" Mary looked over her shoulder toward the bar. "We're not supposed to…you know—"

"To go out with me."

Startled, Mary sucked a moment on her lower lip. "You're…you're—"

"I'm not actually asking you out, Mary. Tomorrow's Bloomsday."

"Ah, so it is. I forgot."

"And I go into Dublin every June 16 to spend a little time with Joyce." Mystic nodded. "North Earl Street."

"The statue." Mary did not speak for a moment, hoping that Mystic was indeed asking her out. She looked again over her shoulder. The few patrons were involved in their own conversations. Liam was wiping some glasses. She turned back. "Do you know his books, then?"

"Well, I…" Mystic rubbed his left arm with the palm of his right hand, leaning forward as though in conflicted thought. He reminded Mary of himself in the drug dealer romance, when he made a similar gesture just before declaring his dangerous love for Jennifer Lopez, who was playing an undercover cop. "I—"

"Finnegans Wake."

"Yeah, I tried. The first page wasn't bad, but the rest of it was the biggest piece of shite I ever read." Mystic looked up.

Mary was charmed by his use of the Irish variant. "Shite, you said?"

"That's it."

"If you think so, why do you visit him?"

He grabbed his arm once again. "Because he was so brave. And, you know, he wrote *Dubliners* too. Now, there, that was—"

"What? Sitting at a desk and writing down words?"

"Exactly. No money. No Dublin. Stuck in Paris. Going blind. And look what he tried to do!"

"But—"

"It doesn't matter to me that *Finnegans Wake* makes no sense, Mary. Joyce plunged into the light. It took him by surprise, and it dazzled him. It riveted him. I think he lost his mind."

"He came out the other end, though, didn't he?"

"Yes. But, electrified. Blinded by it."

Like many others, apparently including Mystic, Mary had given up on *Finnegans Wake* after fifty pages or so, offering Jim Joyce the suggestion that he fuck himself. But she had read his other stuff and walked often beneath the Martello Tower in Sandycove, in which he had once so famously slept for a night or two. Looking out to sea, she had felt that the tower, the cold, the rain, and the darkness had been holding her consciousness from the moment she had been born. The Atlantic. The terrifying deep. The wish to leave this place, like Joyce himself had. The far world.

Mary took up the plate, now empty of its crumble. "Yes, I'd like to go with you." The few stains of blackberries did nothing to quiet the fork rattling against the ceramic. "Just don't tell anyone here, Mystic. Please."

"Not a word." He, too, looked to the front of the pub. "But can I drive you home?"

Mystic had parked his Land Rover a few streets from Finnegan's, and he gave Mary surreptitious directions to where it was. Once she got into it, he asked whether she would like to see where he lived.

Mary thought about it, and was stunned by the brevity of her caution. "I would, yes."

They drove up Dalkey Avenue and then ascended Killiney Hill to Vico Road.

"Do you like living here, Mystic?" Mary's heart fluttered as she looked down at the view of Dublin Bay.

"I do. It's private."

"You get pursued a lot, I imagine."

"I do."

"Everywhere."

"Yes."

A high double gate, wood painted red, opened before them. The wall Liam had described, of yellow sandstone, extended left and right into the darkness. Ahead, the drive turned through a grove of deciduous trees and flowering bushes, all now just coming into leaf, toward what looked like a small castle in the darkness. A broad swath of yellow daffodils bordered each bank of a meandering stream that ran through the property, bordered by the gravel drive.

Mystic leaned forward over the steering wheel, looking out. "You like flowers, I hope."

Mary placed two fingers against her lips, enjoying the small, welcoming spectacle. "'…Lonely as a cloud.'"

They made love, and Mary, in Mystic's arms, fell into floating release, the colors in the candlelit room gathering into swaths of cloud-like warmth. He treated her with close gentleness of touch and startled generosity. Finally, their sighs of shared excitement gave her such joy that she asked him—unexpectedly, thoughtlessly—to please love her.

It rained that night, and now very cold morning light broke up the colors in the still turbulent waters below. They sat on the stairs at the Forty Foot. They would take the train into Dublin, but Mystic had asked her to join him for the one other stop he routinely made on June 16, with the Martello Tower in sight, to look out to sea.

Mystic took her hand. "But why do you want to go to the States?"

"Adventure."

"In the States?" He waved a hand before him. "You don't know what you're talking about."

"That's why I'll be going there, mate."

"Yeah, I know. Everyone thinks that New York's the center of the world. That that's where the action is…." Mystic looked down into the waters as the roughness turned them to white foam and green rivulets, advancing and receding. "But they all think that getting rich is all there is. And they tell you about it."

"What do you mean?"

"Their own importance." Mystic leaned forward and placed his elbows on his knees. He continued studying the tide pools. He tossed a stone into the sea. "There are a lot of schmucks in the United States."

Already, Saul Bellow was one of Mary's favorite American authors. So she well knew from his work what a schmuck was. "There are plenty of those here, Mystic."

"Yeah, I know."

"So what's the difference?"

"The ones in New York are idiots."

"And the ones here?"

"At least they've got that blood…the blood you've got… running through them. The Language. The stories, Mary. Talk."

Mary nudged him. "Shite, you mean."

"No. Myths. The long ago. Blood. Heart."

"And they don't have that sort of myth in New York?"

"No. Their myths are all about J.P. Morgan and those guys. Rockefeller." Mystic tossed another stone. A wave cobbled into the inlet. "Mary." The sound of the wave was full with embrace, the sea's voice. "Will you stay here with me?"

Mary turned her head quickly toward him. She worried that she hadn't heard him right. But Mystic surveyed her now, his eyes engaging hers with not one hint of uncertainty. He held a third pebble between the fingers of his right hand.

Mary glanced at it, its gray surface interlined with light delicacies of white. "But you're Mystic Brennan."

"Sure that's right." With the PS 155 accent, the Irishism sounded loving, as though Mystic were making fun of himself for Mary's benefit.

"You've got nothing but girlfriends, Mystic."

His lips turned down. "Maybe so."

"Comes with the territory, I imagine."

"It did, yes. But please. Mary, stay with me."

Mary's stomach quivered. Suspicions of misuse and arrogance wavered through her. This man was internationally known, and she was a student of business headed for who-knew-what in New York City. He had to be joking with her. This request could not possibly be sincere.

"You think I'm making it up, don't you?"

"Mystic."

"That I'm probably already getting ready to leave you."

"Oh, no, I…."

Mystic stood up and removed his coat. One shoe came off, and then another, plus his socks.

"What are you doing?"

He unbuckled his belt and slid his pants down his legs. Sitting down, he pulled one pants leg from one foot, and then the other from the other.

"You'll catch your death of cold."

"I'm going into the Irish Sea, Mary Dalton."

"Mystic!"

"The waters, see?"

"Please."

"For you." He took the first step down the stairway, toward where the waves rose up to take him. He turned back. "Mary. Stay."

She had to tell him. New York was waiting. She was leaving.

She hadn't seen Mystic for ten years. Her father had died and her mother had moved to New York, to an apartment in Park Slope that Mary bought for her. The two women were in Dublin now for a visit and were staying up Killiney Hill at the Fitzpatrick Castle Hotel. Mary knew he still lived on the hill, but even though she was back in Ireland, she couldn't call him. Not after what he had asked of her, and how she had refused him.

But Mystic knew she was back, and he called her at the hotel, to ask her to meet him at Finnegan's. "Yeah, Liam told me. He said you came in yesterday."

Now so successful a "Yank," as those at Finnegan's who remembered Mary's tenure at the pub years earlier now called her, she spotted Mystic at his table and, when he stood to greet her, she embraced him.

"Look, we're going to be in New York next month." The allure of his eyes summoned even more of a hug. His hair had begun to gray, a feature that made its still-swirling blacks even more attractive than those of the bedraggled rocker who had sat at this table a decade earlier. She had been following his career, and she knew that he had given up music in favor of his acting for some years but had recently formed a new band.

"Manhattan?"

"Yeah, we got two nights at the Beacon Theater."

"Oh, Mystic, I…"

He pointed to the bench. Mary looked over her shoulder. Liam, who indeed still remained behind the bar, smiled at her and gave her a thumbs-up. Mary, embarrassed by her own lack of candor, waved back. The gesture felt listless, as though it were caught in some sort of hidden, unrealized surprise. She sat down.

"Can I see you there?"

"Mystic, it's…"

He took up her hand and looked to the front of the pub. "What, is there something there you don't want me to know about?"

"Please." Mary's heart stumbled.

"Some reason you don't want me to show up?"

She swallowed.

"Come on, Mary. There *is* something else. I'd—"

"I'd love to go. But I—"

"You're spoken for."

Mary's eyes fluttered as though, a little girl, she had been caught in a subterfuge.

Mystic sat back and surveyed her. "I'm surprised to see you without a…without a reply, Mary."

She laid her hands on her lap.

"You're married."

"No."

"Well, at least you're in love."

She recalled the regret that had lingered in her that day at the Forty

Foot, and that returned from time to time, usually in the morning dark in Manhattan, when she would awaken, her throat tight, her breathing hurried. Salt water had been dripping from his hair that day like beads of light itself, and, his face glistening with it, Mystic had asked her, did she still want to visit James Joyce with him.

She had said no, and he had gone alone. Since then, she had regretted her response and missed what she suspected she would have seen that day in Mystic's company. What they would have loved seeing together.

"I am in love, yes."

For a moment, the meandering of other conversations in the pub was the only thing that broke the silence. Mary wished to tell Mystic the truth. But Dermot...*Poor Dermot*...and his feelings for her kept her silent.

Mary walked alone to the Forty Foot. She sat down on the same step from which she had watched Mystic hurl himself into the sea years before. She imagined the falling rain that pummeled these waves. *So much of it, it must add to the Irish Sea itself,* she thought, *an ancient flood.* And she thought of all that black water pushed about by the terrible winds that drub Ireland from everywhere. She imagined Mystic leaving her there on the stair, swimming out until he could swim no more, and disappearing beyond the horizon. The image was a romantic fantasy, she knew, and she was amused by it. It was like some sort of Pre-Raphaelite painting, the young hero poet losing himself in the waters because of love's having abandoned him. Mary smiled. She imagined herself, a ringlet of flowers surrounding her hair, a medieval white gown hanging from her fine shoulders, as she, the lost love, looked out to sea for the drowned boy whose lyric voice she had always cherished. The Lady of Shalott, rendered by John William Waterhouse, only this time seated on the salt-eaten cement at the Forty Foot instead of in a finely wrought Viking boat on a lovely English pond. She wondered if those rains fell across Mystic, too, his hands in the pockets of a heavy coat, his footsteps sodden as he wandered beneath the Martello tower. He thought of her, she knew. At least there was that. And she thought about him.

He phoned her just as she arrived back at the hotel.

"I'll leave a stage pass for you."

"Please don't. It wouldn't—"

"Just in case."

In New York, he called her.

"You've got what you want in Dalkey, Mary, and you don't even know it."

"What about my work?"

"You've got a computer?"

"Of course."

"A cell phone? Wi-fi? The cloud?"

"Yes."

"Then you can work in Dalkey." He paused. "Six months here." Mary awaited what she knew was coming. "Six months in Manhattan."

She recalled the day he had first touched her hand, at Finnegan's, when she asked whether he had been embarrassed by his name. The brief innocence of that caress had thrilled her.

"Besides which, you got me in both places."

She lowered her head, conflicted by the prospect of what he was offering her. She had not lost Mystic as, for these years, she felt she surely had.

Dermot was silent.

Mary gripped the phone, feeling graceless. "I'm in love, Dermot."

He was a fine man but— "And not with me," he finally said.

She looked south to the Hudson River. There was a sailboat here and there, ferries, a couple tugboats, and New Jersey lay beyond all that beneath a covering of roiling clouds. All benefitted from the seeming stillness that their distance from Mary's window afforded them, as though they made up a grand painting of the physical American world in its entirety.

She looked downriver, where it flowed toward the east into the mutinous Atlantic. "That's right."

"But Mary—"

"Dermot, I'm leavin' New York. I'm sorry, but I'm leavin'."

She sat on a stool offstage that one of the hands had found for her. From this angle, the audience appeared like a vast flood of fingerlings clustering at the surface of the sea, seeking food. There were many in their thirties, fans of the now fondly remembered The Yank's Laughter. Mary was startled by the number of much younger people in the audience as well. Mystic Brennan still packed them in, just like he had years ago.

The band came up a hallway from their dressing room. In conversation, laughing and hurrying through the clutter of wiring on the floor, backstage stuff, lighting stands and numerous onlookers, they were clearly excited—way excited—by the prospects for this, their first night of an East Coast tour. She had read the article about it in the *Observer,* in which the writer had extolled the virtues of Mystic Brennan's music from a few years ago. "This new band is new," the critic had written, "and Mystic's public has been waiting too long for his absence to end. His fans now have kids, and we expect they'll be there tonight too."

Hidden as she was to the side, next to a curtain, she watched as the band began passing her by. Mystic, dressed in a slim black suit with a white open-necked shirt, was the last in line, looking about him, carrying a guitar in his right hand, searching the backstage. His face was drawn, worry passing across it and emphasized by his tightened lips. He looked lost, his soul darkened.

Mary reached out and touched his sleeve. "Mystic."

About the Author

TERENCE CLARKE is a novelist (Mercury House, Ballantine Books, Astor & Lenox) and short story writer (*The Yale Review*, *The Antioch Review*, *Kindle Singles* and others), a publisher, editor, journalist (*San Francisco Chronicle*, *Salon.com*, *HuffPost*) and translator of literature and journalism from Spanish to English.

"When I lived in New York City, I learned that about eight hundred different languages are spoken there, from numberless immigrants and others who speak English as a second language. My previous fiction often features Americans living outside the United States, in circumstances in which a major portion of their difficulty is the fact that they don't fit in, linguistically or culturally. That was a feature of my own early adulthood when I lived for a few years in Sarawak, Malaysia. I learned then that to be in a position in which I have to know about how these other people live, speak, feel, think, and treat each other is a true privilege. That understanding has been a major factor in all my writing. With regard to this particular story collection, it was also important for me to realize that New York City itself is its own foreign country."

Terence Clarke lives in San Francisco.

CPSIA information can be obtained
at www.ICGtesting.com
Printed in the USA
LVOW07s0003261217
560794LV00001B/95/P